THE FINAL GOD

THE GODLESS TRILOGY | BOOK THREE

CHRISTOPHER MONTEAGLE

Black Rose Writing | Texas

ISBN: 978-1-68513-600-0
PUBLISHED BY BLACK ROSE WRITING
www.blackrosewriting.com

Printed in the United States of America
Suggested Retail Price (SRP) $24.95

The Final God is printed in Calluna

*As a planet-friendly publisher, Black Rose Writing does its best to eliminate unnecessary waste to reduce paper usage and energy costs, while never compromising the reading experience. As a result, the final word count vs. page count may not meet common expectations.

Praise for
The Final God

Maxy Award Runner Up for Best Fantasy/ Science Fiction 2021

Iron Union
Kovalith
Alovat
Grand Duchy
of Joana
Ironhelm
Ciro
The Shield
Dark Spires
Fortress of Krág
Klyph
(Malene's Fall)
Mac-Soldai
Hammerfall
Arbek
Rhaskitov
Greund
Barrens of Silence
Kardak
The Render

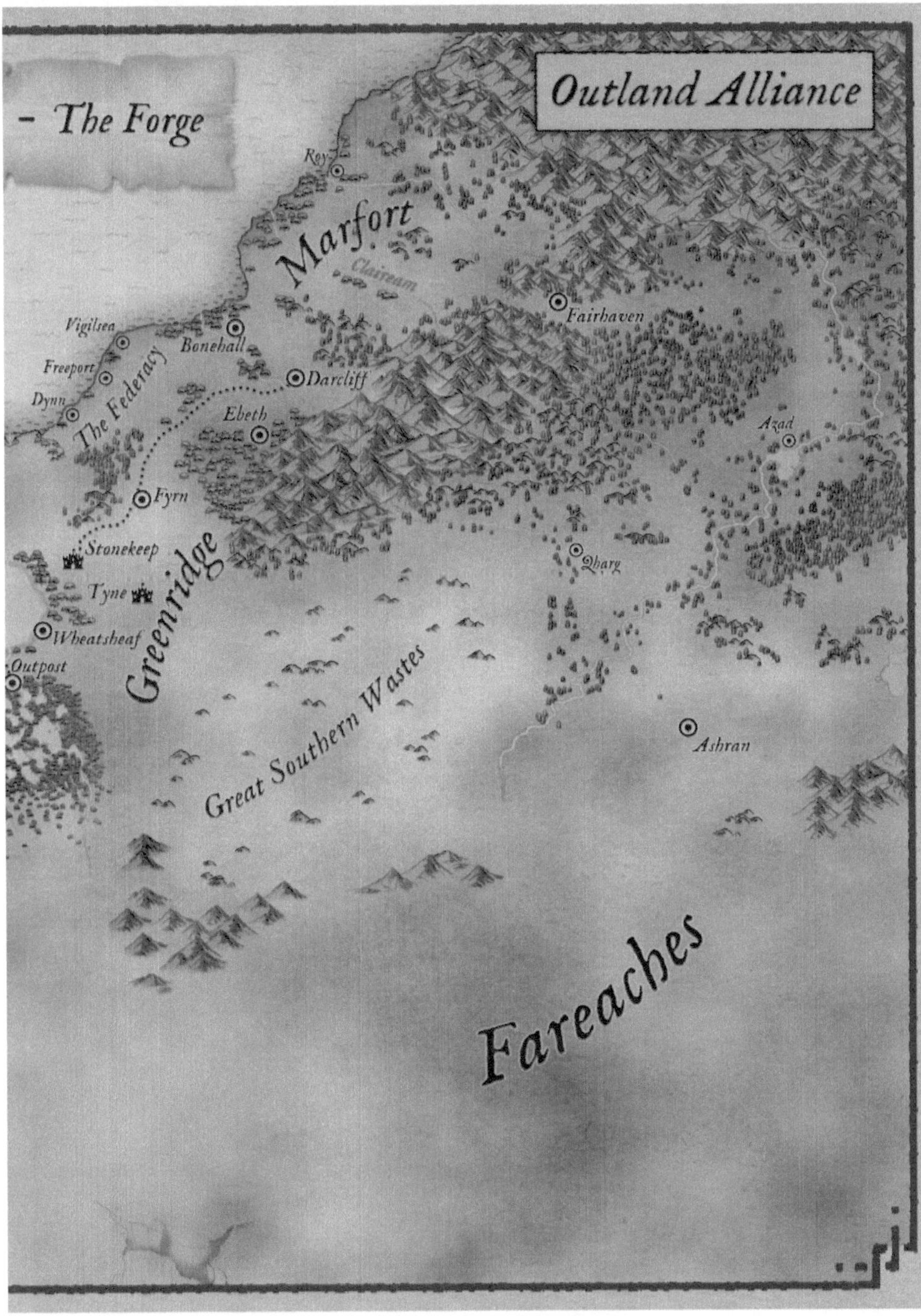

The Forge
Outland Alliance
Roy
Marfort
Clairean
Fairhaven
Vigilsea
Bonehall
Freeport
The Federacy
Darcliff
Dynn
Ebeth
Azad
Fyrn
Stonekeep
Greenridge
Qharg
Tyne
Wheatsheaf
Outpost
Great Southern Wastes
Ashran
Fareaches

To my mother.
Thank you.

THE
FINAL GOD
THE GODLESS TRILOGY | BOOK THREE

INTRODUCTION

The gods have left us. Only two remained – Bythe of the Iron Union and the Blessed Mother Maelene of the Outer Wild. War between these two last gods was inevitable, and after decades of conflict, Maelene was ultimately deceived and murdered by Bythe. The Iron Union has been in ascendancy ever since that black day.

Commander Vale – the young, illegitimate daughter of Bythe – invaded the remote town of Outpost, the home of a young woman named Elyn. A chance encounter between them revealed they were identical in appearance, but before Vale could act, Elyn and her father fled to the remote town of Fairhaven. Over the following two years, Commander Vale chafed under the cruel supervision of Yvorre – Bythe's grotesque Mistress of Spies and Assassins – who dominated and controlled Vale's every move.

Fairhaven was attacked by raiders, and Elyn's father brutally murdered in front of her. In this moment of primal grief, Elyn and Vale's connection was strengthened, and both understood the truth of their existence: they were two halves of the same person – the daughter of Bythe split in two. Mistress Yvorre exploited this tragedy to discover Elyn's whereabouts and sent her fearsome servant – the unstoppable Imbatal – to retrieve the girl.

Deserting the Iron Union, Vale desperately set out in the hope of reaching Elyn. Imbatal and his army descended upon an unprepared Fairhaven, and the city was quickly overrun. As the battle raged, Vale arrived at Fairhaven and found Elyn. Together, they sought refuge with the Ageless – Maelene's followers.

Within the Temple, Vale and Elyn were confronted by the spirit of Maelene and the terrible secret of their birth was revealed. Maelene had not died as the legends recorded, but had been captured by Bythe and forced to bear his child to fulfill a prophecy that their daughter would end the war. When Maelene had tried to flee, their daughter had been split into two fractured godlings: Elyn and Vale. By pure accident – or whim of fate – Elyn had been lost to both of them, leaving the incomplete Vale behind. Over time, Maelene eventually degenerated into the twisted Mistress Yvorre, forever searching for Elyn in order to reunite her daughters as a weapon against Bythe.

Imbatal penetrated Fairhaven and ruthlessly hunted down Bythe's daughters. In order to save her people, Elyn surrendered herself into Vale, and the two reconciled into a new god: Valeyn. Imbatal was defeated and Valeyn quickly fled Fairhaven, fearing she would be used as another weapon in the ongoing war against her father.

Enraged at the revelation of his daughter's existence, Bythe dispatched Royal Inquisitor Exedor to find her and sent Baron Ethan – Vale's loyal subcommander – to march on Fairhaven. Mighty war engines smashed through the defenses of the Outer Wild, forcing Elyn's childhood friends – Jason and Nadine – to lead a failing defense of Fairhaven.

Valeyn reunited with Yvorre and helped her mother overcome the corruption which had poisoned her – restoring her identity as Maelene. With the help of their Ageless allies – Aleasea and Ferehain – they journeyed to Kardak to capture Exedor and free his hostage, a young girl named Naya. Underestimating his unnatural strength, Valeyn and her party were overpowered by the Inquisitor and forced to lead him to the source of Valeyn's secret, and the birthplace of immortal knowledge in Kovalith: The Tower.

In Fairhaven, Jason humiliated Baron Ethan with a stunning defeat, forcing the Baron to use an Ageless traitor to betray the city leaders, including Nadine's father, to their deaths. Devastated by her loss, Nadine miscarried Jason's child. From the wells of despair, Jason ordered the evacuation of Fairhaven and burned the city, remaining behind to face Ethan.

In The Tower, Valeyn was surprised to find the god Nishindra the Crafter still existing in Kovalith. With his help, they were able to overpower Exedor and enter The Tower to learn the truth of Valeyn's existence. To Maelene's horror, Nishindra revealed he had used his power to deceive her. Observing that all gods would ultimately go mad within the mortal confines of Kovalith, Nishindra had intended to manipulate Bythe and Maelene's combined power to summon the gods in the Etherian and call them for judgment – ending the cruel war. Valeyn was not intended to exist at all; she had no preordained purpose.

Consumed with rage Maelene killed Nishindra and summoned the Etherian – starting the final judgment of the peoples of Kovalith. Valeyn and Naya managed to convince Maelene to relinquish her hate and return to the Etherian in peace. However, before Valeyn could join them, she was stricken by a vision of Jason's impending doom and used The Tower to rush to him.

As Ethan stood poised to overrun Jason, Valeyn returned in a blaze of immortal fury and destroyed the Helmsguard war engines. Awed by her display, the loyal Helmsguard supplicated themselves before her, and Valeyn ordered their withdrawal from Fairhaven.

Jason fled to safety with the last refugees of Fairhaven.

Committed by her act of authority, Valeyn found she had no choice but to assume her place as Commander of the Helmsguard and return to the Ironhelm to face her father. In The Tower, Ferehain considered the power that now unexpectedly lay before him, and how it might be wielded to destroy all the gods of Kovalith.

BOOK ONE
RECKONING

CHAPTER 1

"Our gods have returned to us. After centuries of neglect, they now wish to reclaim what they have lost. This Desecration has long been foretold. Its nature has been quietly debated among our scholars over centuries; some claiming it would be an act of judgment for those of us who had followed their teachings, others predicting an elevation of all beings into the immortal realm of the Etherian. All such predictions were wrong. For it would seem we do not understand the true nature of gods."

~The Final Testimony of Aleasea of the Ageless

"Hail, Lord Bythe, our protector and saviour!" The cry rose from a lone speaker buried deep within the rows of soldiers trekking across the dusty plain.

"Hail!" came the reply from hundreds of men.

It was a ritual repeated every hour. A prayer of respect and recognition to their immortal guardian as they crossed over his lands. It was an offering of devotion, of complete unquestioning loyalty. It was a refrain expected from every soldier of the Helmsguard.

Valeyn remained silent.

The Iron Union had always been a frightening place to Elyn, as much as it had been a childhood school to Vale. Now Valeyn found she couldn't reconcile these conflicting feelings as she returned home.

Ahead of them, on a large hill, lay the proud town of Arbek. Like all cities within the Iron Union, it was protected by walls forged from black iron. Within those walls lay wealth – levels of wealth that people living in the Outland Alliance could only dream of. From a distance, it seemed the entire hill was lined with beautiful terraces and rows of ornate archways crafted in intricate detail. Valeyn knew that the illusion was generated by the hundreds of houses built by nobles and aristocrats within those walls – each competing with the other in splendour and grandiosity.

The sky above was polluted by myriad trails of thick, black smoke that curled upward from the countless kilns and refineries below. Bythe had long ago discovered the power of the metals locked within his lands and had learned how to harness it through fire and through force. The dark iron and darker smoke were always present throughout the lands occupied by her father.

It was the industrialised might of the Iron Union. It was her birthright.

"Charming little rat-hole, isn't it?" Ethan's voice cut through her thoughts and she smiled briefly at a memory. He had said those words to Vale a long time ago as they had approached Outpost as completely different people. Ethan had been a confidant then, a warm and reliable friend. Now a chasm seemed to stretch between them and neither knew how to bridge it. Both had betrayed the other in their own way, and neither knew how to atone for sins they did not truly regret.

"We've seen worse," Valeyn answered.

She turned to look at him, and he returned her gaze for a moment, as if he were about to rejoin with another light-hearted remark that had always been the shorthand between them. But after a moment, he looked away, as if further reminiscence were suddenly inappropriate under the circumstances. It had been over two months since she had left the ruins of Fairhaven and agreed to return to the Ironhelm. The experience of riding alongside the Helmsguard had been unusual, and yet it was also strangely familiar. The low scrublands of Mac-Soldai were recalling distant memories of Vale's youth, yet she couldn't recall such dry heat.

"Outrider," she called to a young man riding a few feet to her left. "I need some water, please."

The young soldier glanced sideways at her, and Valeyn could instantly tell he was one of those who considered her more of a prisoner than a

Commander. He looked at her carefully for a moment, clearly weighing his answer before deciding on a neutral response. "I don't have any, sir," he replied.

Valeyn sighed and was about to let the matter drop when Ethan's words rang out. "Then you damned well go and find her some!" Ethan snapped. "And you're pulling a double watch tonight for that little display of insolence, soldier. If I hear you disrespect another of my officers, I'll have you in a cell. Do you hear me?"

The young man stiffened in his saddle and saluted, his face a mix of surprise and embarrassment. He'd seen Ethan's awkward exchange with Valeyn, and obviously thought he'd try to score some points with his Commander, with a disastrous outcome. Valeyn supressed her smile.

"Yes, sir," he called out before wheeling his horse and trotting back down the line to find the water carrier.

Although Valeyn had formally resumed her position as Commander as soon as they left Fairhaven, she found that simply returning to her position of authority had been more complicated than she expected. Soldiers of the Helmsguard viewed her as a saviour or a traitor; there seemed to be no middle ground. The exchange with the sullen Outrider hadn't been the first time she'd encountered such barely repressed hostility, and she knew it would be far from the last.

Valeyn returned her attention to the hill and the opulent structures clinging to it. A lavish manor adorned the crest like an oversized ornament. It was Fullertanse, the residence bequeathed to the Earl of Mac-Soldai – the most powerful house within the Iron Union. It was Ethan's family home.

"How long has it been since you've been back?" Valeyn asked, but Ethan avoided her stare as if he hadn't heard. "Baron, do you have a moment?" she persisted, hoping a little formality might give him the excuse he needed to answer.

"It's Commander now, remember?" Ethan replied, nodding at the gold edging on his black armor. The Ironforgers had been quick to replace the breastplate he had donated to Valeyn, and he once again looked resplendent in the trappings of command. Valeyn noticed how well the look fitted him – it seemed to complement him far more naturally than it had ever done to her.

"How long has it been, Ethan?"

He sighed and seemed to abandon a feigned indifference. "Years. In fact, you were with me the last time I was here – or at least Vale was."

Valeyn recalled that visit. Ethan had been promoted to the rank of Baron and had been attached to Vale as her Chief Officer, despite the fact that she was several years his junior. Apparently, being the daughter of Bythe bumped you up the ranks – even if you were an unrecognized daughter.

"Yes, I remember," she answered then, after a moment, added, "Your family never really liked me, did they?"

Ethan didn't answer straight away, and when he finally spoke, he seemed to choose his words carefully. "They're a proud and noble house. The largest in the union and the greatest economic force by far. You know what's important to those families."

"Prestige? Recognition? An all-consuming need to be better than your peers?" Valeyn said with a smile.

"Well, my brothers thought it was a great honor that I was assigned to your command," Ethan offered with a touch of reticence.

Valeyn nodded. She didn't need her empathy to sense what he was thinking. "But your mother thought the son of the most important house of Bythe's empire shouldn't be relegated to serving a young girl?"

"Something like that. I seem to recall my father thinking that I should somehow culture you and then have you serve me as a respectful and dutiful wife."

An unexpected laugh broke free from Valeyn. "He expected me to wait at the door for you every evening with dinner served and wine poured?"

Ethan smiled and seemed to blush a little. "Again, something like that." He paused for a moment and recovered something of his lost playfulness. "I have to admit, it's something of an unusual mental image. I don't think I know how to picture you with an apron."

She laughed again. "Perhaps we can find one and you can finally present me to your family in the manner they think proper."

Ethan laughed with her. "Oh, I'm sure they'd love that."

Valeyn's smile faded abruptly and she looked about her as if she had forgotten where she was. "Ethan," she sighed, "what sort of homecoming is this?"

Ethan's smile also faded, and he looked at her sincerely for the first time since they'd commenced their journey to the Ironhelm. "It's the one the gods have given us," he replied. "I think we now just have to have faith."

Valeyn swallowed words that rose unbidden. She suddenly wanted to tell him the secrets she'd learned in The Tower. She burned to spill the truth, to throw it at him. She wanted to scream at gods who weren't listening. She wanted to tell Ethan how the gods had deserted them, how they'd slowly been driven insane through their mortal existence. Instead, she sighed and kept her secrets. There would be a time to tell him everything, but it was not now. Not before she had confronted her father.

A horn blew from the wall in the distance and it was answered by a note from their own herald at the front of the party. At this, Ethan rode forward and began issuing orders. Banners were unfurled and the violet standard of the house of Mac-Soldai waved proudly over the heads of the Helmsguard as they marched with unerring discipline.

Within an hour they had arrived at the outer walls of Arbek and the heralds rang their horns in unison. A roar erupted from the battlements of black iron, giving Valeyn her first taste of what awaited her within the Iron Union.

Helmsguard protocol demanded that any delegation carrying an officer of the nobility was to be greeted with a show of respect proportionate to the officer's rank and standing. Baron Ethan had always been well respected, and this had only grown since Bythe had personally assigned him to lead his army to Fairhaven. But the cries erupting from the walls eclipsed any formal salute that Valeyn had ever heard. It was the cries of a mob. And in that moment, she realized the thunderous noise was not coming from the top of the walls, it was coming from beyond them.

Ethan rode back to Valeyn and when he looked at her, she could see anxiety on his face. It was an unusual expression for him. He turned in his saddle and snapped orders to a nearby soldier before returning his attention to Valeyn.

"It seems like you've created a bit of a fuss," he said.

Valeyn turned back to look at the wall. "Are they cheering for me?"

"I'm not sure if *cheering* is the right word. I'm told some of them are. I think some are here to lynch you as a traitor, but I think most of them are just here to get a look at the new god. Either way, we need to take some precautions."

As he finished speaking, a squad of two dozen Helmsguard took up defensive positions around her. Valeyn smiled at the gesture. Although she'd never tested herself against an angry mob, she was reasonably confident that – after destroying a war engine – she could handle a few disaffected commoners. Once the men were in place, Ethan shouted another command that was repeated up the line of men until the column of soldiers began to move toward the black iron gates.

Valeyn looked about as the column moved through the massive archway. The purple standards of the house of Mac-Soldai adorned the parapets and alongside them were the rigid figures of Helmsguard standing to attention – mailed fists placed across their chests in salute. She wondered how many of them were saluting her. The roar of the crowd – previously muted by the walls – seemed amplified by the cacophonous chamber of the tunnel, and for a moment, she was overwhelmed by the sound. When they emerged from the tunnel, she beheld a scene of madness. The civilised people of Arbek were gathered in the hundreds, a clamouring mass of noise and unsatisfied expectation.

"By the gods," Ethan shouted as the column emerged from the tunnel. "Where are the Sheriffs? You there! Find them now!"

But Ethan's orders were impossible to carry out. All around them, the crowd pushed and surged closer – the cheering, yelling, and cursing all combined into one incomprehensible voice. Ethan barked another order, and the party formed a black wedge of soldiers as they slowly forced their way into the promenade. Shouts and cries went up from the crowd as Ethan's men inched through. The soldiers surrounding Valeyn became tense, and their hands constantly flitted to the sabres resting on their belts.

Where were Arbek's Sheriffs?

The Helmsguard pushed through the crowd with angry shouts and threats. Their journey was meant to take them upward through the spiraling promenade that skirted the hill and led to Fullertanse at the summit, but Valeyn could see this would be almost impossible. It was as if an army of townsfolk were opposing them. Their slow progress abruptly halted as some commotion erupted at the head of the party and Ethan's orders to clear the way became more agitated.

"Valeyn. My goddess! Please! Look this way!"

The cries became clearer and the crowd closed in around them.

"The daughter of Bythe is here! Praise our father!"

"Glorious Valeyn. Have you heard my prayers?"

"Traitor! Blasphemer!"

"Witch of Maelene! Execute her!"

Someone shoved one of the Helmsguard before her and the soldier stumbled back a step before drawing his sabre.

"No!" Valeyn ordered but her order was drowned out in the tumult.

"Save us, Valeyn!"

"Burn in the abyss!"

More sabres were drawn by the soldiers. Valeyn could hear Ethan shouting again. He was trying to make his way back to her, but he seemed so far away. The feelings from the crowd began to close around her, suffocating. With a jolt of panic, she realized she couldn't escape, even if she wanted to. The crowd had now enveloped her on all sides – but even worse – their feelings were now flowing unbidden, washing over her like relentless waves over a drowning woman. Each new assault denying her the chance to recover from the last, preventing her from drawing even one desperate breath.

"Help us, Valeyn!"

"Get back, please," she murmured but her heart was pounding. She didn't know where she was. She couldn't see.

"Praise Bythe. His daughter has returned to save us!"

"Stop it."

"Die, you Ageless whore!"

"Get back!" Valeyn screamed with the shrill power of panic and a wave of red force erupted from her. It slammed into the people around her – townsfolk and soldiers alike – and all were thrown away from her, landing roughly on the ground like discarded dolls.

Screams of panic filled the air and within seconds, the crowd had changed from a unified force to a fleeing rabble. People ran heedlessly in any direction, desperate to escape the godly danger that was now seething among them in the crowd.

Valeyn saw none of this. She could only hear the screams as she collapsed to her knees, gasping for air in stricken sobs.

"Vale!"

She could recognize Ethan's voice calling her childhood name, but she didn't respond. All about her, people were running in fear, people wanted to flee from her presence. She suddenly wanted to join them.

"Vale! Are you alright?" Ethan's voice was next to her now. She opened her eyes and saw the promenade was quickly draining. Her guards had recovered from the assault and stood well back, weapons drawn and ready to be used against her, fear radiating from the black helmets. She wanted to say something, to apologize or explain, but she knew it was pointless. She was a god to them now. Gods can never explain their actions; their followers will only hear the answers they need. She took in a deep breath and slowly rose to her feet. The panic was subsiding, only to be replaced by a sudden shame at what she had done.

Is this the onset of madness, child?

She pushed aside the thought – although it felt alien to her. Not yet. It couldn't be. There was still too much to do.

"I'm fine, Commander," she answered, willing her voice to be steady. The poisonous emotions had fled now, but the memory of them still lingered. Valeyn became aware that every eye now rested on her. It was as if the entire town was waiting to see what she would do next. Even Ethan was looking at her expectantly. These people had become so conditioned to accept the random acts of their gods, so desperate to ascribe a higher meaning to them. Revulsion filled her.

"At attention, Helmsguard!" she snapped, and instantly they responded by standing tall, fists across their chests. Ethan seemed to break from her spell and remembered his place. Avoiding her gaze, he barked more orders and the soldiers began to reorder themselves.

The clatter of hoofbeats rang from further up the promenade, as a troop of mounted soldiers rounded the bed and drew up before the visiting party.

Ethan pushed his way through his men and stormed to face the lead rider as he dismounted.

"Where in the hells have you been, Sheriff?" Ethan raged.

The lead Sheriff removed his black helmet to reveal a young face of no more than twenty years. He looked both flustered and contrite as Ethan towered over him and continued his tirade.

"My men arrive in Arbek in search of rest and welcome and are instead greeted by a braying mob. Is this how you acquit the duties of the Union? Is this how Arbek welcomes her knights? Where were you?"

The Sherriff opened his mouth to stammer an answer, but another voice spoke over him.

"Oh, c'mon now, Ethan, let the poor lad go. You're still in one piece, aren't you?"

A tall man with red hair and a thin face smiled down at Ethan from his position on his fine, chestnut horse. A range of different emotions seemed to flash across Ethan's face at the sight of his older brother, but he didn't have a chance to voice any of them.

"Don't tell me you're rattled by a few pushy commoners. I thought you'd faced down armies." The elder brother chuckled as he swung off his horse with natural ease.

Ethan seemed to struggle for the right reply as the man walked over to embrace him. "Rayner," Ethan said at last. "I didn't know you were here."

Rayner smiled again but it gave him a somewhat disinterested air. He very much wore the look of an aristocrat, which contrasted sharply next to his younger sibling.

"Someone's got to look after the estate with you off saving the Union," Rayner replied, looking about as he spoke, as if Ethan wasn't quite worth his full attention.

Valeyn recalled Rayner from their only meeting a long time ago. He was the eldest brother and natural heir to the family estate. Unlike most of the House of Mac-Soldai, Rayner had held little interest in the might of the Helmsguard. He was tall and lean with a dispassionate face marked by early middle years. He wore a fine suit in his family colors of deep violet. Every inch of him held disdain for the vulgarities of war. Even now as he glanced at the soldiers milling about the promenade, he had the look of a man viewing his property. When his eyes found Valeyn, they lingered uncomfortably.

"And here she is, the young Vale. My, you are impressive," he said, appraising her from head to foot. Although Valeyn stood taller than him, the aristocracy always had a way of making others feel small.

"My name is Commander Valeyn, Lord Rayner," she replied evenly.

Rayner smiled. "*Commander*, is it? Well, I'm not so sure about that." He nodded at her emerald-green breastplate. "I'm not a military man like my young brother here, but I'm fairly certain you're not wearing the colors of the Iron Union."

Valeyn opened her mouth to argue but Ethan spoke first.

"Valeyn has returned to us willingly. She's our guest, brother. Please extend her such a courtesy."

Rayner held her eyes for a moment then shrugged. "Guest? Prisoner? It's all a matter of perspective, isn't it? And of comfort, I suppose." He laughed as if he'd made a joke that only he could understand. "But you're right, of course, Ethan. How rude of me. Please, allow me to escort your party for the rest of the journey. Mother and father are so anxious to receive you. Come, they have a reception ready. And I'm deeply sorry about that, but you know our mother."

He clapped Ethan on the shoulder and turned to re-mount his horse. Ethan looked at Valeyn as if to offer an unspoken apology, but she waved it away with a quick nod. She had known that no part of this journey was going to be easy. The soldiers surrounding her regrouped and they all resumed their journey up the promenade. Valeyn glanced north toward the horizon and the black towers of the IronHelm beyond. Reaching her father was all that mattered.

•   •   •

Another shrill whine split the dawn. Jason screamed a warning as the ball of Godfire seared overhead and smashed into the ground a few dozen yards behind him. If there were cries from his men, he couldn't hear them – his focus was set on the Helmsguard rushing forward.

"Engage!" he cried and the men at his side obeyed his order. Figures in gray, blue, and green – the remnant colors of the Outland Alliance – rushed forward to meet their opponents of solid, black iron. Jason rushed with them and raised his weapon – a crude sword that needed both of his hands to wield – and brought it down onto the first figure in black who was unfortunate enough to cross his path.

Jason had learned that brute force was best when it came to fighting the Helmsguard. They were too well equipped and too well trained for him to fight them any other way. They were skilled solders with impressive training and discipline, but they had no passion, no rage. Rage was all Jason had.

The first Helmsguard buckled as Jason smashed his weapon aside and then cleaved into his neck with the second swing. He kicked the dying soldier away and moved to help one of his men struggling with his own enemy. They had the advantage of numbers for now, but Jason knew that wouldn't last. He ran his sword through the back of the Helmsguard, ignored the desperate nod of thanks from the man whose life he'd just saved, and squinted through the dawn shadows. The Cremators were scurrying about the base of the war engine, bringing forth bright, liquid fire to be loaded into its leaded belly for another attack.

"Move!" he screamed at his men and rushed forward again. He knew they couldn't stay in the same spot for more than a few moments. Through terrible experience, Jason had learned the war engines were devastating against anything in their path, but the same experience had also exposed their limitations; their great size meant they had difficulty destroying anything that was not directly in their path. This was the first limitation he intended to exploit on this cold morning.

He led his men across the open space and leaped into a trench that had been built as a network of defensive groundworks in front of Roy. It was the same defense he had used to defend Fairhaven, and although the Helmsguard had learned to no longer charge recklessly into this trap, they were nevertheless forced to maneuver their slow and clumsy machines very carefully. This was their second limitation.

There were two of the Helmsguard waiting in the ditch, but Jason's men made short work of them. The Iron Union had taken these trenches for the third time just two days ago, and while Jason had considered launching another attempt to reclaim them, he had correctly predicted the war engine would be waiting for them. They ran through the sodden mud and hoped they could get close enough before enemy reinforcements arrived or the engine refuelled. Jason had noted that it took them an average of ninety-three seconds to reload the engine with Godfire during most encounters.

He slammed into the timber sides of the trench with a heaving chest and peered over the lip. A few hundred feet away, Helmsguard officers were shouting orders to units, who were quickly forming up and preparing to enter the trenches in pursuit, while lookouts scanned the battlefield, hoping to guide the soldiers to wherever Jason and his men were hiding. Behind them worked the Cremators, clad in protective suits with masks and bulbous eye-glasses. Three of them struggled with an iron cart full of the searing liquid that fuelled the machine, while two more manipulated valves that released a rush of dark steam in preparation for the fresh load.

"Shane!" Jason hissed, and the large frame of his lieutenant joined him at the side of the trench. "Are we close enough?"

Shane's flat, brutish face contorted into an expression of concentration for a moment before nodding. "Yeah. This'll do."

Jason stepped away from the edge and motioned to three other heavy-set soldiers who were waiting behind him. They moved into the vacated space and all four unslung heavy crossbows from their backs and positioned them against the edge of the trench. They were Helmsguard weapons, fairly experimental given what Jason had learned from his confrontation with Ethan, but when they were later given the opportunity to capture a handful of them, Jason had recognized their value. Designed to penetrate armor, they were incredibly difficult to wield by all but the Ageless. The strongest of Jason's men had needed weeks of practice before they could hit any target with consistency.

The four men settled into position and withdrew long, wooden bolts from pouches on their waists and began fitting them into the weapons. The seconds passed interminably, and Jason glanced at the lookouts in the distance, knowing it would only be a matter of moments until they were sighted, and then dozens of soldiers would be upon them.

"Are you ready?" Jason snapped.

"Almost," Shane whispered back. With sharp, metallic clicks, the bolts were snapped into place, but the soldier at the end of the line continued to struggle. Shane gave him a glance. "What's going on?"

"Sorry, sir," he muttered as he continued to fumble with the bowstring. Shane was glaring impatiently, which seemed to only heighten the young man's anxiety.

A shout in the distance caught Jason's attention, and he looked up to see the Helmsguard lookout pointing in their direction. Another soldier was rushing to his side, and within seconds, he would confirm what the first man thought he saw. They were out of time. If they left now, the attack would fail, and if they remained any longer, they would all probably die. And while the second thought gave Jason no anxiety, the first thought rankled ; he dearly wanted to hurt the enemy, and he would not come this close to the opportunity only to let it go. But three crossbows wouldn't be enough.

The young soldier swore as he lost his grip on the bowstring and the bolt tumbled onto the mud at his feet. Shane's look now promised murder. Jason stepped over and retrieved the bolt, wiping the wet dirt from it before handing it back to the young soldier. Jason remembered his name was Sturric. He was a young cadet from Bonehall who had joined them during their retreat north. A young man who should have been chasing young women instead of fighting for his existence in a filthy trench. He looked at Jason with nervous, brown eyes and muttered another apology before turning back to his weapon.

A second shout broke the dawn, followed by several cries, and Jason didn't need to look up to know they'd been sighted. Instead, he placed his hand on Sturric's shoulder. "Breathe easy, cadet. Don't rush it," Jason said, as if they were on the training field with all the time they needed to practice.

Sturric nodded and took a deep breath. He drew back the string and the bolt snapped into place with a click. "Ready, sir," he whispered to Shane.

Shane nodded and all four men leaned over their weapons, taking careful aim at their targets. Jason kept his hand on Sturric's shoulder to offer a reassurance he didn't feel.

"Breathe easy, son," he repeated. "Relax. Don't think."

The Helmsguard's shouts grew louder and the first of their arrows began to land in the dirt behind Jason's position. He glanced up to see a line of more than a dozen Helmsguard heading to an opening in their trench several hundred feet ahead. Another line was heading in the opposite direction in an attempt to enter the trench behind Jason's men and block their escape. Jason took his hand away from Sturric's shoulder and stepped clear. "Fire," he ordered.

The twang of thick cords sounded, and the recoil threw one of the soldiers back a step. The four bolts tore through the morning air toward the mighty war engine. The thick iron plates of the machines stood ready to deflect them. Jason had learned they were completely impervious to infantry weapons – even those as powerful as a Helmsguard crossbow – but the Godfire that powered them? That was their third limitation.

Two metallic carts were each pierced by two bolts, and searing Godfire sprayed out in two glorious arcs of liquid fire. Cremators screamed as they were instantly set alight and began running like grotesque, burning effigies. The abandoned carts were left to topple on their sides and within seconds, the ground under the war engine had become a lake of flame. The Helmsguard started screaming orders to contain the fire, and the soldiers who had been running to block Jason's escape suddenly stopped, hesitated, then ran back to assist their desperate comrades trying to save the precious war engine. Jason could feel the heat searing his face, even from this distance, and he knew the inferno would burn for the rest of the day.

He clapped Sturric on the shoulder and nodded at Shane. "Good job, boys."

Without another word, they reslung their weapons and sprinted back in the direction they'd come, clearing the trench and running back toward their lines in the smoky, gray dawn. Nothing challenged their retreat beyond an occasional arrow landing well clear of them. As Jason had planned, the Helmsguard now had bigger problems to deal with.

They slowed their pace to a jog once they were close to the line of timber fortifications defending Roy, and Jason gave the signal for the barrier to be opened. Two wagons were pushed aside leaving a gap just large enough for the four men to squeeze into, then it snapped shut behind them.

Dirt-streaked faces looked at Jason with measured respect. Soldiers nodded their approval or saluted briefly before returning to their assigned duties. There were no cheers. Captain Jason would allow no such indulgences.

"We'll cheer when those bastards have turned around, not before," Jason had warned every soldier in their dwindling army. Cheers were for victories, and it had been too long since the Outland Alliance had enjoyed a real victory.

He pushed through the men and women in the tight space behind the barricade and out to the churned dirt of the field beyond. He turned to the four men and told three of them to see the medic, then to find a bunk for four hours before reporting in for their next assignments. Four straight hours of uninterrupted rest was a luxury, but there was no doubt these men had earned it. All but Lieutenant Shane. While there was no question of his entitlement to such a reward, Jason was simply in no position to bestow it. Shane followed his captain to a crude, wooden observation platform that had been erected ten feet above the ground and they mounted the steps.

Lieutenant Geordine stood on the platform with a map spread out on a desk before her. Her blue Fairhaven uniform contrasted against her short, red hair. She flashed them both a warm smile as they approached. "Glad to see you both back in one piece. When the flames went up, we thought you might be done for. Nice work, sir," she said.

Jason nodded but didn't reply. He walked to the edge of the platform and surveyed the landscape. Roy – the last refuge of the once-mighty Outland Alliance – was under siege. The Iron Union had arrived eighteen days ago to crush what remained of their enemies, and the small city had not slept since. Black smoke rose from the damaged war engine to the left, but he ignored it and scanned the fields to the right. The barricades that formed the defensive lines of the Outland Alliance stretched across the landscape in a semicircle. Beyond them lay the jagged lines of dozens of trenches that had been dug to slow the Helmsguard's advance. Sedren, the engineer who had assisted Jason in Fairhaven, had taken their idea to another level. The latticework of trenches had been constructed like a spider weaves a web, most of them now supported by interconnecting tunnels that allowed the defenders to quickly redeploy to wherever the Helmsguard chose to attack. It also gave them the ability to repair trenches quickly when the war engines inevitably levelled their power at them. The tactic was working. The Helmsguard advance was slowing. But Jason was still frustrated, he didn't want them to slow, he didn't even want them to stop; he needed them to go backward. And the Helmsguard had not taken a backward step since Fairhaven.

"Where's breakfast?" Shane grunted. Geordine pointed to wooden bowls on top of a barrel to her right and Shane crossed over to it.

Jason continued his vigil over the chaos before him. They simply did not stop. No matter how many defenses he threw up against the invaders, they continued to come, day after day. Roy was a small city positioned against the sea, deep within the Marfort Downs. A small, square fortification crowned the low hill at the center of the town, and hundreds of brightly colored dwellings decorated the streets that led down to the seawall. Jason had thought it must have been a fairly idyllic community before war arrived and the promise of annihilation had shattered such an illusion. They had constructed their defenses a mile out from the city, in a rough semicircle formed against the coastline. It was a smart defense, but it was their last one. With their backs to the water, there was no possibility of further retreat. The Outland Alliance would either prevail here and live, or it would die. And the Helmsguard had not taken a backward step.

Lieutenant Shane swore as he spat the watery gruel out of his mouth and threw the half-finished plate onto the barrel top. "Bloody disgusting. Who needs the Helmsguard? A few more weeks of that crap and we'll all be dead from poisoning," he muttered, wiping his mouth with his sleeve.

"It's all we got, Shane. Just eat up and try not to act like a child," said Geordine as she walked over to stand beside Jason. "You think they're going to try and break through again?"

Jason shook his head. "I don't know. They haven't come in three days so it must be coming soon."

"What in the hells are they waiting for?" asked Shane as he walked up beside Geordine.

"Maybe your antics with their engine are making them nervous," said Geordine. She paused and sniffed the air. "Or maybe it's your smell holding them back. My gods, Shane, do you ever wash?"

Shane shrugged again. "I'll have time to wash when this is over or they'll wash my body, not before."

"How wonderful for the rest of us," she replied, looking away from him. The corners of Shane's eyes tightened which was the closest he ever came to smiling.

"Enough joking," Jason reprimanded them gently.

"Sorry, sir," she answered.

Jason considered the five grotesque spikes of iron that scratched the sky. Those war engines had barely moved in the past four days.

"I think it's starting to have an effect," he said.

"You'd bloody well hope so," said Shane. "That's the third lot of Godfire we've been able to destroy. It must be starting to hurt them by now."

It had been Nadine's insight. While the engines were all but impervious, their source of power wasn't, and the further the machines were from the Iron Union, the scarcer that source of power must be. To that end, their strategy centerd on exhausting the war engines of their Godfire. They had staged diversionary attacks designed to waste the enemy's ammunition, and when the Helmsguard finally understood the ploy, Jason then decided on more creative approaches.

"So, let's keep it that way. I want those bastards so worried about their priceless war engines, that they don't dare risk moving them another step," ordered Jason.

"Well, then, I'd better go make sure they don't put out that fire in a hurry," Shane said.

"I'm going to inspect the southern lines. Geordine, carry on here. Shane, you're in charge of our war engine. If I come back and that thing looks even capable of moving again, I'm holding you personally responsible."

"You don't have to worry. By the time we're through with them, they're gonna hate their own machine, sir."

Jason looked at Shane and tried to recall the young bully he'd bested during the Wellspring Festival so long ago. They had all changed since those days, of course, but age had tempered Shane's brash thuggery into a raw, honest strength that Jason now relied on.

"Good man," Jason turned and left to the sound of Shane barking orders to his men, extending them dire promises of his views on failure. He climbed down from the observation platform and walked south. Everywhere he looked, he saw the hallmarks of war. Aged men tramped over ruined cornfields, carrying filthy sacks of supplies to the front lines, the necessitudes of farming now considered to be a dispensable luxury. Jason barely noticed the group of half a dozen young boys receiving sword drills from an older youth, barely old enough to hold a sword himself. He chose to ignore their idolizing stares as he walked past. He refused to think about them at all; they reminded him far too much of himself. Instead, he continued marching down the field, desperate for a distraction from the memories that began to stir in the corners of his mind, far too eager to throw himself into the dark work of a world that was no place for children.

CHAPTER 2

"Unlike the Outland Alliance, the Iron Union is not an association of independent nations. Where Maelene sowed societal unity through a natural ecosystem of balance and cooperation, Bythe believed that true strength came from unified purpose under a single vision – his vision.

Bythe did not believe in furnishing his empire with the natural wonders we take for granted in the Outer Wild. While other gods decorated the world with deep forests, waterways of crystal-blue or snow-capped mountains, Bythe cared only for metal, and he created a land rife with almost every ore in Kovalith. This made the lands of the Iron Union seem almost barren by comparison.

But while the Iron Union might lack the aesthetic beauty found in the wildernesses of this world, nobody can fault the machinery of its industry, and when it was necessary to organise the people to one shared purpose, Bythe proved himself to be without peer. Through a combination of dominance, intimidation, and guile, Bythe manipulated the nations of the west to accept subjugation as vassal houses, where each could compete for importance within the hierarchy of his empire. The most powerful house is named Mac-Soldai; and the riches they supplied the Iron Union allowed them to cultivate an army far exceeding all rivals. Which is why many of the other houses have often united in plots to undermine them."

~The Final Testimony of Aleasea of the Ageless

Fullertanse sprawled across the hilltop like an extravagant waste. The three-storied manor stretched its dual wings in an almost deliberate attempt to ensure no competing object could share its nest at the height of Arbek. Even during her youth, Vale had never understood the vile indulgences of the Iron Union's nobility. While the Ironhelm had stood as a testament to austere strength, the cities throughout the conquered empire did not all hold to the same values. It rankled Valeyn that these fops were willing to accept the protection of the Helmsguard without sharing the values that sustained them. To Ethan's credit, he had never seemed altogether comfortable with the ostentatious wealth and influence wielded by his family. Influence so pronounced, they were the only house to have their lands named after them, one of the many honors which distinguished them from their rival houses.

The bulk of Ethan's party had been offered rest at the guardhouses some distance away on the promenade below, as it seemed that even soldiers of the Iron Union were not strictly welcome beyond a certain altitude. Ethan had selected a number of his senior officers and Valeyn to complete the journey. Trumpets blared as Rayner and Ethan led their small delegation through the massive iron gates which stood wide and welcoming. Black-clad soldiers lined the path with violet banners of Mac-Soldai held aloft. Valeyn rode behind Ethan and wondered if these nobles even considered themselves to be real subjects of Bythe.

The gravel road to the manor ended with steps leading to a grand balcony adorning the entrance to the colossal facade. Upon this flamboyant platform stood Lord Garde and Lady Sarele along with what Valeyn assumed must have been the entire serving staff of their household. Lord Garde looked almost exactly as Valeyn remembered – tall with red hair, round of body and rounder of face, but with a healthy and exuberant love of life in his expression. Lady Sarele stood in contrast to her husband, short and slender, with stern eyes set in a handsome face framed by dark hair. Valeyn met her gaze and could feel the judgment emanating from the middle-aged woman. Valeyn had always struggled to believe she could be Ethan's mother.

"My boy!" Lord Garde erupted and tottered down the steps as Ethan pulled up in front of them. Lady Sarele seemed about to protest the obvious breach in decorum, but threw up her hands in a slight admission of defeat and descended the steps behind her excited husband. Lord Garde had already embraced his son leaving Valeyn facing Lady Sarele with the slightly awkward task of agreeing on the suitable level on intimacy between them.

"Lady Sarele, it is an honor to be in your house once more," said Valeyn with a formal bow appropriate to their respective stations.

"Young Vale, it is so good to see you again. My, how you've grown," Lady Sarele replied with a faint smile.

Valeyn ignored the refusal to acknowledge her rank – let alone her name – and turned to Lord Garde who had untangled himself from this son and now enveloped her in a comparable embrace. The scent of wine lingered over him and Valeyn understood he had begun his own celebrations some time earlier in the day. After extracting herself from the affectionate greeting, she had a moment to herself as the House of Mac-Soldai was entirely focused on the return of the favorite son. Ethan seemed uncertain how to handle the attention and for a moment, he shot her a look that seemed to be a desperate cry for assistance. Valeyn smiled and shrugged at him.

After the necessary greetings were completed, Lady Sarele noticed the encroaching twilight and declared it was time to attend the reception.

"Really, mother. Must we be put through this? Valeyn and I have had a long journey, and we aren't even in our dress uniforms," said Ethan.

"Oh, nonsense," replied Lady Sarele. "Field armor is a perfectly acceptable standard of dress for any honored member of the Helmsguard."

"Indeed, it's preferred!" said Lord Garde. "What better way to present the victorious Commander Ethan than in his glorious armor, forged in the image of Lord Bythe?"

Valeyn was suddenly confronted with her decision to reforge her armor in the emerald green of her mother, Maelene. It had seemed like a confident assertion of her independence at the time, but in the current setting, she found herself feeling rather self-conscious. Lady Sarele seemed to read her mind as she looked over Valeyn's body.

"That's a striking look you've chosen for yourself, Vale. I'm sure it will cause quite the stir among the nobility in there. Pay them no mind. You're in my house and under my protection," Lady Sarele added dryly. It occurred to Valeyn that Ethan's mother had perfected the art of conveying the exact opposite meaning of the words she spoke. It was bewildering and frustrating all at the same time.

They all moved into a grand foyer, which was flanked by two staircases carved from white marble. The party moved between the stairways, down the center of the room and into an even larger ballroom beyond. The room was packed full of people dressed in the formal black silk of the Iron Union, and Valeyn immediately felt out of place at the sight of them. The impression was only heightened when a bell announced their arrival and every face in the room turned to her. Suddenly, she found it was easier to face down a war engine than to enter this room.

The House Master's voice rang out clearer than the bell as he formally announced the party to the assembled mass of nobility. When her name was finally announced – at the very end of the pecking order of dignitaries – judgment assailed her from every corner of the room. Valeyn's green armor appeared to evoke an equal measure of scandal and bemusement, but most seemed content to stare at the curiosity who had wandered into their predictable and supercilious lives.

I will not be intimidated by these peacocks.

Valeyn didn't wait on ceremony. She stepped forth before Lord Garde and walked into the room with as much forced poise and indifference as she could summon. She took a measure of satisfaction at the repressed indignation she could feel rippling throughout the room at her small act of arrogance. Everything was repressed when it came to these people.

Seconds later, Ethan was at her side, swiftly guiding her into the waiting clutches of a group of men who had clearly been promised the first audience with the visiting celebrity. She contemplated denying them their presumptuous expectation but decided one openly rebellious act was quite enough for now.

A tall man with thinning hair stepped forth and bowed before Ethan. The smile on his face seemed genuine and Ethan's expression brightened in return.

"Hello, uncle," said Ethan, nodding his head in a formal gesture befitting their respective stations. "It's been too long. How is Claryn?"

The older man's smile became wry, and he shrugged his thin shoulders. "She's decided to stay at the estate, so our marriage at this moment is therefore peaceful. But come, Ethan. Let's not talk about an old man's problems. You are the guest of honor, and you must tell us your story first!"

Ethan grimaced in a vain attempt to hide his discomfort. "What are you talking about?"

"What everyone is talking about – you. You destroyed Fairhaven, the home of the Ageless! You've shattered the heart of the Outland Alliance. They're falling now because of you."

Ethan looked uncomfortable as he searched for a reply. "The stories are exaggerated, uncle. There are thousands of Helmsguard all doing their part in the war. My successes are just one small part of the larger campaign."

Laughter erupted from the men around them.

"Oh, Ethan. You poor noble fool," said Rayner, as the rest of the family walked up to join the group. "You're the greatest soldier in the Union right now and you're still too damn noble to take the credit for it. It's just as well that you're a brilliant tactician because you'd be terrible at politics."

Lady Sarele smiled and touched Ethan on the shoulder. "I don't know about that. His humility is refreshing. Perhaps the people need someone who speaks through actions rather than through hollow boasts and displays of wealth."

Rayner's face tightened at this reproach and he fell silent. Valeyn could sense his frustration. It seemed the heir apparent had quickly become the overlooked son, and Rayner was not happy with the reversal.

"Allow me to introduce Commander Valeyn," Ethan announced in a clear attempt to deflect the unwanted scrutiny.

Valeyn met the eyes of every member of the group and challenged each in turn.

I will not be intimidated by these peacocks.

The smiles all held, but there was a wilderness of insincerity on display. She didn't know the people before her and didn't want to. All she wanted was to get through this absurd ritual and be on her way to the Ironhelm.

"Commander Valeyn, my name is Fowles-Marlow of the House of Ciro. It is an honor to finally meet you," said a thin, silver-haired man.

Valeyn noted the usage of the hyphenated name, a complication of the usually simple names chosen by people in the Iron Union and also an unmistakable symptom of pretension.

"Fowles-Marlow, it's a pleasure. You're a long way from home." Valeyn answered. Ciro lay to the north, halfway between Arbek and the coast. It was a simple town by the standards of the Union, administered by even simpler lords.

"I'm staying as a guest of Lord Garde and Lady Sarele. We're discussing the finer points of a trade agreement between our houses. Quite dull, I assure you. You, on the other hand, are far more interesting. You must tell us what you've been up to this past year. You've had the entire Union in a complete state of anxiety wondering where you've been."

Valeyn shifted her weight uncomfortably as she tried to manipulate the conversation to a direction of her choosing. It occurred to her this was not dissimilar to a duel, although she would have been far more comfortable with a sabre than with words.

"I don't think that's as interesting as people seem to believe. I simply needed some time to myself," she hedged. "Really, though, tell me about your business with Mac-Soldai. I'd like to be brought up to date with the economic changes in my father's empire."

The gray-haired man wore the look of a teacher confronted with an overly-inquisitive student. His eyes glossed over with contempt as he slowed his speech into patronising tones.

"The economics of Ciro are quite complex. Forgive me, but I'm not sure I could give you a detailed enough explanation in this reception. And you were last assigned to fight the savages in the Southern Wastes as I recall? I'm not sure you were given the proper education for these matters, but I do appreciate the curiosity."

Valeyn's smile didn't drop. "Forgive my curiosity, sir. My understanding is a little simplistic. For example, I recall the House of Ciro was somewhat behind with their tax obligation to my father, and I was sincerely hoping your fortunes had improved during my absence. But maybe I just don't comprehend the complexity the situation?"

The old man's face flushed an intense shade of red, and he laughed nervously as if Valeyn had made a joke.

"Well, times are difficult, aren't they?" Rayner interjected. "The land seems to have turned against us these past few months. Crops aren't yielding any decent harvests. The weather has turned warmer, then colder.

There have even been stories of water falling from the skies in the south. Strange times."

"Quite right," replied Fowles-Marlow with far less bravado. "The economy has been slow throughout the entire empire. We had all hoped that Lord Bythe's great war would have improved things, but the opposite seems to now be the case."

"That's enough talk of business, Fowles-Marlow," Lady Sarele chided. "We're here to honor my son and his Commander Vale. She has always been a welcome guest in this house."

"Thank you, Lady Sarele," Valeyn answered.

"Oh, I forgot, my dear. Forgive me," Lady Sarele said in a tone that held neither contrition nor regret. "You're not quite Vale anymore, are you? You call yourself . . . Valeyn now. Did I get that right?"

"Yes, that's right." Valeyn stiffened.

"You poor girl. I heard that traitor Yvorre and the Ageless did something quite terrible to you. I mean, just look at you now. You're taller than almost every man and quite intimidating to behold. This must be very difficult for you."

"Was it Yvorre, Mother?" Rayner interrupted. "I heard that she was supposed to be Maelene, now returned to them."

Lady Sarele laughed and several of the others joined her. "Oh please, Rayner. That's exactly what they would believe – that their fallen goddess was secretly living among us all these years and then she returned to save them. No, Mistress Yvorre was a cunning old crone. I'm sure she had some scheme in mind to seize power for herself."

"Indeed," interjected a well-fed, round-faced nobleman. "In fact, I have it on good authority from the Ministry that it was Yvorre who contributed to the fall of the Ageless. She summoned demons from Kardak to try and take Maelene's secrets for herself and was destroyed in the process."

"Yes, quite right. I also received similar reports," agreed Lady Sarele

The proud ignorance and brazen lies assailed Valeyn. How could these people isolate themselves from the world so completely and yet claim to understand it so intimately? She wasn't sure how much people knew, but she was fairly confident the rumors would overshadow any truth. She fished about for the right words but was far too slow. Fortunately, Ethan was more experienced with these situations.

"Valeyn has been through a lot, Mother. I don't think we should pry into her feelings tonight. We've all had a long journey."

Lady Sarele smiled. "Oh, you always looked out for her, didn't you? You know you two would have been such a charming couple back when you were younger. Such a shame now."

"Why is it a shame now?" Valeyn asked.

Lady Sarele looked at her with mock surprise. "Well, of course. Surely, you're not interested in a husband now. I mean, you're clearly not quite . . . feminine . . . anymore. Are you?"

The judgment was meant to sting. It wasn't the assumption of her sexual preference, but the clear rejection of her suitability as a match for Ethan that hurt.

"Stop prying, Sarele. It doesn't matter how she prefers to live," said Lord Garde in joyfully boisterous tones before turning to Valeyn. "Either way, Ethan here would be at home making the beds and nursing your children while you were out drinking and fighting! Can you picture that little household?" Lord Garde erupted with a laugh that filled the room.

Valeyn struggled to find a reply that wouldn't further justify the intrusion into her privacy. Even Ethan was at a loss for words.

"I think Commander Valeyn has far greater ambitions nowadays," said Lady Sarele, skilfully steering the conversation away from Valeyn after having scored such a personal blow. "She's going to return to her father and hopefully convince him to return to his people."

"What do you mean?" Valeyn asked.

Lady Sarele looked at her with mild surprise. "Nobody has seen Lord Bythe in over a year. Why, some are even spreading nasty rumors that he's no longer alive. I'm sorry, my dear, I thought you knew this."

Valeyn hesitated. She knew her father had become more reclusive over the years, but she hadn't known he'd retreated from his subjects so completely.

Seizing the opportunity to join the conversation, a short, middle-aged man pressed forward and gave a small bow to Valeyn. "My name is Dario. I must say I'm extremely pleased to hear that you're returning to Lord Bythe. I think your father needs you now, more than ever."

"Oh, don't start exaggerating, Dario. The war is going extremely well. Reports indicate the Outland Alliance will fall any day now," answered Lady Sarele,

"That's right," rejoined the drunken Lord Garde. "Fairhaven has fallen, thanks to our boy. Bonehall and Darcliff have also been wiped out by those incredible machines. I hear they're marching into Marfort now."

"Even the free ports of the Federacy are under siege. They won't hold out much longer," said Fowles-Marlow, eager to rejoin the conversation after his humiliation.

"The Ageless are completely destroyed, isn't that right, son?" said Lord Garde.

"I don't know that they're *completely* destroyed, but I watched their temple burn. In fact, they burned it themselves before we could claim it. From what the traitor E'mar told me, I think their power is all but gone." Ethan spoke carefully in the presence of Valeyn. He had watched her claim the green *kai* of Maelene in Fairhaven and knew it still lingered.

"A shame you couldn't seize the Temple," sighed Lord Garde with a touch of disapproval. "That was the mission, wasn't it?"

"Stop it, husband. He defeated the Ageless and forced them to burn their own power. That's an outstanding victory by any measure," said Lady Sarele.

Ethan shrugged. "Seizing the Temple would have been desirable, but that was always going to be difficult, even with the Fingers of Bythe. Like Mother said, the destruction of the Ageless was what Lord Bythe needed. The mission was still successful."

"It is a clear victory, and one our Lord Bythe dearly needed," agreed Dario. "The Prodigals will not be happy with this show of strength. It will almost certainly weaken their own sphere of influence at court."

"Please, Dario," said Lord Garde. "Don't start trying to convince us of the existence of the Prodigals. We really don't need more fanciful stories."

"Oh, the Prodigals are quite real. Don't be fooled on that count. My young Valeyn, you must be very concerned about this."

The name of the Prodigals brought back unwanted images of Exedor. He had first mentioned that name at Kardak – a rumored existence of highly-placed conspirators against Bythe. Maelene had known of them, but then, Maelene had always seemed to know of everything. "I really don't know anything about them," she lied.

"And that's precisely their power," Dario answered with the overenthusiasm of the intoxicated. "Nobody even dares mention their name up north, but they exist. There's a ring of very powerful men working to overthrow your father – overthrow him, or worse. It's feared that if you admit to their existence, you'll either be branded a lunatic or be accused as one of them." He leaned forward to whisper the last words at her and the ripe tang of wine assailed her. The others in the group looked on with slightly amused smiles.

"Please, young lady, your father needs to take this threat seriously. Will you raise it with him?" continued Dario.

"I'm sure I will," she smiled, anxious to move away from the subject.

"You'll get her laughed out of court, Dario," Lord Garde scoffed. "Who could kill a god? This is Bythe you're talking about – the last god on Kovalith. He has swept aside all opposition and now stands poised to conquer the entire Outland Alliance. He has never been so powerful. Any attempts to assail him now are simply unthinkable."

"Father, you insult our guest," Rayner broke in nodding to Valeyn with a wry grin. "Lord Bythe is no longer the last god of Kovalith. He has competition once again."

"I can assure you, Lord Rayner, that I am not his competition in any way. My father has nothing to fear from me," Valeyn answered.

Rayner's eyes sparkled as if he were toying with a fascinating idea. "But my father makes a valid point. Bythe *was* the last god on Kovalith, but now there's you. And it's said that a god can only be killed by another of his own kind. Perhaps Dario's Prodigals will seek you out and try to recruit you to their cause. Perhaps they already have?"

Valeyn was briefly stunned by the audacity of the thinly veiled insult, but before she could think of an answer she was cut off.

"Brother, you go too far!" Ethan growled. "Lord Bythe summoned me. I stood before him in person and I heard his commands . . . I heard him . . ." he trailed off as if catching himself saying something inappropriate. Rayner was smiling at his younger brother with that look of condescension back on his face. Valeyn wanted nothing more than to hit him.

"Yes, we forget. You've met our powerful Lord Bythe. You've actually stood in his presence, which is a rare thing these days. We've all forgotten how important you are, little brother, so please remind us. Tell us what he said to you," Rayner prompted.

The group was silent as everyone waited for Ethan to answer. Even Lady Sarele declined to come to the defense of her favorite son and she also waited expectedly. For his part, Ethan looked as if he had been asked to recollect a nightmare. Moments lingered before he finally spoke. "I was hauled in there from a cell in the bowels of the Ironhelm," he answered. "I'd been in that prison for months. You all know this. I'd been accused of treachery, or heresy, and of treason. That bastard Exedor came to me over and over again, with his questions and his . . . persuasion."

Valeyn looked at him with unbidden sympathy, never having heard of his torment. Ethan had never spoken to her of what he endured after she'd sent him away from Fairhaven. She listened to his simple words but knew they disguised so much more. Ethan was never one to embellish. He had always minimised his sorrow as if it were a sin.

"And she abandoned you to that fate," Lady Sarele finally looked at Valeyn with undisguised contempt, as if all cordiality and pretense had been suddenly stripped from her.

"No, *you* left me to that fate," he glared at his mother. "You all did. Where was the powerful House of Mac-Soldai when I needed it? Where was your mighty political influence within Bythe's court? And now you throw me this party and flaunt your influence in front of everyone, but it's all for show, isn't it? When I really needed my family, you were impotent!"

The small group was silent at this eruption of honest fury. Lady Sarele looked away in shock, as if her son had slapped her. Rayner's expression seemed to lie somewhere between anger and unexpected sympathy toward his brother. Even Lord Garde closed his mouth and looked at the floor with unusual sobriety.

Valeyn felt an urge to break the unbearable silence. She reached out and gently touched Ethan on the shoulder. "Ethan, this is your family. Please don't dishonor them in this way."

Ethan closed his eyes and straightened his posture; the noble son replaced the broken one once more. "Of course, Commander Valeyn.

Forgive me, everyone. It's been a very long journey and an even longer campaign. I bear many grievances which should not be directed at you."

There was a round of quiet nods from the group but Lady Sarele still looked away.

"Excuse me, I need to take some air," Ethan sighed and quickly left the gathering. Confronted with the prospect of facing Ethan's family alone, Valeyn also excused herself and hurried after him. Pushing through the crowded room of perfumed aristocrats, she passed through the open doors which led to a courtyard. She acknowledged the salutes of two guards and looked about the square and the magnificent garden lying beyond it. Even by the dim starlight she could make out rows of perfectly manicured hedges stretching far into the distance and for a moment, she thought of Nishindra's work at The Tower. The night was darker and colder than usual. She glanced up at the few stars which now hung in the black sky and wondered again what had happened. She had first noticed Kalte's star vanish back when she was at Tiet, and ever since, the stars had seemed to be departing one by one. The nights were getting darker and the air cooler, and Valeyn couldn't shake a feeling of dread. Was this damage done by Maelene at The Tower when she ripped the *kai* from the world? But she remembered Kalte's missing star had happened long before the events of The Tower, so what forces were at work? She finally spotted Ethan's lean frame silhouetted against the night and walked over to stand beside him. For a long moment they both stood there in silence, staring out across the shrouded hedges.

"You know," Valeyn began quietly, "your family hasn't changed much."

Ethan's shoulders shook and a laugh erupted against his will. Valeyn couldn't help but join him, and the sound of their amusement gave the courtyard a brighter mood for a moment.

"I'm sorry, Vale," Ethan said after his laughter died. "I honestly had no idea they'd be this vicious."

Valeyn ignored the use of her old name and shrugged in reply. "I wasn't really expecting a friendly reception, but I didn't think it'd be this hard on you."

Ethan shook his head. "I didn't think so either. I guess I wasn't expecting it to be this hard . . . so many emotions . . ."

She nodded and both were both silent for a while, as if neither were quite sure what to say. Eventually, Valeyn spoke. "My father, Ethan . . ." Valeyn tried to form the sentence, but found she couldn't voice that which she desperately wanted to know – as if asking the question would, in itself, confirm a weak, needfulness deep within her.

"Yes, Vale, he ordered me to find you. In fact, he made it very clear that finding you was all that mattered to him."

She fought down the fear as it threatened to rise within her again. Her confidence and bravado were impressive, but she knew it was based on a lie. Yes, she was a god, but what greater authority did she claim? What greater knowledge did she wield? The secrets she had learned in The Tower were hardly divine. In fact, they had proven to her there *was* no higher wisdom. The truth was, she had no idea what would happen once she stood before her father. He might strike her down as quickly as he might embrace her. All she knew was that she had to confront him. She had to stop running, take what she had learned from her mother and bring an end to the madness that was infecting the world. She had to try.

Ethan seemed to sense the emotions raging within her and turned to face her. "Family is a complex thing, isn't it? Even though we can love each other, it seems like there are times we shouldn't even be in the same room."

While Elyn had had a surrogate father in Leon, Vale had never known a true father, and Valeyn felt the old tremor of disunity between her twin selves. She took a moment to smooth over the feeling. "What does he want from me?" she whispered in a voice that trembled softly.

Ethan stepped closer and gently took her hand. "I don't know, but I'm sure he doesn't want to harm you. Either way, I'll be with you. I'd never have left your side if you hadn't ordered me away, Vale."

Valeyn could sense Ethan's deep feelings resurfacing. Old passions long denied were now being fed hope. She decided she couldn't be that selfish to him. "Ethan, you know I'm not Vale anymore, don't you? I'm a different woman now."

He snatched his hand back as if he'd been rebuked. "Of course, I know that," he said too defensively.

Valeyn opened her mouth to console him but something stopped her. There was suddenly a chilled edge to the air, and her breath had started to mist. For some strange reason she felt the need to be on her guard. Ethan caught her expression and immediately became alert, instinct earned from years fighting alongside each other taking over. Valeyn was now grateful for the fact that she hadn't been given time to change into a dress uniform as she gripped the handle of her sabre. Without a word exchanged, both soldiers immediately began scanning the night. Valeyn's training took hold, and the sounds of the party were reduced to background noise as she took in every detail of her surroundings, searching for a clue to her disquiet. She examined the potted boskaine plants, the light spilling onto the flagstones of the courtyard, the mist of her beath hanging in the still air before her face, the two Helmsguard standing at attention at the ballroom doors.

Her eyes locked onto the two men as if driven by some unknown need. She saw that mist streamed into the night air from the warm breath of the soldier to her left, but the air around the faceplate of the soldier on her right was free from condensation. It was as if he was holding his breath. Or as if he wasn't breathing at all.

Valeyn suppressed a cry as the figure leapt at her. Despite her preternatural reflexes, she was still caught off-guard by the speed of the attack. It had crossed the courtyard in an instant and Valeyn could sense the black metal cutting through the air toward her throat. She threw herself sideways and rolled onto the grass, the interlinked plates of her armor protecting her like a shell as she fought to free her sabre from its sheath. She had barely time to rise to a crouch before the black figure attacked again. The roll had jammed her weapon into the scabbard, and she tried to pull it free without snapping the blade with her strength. Her assailant made no sound as he flew at her again with the same impossible speed. Realizing the attempt to free her weapon had robbed her of the chance to evade, she held up her armored gauntlets to protect her neck as the black iron blade slashed at her. Her arms shuddered and she felt the iron plates on her forearms break under the force of the impact, but the black figure also twisted with the shock and tumbled awkwardly onto the ground behind her. Valeyn took a moment to verify her wrists hadn't been severed before turning to face her attacker, but that moment of self-concern cost her the advantage. The ground behind her was empty.

"Guards!" cried Ethan, but his voice seemed slow and distant. Valeyn had instinctively accelerated her movements and awareness to a heightened state, yet her attacker was operating at almost the same level. Ethan would be of little help, especially if her suspicions about her enemy were true.

Finally freeing her sabre, she held it before her as she stood motionless, waiting for the attacker to strike again. Footsteps betrayed Ethan's hurried approach.

"Stay where you are, Ethan!" she called out and his footsteps halted. The second Helmsguard was slowly approaching the gardens from her right, his weapon held at the ready as he also searched for the intruder. Valeyn opened her mouth to shout another warning, but there was a flicker of darkness and the man fell to the ground with only the soft clatter of his iron plates to mark his death.

"My gods," whispered Ethan. "Mercurion?"

"I think so," answered Valeyn without taking her eyes from the shadows before her.

The name of Bythe's assassin was spoken with fear throughout the Union. While Yvorre had always been a somewhat public figure, Mercurion had lurked in almost complete obscurity and seemed to enjoy autonomy from the formal ranks of the Helmsguard. His existence was a certainty, yet little beyond that was. Even Vale had been given no formal briefing or intelligence on the details of this spectral killer, only that he rarely – if ever – failed to fulfil the task Bythe set him.

Shouts from within the ballroom heralded the approach of more of the Helmsguard, more lives that would almost certainly fall to Mercurion before she would even have a chance to strike at him.

That will not happen.

Breathing in deeply, Valeyn threw her sabre to the wet grass and stretched out her hands. "I'm here, Mercurion," she called out into the night air.

"Valeyn!" Ethan shouted, but she held out her palm to stop him.

"Hold your ground, Ethan. I can't protect you from him."

"To the hells with that!" Ethan snarled and stepped forward with his weapon held ready.

"No!" Valeyn shouted, but the blackness before her quivered and flailed out at her.

The figure was that of a Helmsguard soldier, but he seemed to glisten as if he were shrouded in the night. Valeyn stood ready for the attack but was unprepared for Ethan's well-intended assistance as he swung his sabre at Mercurion. To her eyes, it was a child threatening a hurricane, and Mercurion barely took notice. He sidestepped the attack and struck out at Ethan with his own black blade. Valeyn rammed herself into Ethan, and her unexpected blow knocked all air from his body – saving his life as he cartwheeled onto the ground, out of Mercurion's reach. She implored all her heightened reflexes to recover, but the single action of saving Ethan seemed to have come at the cost of any other, and Mercurion seized advantage of her mercy. Reversing the blade that had missed Ethan, the assassin directed it instead at Valeyn's exposed side as she tried in vain to reposition herself. Valeyn closed her eyes and heard Ethan scream a warning as Mercurion plunged his sabre deep into her body. A moment passed as they both stood frozen in a horrific tableau. Then Valeyn turned and gripped Mercurion by the throat, holding him above the ground as he wiggled frantically in her grip. Mercurion lifted his freshly melted weapon up to his black, metallic face and Valeyn thought she could see surprise on the featureless visage. Valeyn smiled confidently to conceal her own racing heart – she hadn't known that was going to work, but it was nice to have her suspicions confirmed.

"Mercurion, I'm very pleased to meet you," she forced her voice to be steady. "Tell me, was it your idea to try and kill the daughter of Bythe with a metal weapon, or are you following the instructions of an idiot?"

The courtyard was now buzzing with the sounds of rushing feet and cries of excitement as soldiers rushed into the space. Figures in black iron filled the courtyard but Valeyn barely noticed them, her attention consumed by the creature writhing in her glowing red hand.

Red. The color of her father's *kai*. It pulsed through her like blood, and its energy caused her body to burn with a crimson nimbus that seemed almost murderous. Soldiers moved up beside her, clearly uncertain of what to do yet compelled by duty to at least act.

"Ethan! Vale! What happened?" Lady Sarele pushed her way through the crowd that had formed near the courtyard doors. When she saw Mercurion, her face froze in shock. "Guards, seize that creature."

"Stand back, all of you!" Valeyn commanded in a voice that swept through the space. The guards instinctively obeyed, and even Lady Sarele took a step back at Valeyn's sudden display of authority. Valeyn turned her attention back to the figure squirming in her grasp. "Who sent you to try and kill me? Answer, demon!"

Mercurion's blank face seemed to mock her question as he regarded her in silence. Valeyn tightened her grip on the creature's throat and red fire surged through her. A strange garbled cry came from Mercurion as pieces of metallic liquid began to bubble and break away from his body; floating in the air like dust.

"I am the daughter of Bythe. You dare presume to assault me? Who has ordered this?"

She concentrated on the left arm of the poor, dead solder who had served as Mercurion's host, and with the sound of grating metal, tore the limb from his body. Mercurion screamed his shrill cry again. Drops of black liquid fell from the wound and pooled on the grass like fetid water. Mercurion shrieked and thrashed, but her crimson grip didn't falter.

"I can kill you, demon. I'm probably one of the few who can. I hope you no longer doubt this. Tell me who sent you, or in my father's name, I will rip you to pieces right here."

She focused again and rage surged through her. In that moment, she wanted nothing more than to kill something; Mercurion, Lady Sarele, Rayner, all of these aristocratic fops who swarmed around her like servile animals. They crowded her with their banal questions and puerile attempts at intimidation and manipulation. She suddenly wanted to show them real power. She wanted to strike out at everyone who had hurt her. Mercurion screamed again as Valeyn ripped more metallic chunks from his body and discarded them into the night.

Yes. Show me your true nature, new god.

The voice in her head was different this time. It swirled among the rage that cloyed her mind.

"Vale!" Ethan shouted, and the red mist receded. He was standing beside her and she dimly realized he'd been saying something to her. She looked at him in confusion.

"Commander," he awkwardly corrected himself once he had her attention. "He's worth more as a prisoner."

"A prisoner?" she repeated as if confused. "This creature is worth nothing. All that matters . . ." She trailed off, realizing everyone in the garden was now listening to her.

Disgust gripped her and she concentrated on Mercurion again, only this time she didn't torture him further. Instead, his true liquid form contorted and tore away from the corpse of the Helmsguard he once possessed. It floated in the air like a shimmering pool of oil then immediately solidified into a twisted shape of black iron. It hovered for a moment before Valeyn dropped her hand and Mercurion fell to the ground in a prison of his own body.

"Take him," Valeyn said to nobody in particular and walked into the darkness of the garden. The courtyard behind her erupted into a frenzy of activity and shouted questions, but Valeyn ignored them. She was struggling to supress the crimson rage that still beat within her. Ethan's approaching footsteps were another unwelcome distraction and she turned to face him with frustration.

"Vale—" he began but she cut him off.

"I told you, my name is Valeyn. Stop treating me like I'm still your juvenile infatuation!" She forced all her useless anger into words. Words that could hurt someone and in doing so, achieve something.

Ethan's mouth opened and closed, and a strange expression passed across his face. For a moment he turned to leave, before arresting himself and taking a breath. "Commander," he continued. When she said nothing, he forged ahead. "Commander, I need to know if you're injured."

She sighed and the anger fled, leaving a swell of unexpected tears in its place. She took a moment before answering in a quiet voice. "I'm sorry, Ethan. Forgive me."

Ethan nodded but said nothing. He seemed to understand that his silence was worth more to her than platitudes. She stared out into the rows of dark hedges before her and brought her swelling emotions under control.

"Mercurion tried to kill me." The words sounded like an admission of guilt.

"He failed. You don't need to worry about him. When you're ready, you can punish him publicly. That'll diminish him in the eyes of just about everyone."

Valeyn shook her head. "Mercurion isn't the problem. He was just a weapon. I can't blame the sabre that strikes at me; I need to find the hand that wields it."

Ethan chose his words carefully. "Who do you suspect?"

"I don't know," she confessed. "Someone powerful enough to command Mercurion. Could it be my father?"

Ethan thought about this for a moment then shook his head slowly. "I seriously doubt it, Valeyn. He sent me to bring you back to him; it was all that mattered. Why would he now want you killed? It makes no sense. And besides, why would Bythe choose Mercurion as a weapon against his own blood, surely he'd know how impotent such an attack would be?"

"Perhaps that was the point? Maybe it was a test of my birthright? Maybe he wanted me to prove I really am his daughter?"

Ethan shook his head again. "I don't know. It doesn't feel right to me. Why would he go to all that trouble when you're already walking into his arms? He'll have plenty of chances to test your lineage if that's what he's worried about."

Valeyn felt a sudden chill and pushed the thought away. "What about these Prodigals? I've heard of them before, and I think they're more than the wild rumor your father believes them to be." She thought for a moment then continued. "Or what if this attack was arranged by someone in this very household?"

Ethan's jaw clenched, but to his credit, he refrained from any emotional outbursts of his own. "My family may not approve of you, Valeyn, but that doesn't mean they're ready to have you murdered on their lawn. I think you're going too far with that line of reasoning. Besides, even if my mother decided to assassinate the daughter of Bythe, do you think she would be foolish enough to do it at her own reception? I really don't think tonight's events are going to favor the standing of my house in the court of the Ironhelm tomorrow."

Valeyn nodded. "You're right. I'm sorry again."

"Don't apologize, Commander." Ethan switched to his formal role once more. "You need to examine every possibility with logic, not sentiment. I have to say, it's reassuring to see this side of you again . . . even if you *are* accusing my mother of attempted regicide."

Valeyn smiled.

"We have Mercurion in captivity now. You can question him to see if he gives us any answers," Ethan finished.

"No, I don't think so," Valeyn sighed with resignation. "I doubt Mercurion would confess, and even if he did, what would it matter? I have enemies, Ethan. These Prodigals, the people of the Ironhelm. Maybe even my father? I need to accept that. I want to leave immediately. No more delays. I need to face him."

Ethan nodded and turned to go, but once he'd taken a few steps, he paused and called back over his shoulder. "Well, either way, I think you sent a powerful message to your would-be assassins tonight. The daughter of Bythe is not to be treated lightly."

Valeyn smiled and watched him go, but she wondered if he was right. Would tonight's display deter her enemies, or would it only provide them with better tactics?

CHAPTER 3

"The exodus from Fairhaven had been dreadful. With word that both Bonehall and Darcliff had fallen, the refugees had had little choice but to retreat into Marfort, at the northernmost corner of the Outer Wild, and hope that by extending Bythe's forces to such extreme lengths, a weakness could be identified and exploited. They encountered tired and defeated remnants from other retreating forces but nevertheless combined whatever strength they had in the hope that it would give them a fighting chance.

The Outland refugees had not been welcomed at first. The crushing defeats of Greenridge had all but destroyed the Outland Alliance, and when they had approached the town, the cavalry of Marfort had ridden out to turn them away. It had been Councillor Nadine who had risen to the moment. It was Nadine – last surviving member of the Fairhaven Council – who had personally demanded an audience with Warlord Saldar of Roy. When confronted with the news that Marfort now considered the Outland Alliance to be dissolved, it had been Nadine, in full fury, who had pointed out the hypocritical convenience of such a position. History would record that Marfort watched as the Iron Union butchered the people of Greenridge and the Federacy – and when the hour came for Warlord Saldar to honor his vow and protect his allies, he instead turned his back in fear. It had been a furious young woman, scarred from war and with nothing to lose, who had beaten a mighty Warlord in front of his

Warmasters not through physical force, but with the adroit application of shame and judgment.

Saldar died soon after, of course, like most of the senior leaders of the Outland Alliance. Once the Helmsguard resumed their march northward, the terrible destruction of the war engines brought a swift resolution to every attempt to stand against them. Saldar had insisted on riding out to meet the invaders with an audacious show of force. He, like so many others, had not believed in the might of the war engines until he saw their power for himself, and by then it was too late to save him."

~Kaler of the Ageless

Jason spent the morning commending and admonishing in equal measure. He had inspected no less than five fortifications and received briefings from twice as many soldiers across the trenches, and finally, when he had run out of excuses, he trudged back up the hill to report the morning's progress to the Councillor of Marfort, the acting-leader of the Outland Alliance, Nadine of Fairhaven – his wife.

He found himself hoping they wouldn't be alone. It was very unlikely they would be. He knew they hadn't been alone since Fairhaven, and both of them had seemed very comfortable with the arrangement. They had spoken little since losing their child, both pretending the war and the flight from Fairhaven had been the reason, but Jason knew better. Neither of them seemed willing to face the other, as if doing so would cause them to confront the reasons for what happened and give them the opportunity to hurl their unspoken accusations at one another. And if the unspoken was articulated, things would never return to the way they were. No, Jason had been very happy to leave these things unsaid and direct his energy toward hurting others.

He found the dark green command tent and entered. As expected, Nadine was not alone. Two junior adjutants fussed around the small space while a third conferred with Nadine. She glanced up at him when he entered and then resumed her conversation with one of the aides. Jason waited patiently. Warmaster Zain – a middle-aged man with dark hair and the physique of a soldier half his age – stood next to the table, glaring at the map with a troubled expression. Zain didn't salute; he merely nodded at Jason then refocused his attention on the map. The rankings of Marfort had never been integrated with the rest of the Outland Alliance, and nobody had decided which rank – Captain or Warmaster – was higher. However, there was more than enough work to do, and their mutual respect led to an unofficial accord that they would be equal in authority – at least until the siege was decided.

"Your assault on the machine was brilliant, Captain. I congratulate you," said Zain curtly, his stare still fixed on the map.

Jason had fought alongside the man long enough to be able to read his mood. "Has something happened?"

The Warmaster nodded and rubbed a hand over bleary eyes. "Yes. We lost the shipment."

Jason's expression became stoic, and he rested his hands on the table before him, his head bowed as he fought the frustration welling within.

"What happened?" he asked.

"We're not really sure," Nadine interjected as she walked over to join them. "Somehow the Helmsguard found out about the plan sometime after the ship left Vigilsea. Kaler tells me she's now burning off the coast, about thirty miles south. They probably had one of the war engines waiting for her in ambush. The crew wouldn't have stood a chance once they'd sailed in range."

Jason chanced a glance at his wife, but she was also staring at the map, carefully avoiding his eyes. He felt relief at her silent refusal to connect with him and returned his focus to the problem they all now shared. "How the hells did they find out? We were so careful this time. Even if the Federacy have surrendered to the Iron Union, they hate the Helmsguard almost as much as we do. How could they have betrayed us?"

"We don't know that they did," said Zain. "All it takes is one man to say the wrong thing to the wrong person; then even the best plans can unravel within moments."

"Just like E'mar," Jason muttered.

Nadine shook her head at the mention of the name. The Ageless who had betrayed them all to the Iron Union. The Ageless who had betrayed her father to his death. The memory still cut deep, but she had learned to salve the pain with purpose. She had decided to honor her father by continuing on as he would have, to embody him and his values; but Jason knew her hatred still burned for those who had done this to her.

"I suppose it doesn't really matter how the Helmsguard found out; it seems they finally have some power over the water, and getting supplies by ship was our last option," she said.

"We could've used the weapons for resupply, and the cloth would've helped the civilians, but we can get by without them for now. The grain, on the other hand, is going to be a real problem," said Zain.

Nadine nodded again. Food had become an increasingly serious issue since the Helmsguard had laid siege to Roy. Supplies were dwindling and the few crops left under their control had started to fail without explanation. Rumors had begun to spread that Bythe's witchcraft now poisoned the very land itself and the people were beginning to lose hope. This shipment was supposed to restore that hope, but now both were in flames.

"We need to fix this," Jason said. "We can't let word get out until we've come up with a plan."

"Word is already out, Captain. It's all over the barracks this morning," Zain replied.

"Then tell your men to shut their mouths. Do they want to start a riot? And how the hells did this get out anyway? It seems like nobody can keep a secret anymore," Jason snapped.

Zain turned a stony gaze to Jason but visibly restrained himself from making a justified retaliation.

"Captain Jason," Nadine said with a slight touch of formality, "we can't undo what's been done; we need to focus on what we can do next." Jason's eyes flashed for a moment before he shook his head. Kaler entered the tent without making a sound. His youthful, dark-skinned face was framed by his violet robes and fixed in its usual expression of intense focus.

Jason glanced at him with mild irritation. "And where have you been?" Jason snapped.

If Kaler were offended by the Captain's brusque tone, he showed none of it. "I have been gathering intelligence," the Ageless replied.

"It's a little late for that, isn't it? Intelligence was something we needed before our shipment was sent to the bottom of the sea."

"My apologies, Captain. The Ageless are no longer the force we once were at Fairhaven. We can only do the best we can and hope that it still meets your expectations," Kaler replied with only a hint of bitter sarcasm.

"And that will never be forgotten, Kaler. We thank you," Nadine interjected, defusing the imminent escalation with her usual diplomacy

Kaler inclined his head to Nadine, ignoring her insolent husband for the moment. "I suspected your immediate priority would be to secure another food supply, so I have spent the past few hours attempting to identify alternatives. Regrettably, we do not have many."

"Is there nothing you can do for our crops?" she asked.

"The art of the soil was not a school of study to which the Violari were well acquainted. We left such matters to the Entarion. But even I can sense that the blight plaguing these lands is not of natural origin. It is obscene and contemptible."

"Is it Bythe?" Zain asked.

"I cannot say with certainty. While Bythe the Deceiver would most certainly gain from this, he has never demonstrated such abilities in our known history. The land does not obey a master of iron and industry."

"What about the war engines?" asked Nadine. "Bythe had never displayed that sort of power before, and yet they exist."

"The war engines are constructs of metal which are powered by foul magic. No, they are very much within the realm of our enemy. On the other hand, this sickness that plagues our crops seems to stem from an absence of something more than a presence — as if something that is needed to give life to our harvest has been taken from the land."

"You're talking about what happened back at Fairhaven, when the light shot up from the ground," said Jason. "You think that's got something to do with all this."

"The Desecration," Kaler corrected. "If the *kai* is being drained from the land, that could possibly explain this."

"Either way, we can't let ourselves become distracted with this now," sighed Nadine. "We need to figure out what we're going to do about the shipment."

"As I said before, our options are limited. Were any of the Entarion still with us, we might have had more choices. It is ironic that the militant Violari are less useful to you in a time of war."

"Kaler, we have so few Ageless left to defend us, and your skills have saved us countless times. Don't speak as if you have no use." Nadine's reprimand was kind, but firm. There was no time for regret and even less for self-pity.

Kaler nodded then turned to Jason. "At least your attacks on the war engines continue to be successful, Captain."

Jason waved the compliment away. "Holding off the enemy isn't a *success*. I'm simply delaying a defeat, and besides, I think they're about to try to break through again."

"Where?" asked Zain.

"Along our southern flank," said Jason, pointing at the map. "They've been peppering us with attacks to the north, and I reckon they're trying to get us to divert men up there. I know the southern barricade is a weak point so I'm sure someone over there knows it too. It's where I'd attack next."

"If that barricade is at risk of falling then we should pull our men back now. We need to be cautious, especially after the loss of our resupply," said Zain.

"And while we're at it, why don't we just put up a sign telling the Helmsguard exactly how weak we are?" snapped Jason.

"We will be far weaker if we try to prevent the breach and fail," Zain replied with forced patience. "If we set up a new perimeter a few hundred feet back from the barricade, we can push them back out from an elevated position."

"Warmaster," Nadine interrupted, defusing another escalation. "While your caution is wise, I agree with Captain Jason that it would almost certainly betray our current lack of strength. Please see to it that whatever additional units we have are stationed in the southern positions. We will need to hold that line. We can adopt your plan and defend further back if the Helmsguard break through."

"I'll do it," said Jason.

"Captain," Nadine pressed carefully, "I want Warmaster Zain to see to this."

"And I want to do this. This is my job."

"You haven't slept in two nights and you need to rest."

"Are you relieving me of my command, Councillor?" Jason finally confronted his wife and the tent fell silent.

Nadine sighed. "Everyone, I would like to take counsel with my husband. Please leave us for a moment," she announced. Without another word, the five other people in the tent bowed their heads and left.

"Jason, what are you doing?" Nadine seemed to drop all formality once they were alone, and the two were equals again. "Don't call me out like that, you know I need you leading the men."

"So why are you telling me how to do my job?" The protest was petulant and clearly flawed, but somehow it felt satisfying to use it.

"I'm not doing anything of the sort. I'm doing *my* job by making sure my commanders aren't burnt to the ground with exhaustion."

"I'm fine, Councillor. You don't need to worry about me. Now if that's settled, I need to ensure the southern lines are reinforced."

He turned to leave but a tremulous voice stopped him.

"Jason." She called his name with a soft fragility that almost broke through his bitterness. "Jason, please, I know you're not alright."

He turned back and fixed her with a stare. "And you are?"

"Why are you doing this?"

Words rose within him but were swept aside in a torrent of emotion that choked articulation. "What else do you want me to do?"

"I don't know, not this. The way you've been over these past few weeks. It's like you don't even care if you live or die anymore. Is that really how you feel?"

He grunted a laugh. "That's funny, I was thinking something similar. Do you care if I live or die?"

She lowered her eyes at his attack and didn't rise to it. Despite all that had happened between them, she still knew her husband. "I know I haven't been myself since . . . " Her voice trailed off, as she struggled to give voice to the unspeakable. "Can you please just be patient with me?"

"I've been patient, and where did it get me?" he replied. He knew he was being unfair but he wanted to hurt her. He wanted to hurt everyone and everything. None of this was fair.

"How can you be so selfish? I never knew my husband to be this cruel," she replied.

"And maybe that's why your husband couldn't protect you? Maybe he wasn't cruel enough to deal with life. Maybe that's why we're about to lose this war? Maybe that's why we lost our child?"

"You can't think this is your fault."

"I'm tired of thinking, Nadine! Round and round in endless circles. What if I'd done this? What if I'd done that? It never stops, and there's never an answer at the end of it anyway!"

He could feel something rising within him, and he fought desperately to keep it down. He knew if it broke out here, he wouldn't be able to control it, and he couldn't do this . . . not now.

The tent flap was flung open, and Jason realized there was a commotion outside.

"Apologies, Councillor, but the enemy are moving against the southern lines," Zain announced.

Jason turned and stormed out of the tent. He knew Nadine was ordering him to stay but he ignored her. Zain also shouted something at him, but he ignored the Warmaster as well.

You can both court-martial me when I return . . . if I return.

He ran down the slope as fast as he could and began shouting orders for all able-bodied soldiers to fall on him. In the distance, a black line of Helmsguard cavalry were moving swiftly across the plain, heading straight for the southernmost point of the barricade. Large, timber platforms were being laid across the trenches, allowing the horses and supporting infantry to advance quickly over the makeshift bridges. Jason was already making the mental calculations and rightfully concluded it would take almost a quarter of an hour to redeploy enough soldiers to push back the invaders, and that was assuming this was a genuine attack, not a feint to draw his forces away from the point of a second assault. He paused when he was a few hundred yards from the attackers and assessed the scene. Roughly a thousand Helmsguard had crossed the trenches and were now engaging defenders half their number. A gap had been pushed through the barricades and the black mass of fighters was seeping through like an infection. The fighting was close and ugly – and Jason felt a sudden urge to be in the middle of it; as if the violence itself were calling to him. He glanced about at the soldiers who had followed him and counted roughly three score dressed in the various hues of the Outland Alliance. He noticed

Warmaster Zain several yards away shouting orders to assemble a defense, but most of the soldiers had followed in Jason's wake.

Jason pointed at two young men dressed in the light blue of Fairhaven. His voice was clear and strong. "You each find three hundred more soldiers and send them here within the next ten minutes or the camp is lost. Move!"

The two soldiers sprinted in opposite directions, but Jason had already forgotten them. He turned and cast a critical look over the rest of the soldiers. "I'm supposed to set up a defense here. But our friends are dying, and I'm not standing by, waiting for reinforcements! I'm heading in to help them."

There was no other word or order. He simply drew his sword and ran alone toward the mass of fighting people, but within seconds, he heard the sound of at least fifty other soldiers thundering down the slope behind him. He crashed into the throng and swung his sword at the nearest figure in black. The fighting became a blur. It always did these days. In some distant part of his mind, he remembered strict training drills and tight technique based on some combat theory or whatever it was that he'd been taught. Why had they bothered? All he really needed was enough anger and enough will to harm. All he needed was enough hate.

Almost half of the enemy had pierced the barricade when Jason arrived, but the fury of his assault had an immediate effect on them.

"Get them! Get them now!" Jason was screaming without discipline or decorum. He wasn't commanding a unit any longer, he was leading a wild mob who's only chance for survival was to throw themselves on their enemy as savagely as possible. The Helmsguard looked around in surprise as they came surging down the hill with their swords raised. There was no logic to the attack. No strategy. They didn't even choose their targets evenly. A small mob swarmed upon the first unfortunate Helmsguard soldier they reached. The closest rider raced over to help, his sabre falling savagely as he felled two of Jason's men, but on trying to land a third blow, his wrist was caught by Jason. As Jason struggled with the rider over the weapon, two soldiers reached up on the far side of the horse and pulled the Helmsguard rider from his mount.

"Kill him!" Jason yelled. "Don't let him get up."

His heart felt like it was about to explode in his chest and his vision was strangely vivid. The sounds of metal striking metal and the cries of dying men seemed to fill his head. He saw two riders closing in and he ran at them. He heard someone screaming and recognized on some distant level that it was him. He ran at the Helmsguard without a thought or care for his own safety. If he was to die, then let it be here. He swung his sword with an animalistic ferocity. The rider tried to defend himself, but he'd allowed himself to become a slow target and no horse is protection enough from a braying mob. Jason slashed at the man's armored legs with both hands on his sword. He didn't try to deflect the rider's sabre as it cut across his back. He simply hacked at the man's legs like he was cutting wood. The Helmsguard screamed – either from Jason's strikes or another unseen injury – and the rider lurched forward in his saddle.

Jason wasted no time. He dropped his sword, grabbed the rider by his metal breastplate and pulled him to the ground. Then he simply kicked him. He kicked until the metal faceplate broke. He kicked until he felt flesh and bone crunching beneath his armored toecaps. He knew others were kicking too. They kicked until the rider stopped moving. Then they stopped. Jason looked about him

The Helmsguard had been pushed back through the hole in the barricade and seemed to be on the verge of retreat. Jason felt a strange anger at this, as though it were an injustice for any of them to survive. As though it were an injustice for him to survive. He lifted his sword again and ran through the barricade into the open fields. Most of the Helmsguard's cavalry had been killed and those who had survived were regrouping beyond the trenches. Half a dozen infantry were slowly retreating in a rear-guard formation. Jason ran at them.

He sprinted across the field with his sword above his head as another battle cry tore from his throat. Three of the soldiers saw him approach and readied their weapons. Jason felt a strange comfort in this, as if he were greeting old friends.

The dirt hit his face and the sky rolled before him. He finally settled on his back and marvelled at the blue color in front of him. A distant pain broke though the peace and it took Jason a moment to understand he'd been injured. He looked down at his body and beheld an ugly thing. Blood and sections of his innards were leaking onto the grass. A black, iron crossbow bolt had apparently ripped through his stomach and lay embedded in the ground – along with some cords from his intestines –

some feet away. He looked at this in confusion for a moment, dimly aware that this was a lethal injury and that he was going to die – and yet it didn't seem real. It was as if he were in a dream or the violence had happened to somebody else. He couldn't quite comprehend the finality of what he saw.

And so he laughed. He laughed at the blood, at his intestines lying in the dirt, at his killers who were retreating further across the field, at his comrades who hadn't followed his mad suicide run. But most of all he laughed at himself – dying alone on a battlefield after an act of complete stupidity. After all that had happened – it was the most fitting way to end.

"Why do you laugh?" A feminine voice cut across the blue sky.

Jason didn't answer. He wasn't even sure if the voice was real. How could it be? What sort of well-spoken lady would be standing in the middle of a battlefield having a casual conversation with him? The mental image sent him into a fresh peal of laughter. The bright blue of the sky was beginning to darken.

"Again, you laugh. What humor do you find in this moment? I would know. Would you please tell me?"

A shadow blocked the sun and a young woman with long, fair hair peered down at him.

Jason smiled and tried to sit up, but his body wouldn't obey him. That was irritating.

"Please do not try to move," the young lady said as if she were attending him. "You are on the cusp of death. There is very little time left. Any energy you spend will simply extinguish your light from the world, and I do so want you to answer my question before you go."

"Who are you, my lady?" Jason asked. He felt as if he were drifting off to sleep.

The woman giggled. "Such manners. Even when you are about to die, you still stand on ceremony. I always found that very endearing." She crouched down on her haunches and her white dress clustered around her. Gently, the young lady took Jason's hand and clasped it in her own. "Your people used to call me Romona."

"Romona," Jason repeated lazily as if he were drunk. "Your parents named you after the Goddess of Death?"

She smiled and genuine compassion filled her eyes. "No, Jason, I am she."

Jason tried to laugh again but the sound wouldn't come. "Romona's gone, I'm afraid. They're all gone now. Even Valeyn. She's gone too."

"Oh, we have all returned now. Well, most of us anyway. I imagine the rest will be along soon," Romona answered.

On some level, Jason knew this statement should have bothered him, but it was so difficult to think clearly.

"But tell me, Jason," Romona continued, "why have you sought out death in this way? And why do you laugh when it is upon you? I have seen many men die, older and braver than you. I have seen men weep and beg me for life. I have seen men curse my name and spit at me, but rarely do I see a sane and strong man seek me out and then laugh when he has found me. And I am so very curious . . . why did you do this?"

"I don't know," he replied. "I'm hardly strong, and I don't think I'm even sane anymore. Perhaps I'm just another raving, madman looking to die."

Now it was Romona's turn to laugh. The sound was dark and delicate, and it made Jason sad. "No, Jason. You are not mad, and you are indeed strong, — far stronger than you realize. Valeyn will yet need that strength before she is judged."

Her words cut through Jason's fog and he struggled to latch onto them. "Judged?" he repeated. "What does that mean?"

"You are all going to be judged, Jason, but her most of all. For while we all anticipated this time would come, we did not anticipate her. A new god born of this world. How delightful! It makes me regret leaving this place so soon."

Jason looked at her with failing eyes and decided he no longer cared if she was a hallucination or real. If she really was the Goddess of Death, then so be it. "So, you've all come back, just like Valeyn said you would. Well, you're too late. It's all over anyway. Bythe has won. He's taken everything. He was right."

Romona's expression hardened, and for a moment, Jason knew an unnatural fear. "Do not speak so. Is this the reason you laugh? Are you little more than another defeated man who surrenders all at the moment of his death? I had thought more of you, Jason, son of Caydyn." She raised her head and looked about her. "My kindred, Bythe, has not yet made his point. There are still many parts to play before this ends, and we intend to observe, for these will be the hours in which you prove your worth, or fail to."

Jason shook his head weakly. "I'm afraid you'll have to let me know how it turns out."

Romona returned her gaze to him and the smile returned also. "No, young Jason. You and Elyn are inextricably linked. It has always been thus and so shall it continue until the end. While I would dearly love to take you into my embrace, it is not yet time." She leaned forward and gave him the softest kiss on his forehead. "Remember, I was named Romona: Goddess of Death *and* of Regeneration. You are fortunate to have met me this day. Rest now. I will see you again."

Darkness swept over Jason for little more than an instant, but when he opened his eyes, the sun was low in the sky and orange twilight bathed the battlefield. He felt refreshed, as though he had slept for days, and yet he'd only closed his eyes for a moment. With a jolt of panic, he looked to his injuries, expecting to see his ruined stomach, but was met with smooth, unbroken skin. While his Captain's uniform was ripped and bloodied beyond repair, his body beneath the clothing was completely unharmed. He sat up without the slightest discomfort and patted his back and stomach to confirm what he'd seen – there was no injury. Had he dreamed it?

Turning to his left, he saw the ugly, iron crossbow bolt adorned with his entrails – now covered with flies – and knew it had been no dream.

"Captain!" a voice shouted, and he heard footfalls rapidly approaching. He didn't react. He simply stared at the crossbow bolt that should have killed him – that *did* kill him, and tried to understand what had happened.

"Jason, oh, thank the gods. We've been searching. I thought you'd been killed," Lieutenant Geordine gasped as she ran up with two soldiers in tow. She looked at his bloodstained clothes with dismay. "You're injured?"

Jason looked blankly at his lieutenant. "No. It doesn't make any sense."

"I know it doesn't, sir, but we're not going to argue with it."

"Did you see what happened?"

"We all did, but we don't know how it was possible. We were hoping you could tell us, sir. Perhaps the gods have intervened after all. Do you think this was Valeyn's doing?"

"Valeyn? No, that wasn't Valeyn," Jason said distantly.

Geordine looked confused. "Of course, that wasn't Valeyn, sir. We all knew who that was. But you've actually seen him before, haven't you?"

Jason looked at her. This wasn't making sense.

"Him? Who are you talking about?"

Geordine looked at Jason in confusion then pointed behind him, toward the Helmsguard lines. Jason turned to look, and his questions died in his throat. Smoke shrouded the scene, and Jason realized the orange glow was not coming from the setting sun, but from fires raging uncontrolled throughout their camp. Bodies of Helmsguard soldiers lay everywhere and the few surviving men were running about in a disorganised mess. But what drew his attention most of all were the ruined skeletons of five war engines, towering above the chaos below and burning in a conflagration of Godfire. A scene of destruction that was explained in one name.

"Imbatal, sir."

CHAPTER 4

"It is difficult to translate concepts held by the gods into the consciousness of mortals. Even the Ageless struggle to comprehend the realty of existence beyond Kovalith.

The Tower was a bridge between the Etherian of the gods and the physical lands of Kovalith. Lands that cannot exist if the Etherian is brought to occupy the same space as Kovalith – an act known as the Desecration. This cataclysm has been closely guarded by the Ageless. Even the great Veroulle rarely spoke of what Maelene had taught him. Nonetheless, the knowledge that the gods would one day return to judge their creations has been the burden of all Ageless, even as we strove to prepare for it. We all held different views on how to achieve this, some through compassion and teaching, some through strident use of discipline, but always to prove ourselves worthy of their judgment.

Ferehain never truly accepted these views. After Maelene fell, he believed the gods would only respect us if we proved we were their peers in some measure. Such a thesis was rejected on the merits that it would be impossible for any mortal – Ageless or human – to challenge the gods directly. The inequity of power was simply too great.

Ferehain discovered how to overcome that limitation."

~The Final Testament of Aleasea of the Ageless

Ferehain ripped another fragment from the soul of the land and The Tower trembled in response. Elsewhere, Aleasea paused in her journey through a corridor and glanced about cautiously. The walls that seemed carved from clouded glass began to ripple and shimmer in concert with the unsettling rumble sweeping toward her. She steadied herself as the wave of vibration washed over her and continued its journey through the massive corridor behind her. Aleasea sighed and carefully scanned the walls, already littered with webs of small fissures, searching for any sign of imminent collapse. When she was convinced of her safety, she resumed her slow journey.

Another god's power had been unlocked. Another piece of *kai* was now under Ferehain's command. In the months she had been trapped in The Tower, he had been relentless in his pursuit of knowledge of the gods – and he had proven himself very effective at forcing The Tower to reveal its secrets. She glanced to her left as she crossed a connecting hallway and allowed herself the indulgence of contemplating the large doors leading out to the freedom of Render – doors now sealed by Ferehain. Aleasea knew she might once have been able to breach those doors had Ferehain not blocked her access to whatever remained of Maelene's *kai.* The doors now seemed to mock her. She turned her back on them and walked in the opposite direction, toward the heart of The Tower.

Cracks gaped in the obsidian floor forcing her to carefully navigate her way around them. Ferehain had not concerned himself with repairing the damage he had wrought on Nishindra's creation, his only focus seemed to be his quest for power, and the rape of such beautiful work was of no consequence to him. Aleasea passed under an archway and entered a cavernous room. A central path split the area into two equal halves, and on either side lay the dozens of empty caskets that had once housed the copies of Imbatal. The gods only knew what Ferehain had done with those clockwork monstrosities. As if prompted by the memory, a pain lanced through her right shoulder, forcing her to pause for a moment. She raised her left hand and massaged the injury that had been wrought by Imbatal four years ago, and her face tightened in discomfort.

"Another attack? I hope it's not too uncomfortable, my dear Ageless?" Exedor's voice rang out across the chamber.

Aleasea shook off the pain and continued walking in his direction. "I thank you for your concern, Inquisitor, but the pain is diminishing."

Exedor sat on a large daybed of crimson leather, semi-reposed and wearing a dark blue robe. He would have looked almost relaxed if not for the bandages visibly wrapped around his stomach. An adjacent bench was littered with bottles, filled with liquids of different colors, and a seemingly random assortment of jars, creams, and powders

"Well, that is a shame," Exedor replied, his smile distorting the face lightly scarred from Ferehain's blades in Kardak. While Exedor had ultimately triumphed, victory had come at the cost of his eyes. At the time, this had been a small price to pay as Exedor had infused himself with a perversion of the same clockwork *kai* that had powered Imbatal. But now that power lay in the hands of Ferehain, and Exedor had been left behind as human wreckage.

"I trust it is the same with you?" Aleasea asked as she crossed to stand over him.

"Yes, I suppose it is," he answered. "A somewhat unexpected benefit from all of this."

Aleasea knelt and began inspecting the bandage tied around his midsection.

"So, given our latest brush with destruction just now, I presume that Ferehain has successfully unlocked another Artefact?"

Aleasea ignored the question and focused on Exedor's injuries. When Ferehain first ripped the machinery from his midsection, Aleasea assumed Exedor had mere days to live, if not hours. But he had not died and, contrary to all her experience, he had not only clung to life – but his horrific injuries had somehow begun to heal. Slowly at first, but over the interminable days in the Render it was becoming increasingly obvious that Exedor was going to survive. Even his terribly scarred face was now handsome again. Ferehain had regarded the inquisitor's impossible recovery as little more than a passing curiosity – but still did not interfere with it, as if this was yet another secret he needed to understand.

"So how many is that now?" Exedor persisted. "Twelve? If he's distilled the essence of their *kai*, there's no telling what he might be cooking up."

"I cannot say," she answered.

Exedor gasped in pain as Aleasea removed the last of the bandages to reveal a jagged line of mottled flesh across his stomach. Blood had seeped through the injury and crusted its edges.

"You have been walking too much," she said with disapproval.

"The wise and powerful Ageless can truly see all," Exedor replied through a pained smile.

"You need to be careful," Aleasea chided. "Although I cannot explain the nature of your recovery, I do not think it wise to press it too quickly."

She turned to the table and collected a clean dressing along with several of the bottles. After a few minutes work, she applied a salve to the fabric and pressed it gently across Exedor's wound. He watched her silently for a moment and the mocking expression slipped from his face.

"Why do you do this, Ageless?" he suddenly asked with a touch of bitterness. "Why do you tend to me? You should have let me die a long time ago. I would have done the same to you."

Aleasea's mouth tightened and she took a moment before answering. "In truth, I do not know. You are correct. You should be left to perish, and in earlier days, I would have gladly seen to it. You are a Royal Inquisitor of the Iron Union, and my sworn enemy." She paused and looked up, her eyes attempting to seek out Ferehain somewhere in The Tower far above them. "However, so much seems to have changed since those days. People I once understood so well have revealed themselves to be alien and others I once followed without question are betrayed as flawed. I wonder if I am in any position to judge anyone. I am certainly no longer willing to condemn anyone to death – not even you, Inquisitor."

Exedor laughed and gestured to the bandage around his eyes. "I agree with you, Ageless. It can be dangerous to be too blind."

They were quiet while Aleasea finished changing the bandages. When she was done, Exedor tested their fitting while she cleared the waste left from her ministrations.

"So, have you considered my suggestion?" he asked.

Aleasea sighed and got to her feet. "No, Exedor. I am not interested in aiding you and your conspirators, even if Ferehain did not have us trapped in this place."

"I don't believe we will be trapped here forever. I will find a way out for us, and when I do, you will need to decide where you stand in the war."

Aleasea raised her eyebrows. "You can barely walk, Inquisitor. How do you propose to escape from a man who is harnessing more power than anyone on Kovalith has ever wielded?"

"You may let me worry about that," he answered with a smile.

"Well, your fantasies aside, even if we were to escape, I cannot assist you. I am no agent of the Iron Union."

"Nor am I! The Prodigals seek to bring down Bythe and his empire. We are not so dissimilar to you in many ways."

Aleasea shook her head. "The Ageless serve a higher purpose. We do not seek to merely destroy."

"No, that's incorrect on both counts. You said yourself that you would have gladly destroyed me not so long ago and that your higher purpose has now been proven fraudulent. Like the Prodigals, the Ageless have labored under an illusion. We are not so different at all."

"I do not see it that way, Inquisitor," she said tersely and turned to leave.

"Please, Aleasea. I think it's time we all started seeing things more clearly," he said as he reached behind his head to undo the bandage wrapped around his eyes.

Aleasea stopped. "Do not do that."

"It's quite alright, my dear. Once you have been blinded, you have a unique opportunity to reevaluate your perspective on so many things."

The bandage fell to the floor. Exedor stared at her with cold brown eyes set in a smooth, handsome face. "I tell you with certainty that my vision is clear," he said with a smile.

Aleasea stared at the handsome face. "This is remarkable," she whispered and walked over to touch his face in an almost involuntary act of disbelief.

"Indeed, it is," he said.

Aleasea had suspected the Render was the reason Exedor had clung to life and that it was healing him at an unnatural rate. It was as if pure life essence was amplified by the raw *kai* which underpinned this place. Even still, the full restoration of his sight was beyond her expectations.

"I feel stronger by the day, but lately it has quickened. The spasms come more frequently but they're also less potent, and in their wake I feel rejuvenated. I felt my eyesight begin to return three days ago."

Aleasea felt a spike of excitement and forced it down, but it seemed that Exedor read her thoughts.

"My dear, Ageless," he chided softly. "I suspect you conceal your own little miracles. May I see?"

She hesitated for a moment, then pulled back her green cloak to reveal an emaciated, pink limb hanging by her side. Exedor nodded.

"The arm began to grow some weeks ago, but in recent days it has . . . accelerated." She had not dared to believe her ruined arm could ever be restored but after witnessing Exedor's recovery she felt hope struggling to break through her wall of discipline.

"Can you move it?" he asked.

Aleasea met his newly born eyes. "I do not know. I . . . have not the courage to try."

Exedor reached out slowly and took her tiny, pink hand in his own. He lifted it gently and heard Aleasea gasp. "Can you feel this?" he asked.

"Yes," she whispered.

Slowly, he removed his hands and let her arm hang suspended in the air before her. It did not fall uselessly to her side like a mockery of life. Instead she found it had strength – slight strength, but strength all the same. She willed the arm to turn and it responded. Delight flashed across her face and for a moment, she looked as though she were a child. "It is growing, even now. I can feel it," she said with wonder.

"You see? You shouldn't give way to despair. Almost anything is possible."

Aleasea looked at the thin limb, and a slight sob of joy broke from her lips as she flexed the fragile fingers.

"He is right." Ferehain's cold voice broke through the intimacy.

Aleasea stepped away from Exedor and covered her arm with her robe as though she had been caught naked. Ferehain swept into the room, covered head to foot in his flowing black robe, and strode to where Exedor sat. He reached out and gripped Exedor by the jaw, forcing his face upward. Ferehain's piercing black eyes met Exedor's dark brown, and neither broke the stare. Eventually, Ferehain grunted and withdrew his hand, yet Exedor's face remained upright and defiant.

"I trust this meets your approval, Inquisitor," Ferehain said evenly.

Exedor looked at him with suspicion. "How did you know?"

"How did I know?" Ferehain repeated. "Did you think it a coincidence? Did you not wonder why you still live? Did you sincerely believe I would sustain your life if it did not serve me in some way?"

A sense of understanding settled over Exedor's expression. "What do you want in return?"

"I am about to make that clear to both of you." Turning to Aleasea, Ferehain extended his hand. "Show me," he ordered.

She took another step away from him. "No."

It was a pointless defiance, a petty one, and yet it was all she could offer. Ferehain showed neither frustration nor hesitation as he stepped forward and struck her across the cheek with the back of his hand. Her head snapped sideways and yet she refused him the satisfaction of a sound. Ferehain pulled the robe aside and gripped the newly born limb. He glared at it without passion, and for a moment, Aleasea feared he would rip it from her shoulder like a curiosity to be studied; but after a time, he simply let it drop as if it held little fascination for him.

"You are both very fortunate. All of Kovalith was created here. All the energy to create and sustain life flows from this place. It would seem the Render naturally wishes to sustain you both and restore you to your full potential. As do I. As I said, fortunate."

"And what is the point of such fortune, Ferehain? We are both your prisoners, and you have deprived me of my own gifts. Why do you heal my body and yet disable me in other ways?" said Aleasea.

"I will tolerate no treachery nor interference, Aleasea. I will not apologize for the measures I must take. However, events have transpired, and we are now at a nexus. There may be one final opportunity for choices for you both."

"What do you mean?" she asked.

"Come, both of you," he ordered, then turned to leave.

"My apologies, Lord Ferehain," Exedor called. "I am somewhat incapacitated since your brutal attempt on my life. Perhaps, during your pursuit of godly power you could find a way to restore my mobility?"

Ferehain crossed the floor to where Exedor reclined and, reaching down with one arm, gripped a handful of his robe to lift him without difficulty. Aleasea had never seen Ferehain display such raw strength and wondered at the power he had amassed in his time at The Tower.

"Do not try my patience," Ferehain hissed, before walking out of the chamber, dragging a protesting Exedor along the floor behind him. Aleasea waited for a moment before following the pair out into the massive circular space that formed the center of The Tower. Archways of clouded glass surrounded the space, and, unlike the other areas, Ferehain had gone to great lengths to repair the damage that had been done here. Cracks in the glass were sealed, reminding Aleasea of faded scars.

Ferehain dropped Exedor at the edge of the room and walked to its center. He stood with his legs spread wide, as if bracing himself to lift some unseen weight, then he extended his hands skyward and began to mutter something under his breath. One by one, tendrils of color fluttered down from the great space above and wrapped around his extended wrists. The archways above them began to warp and coalesce into a single, larger frame that formed the window into the Oraculate – one of Shin's greatest creations. Aleasea watched her one-time lover and felt a chill at how easily he now manipulated the immortal energies.

Exedor slowly rose and checked his bandaged abdomen for any fresh injuries. Once satisfied, he turned his attention back to Ferehain. "It appears the Render favors you as well. You seem to have become quite powerful."

Ferehain shot him a glance before returning to his work on the Oraculate.

"The Render has nothing to do with my progress," he snapped. "I manipulate this Tower through the force of will alone."

"And to what end do you do this, Ferehain?" Aleasea asked. "How long do you intend to keep us trapped here? Where have you sent those clockwork demons?"

"You need not worry about the term of your incarceration, Aleasea. I sense it is coming to an end, along with everything else," Ferehain replied.

"What does that mean?"

Ferehain looked at her appraisingly. "Are you playing the fool again, or has your mind legitimately diminished?" He paused for an answer, but she refused to indulge him. With a slight shake of his head he looked away from her and focused on the work above him. "You were here when Valeyn unwittingly called the Etherian and started the Desecration. Have you forgotten this? Or do you genuinely believe the gods have forgotten this?"

Aleasea remembered how Shin had tricked Maelene into calling the other gods when she activated The Tower. "But we stopped it. We closed the gate from Kovalith."

Ferehain shook his head again. "The Desecration is a signal, not a doorway. A bell cannot be unrung. The gods are already returning."

"How do you know this?" Exedor asked.

"I know this through many means you could not possibly understand, Inquisitor, but one like you must only look to the sky to know this is true."

"The stars have been fading," said Aleasea.

"The constellations of the gods have been fading. The lighting of The Tower was but a final guidepost. Their return is now imminent. We have little time to act," said Ferehain.

Aleasea's mind worked quickly. "And this is why you have been obsessing over the *kai* of the gods, learning all you could from whatever power they left behind. You mean to fight them?"

"In a way," he answered. "I mean to destroy our hated enemy. I mean to annihilate Bythe and his empire, and when that happens, even the gods will be forced to respect us."

"How do you intend to do this, Ferehain?" she asked cautiously.

Amusement flickered in his black eyes for an instant. "You need not try to manipulate me, Aleasea. I have brought you here to freely tell you my intentions. Even better, to show them to you. I will then offer you one final choice."

"What choice?" she asked but he ignored her. Closing his eyes, he tightened his brow and the colors wrapped around his arms solidified into a solid band of pure white brilliance. Aleasea shielded her face as the room about her began to hum in unison to the torrent of energy now pouring into Ferehain. "Your work has accelerated the Render. This is how we have healed so quickly; you have been increasing the flow of *kai* into the world," Aleasea said.

"If Bythe is to be destroyed, we will need every last drop of power that is available to us. If we do not claim the *kai*, then the gods will simply take it back."

"Ferehain, this is dangerous. You are acting irrationally."

"No, the danger has already been thrust upon us. This is a completely rational response."

"He's right," said Exedor. "If the gods are returning, then we must be ready to fight them all."

Aleasea turned to Exedor. She had all but forgotten he was there. "You, of all people, cannot agree with Ferehain – not after what he has done to you."

Exedor shrugged. "I can't pretend he'll ever be my closest friend; but when it comes to enemies, we seem to have quite a few things in common."

"You see, Aleasea?" Ferehain's voice had that slightly mocking edge she knew so well. "Even a servant of Bythe can see the wisdom in what I do. How can you, my ally and oldest friend, be blinder than he?"

The Oraculate shimmered and an image snapped into focus. An overcast sky covered a seaside town. Gray, choppy waters lapped against stone breakwaters and a high seawall protecting the town from the ocean's constant intrusion. Colored buildings dotted the laneways and esplanades along the water, and a small hill rose behind them all, upon which stood a square, fortified tower. The scene would have been pleasant, if not for the rising streams of smoke from hundreds of campfires in the skies beyond the hill.

"The city of Roy," announced Ferehain. "The last bastion of the Outland Alliance. It is about to fall."

The image broke and shifted to view the eastern side of the hill. Thousands of black-armored figures filled the plains beyond. Organised ranks of the Helmsguard were camped in white tents with banners of black and gold flying in the breeze, and looming above them all were five war engines – steam rising from their terrible depths. It seemed that a battle had just concluded, several dead soldiers from the Outland Alliance were visible on the fields outside the city.

Aleasea felt despair seize her heart. While she had long suspected the struggle against the Iron Union was doomed, to see it confirmed with such certainty was an unexpected blow. She clenched her jaw and tried to contain the emotion. "Is this why you summoned me? Do you wish to torture me with cruelty?"

"Not at all. I have summoned you to give you a most precious gift – the gift of hope. Watch."

At first nothing happened, but after a few seconds, a ripple of agitation seemed to disturb the soldiers stationed next to the first war engine.

Helmsguard started to jostle in a commotion that slowly increased. A similar scene started around the second war engine, then the third, until all five machines were surrounded by a rippling sea of moving soldiers. Aleasea stepped forward and looked sharply into the image, trying to discern the source of the disturbance. A flash of white among the shades of black armor made her gasp and the image of Imbatal leapt sharply into view. It spun through the men, cutting them down effortlessly as they flailed about in disarray. Another Imbatal appeared, then another, and specks of white started to slice through the swarm of black. While no sound came from the image, the cries of panic from the Helmsguard seemed to echo in Aleasea's mind. The closest war engine started to tremble, then sway, and finally it tilted sideways, crashing to the ground in a violent explosion of steam and fire. As panic started to sweep through the Helmsguard, a dozen white figures leapt onto the remaining war engines and began to dismantle them, swarming over the figures like ants and ripping chunks of metal from their towering frames. A second engine collapsed, followed by a third, and within less than a minute, all five machines lay burning in ruin.

Aleasea watched the scene with a sense of wonder. A smile touched her lips and she felt the touch of joy like an old, forgotten friend.

"You can save them," she said. "We can coordinate with the leaders of the resistance and push the Helmsguard back. There is hope."

A yellow glow emerged beyond the ruins of the last engine, and the Imbatals quickly moved toward it, vanishing one by one into the light as if they had never been there. Hundreds of Helmsguard lay fallen in their wake, and the desolation of the ruined war engines spread fire and chaos among the gathered men.

"No. This was but a test, nothing more. I will leave the defenders of Roy to master their own fate."

Ferehain's blunt denial shattered her joy.

"How can you say that? Look at what you just saw. They swept through the Helmsguard as if they were children, even the war engines fell. You could destroy them, Ferehain."

"While my new Ageless are more powerful than Maelene's, they are not an army. I will not squander them with an assault on vastly superior numbers."

"That is not what I meant. Use our methods, Ferehain. Strike them as you have just done, using stealth and surprise. You know that over time these tactics will destroy any force, no matter the size."

"You are correct that, with careful coordination and planning, we might eventually repel the forces at Roy and possibly even put them into retreat. But such a stratagem would take time – time that we simply do not have."

"You are talking about the Desecration?" she asked.

"Their coming is at hand. It may be a matter of months or perhaps days, but I have no time to indulge vendettas. The siege at Roy is the strongest concentration of Helmsguard outside the Ironhelm, my success here has proven my new Ageless are capable of executing my agenda."

"So, you have exploited the peril of our allies and used them as a test, and now you leave them to perish? Are you really that cold?"

Ferehain raised an eyebrow. "You have always been too emotional, Aleasea. They are no longer my allies. I am no longer a member of Maelene's cause, and while it gives me no pleasure to watch Bythe's forces claim any victory, there are far larger concerns. I cannot afford such a petty indulgence."

"Petty indulgence?" she repeated the words in horror and dropped all formality. "You know some of the people at Roy. I'm certain there are survivors of our brethren who still fight. Even your pupil Kaler is probably still among them."

"Kaler is an excellent warrior. He will act as he judges best and will live or die accordingly. Either way, he is no longer my responsibility. We must all make new choices now."

"Then why do this? Why show me hope and then take it from me? Are you now cruel and petty, Ferehain?"

"Again, you are too emotional. I am not here to mock you. I wanted you to witness my test. I wanted you by my side at the moment of truth so there would be no doubt nor misunderstanding regarding the choices we must now make."

"What are you talking about?" she asked.

He moved closer and for a moment, she was reminded of their ancient intimacy. "I can see now that we were all pawns of the gods for their own twisted ends, even Maelene had used us in such a way. We were told we were fighting for something greater, we were told we were fighting the evil of Bythe, but it was a lie; we were simply prosecuting their trivial feuds."

"They were more than trivial feuds. We stood against evil."

"Evil? What does that mean? There was no good nor evil, only Maelene and Bythe, and Maelene fell to corruption, so only Bythe remains. He is the one, last constant. Bythe is our enemy. He has always been our enemy. And now he thinks he has won. The Outland Alliance has fallen, and the Iron Union will stand as the last dominant force across all of Kovalith."

"Why does this concern you? If the Desecration is truly upon us, Bythe's victory will mean nothing."

"Nothing?" Ferehain looked at her with rare incredulity. "It will mean *everything*. The gods will return and will see he was right, that we were wrong. Who can tell what this will mean for us? No, it cannot be permitted. He cannot be allowed to win. I will not permit it. Not after all we have sacrificed."

"What are you proposing?" she asked carefully.

Ferehain appraised her for a moment before proceeding. "Valeyn has returned home. She has now reached the Ironhelm."

"And how do you know this?"

Ferehain nodded toward the Oraculate. "I have seen it. I have also foreseen the damage her homecoming will inflict. It is somewhat ironic. Bythe has summoned his daughter home, and it will prove to be his undoing." He paced to the center of the room and spread his hands wide to The Tower above them. "I have used these past months fruitfully. I have researched the secrets of The Tower and unlocked as many of them as I could. I have learned to access *kai* directly, and I have discovered something greater. My power is increasing, Aleasea; however, even with such might, I can never reach the potential that Maelene bestowed upon you."

Aleasea abruptly looked away. "Don't speak of this, Ferehain. That was a long time ago and we swore we would never revisit those days."

"You need to stop denying yourself, Aleasea. You were the first born among the Ageless, born in the image of Maelene's beauty, and infused with more power than any who came after. You could touch the essence of *kai* directly, and you could also reach the *ovoid*."

"Yes, I could do all those things. And when we tried to truly test my power, when we tried to create life, you know the price I paid for that gift, the price we both paid."

Ferehain nodded. "Our desire to create life of our own was just, but Maelene's containment of your power was wrong. You were meant to be greater than what you are, you always were. She had no right to take that from you."

Tears stung Aleasea's eyes, and she shook her head violently. "She was trying to protect us from ourselves. Don't discuss this. I won't hear it."

"No, she was trying to control us. She took away your power so you would never disobey her again. And now only the echoes of your exceptional gifts remain."

She never spoke of the abilities that set her apart from her brethren. Even the mighty Veroulle had never mastered the ability to slow time as she still could. But Aleasea remembered a time when she could do so much more – a time when she could touch the very essence of the gods, when she had chosen to create a daughter with Ferehain, and after that daughter had failed to live, when Maelene had taken those gifts from her.

"Aleasea, I come to you now with good news. I believe I can restore what Maelene has taken from you, I can heal your connection to the Etherian. Our minds complement each other greatly. Despite your penchant for sentimentality, you recognize things that I do not. With your help, we can use the weapons of The Tower against Bythe and his machines of battle. We can wage war on a level undreamt of by Maelene. I make this offer, not out of sentimentality, but out of respect and logic. Stand at my side and support me as you once did, and in return, I will make you the most powerful Ageless who ever existed."

"Ferehain, we need peace, not power. And if what you say it true, then we can achieve this, but we need patience."

"There is no time!" Ferehain snapped. "Can you not sense this? Time is now your enemy, and mine. The Desecration is here. You witnessed its beginnings in this very room, and I have watched it flourish. The gods are already here. They have returned to judge us."

"Then we can make contact with Valeyn. With her help, we can negotiate a truce with Bythe and form an alliance against the Desecration."

Ferehain looked at her and for a moment, sheer disbelief flashed across his face. "You expect me to ally myself with Bythe? Do not assume everyone else holds your virtue. Bythe has shown very little interest in the lives of his people, even in the life of his own daughter. He will never help anyone but himself."

"You have a common interest with him, Ferehain," Aleasea answered.

"I have *nothing* in common with Bythe!" he snapped with an unusual display of emotion. "Bythe wants to stand before the gods and declare himself right and just! He wants to pretend that all he has done was justified. He wants to prove that everything I have struggled for, everything that I valued, was wrong and evil. I will never allow that. I will never give up. I will destroy everything he built and stand before the gods when they judge us and I will force their respect! They will behold my power and Kovalith will be spared."

She could see a hint of madness in his eyes that made her want to recoil. Nevertheless, she drew a breath and spoke slowly. "Ferehain, you can't know if any of what you've seen is true. You remember how Shin sabotaged his own creations to manipulate Maelene. You may be a victim of the same deception."

He shook his head and breathed heavily, regaining control of his anger. "I know this to be true. Although I dare not face Bythe directly, I know he will fall, and I must be there to destroy his empire when that day comes. The time of gods is over."

"He's right," said Exedor. "As much as I hate to admit it, he's correct. He's uniquely placed to bring down the last god of Kovalith. He can accomplish what no one has been able to achieve – he can free our land from tyranny."

"Do not be naïve, Exedor. Have you not listened to what he has been saying? Ferehain will not deliver what you seek. He would depose Bythe and take his place. You would simply replace one god with another!"

Exedor shrugged. "The Prodigals fight to overthrow Bythe from within. It's like Ferehain says – Bythe is a common enemy and we can help in this. The Prodigals are highly placed within the Ironhelm. There are many of us who Bythe would not suspect."

Ferehain glared at the Inquisitor. "Do you think me to be a fool? You would make for a most untrustworthy ally, Exedor. You and your conspirators would turn on me the moment it suited you."

"It's true that we would have much to discuss once Bythe is removed from his throne, but we can debate such details later," Exedor replied smoothly. "I suggest that for now, we focus on our mutual objective. As I said, there is much we could achieve if we worked together. You do not have the intricate knowledge of Bythe's empire that I have, and you cannot influence his bureaucracy as I can. I still have the means to contact a powerful ally seated high within the Ironhelm. While you attack from without, I can attack from within."

Ferehain looked hard at Exedor but did not answer.

Aleasea felt a growing dismay at the alliance forming before her. "I don't deny that I would like to see Bythe fall, he's caused us too much pain over so many centuries for me to forgive him, yet what of Valeyn? Is she not a god also? What do you intend to do with her?" she asked, taking Ferehain's attention.

Ferehain broke his gaze from Exedor and returned it to Aleasea. "You need not concern yourself with Valeyn. I have seen her doom. It was inevitable."

Aleasea felt a sudden stab of alarm. "What has the Oraculate shown you?"

"Valeyn is a divisive figure – she always has been. Her very presence will weaken her father and split the power he consolidates. She will diminish him, then diminish herself."

"Could we save her?" Aleasea asked.

"As always, she is the daughter of our enemy. Even worse, she is also the daughter of our treacherous mother. Pure deception flows in her veins. She is beyond redemption. Her destruction is already written."

Aleasea walked up to Ferehain and stared directly into his expressionless face.

"You will not harm her, Ferehain."

"You will not need to concern yourself with that."

"Nor will I stand by and allow you to harm her. She is a sister to me. No, a daughter. I share a bond with her that you cannot understand, a bond we forged in Sanctuary long ago."

Ferehain stepped toward her so their faces were now mere inches apart. "And what of the bond we formed centuries ago? What am I to you now?"

Aleasea shook her head. "I no longer know."

Ferehain nodded. A strange expression swept across his face for a moment, but he turned away from her and crossed to Exedor. "I may have use of your service after all."

Exedor smiled. "As your second choice? Ah, Ferehain, you have an odd way of making your allies feel important. Fortunately for you, my pride and self-esteem were crushed quite some time ago. I will aid you." Exedor bowed his head and Ferehain nodded curtly with satisfaction.

"Ferehain, no," Aleasea protested. "Don't you see the madness of this? How does this honor all you've fought for over so many years?"

"I am no longer interested in salvaging the dreams of Yvorre. I no longer bend my will to any of the gods, quite the opposite is now true," Ferehain snapped. "The Tower is a conduit to the Etherian and to the *kai* above and the *ovoid* below. I have now found this bridge."

"The *ovoid?*" Exedor asked.

"Kovalith was built on the balancing point between immortal existence and nonexistence, between *kai* and *ovoid*. And if the balance between these two forces was upset—"

Alarm gripped Aleasea as she interrupted him. "Ferehain, if you interfere with that bridge, you could tip that balance. The *ovoid* would infect this world."

"Indeed. Which is where you could help. You once were able to influence *ovoid* and *kai* directly. You could ensure the *ovoid* is contained and directed where we will it — at our enemies."

"I don't have that power anymore. And even if I did, I would not let myself be used as a weapon!"

Ferehain shrugged. "The weather and the harvests have slowly changed these past months as the *ovoid* has begun to leech into the lands after the start of the Desecration. The very soul of Kovalith is wilting. It is only a matter of time until the *ovoid* begins to do its work and this land becomes completely incapable of sustaining life. And if you are not willing to seize the opportunity this presents, I must act in your stead." He removed a small, auburn object from within the recesses of his black robes and looked at it thoughtfully for a moment. "Do you remember Ceriv? She was known as the Goddess of Hope. Her followers withered and died out not long after she left them. They spent their days dreaming of nothing more than pleasant thoughts, without the will to execute any of them. Such a pathetic lot."

"I remember her," said Aleasea. "What is this?"

He held up a small, orange sphere that glowed faintly in the palm of his hand. "This was her only relic — a *cour* for her power, much like we crafted back in Sanctuary. Her followers called it the Anticipus. I believe it translated to *the light of all need*. It preserved her capacity for endless hope and in doing so, fed their relentless addiction to it. They all thrived on such a small thing. They crowded around it for sustenance and dependence, and when they all eventually withered and died, it made its way here, like so many Artefacts."

"I don't understand how this is relevant," said Aleasea.

"You have told me of how you have lost hope, of how the years have robbed you of it. Well, I can now remedy that."

He extended his arm and pointed the Anticipus at her. A golden light – like a lance of bright sunshine – washed over her and in that moment, she felt a warm sense of joy permeate her being. Happiness seemed to unfold in her heart like an opening flower, and she took a sharp breath at the unexpected beauty of it. Then it was gone. Ferehain closed his fist and the light vanished. Aleasea had to fight down a compulsion to cross to where he stood and pry the sphere from his hand so she could bask in the glow once more.

"I have now mastered this, like so many of the others. While I cannot generate the *kai* directly, I can wield it through this *cour*. It is quite a beautiful feeling, is it not?"

"You will not manipulate me through the use of false hope," Aleasea grated.

"No, I could not do that," Ferehain agreed. "Hope is your greatest asset; you understand it far more than I can. Your optimism – and the naïveté it brings – are also your greatest flaws, and they expose your greatest weaknesses."

He opened his hand and the orange light washed over her once more, only this time the light was cold. It seemed to flow not toward her, but back into the orange sphere in his hand, and with it, fled all the joy in her soul. She gasped as if she had been doused in ice-cold water and fell to her knees as the light continued its cruel assault.

"Shin was quite learned in the construction and use of these Artefacts, and he kept many records. I have been able to understand how to manipulate some of them, to broaden their purpose beyond their creators' intent."

Ferehain's words floated to her but she could barely hear them. Instead, she grappled with a suffocating weight that had settled across her mind. The world suddenly felt gray and tears pressed against the corners of her eyes. She wanted nothing more than to sleep. Then the light was gone, and the weight lifted.

"Hope can be twisted; it can be given and it can be taken. This is the true lesson of the gods. They are corruptible, as is their legacy."

"What are you doing?" she asked.

Ferehain stepped forward and raised the horrible, orange orb once more. "This gives me no pleasure, Aleasea, but I have given you a choice and you have made it. The *ovoid* must be directed where I will it. I will return your power to you and you will still serve my ends, but not in a manner either of us desired."

The cold light struck her again and the weight settled in against her mind once more. She struggled to remain quiet, to deny Ferehain the satisfaction of the slightest sound as he slowly drained any sense of contentment from her being. Exedor stood behind Ferehain, watching her for a moment, before turning his healed face away.

CHAPTER 5

"The nation known as the Ironhelm is marked by four identical iron citadels, positioned to form a precisely aligned square on a vast plain, all in accordance with Bythe's specific design. They towered high over the cities that were built to support them, only to be dwarfed in turn by Bythe's personal citadel – a fifth spire built at the center of the others – so tall it looked as if it sought to puncture the sky. It was named Domitus, and its girth was so immense it could have almost housed the other four towers within its black iron walls. The design was purposeful; all spires could be viewed by those who dwelled within their perimeter, such was the scale of their design and the scale of the god who had built them. Smoke hung in a permanent blanket over the skies as thousands of fires and forges spread their wastes above Obduratev – the city that surrounds Domitus. The fires never died, and the forges were never cold. The will of Bythe never rested."
~Kaler of the Ageless.

Valeyn was home. She had felt it as soon as the soaring black towers pierced the horizon. Those citadels had been burned into Vale's earliest memories – unpleasant memories from a besieged childhood – but they were a strangely reassuring sight to her. As they had approached Sturmm, the first city on the southeastern edge of the Ironhelm, Valeyn had declined the Secretariat's invitation offered by the ubiquitously obsequious diplomats and instead, passed around the square, iron walls that surrounded the city in perfectly symmetrical dimensions. Valeyn's business was with Bythe, and no preliminary customs would delay her arrival any further; nor would she permit her enemies another opportunity to test her. Her entourage now obeyed her commands without question – and she ordered them to take her into the heart of the Ironhelm.

It had taken several more days to travel the final leg of their journey to Obduratev, and to Valeyn's eyes, its distant citadel seemed to grow larger with every step. On occasion, abandoned villages could be seen in the distance. They would pass rotting timber frames and decaying sheds which were now the skeletons of abandoned lives, and Valeyn would wonder why they were no longer needed. While the polluting industry of the Ironhelm had meant the surrounding lands had never been lush and beautiful, Valeyn had never seen the Ironhelm this barren. Grass seemed to be a rarity and wherever it appeared, it was brown and hugged to the dirt as if clinging to life. Unlike the Outer Wild, the Iron Union didn't support farmers. Instead, massive stations organised and coordinated the production of livestock and distributed the produce across the empire. When Valeyn had passed by the two stations that lay between Sturmm and Obduratev, she was surprised at the small number of cattle scattered around the enclosures. Perhaps Fowles-Marlow's claims of hardship hadn't been as exaggerated as she'd assumed. Yet, as she cast her eyes over the emaciated animals, an uncomfortable feeling gnawed at her. Her connection to Maelene's *kai* seemed to be restless, as if the starvation of the land betrayed a deeper corruption that Valeyn had failed to recognize.

The final days seemed to take longer than the entire journey itself, and there was a strange sense of relief when the anticipation was over. They rode to the gates of Obduratev in silence. They hadn't been greeted by a Secretariat this time, but that was hardly surprising; the Iron Union was administered with precision and order reigned supreme within Bythe's cities – there was no need for superfluous gestures and certainly no need for protection now that she finally stood on Bythe's threshold.

"Last chance," Ethan said from his horse alongside her. "Do you want me to distract them while you make a run for it?"

Valeyn knew that any fantasy of retreat was an illusion — she had committed herself some time ago — but the offer still held some appeal. She smiled and shook her head. "Why don't we head in?" she replied.

Ethan shouted the order and the banners of the Iron Union were held aloft, signifying their request to enter. Without a moment's hesitation, a deep note surged from the top of the battlements, rattling the plates of Valeyn's armor as the sound washed over them. The gates – towering sheets of reinforced iron forged within the industrial smelters of the Union – slowly began descending vertically into the ground. As they lowered, Valeyn could see her home city revealed once more, and a surge of emotions fought to unsettle her. She pushed them away and nudged her horse forward.

The deep horn blasted again as Valeyn led her retinue of Helmsguard under the rectangular portal that now appeared in the otherwise solid surface of metal surrounding the city. Once she had passed within the walls, Valeyn – Daughter of Bythe – was welcomed home.

Cheers erupted from the thousands gathered in the streets before her. Unlike her reception at Arbek, this was no unruly mob. The boulevard leading into the city was lined with countless Helmsguard. A corridor of armored men marked her path forward. Behind those soldiers stood the citizens of Obduratev, emotional, yet civil. Valeyn readied herself for the insults as she entered the boulevard, but when the cries fell on her, they were shouts of praise and gratitude.

"Well, it looks like you might have a few admirers," Ethan shouted to Valeyn over the din.

Valeyn was stunned. After Mercurion's attack, the best she'd hoped for was the mixed reception she'd received in Arbek, and despite her façade of confidence, this outpouring of praise was far from the tepid homecoming she'd braced herself against.

Within the walls, the city was no different than Vale remembered. If Fairhaven had been built as an organic testament to growth and necessity, the Ironhelm was a tribute to exactitude – a completely precise grid of well-paved streets and boulevards leading toward the tower positioned at the center of the city. Valeyn noted the commitment to symmetric perfection was nothing short of beautiful. All of the buildings within the walls were also built to exact specifications. Five stories high, they flanked the streets in corridors of dark stone and metal. However, while the design of Ironhelm's cities may have been meticulously controlled, their structures were by no means austere. Art flourished in the Iron Union, and here, it was given full expression. The square buildings were adorned with angular facades and ornate sculptures. Small towers crested some roofs and almost every building bore statues of soldiers or creatures with sweeping wings. The city was a collection of carved black marble, bronze furnishings, and sculpted bas-reliefs. Enormous faces stared balefully down at those in the boulevards beneath them, their stoic expressions offering both judgment and security. Bythe's citadel towered over everything else. The construct was immense, and even Valeyn found herself overcome with mild awe as she beheld it from the back of her horse. While Vale retained memories of the structure, Elyn had only heard stories, and Valeyn was surprised to feel the shocked reaction of the young girl from Fairhaven stirring within her. The spire was built from reflective black metal, polished so intensely that it seemed to be constructed from dark glass. Its surface reflected the thousands of lights burning in the city so that it seemed to almost glisten with life.

With slow and deliberate confidence, Valeyn led her party down the boulevard. She did not look aside at the crowd nor acknowledge them in any way. Instinct told her it was unseemly. Perfection was now expected of her; it was demanded of her. The cheering of the crowd increased in intensity and for a moment she wondered if they would break loose and repeat the actions of the mob at Arbek, but they held their poise as refined members of the empire. For the first time in her life, Valeyn felt grateful for the discipline engendered by her father's presence.

Bythe.

She could feel him. With every step the spire grew larger and the red pulse of his *kai* surged stronger within her. And yet, there was something more than that — an indescribable sensation of pending reunification and of reckoning.

After long minutes of marching, the boulevard led to Domitus and an immense walled square paved with polished flagstones beyond which lay the steps of the citadel. Now that they were close, the tower seemed to stretch endlessly in both directions, forming an impassable obstruction. The walls surrounding Domitus prevented citizens from encroaching any further, and the square itself was filled with ordered lines of soldiers in black metal. Every one of them stared forward, resisting the temptation to steal a glimpse of the new god as she proved her existence to the civilized world.

Horns sounded from the tower above and Valeyn signalled the party to halt. Thousands of Helmsguard turned as one and faced her, placing their fists over their chests in one synchronised movement. Valeyn dismounted with Ethan. The two senior officers stood at attention and returned the salute to the small army assembled before them. Besides the lines of soldiers and officers, there was no official dignitary or party to greet them. The dozens of steps leading to the platform before the citadel were empty, and the doors beyond were sealed. Both Valeyn and Ethan stood at attention patiently as the long minutes dragged out.

"Do you think he forgot?" Ethan murmured, giving Valeyn a brief smile to break her tension.

"No, he's coming," she answered. The weight of his presence grew heavier within her. Valeyn knew that Bythe's mind was fixed on hers.

A crack split the tower's doors and they silently swung inward. Valeyn could feel Ethan tense, and she had to force herself to repress a sudden urge of panic.

Figures in white robes began filing out of the citadel, taking up position along the platform. At the end of the procession walked a bald-headed man with pale skin. He wore the same pristine white robes as the rest of the retinue, but his clothes were lined with crimson flourishes and he carried a metal staff adorned with the horned symbol of Bythe. His stooped form shuffled to the front of the platform where he paused to stare down at Valeyn.

"Udrax." Ethan spat the name as if it were a curse.

Udrax the Oppressor was Bythe's High Priest, and as such, wielded almost unrestricted power within the Iron Union. He existed to spread the word of the glory of Bythe and to identify those who refused to hear it. Udrax was known to routinely order inquisitions throughout the Empire and take a well-noticed pleasure in personally overseeing them. Deliverance of the glory of Bythe was his sole ambition, and as a result, few men in the Empire were feared more.

"Wait here," Valeyn said then strode forward before Ethan could object. She marched between the rows of Helmsguard still frozen in salute.

As her foot touched the first step, the silence was broken by a cracked voice above her.

"Commander Vale, stop where you are. You may come no further!" Udrax barked from his position above.

She stopped and glared up at him. "You dare prevent the daughter of Bythe from returning to her rightful place?" she replied. The words carried a confidence she certainly didn't feel.

"*You* dare," Udrax began, using a well-rehearsed voice that was low and yet somehow carried across the entire assembly. "*You* dare to return, with the trappings of an office you scorned and a position of honor and privilege you willingly discarded. *You* dare to walk through these gates and bask in the exultation and praise of a people you abandoned? And now you presume to walk into the sacred grounds of Domitus and seek a personal audience with our Lord Bythe? What arrogance has overcome you? You will explain yourself, Commander Vale."

Valeyn rose to her full height and met his gaze. "I do not explain myself to you, Udrax." There was a murmur from the collection of priests behind him at her failure to use any honorific.

Udrax's expression darkened. "You will address me by the titles our Lord Bythe has bestowed, young lady." His words seeped patronisation, and Valeyn felt any lingering indecision swept aside by frustration.

"I will address you in any manner I please," she replied and defiantly placed her foot on the next step. When he said nothing, she continued ascending. Her steps were slow and methodical, and she mounted the platform without a glimpse of emotion. When she finally stood before Udrax, her powerful form towered over the stooped man, and yet his shrewd gaze betrayed an intellectual cunning that urged caution. He waited patiently.

"I am here to see my father," Valeyn announced. "Stand aside."

"Look at you," Udrax sneered. He walked around her and gestured theatrically, speaking to the crowd rather than to her. "You wear the colors of our enemy and you desecrate our sacred armor with the filth of Maelene. You return to us demanding respect, and yet you bring with you the stench of betrayal."

Valeyn suddenly understood she was on trial, either through the will of Udrax, or possibly through the orders of her father. Her self-assurance faltered. Why hadn't he appeared? Had she walked into an elaborate trap after all? While she had no doubt she could overcome whatever power Udrax possessed, what would she do next? Would she fight the soldiers who would most likely come to his aid? Had she returned home merely to bring violence? She recalled the lessons of Vale and slowed her racing mind, calming it to reflect the unbroken surface of a still lake, and then she spoke in a voice that also carried across the square.

"You address me as though I were still the young Commander Vale, and if I were that same woman, then your claims against me might hold merit. But I am not her. I have not been her for a long time. My name is now Valeyn. I am the daughter of Lord Bythe, and I repeat my demand to see my father."

"Indeed, word has reached us of your feats at Fairhaven, Commander Vale. Your petty tricks and illusions are impressive, yet we all know there is only one true power in this world, and it flows from Bythe, our master." He stepped closer and eyed her with exaggerated suspicion. "And yet somehow you have managed to learn the crafts of our enemy. You have been witnessed by our own men. You wielded the black arts of Maelene against one of the Ageless."

"I will not explain myself to you, Udrax," Valeyn repeated, but the words sounded too defensive in light of his mounting attack.

"I have a theory, Commander Vale," he continued, turning from her and addressing the assembly before them. "I believe I can explain what happened after you deserted us. It is well known that you are the unrecognized daughter of Lord Bythe, that is true, but it is equally known that you are a failure to him. You are no god. You cannot bear to stand in his light for it forever reminds you of your own shortcomings. And so, when the opportunity presented itself, you deserted your men and defected to the Ageless. You misled Baron Ethan and his soldiers and used them to secret you into Fairhaven where you could be delivered to your conspirators. It was only through the untimely intervention of the Northmen, that Baron Ethan was able to escape before you could execute him and his men."

"That is not what happened," Valeyn answered. "Commander Ethan can verify this account."

"Commander Ethan is not accused of treason, you are. Do not try to hide behind him, stand for yourself."

Valeyn looked down at the assembly and could see Ethan stepping toward her but she held out a hand to stall him. Udrax was right about one thing; Ethan could only be harmed by publicly defending her – especially if this examination was the scripted farce she was beginning to suspect. Udrax was letting Ethan escape punishment, and she had no intention of interfering with that.

"Hold your ground, Commander Ethan," she declared. "Udrax is right, I will defend myself."

Udrax smiled and his expression resembled a cat eyeing an unsuspecting bird. Valeyn knew he had no interest in reaching the truth, only in weaving a narrative that people would want to believe.

"It is clear that you are a treacherous disciple of Maelene, who defected to learn her secrets, only to betray her in turn," Udrax continued, his argument reaching full stride. "Who knows why you did this? Perhaps you witnessed the mighty war engines, the Fingers of Lord Bythe, and you again quivered in his presence? Perhaps you finally understood that the reach of Lord Bythe is endless, and that his justice can never be outrun. And it was in that moment of terror, that you devised a new plan. You took the power of Maelene for yourself, you betrayed the Ageless and killed them all."

Valeyn shook her head. "These are mere fantasies, Udrax."

"Fantasies?" he repeated in a mocking tone. "We have sworn testaments from dozens of loyal Helmsguard who witnessed you wielding the green light of Maelene against the Ageless in Fairhaven. They watched you attack one of them and seize the power for yourself. Do you deny this?"

E'mar – the deceitful Ageless who had conspired with the Helmsguard to betray his own people. It was ironic that Udrax was so effectively reversing their roles. She wondered if the High Priest knew the truth or if he was only fabricating an elaborate fiction based on the few facts he possessed.

"Yes, I wield the power of the Ageless, just as I now wield the power of my father. I do not deny who I am, nor do I deny my heritage. I am the daughter of Bythe," she took in a breath and then plunged ahead with words she knew would change everything, "and I am also the daughter of Maelene. I am the offspring of their union."

At this declaration, even the steadfast discipline of the Helmsguard faltered, and a ripple of astonishment swept through the crowd. The priests looked at one another in outrage. Udrax took a shocked step backward – his first reaction that hadn't been rehearsed – and he looked at her with open hatred on his pale face.

"Blasphemous witch!" he snarled in fury. "You stand on Lord Bythe's doorstep and accuse him of fornication with the mistress of evil?"

Valeyn opened her mouth to reply but was silenced by a growing presence within the citadel. Udrax – mistaking her silence for contrition – redoubled his tirade.

"You are nothing more than an unscrupulous opportunist, looking for personal gain and power wherever you might find it. You have spread your poison among the Ageless and now you seek to spread it here. But no, my young Vale. We are aware of your perfidy and we will not allow you to bring it another step closer. Guards, chain her!" he screeched in an escalating crescendo, and yet before his cries had echoed, they were crushed by a stronger voice.

"Silence."

The voice was like stone. A moment passed as the order carried across the square and within that instant, every person who heard it dropped to their knees without hesitation. Thousands of Helmsguard genuflected in the square, arms crossed against their chest, eyes fixed on the flagstones before them. The priests on the platform had assumed the same prostration. Even Udrax had arrested himself from his ravings and immediately sunk to his knees.

A large mass was moving toward Valeyn from the darkness of the doorframe. Conditioned childhood terror flooded her, and she instinctively wanted to cower in fear and supplication. She clenched her jaw but resisted the urge to kneel in the form she had been taught to follow since her earliest memories.

Bythe stepped out of the shadows.

He was as tall and as fearsome as young Vale had remembered, as if the distorted lies of childhood memory were suddenly revealed to be true. His black armor shimmered across his massive bulk as he loomed twice the height of any man. Arms the width of tree trunks swung at his sides as he crossed the space with only a few slow strides. A black cape framed him and seemed to enhance the shadow he cast. His face was concealed behind the black iron helm he had always worn, full faced with dual curved horns – the universally respected symbol of Lord Bythe the Immortal. He stood before Valeyn and the weight of his gaze was almost palpable upon her, but she refused to kneel. Instead, she forced her face upward and her eyes found the black holes in his helm that marked his eyes. She stared into the hollows and fought the fear that screamed within her.

I will not kneel.

"Prostrate yourself before your Lord Bythe!" Udrax rasped from somewhere beneath her. She ignored him and continued to meet the judgment of her father.

"Blasphemous witch," Udrax snarled again, getting to his feet. He pulled the iron staff over his shoulders and swung it viciously at Valeyn's head. She sensed the lethal metal closing in on her temple but refused to break her father's gaze.

Bythe made the slightest movement of his head, and Udrax yelped in pain as the staff resisted his swing. He lost his grip on the weapon and stumbled onto his knees, the staff hovering in the air for a moment before falling to the platform with a shrill clang. His empty stare remained fixed on Valeyn and she resisted the compulsion to cower, to scream, to rage; instead, she feigned stability and continued to return the silent stare. After an eternity, she felt Bythe's gaze pass from her like a weight lifting, and instead it fell on the grovelling priest. The unspoken judgment was now turned on Udrax, and he quavered under the same power Valeyn had endured. Anxiety passed across his face as he desperately fought to compose himself. He stared at Bythe's armored boots and spoke in a quivering voice. "But my lord, look at her. She does not give you the proper respect. She is unrepentant. She marches back into the Ironhelm as if it is hers. She does not even seek your forgiveness."

Bythe's response was swift. His armored hand gripping Udrax by the throat and lifting him to meet Bythe's dark eye slits. Udrax's mouth moved silently as Bythe pulled him closer to his faceplate. When Bythe spoke, the words rumbled from somewhere deep within the cavernous helm.

"Of course she is defiant. Of course she is arrogant. She is my daughter."

He dropped the terrified priest, who landed on his back, gasping desperately.

"I accept her. Respond accordingly," Bythe commanded. Without another glance at Valeyn, he turned and walked back toward the citadel. She watched him retreat, almost entranced by the black cape which trailed him.

When he had vanished, there was a moment of silence before the machinery of his empire responded to his orders. Orders were issued and the square erupted into a frenzy of organised activity. The priests rushed to aid Udrax, who was lying in a state of shock, and helped him to his feet. He brushed them aside and cast a hateful stare at Valeyn, gesturing to a scaffolding erected to the side of the square.

"Your father's will cannot be questioned, but I am not fooled. One day you will hang on that scaffold along with the other traitors. Mark my words, Commander Vale," he growled before turning and retreating into Domitus

Ethan mounted the steps and walked quickly to her side. To his credit, he didn't patronise her with enquiries about her well-being; he merely watched the retreating backs of Udrax and his priests with the same thoughtful silence that possessed Valeyn.

"I suppose that could have gone better . . . or worse," she said after Udrax had vanished.

"I think it could have gone a lot worse. You may only have one ally, but he's the only one who counts," said Ethan.

"I'm not sure. I think my job is going to be a lot more complicated than I expected."

"Well, I should be able to help you," said Ethan.

"Please do, Ethan. I think I need every friend."

Ethan nodded grimly as they let the surrounding guardsmen usher them into the darkness of Bythe's citadel.

CHAPTER 6

"It is believed that Bythe travelled alone to the desolate plains in the northwestern corner of Kovalith, and there he built his empire with his own hands, raising the mighty citadel of Domitus from the metals of the land and forging it into a construct befitting the majesty of the god who would occupy it. Over the following centuries, the remaining towers of the Ironhelm were built, and the men and women of Kovalith would come to see the miracles of Bythe and bow to worship him – for such was the purpose of his existence.

While force was required to begin his campaign of authority in the early decades, it was not his only means of asserting control. Some nations, understanding the protection and stability he offered, willingly agreed to submit themselves to the rule and protection of the Iron Union. These houses often found themselves in positions of favor within Bythe's court.

As the Iron Union expanded in size and influence, a form of bureaucratic governance presented itself as the ubiquitous necessity of all leaders; both aggressive and benign. Bythe selected favored houses of his court to manage the trivial management of his empire, tasks that were beneath his notice or too administrative for his station. This group was known as the Unity Assembly.

But as Bythe's focus moved away from his people and on to other matters, the Unity Assembly's influence gradually expanded to fill the vacuum of his inattention."

~Kaler of the Ageless

Valeyn's father had welcomed her home, recognized her standing in his empire, and had not appeared again.

She had chosen to spend the first two days confined to her lavish apartments, waiting for the summons from Bythe that would surely come. But no message arrived, nor any formal visitor besides the servants who waited on her every hour of the day or night. Only Ethan kept her company, but even he hadn't been able to learn anything that would explain Bythe's reaction. The city – if not the entire empire – was buzzing with the gossip of Valeyn's return and of Bythe's recognition of her. The Unity Assembly was said to be deeply concerned with the news, but had failed to take any action – so far. It seemed as if the entirety of the Iron Union were waiting to see who would act next – Valeyn or her father?

After the second day, she had grown tired of her apartments and decided to rediscover her home city with fresh eyes. It was only then that she realized that a personal guard would escort her whenever she left her rooms. Was her apartment a home or a prison? Were the men assigned to her guards or jailers? Who could honestly say?

It's all a matter of perspective, isn't it? And of comfort.

Valeyn recalled the words of Ethan's brother and smiled. Perhaps he was wiser than he knew?

But once Valeyn was outside, her anxiety was washed away by the glory of Obduratev. It thrilled her to be home again and she surrendered herself to the city. Although guarded on all sides, she was still able to move down the streets unimpeded. All of the citizenry parted as her retinue approached, many of them crossing their fists across their chests and bowing their heads as though she were her father – acts which made her uncomfortable. She tried to distract herself with the beauty of the architecture she remembered, but once she glanced down the ordered alleyways that connected the main boulevards, she sensed something else. Empty shopfronts and rusted iron archways cast a pall over the laneways, which looked eerie compared to the bright, broad streets. It was as if she peered into a different city, one which was hidden by the glamour of a magnificent façade. Fairhaven had always bustled with life from every class of society — the nobleman through to the destitute. Obduratev's streets were filled with signs of wealth. Men wearing coats of dark silk and women with flowing dresses of equally dark lustre. Many of the heads Valeyn saw were shaved clean – both men and women – as was no doubt the fashion of the season. She wondered which aristocratic house has started such a trend and were now enjoying the flattery of such a following.

There are no beggars. Is there really no poverty here?

The alien thoughts broke through the reverie, and Valeyn felt a stab of shock. It was as if someone were viewing the city through her eyes. She paused mid-stride and turned her thoughts inward.

Elyn? Is that you?

There was no answer. How could there be? She returned her attention to the present and realized her guards were looking at her with curiosity. Even the citizenry around her were now starting to gather, as if her abrupt pause had meant she had been about to address them. As they gazed at her expectantly, Valeyn was sharply reminded of a truth Vale had forgotten. There was no poverty in the Iron Union for a simple reason: any man or woman unable to provide for the empire was *liberated* from the city and provided shelter in one of the Union's production camps in the west, close to the Dark Spires.

"Lady Valeyn?" a girl cried from the front of the onlookers. She was a young child, no more than ten years old, with short, dark hair and the enquiring eyes that only the very innocent can possess. The young girl looked at her with such hope and admiration that for a moment, Valeyn was moved by her. The young girl's face brightened as their eyes met, and she took a small step forward. "Lady Valeyn, I prayed to you. Are you going to save my grandma?"

"I'm sorry?" Valeyn asked.

"Grandma's farm vanished. Mama said the gods took it away. I was wondering if you could return grandma to us, please? You can still keep her farm."

"Tala, no!" the girl's mother warned and pulled her daughter back. "Don't ever question the actions of Lord Bythe! Please forgive us, Lord Valeyn."

Tala seemed shocked to learn she'd done something wrong and her face fell. The expression abruptly reminded Valeyn of Naya, and her own mood faltered. A guard stepped between them and signalled for the woman and child to leave. Tala's confused look haunted Valeyn as the young girl was pulled away by her grateful mother.

"Apologies, Lord Valeyn," the guard said. "You should know you're going to be petitioned by anyone with a problem. I suggest you shouldn't be out here long, my lord."

"What was the girl talking about?" Valeyn asked.

The soldier shrugged. "There's always a rumor doing the rounds. It seems to change every week. Right now, people are spreading stories of evil spirits wiping entire settlements away. It'll be something else next week, my lord. Pay no attention."

She watched the young girl vanish from sight, and the quiet alley now seemed haunted by those who should have been there. "Let's go back to the apartments," she ordered.

On the fourth day, a messenger arrived bearing a Royal Directive. Valeyn – Daughter of Bythe the Immortal – was formally recognized as Heir Designate and appointed to the Unity Assembly effective immediately.

Heir Designate.

Valeyn stared at those words for a long time. It was a new title, and the responsibilities and details of the role were almost certainly undefined, but the implications were clear; Bythe was formally recognizing Valeyn as his daughter. And yet, still no summons had come forth. The messenger dutifully informed Valeyn that the Assembly was due to convene the following day and that her presence would be greatly anticipated. These words turned her stomach, yet she dismissed the page with the answer that she would be honored to take her place at the Assembly.

On the following day, Valeyn surveyed the great expanse of the Ironhelm as she waited for the appointed hour of the meeting. From her apartments high in the citadel, the ordered lines of the boulevards appeared even more impressive. The squares formed by the streets built upon each other in a pattern of fractals than confounded the mind, and Valeyn felt herself start to lose focus on her surroundings if she stared at them for long enough.

"It's a trap, Commander," Ethan repeated for the third time as he adjusted the fittings on the backplates of her green armor. "You may not be in physical danger, but trust me, these political battlegrounds can be even more dangerous than real combat."

"I don't think that's correct, Ethan," she smiled as he completed the adjustments. "The title, I mean. I don't think I'm Commander Valeyn anymore. I believe I'm the Heir Designate."

Ethan paused. "And what's the correct honorific for that?"

She shrugged. "I think I'm the first person to ever hold the title, so I don't think anyone knows."

"My lady, then. One rule I learned as a young nobleman, when all else fails and you have no idea to whom you might be addressing, you can never go wrong with *my lady.*"

"No, Ethan. You'll call me Valeyn. Hells, I'll even accept Vale, but if you call me *my lady*, I'll have you executed."

"Very good, my lady," Ethan answered.

She sighed and ignored the bait. "And we haven't spoken about your new position. Royal Watch to the Heir? You used to command an army; now you're my glorified babysitter."

Now it was Ethan's turn to shrug as he made the final adjustments to her shoulder pauldron. "I don't know. To be appointed as a member of the Royal Guard is an honor many aspire to."

"To many soldiers who are aspiring politicians, yes. But to you, Ethan? You're not like your brother."

"If your star is on the rise in Bythe's court, then I could do a lot worse than attach myself to it. I now command your retinue and oversee your protection."

"Oh yes, my retinue. I have staff now. What am I supposed to do with them? I don't even know their names, let alone their positions."

"You were raised in the Iron Union; it'll come back to you. If it doesn't, you can just call them by whatever name you want and whichever position you choose. They're not going to correct you. Politically, this could be a great opportunity for both of us. I'm sure my mother will be overjoyed when she sees us in the assembly today."

She laughed with a touch of venom. "And that just confirms it. This isn't a good change for you, Ethan."

"Valeyn, I'm a soldier. I do what I'm told. I've been doing it my whole life. Don't worry about me. It's you we need to worry about. Politics is a dangerous game. My family has schooled my brothers from a young age, and you haven't been prepared for it."

"They're bureaucrats and dilettantes," Valeyn snapped.

"They're dangerous, Valeyn," Ethan replied and suddenly he was a tutor instructing an unwilling student. "The sooner you respect that, the wiser you'll be. Mother arrived yesterday, and I don't like what I'm hearing — or rather, what I'm not hearing."

"What do you mean?"

"I'm being told very little. It's as if I've been shut out."

"Even by your mother?"

"I don't know if she's deliberately keeping me in the dark or if she's out of the loop herself," Ethan sighed.

"Why would she keep you in the dark?" Valeyn asked and immediately rued the question. The answer was obvious.

"My mother is a complicated woman," Ethan muttered, then resumed in a brighter voice. "On the other hand, she's been happy to share that the entire court has been stunned by the events of your return."

"You mean when Bythe recognized me as his daughter?"

"I mean when Bythe appeared in public. People are astounded, and it's raised your standing quite a bit."

Valeyn paused. While she had known that Bythe had become increasingly withdrawn in Vale's later years within the Iron Union, he had always ensured his presence had been widely felt. Now his presence seemed to have diminished. She thought of the deserted towns she'd seen on their journey here, and the young girl's desperate question two days earlier. It felt as if the two events were linked, but she just couldn't see how.

There is nothing but madness for you here.

Maelene's parting warning of the insanity of the gods returned to her and she felt uneasy once more.

"Are you alright?" Ethan asked.

"We're late," she deflected and walked to the door. Two servants in white bowed as she approached and opened the large door to the hallway beyond. Another pair of guards dressed in the standard black iron of the Helmsguard snapped to attention as she crossed the threshold. Ethan hurried to join her.

"Take me to the Unity Assembly," she ordered, and the guards immediately began moving. For the next twenty minutes they led her through the ordered lines of Domitus's hallways and through to the axis – the wide central shaft that soared through the center of the citadel – where they mounted the seemingly endless steps that spiraled upward. Black square archways lined the levels along with the immense statues and dark faces that seemed to watch Valeyn wherever she went. The central void was filled with the sounds of hundreds of feet and of subdued voices. She followed her guards around the passageway skirting the void until they reached a large square platform attached to an immense gantry. The sheer size of Domitus had made physical ascent impractical to the point of impossibility, and these feats of engineering had become a necessity. The party positioned themselves on the center of the platform and the safety railing was swung into place. Moments later, the platform jerked its way on a slow journey toward the summit of the citadel. Valeyn looked up into the dark recesses of the portal above and was reminded of The Tower. For the first time, she realized her father had probably mimicked – or even mocked – The Tower when he'd built his citadels. Perhaps this had been some grand statement to his peers. Who could tell what his peers must have thought in return?

Finally, they alighted on a landing and the guards led them down another hall, larger than those on the levels below. Valeyn knew the trappings of a space denoted the importance of those occupying it, so she wasn't surprised at the ostentatious banners lining the imposing corridor. Bythe's black helm against the red banner was a ubiquitous decoration along the walls leading to the Unity Assembly. No less than ten soldiers stood before the doors. One of Valeyn's guards identified her – a formality, she was certain – and the soldier closest to the door saluted before opening it and stepping through ahead of her.

"Announcing Valeyn, Heir Designate to Lord Bythe the Immortal," his voice rang clearly through the doors.

Valeyn nodded once at Ethan, took a breath, and strode into the room.

The chamber of the Unity Assembly was even larger than the audacious hallways. A vaulted ceiling hung high overhead, and the opposite wall was comprised entirely of glass, revealing a breathtaking view of the city and of the brown lands stretching beyond. The rectangular chamber itself was slightly curved as it traced the outer perimeter of the citadel's wall. A massive table of black marble was positioned at the far end, yet only a few figures were seated on the red leather chairs flanking it. The majority of people were seated on an array of high-backed chairs and plush couches in a sitting area directly before the meeting table. Six men and one woman – the Lady Sarele – looked up at her from where they lounged. Three more regarded her stiffly from behind the table. None made a move to greet her. The door closed behind her with barely a click.

The room had fallen silent. Valeyn could feel a mixture of emotions emanating from the people around her: amusement, curiosity, disdain, and even hatred. The last sensation was rippling across the room in almost palpable waves. She looked over at the source of the animosity and was mildly surprised to see the bent form of Udrax the Oppressor glaring back at her. Fully aware this silent greeting was a test from everyone, she decided to meet it aggressively.

"You seem to forget your courtesy," she announced. "Do you not stand in the presence of the Daughter of Bythe?"

Sarele offered a thin smile. Udrax shook his head and muttered something venomous. A couple of well-dressed officers lounging on the couch glanced at each other, while three of the younger men rose to their feet and saluted with their fists across their chests. An older man sitting opposite laughed and shook his head.

"Look at them! What did I tell you? They'd be the first on their feet, begging for approval. Well done, boys. Why don't you roll over and see if she'll rub your bellies? Any others?" He looked around the room theatrically before laughing again and taking a sip of grainmalt from the glass in his hand.

"My Lady," declared Ethan, "permit me to introduce Snyed – High Minister of War."

Valeyn didn't need the introduction but she appreciated the cover it granted her. The Lord of Fortress Krag had long been a rising officer among Bythe's senior staff, and his reputation for brutal discipline of his men was well known, along with some of his vices.

"I'm delighted to meet you, Heir Designate," Snyed toasted her with a half-empty glass and even emptier words.

"I can assure you, our feelings toward each other are mutual," Valeyn replied.

Snyed's grin broadened and he nodded his head. "That confidence might have worked at the young Baron's estate, but you need to be mindful of how you conduct yourself here. Even Lady Sarele and her son won't be able to protect you."

Valeyn bristled at the veiled threat, but before she could respond, Ethan stepped forward.

"Indeed, Minister, the House of Mac-Soldai offers our Heir Designate every protection befitting her station. And we note your concern about our resolve, but let me reassure you that my house will deal with anyone foolish enough to threaten her."

Snyed's smile tightened but he turned to Sarele. "I seem to have gotten your little boy all worked up, Sarele. Perhaps you can calm him down?"

"Alright, I think that's enough, Snyed," said another officer of late middle age. He had a bald head, in line with the fashion, and piercing blue eyes. He rose from the couch and inclined his head in greeting. "I am Habistich, Lord of Cavalry. Welcome, Valeyn. Don't be put off by Snyed and the others. Some of us have been looking forward to meeting you."

"Thank you, my lord," she answered.

"Please. We're all equals at the Unity Assembly. Even you, Valeyn. We don't stand on titles here," said Habistich.

"You might want to tell that to our Minister of Intelligence," said Snyed. "He seems to think he runs this show. He certainly doesn't see fit to arrive on time so we can begin."

"He'll be here. In the meantime, I suggest we make a start so we can get back to doing our jobs at some point today," answered Habistich.

"If the Assembly is such a burden on your schedule, you can always resign your seat at the table, Habistich. You want to be here. Don't pretend you don't enjoy the importance," answered Snyed.

Habistich ignored the comment and instead turned back to Valeyn. "Allow me to introduce you to the rest of the Assembly," he announced, and began pointing out the identities of the other men in the room. The three young men who had saluted her were all Ministers of War, high-ranking officers from noble houses across the Union who reported directly to High Minister Snyed – or at least they were supposed to. They were complemented by two older Ministers of War who didn't seem to share their colleagues' religious fervor and were not afraid to display their reservations toward her.

Udrax didn't need an introduction, but was nevertheless pointed out as the Minister of Faith. He didn't look up from the papers spread on the table before him. Finally, Langguinet, Lord of Infantry, was introduced, and the silver-haired man of senior years took Valeyn's hand and kissed it gently.

"I'm honored, my lady," Langguinet said with a strong Joanan accent.

Valeyn couldn't help but warm to the gentleman and bowed her head in return. "You come from the coast?" she asked.

"Indeed, my lady. A beautiful land, made even more beautiful by the work of your father. Have you ever seen it?"

"Sadly, I haven't had the opportunity," she answered.

"Ah. Then that's a crime we must surely address as soon as we can, my lady. I would be honored to host you in my house and personally show you the wonders of my country."

"Now that our pleasantries are done with, perhaps we can all commence work?" Udrax snapped from across the table. He had stopped focussing on whatever he had chosen to distract himself with and now levelled a baleful stare at Valeyn.

"But what about the Minister of Intelligence? Won't he be upset if we start without him?" asked Langguinet.

"Let him get upset. If he doesn't care enough to get here on time, then he doesn't care that much. We have a quorum, let's start. We've got a lot to cover," said Snyed.

The mood of the room seemed to be with Snyed, and slowly, the men moved to the large table at the back of the room. Valeyn gestured for Ethan to take a seat, but he moved instead to stand by the entrance where he would have a clear view of the entire room. An attendant escorted Valeyn to an empty chair, which had apparently been reserved for her. Various papers were arranged in piles before her, and a writing quill and inkpot had been placed for her use. She somewhat awkwardly lowered herself into the seat, adjusting her emerald-green armor as she struggled to find a comfortable seating position. Valeyn had thought her refusal to relinquish her suit would be a sign of strength, but now, in the presence of these formally dressed men, it seemed to betray her. It was as if the armor were shielding her — hiding her inadequacies. She silently cursed her naïveté.

"Perhaps the Heir Designate would like a moment to change into something more comfortable? I'm sure I can find a fashionable dress around here somewhere?" said Snyed.

Valeyn glared at him but kept her temper. "I'm fine, thank you, High Minister. Although I'm impressed by your keen interest in women's fashion."

Snyed's grin fell from his face as chuckles rippled around the table. Even Lady Sarele's stern face broke into a smile.

"Enough!" barked Udrax and clapped his staff on the marble tabletop. "We have serious matters before us."

The room fell silent and all around the table bowed their heads. Valeyn did the same.

"We commence this meeting by recognizing the great and powerful Lord Bythe the Immortal. We praise his deeds and his will. We recognize his lordship over this land and over all of us. May Bythe rule forever."

"May Bythe rule forever," Valeyn answered the prayer in the dutiful way, but was conscious there were several indistinct mumbles — or no replies at all — from several people around the table.

"Now, to business," said Udrax. "You will find before you copies of reports received overnight concerning the campaign in Roy. I trust you have all been briefed by your staff?"

Heads nodded around the table, and Valeyn felt exposed again. She glanced at Ethan, but his look told her he was also ignorant of what everyone else seemed to know. Valeyn picked up the first of the papers before her and began to skim them quickly.

"Are these reports accurate? asked Langguinet in his thick accent. "This wouldn't be the first time our Minister of Intelligence has acted on bad information."

"They've been cross-referenced by five different sources. I have verified this myself. They all agree on the key facts summarised before you. Our forces at Roy have been routed and are in full retreat," answered Udrax.

"How is this possible?" asked Habistich. "Snyed, as High Minister, you are accountable for this humiliation."

"Well, that was quick, Habistich," answered Snyed. "I haven't been in my seat for more than a minute and you're already accusing me of losing the war. You're full of energy this morning."

"This isn't a joke," Habistich shot back. "You have constantly used your rank as High Minister of War to take full credit for every victory so far. You must now take responsibility for this defeat. I have pressed my views onto you for the past six months, but you've rejected every petition I've made. Our forces are exposed, without a greater cavalry presence, the further north they press, and now the defeat that I foresaw has come to pass. Why did you not heed my advice?"

"You almost sound glad that we lost. Is that how you feel? Are you so eager to smear my name that you'll applaud the rare occasion our enemy prevails?"

"Are you calling me a traitor?" hissed Habistich.

"Stop it," interrupted Langguinet. "You cannot be suggesting the presence of your cavalry would have done anything to win this battle. Although I agree, this failure should be placed at the feet of our High Minister."

Snyed smiled and Valeyn could see he was prepared for this coordinated attack. "I can only work with the tools I'm given, and we all know that the soldiers from the House of Mac-Soldai have fallen well short of our standards of late."

Sarele's face had resumed its hardened exterior and for the first time, Valeyn understood how useful it was as a shield against these aggressive men.

"Perhaps, High Minister, if you weren't so reliant on my people, you might be able to find troops to your satisfaction. Perhaps you might even find them among your own house instead of bleeding the lands of Arbek of all its youth." she replied evenly.

"Don't start with me again, Sarele. You never cease to lecture us on the might of your house. I'm only taking you at your word by using that might to defend the Union. Are you saying the great house of Mac-Soldai is now not as strong as you claim?"

"I'm saying that if you continue to weaken Arbek, then you risk destabilising the entire Union," she answered quietly.

"Careful, Sarele. Are you suggesting insurrection again?" asked Snyed.

Sarele met his eyes squarely and didn't flinch. Valeyn couldn't help but feel a sense of admiration for Sarele's cool resolve under such pressure.

"Calm yourself, Minister," she said. "I am simply stating the facts — that a weakened part weakens the whole. Surely, even you can understand this?"

Although Valeyn had known that Bythe encouraged competition between his senior ministers, she hadn't appreciated the intensity of the rivalry until she shared the room with them. She scanned the pages for details of the defeat, but they were filled with the usual bureaucratic formatting and bloated paragraphs that did little more than conceal the clear facts she needed.

"And what does our Lord Bythe say on this, Udrax? Has he said anything at all?" asked Snyed.

"Our Lord Bythe will share his wisdom when we are ready to receive it. We do not impose our will onto his," replied Udrax.

Snyed swore and threw his inkpot across the room. It smashed on the glass wall, and a trail of black liquid started to slowly bleed down the window like an injury.

"We've just been impossibly routed on the cusp of victory by some secret weapon of our enemy, and our great lord still says nothing? What will it take to get his attention, Udrax? Do I need the armies of the Alliance to be marching on Krag before he starts to pay attention?" shouted Snyed. Several members of the Assembly were nodding cautiously.

"Be careful what you say, Snyed. Lord Bythe hears and sees all, and he will not hesitate to strike you down should you overstep your place," snarled Udrax.

"Good! That would at least be something from him! When is he going to act? If it wasn't for his bastard daughter coming home, I don't think we'd have seen him at all."

Valeyn decided she'd indulged them enough. She threw the useless documents onto the table. "Watch your mouth, Snyed! If you insult me again, I'll take your head right here."

The room fell silent and the guards instinctively placed their hands on their weapons. It was a dangerous tactic. While there was no doubt, she could kill Snyed without a thought, she was less certain of the implications of such an act. It was legally permissible for the nobility to defend their honor to the death if need be, but such actions rarely ended there, and the Fortress of Krag was a very powerful house.

"Don't be so sensitive, Valeyn. You're in the Assembly now, not a children's prayer meeting." Snyed threw up his hands as he turned to her. "Yes, you're a bastard. That's just a fact. You're also the Heir Designate. Nobody's denying your claim, but you can't deny your heritage."

She was torn for a response. While the man was crude and insulting, he also wasn't wrong. Suddenly she felt shrill and oversensitive — a delicate girl trying to sit at a table of hardened adults.

"He is correct in this," joined Udrax. "Lord Bythe has no consort, certainly no queen. And Maelene the Wicked is recognized as the Enemy of the Union. Your claim and title have been accepted, as has your ancestry. You are a bastard of the empire."

She resisted the urge to look to Ethan for support. He'd been right. All the physical power in the world couldn't help her on this battlefield. If she didn't find a way to prevail in this form of warfare, then everything would be slowly taken from her.

"Be this as it may, I will not abide such language," she said. Udrax opened his mouth to overrule her but she pressed on. "For such derogatory speech shames the actions of my father. And we know my father's will is above question. To speak of Lord Bythe's will in such insulting terms is blasphemy, is it not?"

Udrax closed his mouth and stared at her. Valeyn could feel he was searching for the right words that he could twist into an escape from her trap, but time was against him and his silence betrayed and magnified his hesitance. Finally, he relented.

"The Assembly will not refer to the actions of our lord in a vulgar or derisive fashion. We acknowledge his deeds and his will as holy and just."

Snyed swore again, but let it drop. Sarele was watching Valeyn with an unreadable expression. But Udrax was not finished.

"Since the daughter of Maelene is so eager to be respected, perhaps she can help us understand what has happened here. I'm sure you can provide us with some insight."

"What do you mean?" she asked, still unaware of what they all seemed to know.

There were murmurs around the table and several men shook their head in frustration or disbelief.

"Are you playing games with us, Valeyn, or are you simply unprepared for this discussion?" asked Udrax.

Eager to retrieve her civility after her previous outburst, she reined in her anxiety and spoke with as much poise as she could. "Forgive me, I have not yet had the time to be briefed by my staff as I was only assigned to this position yesterday."

"Don't apologize. That's perfectly reasonable," said Langguinet

"No, it's not!" roared Snyed. "Imbatal has razed our army and destroyed the Fingers of Bythe! The least she could do is take an interest. Especially since her own mother gave birth to that demon."

"Imbatal?" she asked as shock swept over her.

"Yes, Imbatal! By the gods! Can you please read the briefing?" shouted Snyed.

Valeyn struggled to arrange her thoughts. Imbatal had attacked the Iron Union at Roy. She knew this must be the army she'd seen at The Tower. But who had woken them? Who could? Shin was dead. Exedor had also been killed. Maelene had returned to the Etherian and taken Naya with her. Aleasea and Ferehain had returned to Fairhaven. Valeyn stopped and felt cold.

What if Ferehain hadn't left?

Shin had told her it would take the unified *kai* of both Bythe and Maelene to unlock the Imbatals. Ferehain already had mastery of Maelene's *kai*; what if he had taught himself mastery of Bythe's? He was certainly intelligent enough. She cursed herself for her stupidity. In her haste to leave The Tower and aid Jason, she'd never stopped to consider the position Ferehain had been placed in. The most powerful Artefacts at the fingertips of a ruthless idealogue. Valeyn felt a slow horror swelling inside her.

What have I done? What has he done? Where is Aleasea?

"Do you have anything to say, Valeyn?" Udrax interrupted her thoughts.

Valeyn considered the possibilities. If Ferehain and Aleasea had taken control of the army and were using it to defend the Outer Wild, then it could be welcome news. But if Ferehain had more ambitious plans, this could be a dire escalation for all.

"I don't know how this has happened," Valeyn replied.

"I don't believe her," said Dox, one of the junior ministers she'd met earlier. Most heads around the table nodded in agreement.

"It's true," Valeyn answered.

"You cannot expect us to believe such a thing, Valeyn," Udrax answered. "As you proudly confess, you are the daughter of Maelene, who walked among us disguised as Mistress Yvorre. Her cruel deceptions are well known. And you were her prized pupil. You must have learned the secrets of this creature, Imbatal."

Valeyn had to restrain herself from smiling. *Prized pupil?* Yvorre had banished Vale to the corners of the empire while she searched for Elyn. Vale had been more of a pet than a pupil, a pet to be cowed and beaten until its master was satisfied.

"You can guess all you like, but you're wrong," she said. "As you say, Yvorre and I were close, and I can tell you, she didn't share her power or her counsel with anyone. You can speculate on what I did or didn't know, but there's not a single one among you who was with me."

"Well, that's not entirely true now, is it?" The familiar voice floated from the door and Valeyn's head snapped around in disbelief.

"Hello, my dear Vale," said Morbus. "It's such a pleasure to see you again."

The fat man was standing in the door, dressed in his usual black silk finery. A white cravat buttressed his already bloated chin, which made his condescending smile even more pronounced and repellent.

"Ah, the Minister of Intelligence has finally decided to honor us with his presence," cried Snyed, but Morbus ignored him. In fact, Valeyn appeared to be the only person Morbus could see. Valeyn couldn't find words. She glanced at Ethan only to find her shock mirrored on his face. Morbus followed her gaze and his grin widened.

"Ah, Baron Ethan! Or is it Commander Ethan? I'm so sorry, my dear boy, I do struggle to keep up with your career. It has taken so many strange turns these past few years. I trust you've been treated well this time?"

Valeyn could see the anger simmering on Ethan's face, and she dearly hoped he would keep it restrained. She had no doubt he was recalling

Morbus's attempt to have him killed during the Rak'Tunga engagement in the Great Southern Wastes, and the torture when he'd been imprisoned in Domitus afterward. She still knew very little of what had transpired after she'd left the Helmsguard. Both Morbus and Ethan had been interrogated, but she'd always assumed Morbus's open association with Yvorre had meant the end of his career. She should have known better. If Ethan could survive the political ramifications, then Morbus could do the same. Indeed, it seemed that Morbus had done more than just survive – he had thrived.

His thick form waddled across the room, and Valeyn noted he hadn't exactly wanted for much during his time back in the Ironhelm. He took a seat at the far end of the conference table and wore a look of glorious contempt when he turned his eyes back to her. She wondered how long he'd been planning this confrontation.

"But, my esteemed colleagues, you are wrong and the Heir Designate is correct. She was no prized pupil of Yvorre. I was the one who shared her confidences, as you all know, and I was the one to expose her."

Incredulity washed through Valeyn, and the emotion clearly betrayed itself on her face, causing Morbus to pause and look at her.

"I'm sorry, Vale. Do you have something to add?"

She drew another breath and calmed herself again. Morbus had been poisoning this group for months, if not years, and she had no idea what traps he had prepared for her. A rash word, carelessly placed out of ignorance, could condemn her.

When she didn't reply, he decided to press his line of attack. "Are you suggesting I'm wrong? Are you saying that you *do* hold intimate knowledge of Imbatal? That you can explain his sudden return?"

"I destroyed Imbatal at the battle of Fairhaven years ago. I even took its weapon as my own. I had no love for that creature nor any desire to understand it."

"Well, we know you destroyed Imbatal on the day you deserted your post as a Commander of the Iron Union," Morbus answered, relishing the opportunity to recall Valeyn's past offences. "However, we have little intelligence on what you did afterward. We're told you fled Fairhaven and travelled into the east. Some say you journeyed deep into the forbidden lands to the south and learned dark secrets in the Barrens of Silence. Perhaps you know more than you say?"

"Perhaps *you* know more than you say, Morbus," Valeyn replied. "Was Royal Inquisitor Exedor sent on your orders? Is it his intelligence you're relying on? You should know that he betrayed you in the end. That he . . ." she trailed off, suddenly unsure if it was wise to mention the Prodigals before these men.

Morbus seemed to know what she had been about to say, and the grin smeared his face once more. "That he . . . what? Had another motive? Please, young Vale," he leaned in conspiratorially and lowered his voice, "are you going to tell us about . . . the Prodigals?"

There were murmurs and some laughter around the table. Snyed shook his head in frustration; Habistich smiled underneath his huge moustache. Only Udrax looked to be unimpressed.

"I don't know what you mean," she replied.

Morbus barked a laugh that sounded a little forced, but several others around the table joined him. "Oh, you're an excellent warrior, but a terrible liar. I don't think you're very well suited to be in our company; you clearly have too much virtue. No, we've all heard the stories of the great Prodigals. Of how their grand and secret society has penetrated all layers of Lord Bythe's empire and how they have eyes and ears everywhere. They're an amusing story spread by bored nobles and believed by their vapid children. I sincerely hope you weren't thinking of coming to us with these absurd conspiracy theories."

Udrax slammed an open palm on the desk. "I warn you, Morbus, the Lord Bythe has many enemies, and a common agenda between them should not be dismissed as a *conspiracy!*"

"There you go, dear Vale," Morbus answered. "You have at least one believer behind you. Yes, Udrax, we know; a shared agenda is not a conspiracy. Well, until you can find a Prodigal or two for us, we won't be able to test that."

Udrax sank back into his chair but kept his eyes fixed on Morbus.

"Gentlemen," said Sarele, "could we please return to the matter at hand?"

"Some of these reports say there was more than one demon. Is this true, Valeyn?" asked Habistich.

"I know that Yvorre only ever kept one at her side," Valeyn lied carefully.

"But that doesn't mean there was only ever one of them. No, I long ago suspected her treachery and sought to uncover as many secrets as I could without being discovered. I personally saw several of the creatures — an army of them in fact."

Valeyn felt revulsion at the brazen lies this little man told, yet she held her tongue. Until she knew more, she had no other choice. She knew she was deep in hostile territory and defense was the only strategy.

"And you kept this to yourself?" asked Sarele. Valeyn could sense her subtle attack, and judging by the sly grin on Morbus's face, so could he.

"I informed Lord Bythe. She had sent them to the Render, far beyond our reach. There was nothing more we could do."

"You could have informed us," Sarele pressed.

Morbus sighed and leaned forward onto the table, clasping his hands together in an overt act of patience. "Lady Sarele, I understand you are frustrated that you are no longer leading this assembly, but you must put that behind you. I am in charge now and I take my orders directly from Lord Bythe. You must learn to accept this."

Fire flashed in Sarele's eyes but she said nothing. Valeyn suddenly understood the game Morbus was playing. By using Bythe's name as a shield, he could cover any number of lies, and it was very unlikely he could ever be contradicted. He had done the same to Vale by invoking Yvorre. Valeyn felt a swell of confidence as she realized the daughter of Bythe was now uniquely placed to expose him.

"But now, Vale returns to us from Kardak and behold! These demons also return to plague us. A strange coincidence, wouldn't you say?" Morbus returned the focus of the discussion to her.

"My name is now Valeyn, as I'm sure you know," she replied. "Do not continue to refer to me by my childhood name, Minister."

"Noted, Heir Designate Valeyn. We all understand your need for respect," Morbus sighed with a patronising wave of his hand. "But the morning is wearing away, so could you please answer my question?"

"I didn't send the Imbatals after our army. I've had nothing to do with them."

"Have you seen them before?"

"No," she answered and tried to repress the flush of the lie within her.

Morbus eyed her shrewdly and a grin crept across his face. "No?" he repeated. "Not once?"

"No," she grated and began to feel increasingly uncomfortable. Morbus had her in a trap and he seemed to know it.

"So, you haven't been to Kardak?"

She sensed he somehow knew the answer. Perhaps he had been in touch with Exedor during his time at Kardak. She decided truth was best. "Yes, I've seen Kardak," she answered, and a ripple of surprise swept around the table. "But I saw no army," she added quickly.

"I see," Morbus said, then paused for a moment as if in thought. "And what next? Where did you go after Kardak?"

"I don't answer to you anymore, Morbus, and I will not explain my comings and goings."

"Did you discover The Tower?" he asked.

Valeyn's mouth was suddenly dry. *He knows.* "I said, I will not explain."

"Did you gain entrance to The Tower and discover these demons?" Morbus pressed.

Every eye was now fixed on her. She struggled for the right answer, but her mind wouldn't function properly. Panic disrupted her thoughts and endless seconds of silence condemned her just as they had condemned Udrax.

"Yes, you were there, weren't you?" His words rang with satisfaction.

"Valeyn, is this true?" asked Habistich.

Valeyn decided to counter the attack with one of her own. "Yes, it's true. I travelled the Render and discovered The Tower. That is my right and I will not apologize for it."

"Did you see these demons in The Tower?" Morbus pressed her.

"And how do you know this?" she snapped.

Morbus shook his head like a disappointed teacher. "I am the Minister of Intelligence. It is my job to know these things. I had hoped you would join the Unity Assembly as a loyal member, but I can see your loyalties lie elsewhere."

"That's not true! I didn't awaken the Imbatals. I rejected them and left them behind. This is someone else's work."

"Are we supposed to believe you? I asked you plainly if you had seen the Imbatals not two minutes ago, and you lied to us."

"I didn't see the need to divulge the secrets of The Tower."

"You didn't see the need?" Morbus repeated in disbelief. "These Imbatals have just routed our army and yet you didn't *see the need* to share all you knew about them? Where are your loyalties?"

"I am loyal to my father!" Valeyn stood.

"Are you?" Morbus rose to match her. "And with whom did you visit The Tower? Did you take my traitorous Inquisitor? Two of the Ageless? Yvorre?"

"What?" gasped Snyed. The rest of the table was in an uproar.

"She wasn't Yvorre, she was Maelene. And your Inquisitor imprisoned us after becoming a slave to the dark secrets of Imbatal. He was a Prodigal!"

"It seems as if I owe you an apology, Udrax. Valeyn is giving us your first Prodigal," Morbus said.

"I'm not inventing this. He was a Prodigal and he took us all to The Tower to unlock its secrets. We stopped him." Valeyn answered.

"We?" asked Snyed. "You mean, you and Maelene?"

Morbus closed his eyes as though he'd heard grave news. "So, you journeyed to The Tower in the company of traitors and sworn enemies of the Union. You admit to collaborating with Maelene, the Ageless, and even with the Prodigals to an extent. Not long after this, weapons you discovered in The Tower attack our forces, and when confronted with this, you openly lied to us of what you knew. And now you expect us to accept you?"

The undeniable truth of his statement was now a damning judgment of her guilt. Valeyn had been disarmed and defeated on this battlefield within a matter of minutes. She could think of nothing to say. The more she divulged, the more it was used against her. Morbus sat down and Valeyn found herself standing alone against a room of condemnation. With no other option left, she played her last card.

"I said before, I don't answer to any of you. I answer to my father."

"And how is your father these days?" Morbus asked smugly.

Valeyn paused. "I haven't yet seen him but when I do, you can be sure—"

"Wrong, Vale," he cut across her bluntly, all pretense of civility now gone. "You can be sure that you won't see him."

"He's recognized me as the Heir Designate."

"A lofty title, indeed! But he'll do little more than grant you that. Our Lord Bythe takes little interest in the running of his empire these days. He's let that responsibility fall to us. We hold the real power in the Iron Union, and you've disappointed all of us."

She looked across the table and judgment assailed her. Even Sarele refused to meet her eyes.

"I call for a vote to suspend the Heir Designate from her duties at the Unity Assembly, until these matters regarding her integrity and allegiance can be resolved," announced Morbus.

"A vote? Does anyone here defend her? Speak up if you do!" said Snyed, glaring across the table at Sarele.

"I'm sorry Valeyn, but your lack of honesty this morning is a problem. I think you should take a leave of absence until we can sort this out," said Sarele. The touch of contrition in her voice was surprising to Valeyn. The rest of the room was silent.

"You recall you once removed me from my position, and I accepted the decision with professionalism and maturity. I suggest you now do the same," said Morbus. The satisfaction on his face was absolute. She fought down an almost irresistible urge to lunge at him, but she knew that killing him at this moment would only complete his victory. She would be a villain in the eyes of everybody but her father; and Bythe might not even help. Turning from the table, she signalled to Ethan and strode toward the exit.

"I'll take this to Lord Bythe," she said over her shoulder as they left, but the words were juvenile now, and she knew it.

"Be sure to pass on my best wishes when you do," Morbus answered as the doors closed behind her.

CHAPTER 7

"The differences between Maelene and Bythe are many. Where Maelene presented herself openly as a beautiful figure of peace and understanding, Bythe assumed a shell of iron to project strength from his earliest days on Kovalith. There are no reliable records of the face of Bythe, nor any stories of his appearance without his armor of black iron.

Although I cannot agree with the methods and beliefs of Bythe nor with the indoctrination he would visit upon his citizens, I confess his stewardship of his people was not entirely without merit, as many of them lived peacefully and slept well under the blanket of his protection. And it would seem the practice of indoctrination was not exclusive to the Iron Union.

It is difficult to understand how Bythe viewed his subjects. Some claim he genuinely cared for them, others assert that Bythe viewed them only as collections – trophies as testament to his prestige. It is possible the two views are not mutually exclusive, as the madness which slowly infected all gods twisted one aspiration into another."

~Kaler of the Ageless

Valeyn ignored the salutes from her guards as she stormed into her apartments. She had spent the rest of the day trying to find some task to distract her, but it had been no use. Eventually, her thoughts always returned to the confrontation with Morbus – and his smug grin. She closed the doors to her bedchamber and rested her forehead against the closed door.

Why? Why is he doing this? Why recognize me, then do nothing else? Was it a mistake to return after all?

She tried to push the doubts aside and calm her mind, but it was hard. There was a touch of guilt over the way she'd dismissed Ethan – as if he were just another servant – but the rage burning within her needed to be released, and she feared her oldest friend might be the undeserving target of her wrath if he stayed by her side. Closing her eyes in the dark room, she breathed in the cool air and was thankful for the solitude – before her senses told her she wasn't alone. Valeyn swung around and unsheathed the sabre at her side. A young woman, dressed in the white robes of the Epistemal Order of Bythe was standing silently in the shadows at the rear of her bedchamber. Her head was bowed and her arms crossed in a silent mark of respect and acquiescence. Valeyn scanned the room but found no sign of any other intruder.

"How dare you enter my chamber?" Valeyn snapped, but the acolyte didn't respond. She remained in her place, facing the floor with her arms crossed. After a moment of prolonged silence, Valeyn realized the acolyte was trembling. She was waiting for permission to address a god – she was terrified. Valeyn sighed, sheathed her weapon and forced her voice into gentler tones.

"You may address me, Acolyte."

"Forgive me, Heir Designate and glorious Valeyn, but I was ordered to approach thee in this manner," the young woman whispered without raising her eyes.

"Ordered by whom?" asked Valeyn.

"Ordered by the most glorious and powerful Lord Bythe the Immortal, my Heir Designate. He commands your audience."

Valeyn didn't reply. She walked to the window and stared out over the city. The sun had sunk beneath the horizon, and the Ironhelm was now bathed in the warm glow of twilight. Here and there, lights flickered to life as they prepared to ward off the long night ahead. A sense of complete anxiety assailed her, and she summoned all her will to keep it at bay.

"Take me to him," she said, motioning to the door.

The acolyte bowed lower and turned to walk toward the rear wall of Valeyn's bedchamber.

"Where are you going?" Valeyn asked.

"Apologies, Heir Designate, but I am ordered to use the Sacred Paths. We are not to be seen."

Valeyn watched with growing unease as the acolyte motioned at the wall of her chamber, causing a large wooden panel to appear in the smooth surface. The acolyte pressed against the rectangle and it sung inward without a sound.

"If it would please the Heir Designate, I will take you to Him."

Valeyn wanted to ask the acolyte who had been using this passage, but she knew it would probably be useless. Instead, she nodded and allowed the acolyte to lead her into the passageway. She looked at the high arches and was immediately reminded of the tunnels underneath Sanctuary. It seemed that Bythe and Maelene had shared common ideas at one time. The passageway was dim and lit by recessed lights glowing in the walls every few feet. As they began their ascent up the gently curving passageway, Valeyn experienced a feeling of vertigo and was reminded of her sensations in The Tower.

"We're outside the realms of Kovalith, aren't we?" Valeyn asked the back of the acolyte before her.

"Apologies, Heir Designate, but I have no wisdom of such things. These are the Sacred Paths I have been instructed to use. I do not seek to understand the power and glory of Lord Bythe. I merely worship his works and obey his will."

Valeyn understood she would get very little knowledge from her guide. Like all fanatics, she only sought reassurance on how things should be. Valeyn settled her mind and adjusted it to her new surroundings – just as she had done in The Tower – and she wondered if Bythe and Maelene employed the arts of Shin in many of their creations. The fabric of Kovalith curved under her feet, and she knew that every step in this tunnel was worth dozens outside. The size of Domitus had necessitated the use of the gantries to reach the higher levels, but the inclusion of these Sacred Paths would allow Bythe and his priests unrestricted access across the entire Ironhelm. Just as the Ageless traversed Fairhaven.

They continued their climb, ignoring side passageways and alcoves which no doubt led to other secret ways within the Ironhelm. After a short time, the passageway ended at a vast, rectangular archway, which was veiled by a black curtain. Here, the acolyte again prostrated herself with two fists crossed firmly across her chest.

"Dear Lord Bythe, please grant me the honor to enter thy house. Forgive mine sins and dark thoughts, and cleanse me of any offense in thine eyes."

Valeyn stood by awkwardly as the acolyte listed a litany of self-imagined sins in hushed undertones before rising to her feet and pulling back the black curtain.

"Please enter the House of Lord Bythe, Heir Designate."

Valeyn stepped through the veil and entered the home of her father. A vast space spread out before her. A glass dome, high above, opened onto a sea of stars that were circling overhead even as she watched. Beneath this, the topmost walls of Domitus stretched down to form the colossal room in which she now stood. Everything shone in the glow of monochromatic white covering every inch of the space around her. The walls were decorated with relief panels and long, sleek geometric lines, completely symmetrical and absolutely precise. There was a feeling of perfection, of unspoiled purity, and of all the expectations she had held of her father, this had been the least.

"Where is he?" Valeyn asked the acolyte, but immediately regretted the question and its predictable response.

"My apologies, Heir Designate . . ."

"But you don't presume my father's will. Yes, I understand."

The acolyte hung her head even deeper in shame, and Valeyn sighed in equal parts sympathy and frustration.

"Look. It's alright. Can you please just take me to . . . wherever I'm supposed to be?"

"Heir Designate, I am permitted no further inside my lord's house. Indeed, very few of us are permitted this far. I must return to my station, if you will excuse me?"

Valeyn nodded, but when it became clear that the acolyte wouldn't leave without explicit permission, she sighed again.

"You may leave me, Acolyte. You've done well. Good work."

The smile that lit the acolyte's face filed Valeyn's heart with warmth and pity. That she could control a person's self-worth so completely and with such little effort felt completely wrong. She considered this as she watched the young woman return to her life of willful submission.

The chamber was immense and as she crossed the floor, the fall of her boots rang out clearly across the empty space. Gleaming white steps led up to a mezzanine level, which led to another corridor. This one looked as though it were a great plaza, or marketplace, but it was completely deserted. Rows of glass lined the passageway like shopfronts, and inside each one lay various objects. A statue of marble was in the first, clean and white and featureless. It stood alone and unadorned and for a moment, Valeyn was reminded of Imbatal. In the next room were paintings, mounted on stands and positioned for viewing, and in the next were a range of stringed instruments, aligned in order and shining with polish. In every space, lay some item of beauty or significance. Valeyn wondered at this as she passed each pane of glass. Finally, the corridor ended and another set of steps led down into a room that was set against the summit of Domitus. The entire wall was a sheet of clear glass overlooking the dark expanse of the Ironhelm at night. Valeyn sensed the work of Shin and wondered how far the view from this citadel might actually reach.

A circular table of polished wood stood in the far corner of the room, surrounded by two dozen chairs. It was set with plates, shining silver cutlery, and large goblets that glistened in the light, and yet Valeyn knew this table had never been used for any such festivity. High-backed chairs were set at the other end of the room, and a fire roared in an open hearth on the far wall before them. There was a sense of perfection about the scene, as if it had been constructed simply for appearance. As if for all of its grandeur, the home of Bythe seemed completely unliveable.

Bythe himself stood against the window. His hands were clasped behind his colossal back, constricting the cape that flowed over his shoulders. He wore his horned mask of black iron and stood unmoving. Valeyn wasn't sure if he knew she was there.

She descended the steps leading down to Bythe's living quarters and let her footfalls ring clearly. He didn't respond. Eventually, she reached the bottom of the steps and walked slowly to the center of the room. Neither of them spoke, and for Valeyn, the silence was terrifying. It seemed that every second was smothering her breath, and now that she had come so far to face her deepest fears, she wanted nothing more than to run away from them. When she was on the verge of speaking out, simply to quell the shrill rantings of her mind, Bythe broke the silence.

"Is she truly gone?"

The words took her by surprise, and she fumbled for their meaning.

"I'm sorry, Father. Who?"

There was a pause and Valeyn could sense the disappointment within him. She hadn't known how she'd upset him, but she knew she had, and the sick clench of fear crept back into her stomach. After agonising seconds, his deep voice rumbled again.

"Maelene. Is she gone?"

"Yes," she answered after a moment. "She returned to The Tower and journeyed back to the Etherian."

"Did you witness this?"

"Yes, I was there."

"Why?"

Again, she felt as though she were being tested, but wasn't sure what to say. "We'd been forced to travel to The Tower against our will by your Inquisitor—"

Bythe's raised voice sharply interrupted her. "Why did she leave?"

Again, her mouth went dry and her confidence faltered. She knew she couldn't please him — that anything she said would be wrong. She wished she'd never come back. "She wanted to leave, in the end. She saw the person she'd become, and I think she hated it. She hated Yvorre."

"Yvorre." Bythe repeated the name as though it held great meaning to him. "Yvorre was her own creation, her own weakness. In the end, she destroyed herself."

Valeyn knew she had to try to take control of the conversation and took a step forward. "I've come home, Father. I've chosen to come back."

"Why?"

Another test. She was a student again, struggling against an unforgiving teacher. "Because I'm not afraid of you anymore."

The lie sounded weak, and she regretted it as soon as it left her lips. Bythe slowly turned and the full force of his authority was finally brought to bear upon her. Although his face was hidden from view, she could feel the weight of his look. Any confidence or illusions of bravado were immediately dispelled. It felt as if his presence could eclipse the sun if he simply willed it, and she lowered her eyes under the intensity of his gaze.

"Do not disrespect me with such falsehoods," he said.

"I'm sorry, Father." The apology was instinctive — a reflex attempt at self-preservation — and she hated herself for it.

He stared down at her for a moment before speaking again. "You have returned to me because you must, because you are my daughter and you know your place is here."

Valeyn knew she had to act, that if she didn't find the will or the courage to push aside her childhood fears, then she would be forever bound by them. She took in a breath and tried to clear her mind. The ripples of anxiety settled, and a sense of conviction returned to her as she raised her eyes. "I've returned to you because I've chosen to. I could have stayed away. I did stay away for many years, and everyone's attempts to capture me failed."

Again, he considered her in silence, and it seemed his unseen eyes were weighing her worth. "You have grown stronger, this is true, but you are wrong on one count; you could not have stayed away. You might try to run or to hide in the corners of this land, but your path would bring you inexorably back to me."

Valeyn decided to walk to the glass in the hope that the act might stir her self-confidence. She looked out over the smattering of lights in the city far below and noticed more red lights glowing in the distant recesses of the night – no doubt the other towers of the Ironhelm. Bythe's reflection was still visible in the glass, his judgment inescapable.

"There are answers you seek of me. I can feel them burning within you. Why do you hesitate?" Bythe's voice echoed across the room.

"I was removed from the Unity Assembly today, on my very first meeting. Why have you named me Heir Designate, only to abandon me?"

"And why do you need me to defend you? Are you incapable of acting for yourself? Do not bore me with petty squabbles and the politics of small men. Such matters are beneath us. This is not the question you wish to ask. Why do you waste our time?" Bythe admonished her.

She was angry at herself because she knew he was right. She was acting like a child. "So, answer me, Father. Why are you interested in me now? I lived here as Vale for most of my life, and I've never stood in this room. In fact, as far as I remember, you haven't spoken this much to me in my entire life."

"As Vale, you were a broken child."

"Broken?" Valeyn repeated the words in disbelief. "I was your daughter."

"No, you were not. You were a fragment of my daughter, corrupted by your mother. You were weak and unworthy of me. However, I now understand you were not to blame for this, and I have forgiven you."

Frustration welled in her and for a moment, she forgot her fear and turned to face his black mask. "You've forgiven me? How dare you."

"I can see you hold me responsible, but I was not to blame for this. I could not have foreseen the treachery of your mother."

"You still could have acknowledged me!"

His helm turned away from her. "And is that why you returned to me? For attention? For my acceptance? Perhaps I have misjudged you."

She felt dizzy and needed to reassert control of herself. "I'm not here for your love. I don't need it." Again, the lie sounded false, but she quickly covered it with more words. "I'm here out of curiosity. I want to learn about you. I want to know more about our people."

He was silent for a moment before answering. "This is more commendable. You may sit if you wish."

She looked around at the pristine collection of furniture and understood her father had no comprehension of their true purpose. These were crude artefacts to him, mere objects and prizes. She took her place among them.

"Did Shin help you build this place?" she asked but Bythe didn't react. "Did Nishindra help you?"

"You have met Nishindra? I thought him gone."

"I met him briefly, but he's gone now."

"You killed him?"

The question shocked her, not just for its nature, but for the sense of approval Valeyn could feel behind it.

"No, it was . . . something else." She decided it was best to avoid mentioning anything that could further condemn Maelene. She searched for a lie to cover the story, but her father's indifference to Shin's fate soon made the effort redundant.

"Yes, he aided me. There was once a time when he shared my vision, but he, like all the others, fell deep into madness. I am not surprised to learn of his passing."

"Is the madness something we'll all succumb to?"

"The madness claims only the weak-minded. I have suffered no such malady, nor will I. My will is absolute, now more than ever, for you have brought news of the fall of Maelene, and my supremacy is now all-embracing."

"How can you know this? They've all fallen. Dahz, Narak, Romona. I've learned things, Father. This world was not meant to contain the will of gods. It rebels against us. It poisons us."

"You speak much like the others. They believed as you do now, and one by one, they all fell to madness. They simply do not understand the meaning of strength and what can be achieved through a focused will."

He moved slowly and deliberately, and every step resounded across the room as he strode to the window. Without a gesture from him, the glass shimmered and the black night beyond was replaced with a clear view of the Ironhelm. A vast iron tower soared over a beautiful city, bustling with people moving through the city under a blue sky. The image moved, and it seemed as though she were looking through the eyes of a bird. She could see beyond the walls of Domitus and over lush, green fields where cattle and livestock grazed on the plentiful land. Small stations dotted the landscape, filled with huts with smoke rising from dozens of tiny fireplaces. She remembered the brown fields and the deserted cattle stations from her journey home and knew the image couldn't be real. This was a projection of her father's ideals, of his dreams.

"This is what I have created. Order out of the chaos that plagued this land, much like the chaos that plagued the minds of my brethren and that may yet plague yours. I have established order and dominion over this. It is not only possible, it is necessary."

"What do you mean by necessary?"

"When we first chose these forms within the forge of Kovalith, we became conscious of a . . . change. Our awareness had become altered. At first it was a novel thing, to see a world through eyes unconstrained by omniscience. However, there was a darkness behind it also, an ever-encroaching darkness that would well and stalk the mind at every moment. It was then I realized there was but one way to keep this malady at bay. We all needed a focus; we required drive and we required sheer will. Only by driving forward, constantly and unrelentingly, could this darkness be fought back."

The image shifted again and the Shield filled the glass. The mighty wall of Iron that had been constructed three hundred years ago to mark the old boundaries of the Iron Union, before Bythe had extended his empire eastward. Today, it was more symbolic than strategic, but it was still an impressive work of engineering to behold.

"And upon sharing this insight, I directed my brethren thus. We must remake this world in the image of order and strength. Only by driving this land toward the unrelenting pursuit of peace and harmony will we find that within ourselves, for it is the struggle and drive to achieve order that in turn creates order."

Valeyn recalled her time in Tiet and the deep dissatisfaction it had ultimately brought her. "I came to a similar conclusion once, when I was in the Fareaches."

"And yet, they did not understand me," Bythe interrupted as if he hadn't heard her. "Many of them believed incorrectly that such darkness and chaos could be averted by the pursuit of merely any craft. Facile self-indulgence that would achieve no lasting result. Pursuits of pleasure or of hedonistic beauty that would serve no underlying purpose. And one by one, they all fell into madness. Naïve Romona sought to understand mortal death only to find she could not, and death claimed her instead. The vain Lubalt-Teble pursued pleasures and in doing so, doomed himself to a life of endless consumption. No one ever discovered his fate, so obscure and irrelevant did his existence become in the end. There were many others."

"You could've worked together. Maelene told me that you both allied yourself with Nishindra to argue in defense of this world," said Valeyn.

"That is an oversimplification of a very complex history. Do not take the words of your mother in a literal fashion."

Valeyn recalled that Maelene also hadn't mentioned Romona during her story in Sanctuary. She shook her head as she was reminded of Yvorre's teachings – a lie is most convincing when it is barely a lie. She rose from her seat, suddenly unwilling to play the role of a passive audience to her father.

"How do you know you were right? The madness could simply affect all gods differently. You don't know your answer was right."

"We all embraced different ideals, and yet I am now the last of all the gods. I am still sane and I am still powerful. My values have been proven supreme through consequence."

"If you were so convinced of your superiority, then why did you conceive me? Was that also part of your plan?"

Bythe was silent for a long time, and Valeyn realized she was sensing something emanating from him. Feelings of distant regret, smothered with anger and pride, radiating from the massive figure before her.

"I was given a vision by Nishindra. You were supposed to . . ." Bythe stopped and seemed to hesitate. For the first time in her life, Valeyn saw her father unsure of himself, and in an imperceptible way, he changed forever. "You were meant to be the best of us. You were intended to be the best of me. Your perfection would mirror my own and we would serve as the example to the rest, to the people of this world and to our own brethren. Your existence would prove me right. But in the end . . . you were not what I expected."

"You mean, when I turned out to be imperfect, you decided I wasn't worth it," she replied, trying in vain to keep the bitterness out of her voice.

"I understand now that your mother intervened in this. Her deceptions came between us. We are not to blame for failing to recognize your true nature."

She opened her mouth and wanted to accuse him again. She wanted to attack him for failing to protect her, for failing to accept her – but she caught herself. This would only be seen as more self-indulgent weakness, and for some unfathomable reason, she still needed him to be proud of her. She decided to take an indirect approach.

"My mother felt corrupted by her captivity here. She became the entity known as Yvorre. I don't think she's completely to blame in this."

A dull rumble echoed from Bythe.

"*Yvorre* was a mask, a shield your mother chose to hide behind rather than face the truth."

"What truth?"

"The truth that she was simply weak and simply wrong, and that I had always been right. Maelene was beautiful, she was kind, but she was also fragile. She lacked the strength required to remake this world. I admit she possessed qualities I did not. She understood the raw power of this land and knew how to wield it, but she would not accept that this power had to be funnelled and contained. Much like the madness that eventually overtook her, the power of this land is a disease that will grow and spread if it is not controlled through a strong and inflexible will. And when she slowly understood this, she still could not accept it. Instead, she created the persona of Yvorre and chose to hide from me within her."

"Then why did you keep Yvorre as your servant? Why didn't you just let us go once you thought I was a failure?"

"The arts of your mother's deceit run deep. I believed she had finally subscribed to my ideology and did not perceive the mask of Yvorre until it was too late. I did not appreciate the game she still played, and I was not aware of your true nature until that day you reached out to me from Fairhaven. That was a bold and audacious gambit, daughter. Well done."

She recalled that terrible moment in Sanctuary, when Yvorre had been torturing both Elyn and Vale in an effort to force them to reconcile, and felt an unbidden swell of pride at the words of praise. She fought to keep the feeling contained.

"When I became aware of your existence," Bythe continued, "I understood that I had not erred in my judgment. I had always believed the union of myself and Maelene would prove the triumph of order over disorder. That my child would resemble me and would reject Maelene. That she would prove my superiority. And so, once I learned the truth, I dispatched my full might to find you."

She thought of the war engines and the renewed assault on the Outland Alliance. "Where did those weapons come from? The Godfire . . . I'd seen nothing like it before."

"What you label as Godfire was my own direct life force, my own power. I summoned it and fashioned it into a weapon, one that would end this war once and for all and bring you both to me."

Valeyn understood he was referring to his *kai*, but such a direct and raw use of such power was unheard of. "That makes no sense, Father. Why not make use of that power decades ago? You could've won the war easily."

Bythe paused as though he had been confronted by a difficult question. "The price for such an intervention was high. I will speak no more of this."

The glass flickered and the bright images of the idyllic Iron Union were replaced with darkness. "She has gone now, and you are with me. I have won. It is over."

"What does that mean?" Valeyn asked with a growing sense of unease.

"Her creations have failed, and my armies have overcome them. Within days the Outland Alliance will be destroyed, and my Union will cover the civilised lands of Kovalith."

Valeyn realized Bythe had no knowledge of the Imbatals' attack. "Father, your forces – our forces – have suffered a defeat at Roy. I believe some remnants of Maelene's followers have unlocked the weapons of Nishindra and Romona and are using them against us."

Again, Bythe didn't answer and seemed to gaze out the window at something unseen, far in the distance. She wondered if he'd even heard her or if he was simply comprehending the news. When the silence extended, she felt the need to fill it. "I've been to The Tower. I've seen some of the Artefacts Shin constructed, and I suspect they may have fallen into the hands of the Ageless, Maelene's disciples. These should not be underestimated, Father. I think there's a grave threat to our army."

"If I am truly the last, then my victory is complete, and I now play a game with no opponent."

Valeyn was unsure if he'd understood what she'd said, or if he was simply dismissing it. "Father, the Imbatals are—"

"I want to know what became of her in the end. Tell me."

"Maelene?"

"Yes."

In that instant, Valeyn understood. The war was secondary. The lives of the soldiers, officers, and bureaucrats were mere playthings. Bythe existed on a higher level than all of them, and any interactions with mortals were like a father indulging himself with the games of his children before returning his mind to real work.

"Yes," Bythe repeated, but this time Valeyn knew he was answering a different question. He knew her mind. He could read her as well as she could read others. "You must learn this, daughter. It is important. No, it is crucial. I do not want you to be me. You cannot understand me. You cannot know what it is like to be me. However, I understand you, and you can serve a role that I never could. Your allegiance is to me, not to the people of this world. You must reflect my perfection. You must stand as evidence and testament to the righteousness of my way."

"Why? For what purpose?"

"For the highest purpose of all; your function is to prove that I am right."

It was a savage and brutal truth, and she grappled for a response to it. "What about us? You and me?"

Bythe turned his head toward her and it was though he were looking at her for the first time. "I am your father. You both love me and hate me, and this confuses you."

She stepped back under his unseen eyes, shaking her head in an attempt to comprehend the truth of her world. "I don't know anymore. I just want to stop being afraid of you," she answered quietly

He took a step toward her and for a moment his giant form almost seemed compassionate. "I will give you more than this. You shall stand before our people, and all shall see that you are created in my image. They will see my perfection reflected in you, and they will love you and fear you as you love and fear me. This is the best gift I can give you. It is the only gift I can give you."

She lowered her eyes and fought back against her disappointment. "Thank you, Father."

He turned and resumed his vigil over the lands of his empire, and in that moment, the father vanished and there was only a god before her. "Now, tell me of your mother."

Valeyn took in a breath and began telling him of Maelene's final days. She told him of Maelene's restored beauty and of her return to compassion and love. She told him of all the things in the world that were of interest to him.

She didn't mention his daughter.

CHAPTER 8

"It would seem that a natural law of Kovalith is that there is a direct and proportionate response to the level of control imposed upon its people. While unlawful activity certainly existed in the Outer Wild, there was little structure or organisation behind such activity. Within the Iron Union, the matter was entirely different. The tight controls decreed by the Unity Assembly – and presumably from Bythe – seemed to result in a natural resistance from those who chafed under such direct intervention; and the systemic nature of the perceived oppression necessitated an equally systemic solution.

The smuggling of contraband and other vices necessitated a higher level of organisation in such a tightly controlled environment, and the Black Chamalas formed to meet such a need. While the Helmsguard were constantly alert to the activities of this group, a natural balance seemed to exist between them in order to service the daily lives of people within the Iron Union.

Leon – the surrogate father of Valeyn – was a smuggler and affiliate of the Black Chamalas during his wayward youth, and it is an irony that the unpredictable resistance to Bythe's intractability would influence the life of his daughter in equally unpredictable ways."

~Kaler of the Ageless

Jason reached over and poured another glass of grainmalt from the decanter on the small wooden table before him. The dark brown liquid ran into the glass and a strong scent like old, burnt wood filled the air of the small room. It was incredible that grainmalt could still be found in these times, especially in Roy. But then, it was rumored the distillation of grainmalt originated in these remote, northern lands and that traders had brought the craft of its making to the more civilised parts of Kovalith. Jason inhaled the aroma in the glass and took a deep swallow of the liquid within. The intense flavours that seared his mouth and throat convinced him that such rumors were probably true.

It would be dawn soon. Jason absently stroked the sleek, gray fur of the cat that had made a home of his lap and took another sip of his drink. Captain Lewis's pet had somehow survived the long exodus from Fairhaven and had since decided to claim Jason and Nadine among his possessions. They had been given use of this house as a mark of respect, both for their station and also – Jason privately suspected – because of what they had endured. He still shook his head at the thought. What they had endured.

Show me one family here that remains unmolested by this war and all its mockeries.

His convalescence over the past few weeks hadn't strictly been necessary – there was no physical evidence of his ordeal – but the memory of the events which should have led to his death still clung to him viciously. He hadn't spoken of this, of course. How could he? And while this brief respite had given Nadine and Jason their first hours alone together since Fairhaven, it had been both a relief and dread to each of them. They had resumed a bed together but hadn't resumed their love, and in some ways, Jason thought it would be better for them both if he'd slept forever on the battlefield.

The cat, seeming to sense his mood, looked up into his face before nuzzling into the crook of his arm. He smiled at the affection. They had never named the animal. Neither he nor Nadine had dared suggest such an audacious idea. As if the act of acknowledging the adoption of a simple pet would touch upon a topic too terrible for either of them to face. Like the weight that hung over them every day. And so their pet, like the nature of the growing distance between them, had remained unnamed.

I grant you the gift of life, and yet you still dwell on the embrace of death.

Romona's voice echoed in his mind, and Jason closed his eyes as if he would will the intrusion away. Was she real? Or was she a lingering result of his grief made real by his mind. He'd seen it before, of course. War did terrible things to the minds of some soldiers; far too many more suffered silently, too afraid or too proud to voice their pain. Was he simply another of them now?

A noise in the next room made Jason realize his wife was awake. He finished the contents of his glass and set it next to the nearly empty decanter. A moment later, the wooden door opened and Nadine crossed to where he sat. He looked up at her, draped in a simple blue dressing robe with her blonde hair tied back over her shoulders. Jason had always thought she was most beautiful at this time of the day. While the war had certainly taken a toll on his appearance, it had seemed to only enhance hers. Her beauty had not given way to the strains of leadership, but had now been enriched by a strength of purpose and being that lingered in every expression. Her eyes fixed every subject they beheld with an unquestioning resolve that Jason both admired and envied.

She reached over and gently placed her hand on his shoulder. "Have you slept?" she asked.

Jason shrugged. "A little."

She glanced at the decanter but didn't give voice to her silent judgment. Jason appreciated the restraint.

He rose and crossed to where his blue coat hung on the wall, a relic of Fairhaven now, but still meaningful to the soldiers left under his command. He pulled it on and buttoned it with a slightly careless air. "I'm going to meet with Zain and Kaler. They should be ready to report."

"You've barely slept. Go to bed and let me handle this, please," she said, crossing to where he stood.

"I can't sleep, Nadine."

"Jason."

Her voice took a gentle tone and for a moment he was reminded of the young, noble girl from Fairhaven. For a moment he forgot where he was and he saw tender, blue eyes set in the face of a woman he deeply loved but could no longer reach. For a moment, he cursed the war and every ugly thing it had forced between them.

"Jason . . ." she repeated, but halted, the words freezing in space and becoming lost in the wave of emotions it brought with them. She looked at him wordlessly and he returned the stare. He reached out and took her into his embrace. She folded into him, crumpled against his solid body with a heaving chest. With their faces averted, the deepest of feelings could pass between them unspoken. They stood that way for an eternity.

"I'm coming with you," she announced and broke from his arms, heading back into their bedroom without another glance at him. Moments later, she emerged, dressed in a black tunic and pants with a gold chain across her shoulders. The girl from Fairhaven was gone, his broken wife was gone, and the leader of the Outland Alliance strode across the room and opened the door.

"Let's go," was all she said as she led them into the frost of morning.

They walked in silence as they crossed the distance to the command tent. The town was mostly empty at dawn, but for the occasional pairs of soldiers dotted through the mist. They reached the tent and Jason half-saluted the guards holding the flap open for them as he entered. Inside, Kaler and Zain were deep in conversation. It was mercilessly cold, and Jason silently cursed Zain's harsh discipline combined with Kaler's complete lack of sensitivity to comfort. Thankfully, Nadine rescued his pride.

"Guards, light the brazier so I don't freeze to death during the briefing, please," she commanded. A guard entered the tent and began loading the brazier with wood and oil. Zain glanced at it with mild irritation, as if recalling a forgotten chore, then shrugged it off.

"Councillor, I wasn't expecting you, but I'm glad you're here. The scouts have returned on schedule throughout the night, and the news is welcome," said Zain with the emotion expressed reading a shipping inventory.

"Do you think our forces will be able to mount a counteroffensive?" asked Nadine with an edge of hope in her voice.

"More than that; the Helmsguard seem to be in full retreat," answered Zain in the same impassive tone.

"What do you mean, full retreat?" Jason asked in disbelief. "We've barely provoked them."

"They fell back to regroup at the Pirgem Ridge after the destruction of the war engines and then moved further south one week later, after we initiated three surprise attacks on their eastern flank," said Kaler, outlining the events in rational sequence to make sense of them. "However, now it seems they have continued their retreat and have repositioned their forces south of the River Claiream."

Jason stepped forward and looked at the map spread over the table. "They're out of Marfort?"

"It looks that way," answered Zain. "We've had the reports confirmed by four separate scouting parties, and none have found any trace of the Helmsguard north of the river."

"It could be a trap," said Nadine. "Maybe they want to lure us over the river, leaving Roy's defense weakened?"

"We considered that, but we cannot find any evidence to support the theory," said Kaler. "There appears to be no force left in Marfort — at least none that we can detect. And the casualties they've suffered also do not support this theory."

"What casualties?" asked Jason.

"Helmsguard dead, dozens of them, and not by our hand," said Zain.

Silence hung inside the tent as they all processed the implications.

"Imbatal has continued to attack the Iron Union?" asked Nadine.

"We believe there is more than one Imbatal," answered Kaler.

Jason shook his head. He clearly remembered the damage caused by just one of those creatures. Imbatal had been an unrelenting force when he tore through Fairhaven, and only Valeyn had been able to eventually stop him. And now there were more of him. He repressed a chill and took solace in the one unexplainable fact that seemed to shelter them. "Why are they attacking the Iron Union instead of us?" he asked.

Kaler shook his head. "We do not know. Imbatal was always a mystery to the Ageless. There were rumors of his creation deep within the Render. However, we know that Imbatal was designed as a creature of war, appropriated by Maelene once she became corrupted by Bythe's influence. We did not know there were more of him."

"*How poorly they understand my masterpieces,*" Romona's words sang in Jason's mind. "*How savagely my brethren corrupted my work. This saddens me deeply. Will you not intervene?*"

"It doesn't matter what the reason is," said Nadine, "if these Imbatals have turned on the Helmsguard, that effectively makes them our allies."

"I advise caution, Councillor. We do not know this for certain," said Kaler.

"Either way, Nadine's right," said Jason, failing to acknowledge the slip in decorum. "This gives us a chance to hit them hard, they'll need to deal with two enemies instead of just one."

Zain's cold eyes scanned the map, then he spoke formally. "That is one option; however, we could also make use of this time to develop a strategic advantage. Our forces are inferior to our enemy and we have endured a long siege. If the Helmsguard are fighting on a southern front, we could commit a small force to harry them while we take the time to regroup for a larger offensive in two months when the weather is more favorable."

"*This man gives wise advice, although it sounds predictable to me. I have given you the gift of a second life. How will you choose to spend this gift?*" Romona's voice sounded as if she were over his shoulder. It took an act of will for Jason to keep his attention on the people before him.

"So Marfort's free and the job's done, is it?" asked Jason. "Well, for the rest of us, we still have our homes to reclaim. It's not time to lick our wounds and call it even."

"I was not suggesting that, Captain. I am suggesting a cautious approach. I am more than willing to take the fight to these invaders and push them out of the Outer Wild."

"Further than the Outer Wild. Back into the pits of the Ironhelm," growled Jason.

Zain looked at Jason carefully. "I am willing to defend our lands, and the lands of our allies, but we are not like the Helmsguard. We do not invade the lands of others."

"We'll worry about that when the moment comes," said Jason.

"There is sense in what the Warmaster counsels," said Kaler.

"*And so, will you seek out happiness and contentment with this second chance? Or will you court death once more?*"

"And there's sense in striking now while we've got the advantage," replied Jason. "We don't know how long these attacks will last, and if we hesitate, we might be standing here in two months regretting we didn't act when we had the chance."

Nadine's brow creased with concern as she looked at her husband. "There's risk either way," she conceded.

"I could promise you a grand destiny — a confrontation with the man who has caused you so much pain. I can deliver Commander Ethan to you and promise you his death at your hands."

Jason looked at Nadine and his tone left room for neither ambiguity nor argument. "Do what you want, but I'm going after them. I'll go alone or I'll go with whoever chooses to follow me. I'll hunt down the bastards who took our family and kill them one by one if I have to, but I'm going."

Nadine raised her hand in appeasement. "Jason, don't be rash."

"I'm not being rash, Nadine. I'm just being honest. I can't sit here for two months and hope for the best. Not when this could be our only chance to drive them away. I'm sorry. I'll resign my commission and head out as a free agent if I have to, but I'm going"

"You'd split our army? asked Zain.

"That's not what I want. But if people choose to follow me, it'll be their decision, and it'll be because they know I'm right, Zain. Do you want to put it to the test?"

Zain shook his head and turned to Nadine. "This is dangerous, Councillor. Captain Jason's tactics may prove to be right, but his reasoning is irrational."

Jason laughed. "There's nothing rational left in this world, Zain."

There was silence in the tent as Nadine held Jason's eyes for a long time. She seemed alien to him in those moments, as if she'd never shared herself completely with him, as if he were just another man.

"Very well, Captain," she said at last. "I'm ordering you to work with the Warmaster and start drawing up plans for an immediate counteroffensive. We'll drive these murderous bastards back to the hells they came from."

"Ah, my Jason. You are truly a mortal I could love."

Jason looked at Romona. She was visible now, standing behind Nadine and favoring him with a smile that was as affectionate as Nadine's was cold. He wasn't sure if she was a vision from the gods, a fever-vision from his battle injuries, or if he was simply going mad. He didn't care. It didn't really matter anymore. He knew he wasn't going to stop until either he or Ethan was dead.

• • •

"Is anyone following?" Valeyn asked Ethan, as she adjusted the black silk veil in front of her face.

"No, my lady. Nobody's following," Ethan replied.

"You didn't even look!"

"Valeyn, if a nobleman wants to attract unwanted attention on the street, then the absolutely best way for him to do that would be for him to look over his shoulder precisely every fifteen seconds – as you keep ordering me to do."

Valeyn went to turn her head but Ethan's words caught her.

"And the same goes for his companion. Eyes forward please."

She shot him a black look from under her disguise but obeyed. It had been two days since her humiliation at the hands of the Unity Assembly, and at the hands of Bythe, and over that time she'd felt her legitimate depression descend into an inexcusable self-pity. She needed to do something. She needed to escape the confines of Domitus and of her position as Heir Designate and simply be herself for a time, but she had no idea how to do this. Surprisingly, Ethan – Baron of Mac-Soldai – had provided the solution.

"How do you know they're not behind us?"

Ethan furrowed his brows in a theatrical display of concentration and began enumerating on his fingers. "Let's see. Point one, I've been glancing at the reflections of every window we pass, and I haven't seen anyone suspicious behind us. Point two, I haven't heard anyone shouting at us to stop, which completely eliminates the possibility of any guards running after you. And point three – the most important point – we've passed no less than six other noblemen engaged in similarly clandestine activities tonight."

"Really? Where?" She went to turn her head again.

"Valeyn," he warned.

"Sorry." She returned her gaze to the well-lit street before her.

"We passed one just a few moments ago."

Valeyn cast her mind back, recalling her training to observe every detail. "The man who was standing on the corner in the black coat?"

"That's the one."

"Sorry, he looked more like he was just another commoner in the street to buy something the Iron Union doesn't approve of being sold."

"I'm sure that's what he wanted people to think, but the cut of his hair, his posture — little things like that marked him as a nobleman. I'm sure he recognized the same in me. So, despite your conviction that we're the center of everyone's focus, I really don't think anyone is paying too much attention to us."

"So, what is this? Some kind of secret nobleman's club?" she teased.

He smiled. "Something like that, but there are no membership slips."

"And what are these noblemen all doing out here?"

"Well, that all depends on the nobleman in question. Our friend back there was in all likelihood waiting to meet a companion for the evening."

Valeyn raised an eyebrow. "A . . . *paid* companion?"

"Oh, probably not of that variety, not out in the open street anyway. No, I'm sure he was just waiting for his . . ." Ethan gestured in the air as if searching for the right word. ". . . acquaintance."

"Acquaintance?"

"Acquaintance."

"I think the word you're looking for is mistress."

"Well . . ." Ethan smiled as if he were dancing around a delicate subject. "It's not unusual for noblemen to be born into strict households with arranged marital unions, and it's not unusual for those noblemen to also desire companions of their preference. It's not unusual for noble*women*, for that matter."

She looked around the street. People walked past her alone or in pairs, some gathered at tables in shopfronts. All of them had the look of common citizenry of the Ironhelm; appropriately dressed, well behaved, but she could also sense something else – a feeling of mischief that belied the civility of the scene. "So, your plan to sneak me out of the citadel was to have yourself pose as some roguish nobleman and I'm your secret lover?"

Ethan shrugged and smiled. "Allow me this fantasy, please. It's the closest I'm ever going to get to the real experience."

Valeyn raised her eyebrows but couldn't supress a smile at his honesty. "I could have you imprisoned for that comment, you know?"

"Well, keep looking back over your shoulder and that's exactly what'll happen to me. But I'd prefer you didn't. One prison stay was quite enough for my liking."

She sighed and assumed a casual air. "So be it. Tonight, I'm just a careless young woman out to enjoy life."

"Now you're getting it," Ethan said. "When was the last time you really relaxed?"

She paused as memories of Tiet intruded on her. She recalled where a life of careless pleasure had taken her and what it had done to those around her. She thought of little Naya in the clutches of Exedor and his Faedes.

"What's wrong?" Ethan asked, sensing her disquiet.

"Nothing. Where are we going, anyway?" she deflected in an attempt to change the subject.

"I have a small errand I need to run and I thought you might enjoy tagging along."

"What sort of errand?

"A sensitive one. Not something I'm able to talk about, I'm afraid."

Valeyn looked at him in surprise. "You're keeping secrets from me?"

"Well, that all depends on who I am to you tonight. If I'm your loyal officer, then we shouldn't discuss anything personal so there's no matter of secrets. And in that case, I should return you to the citadel right now."

"No, Ethan, I didn't mean . . ."

"But if you're here as my friend, then yes, I have my secrets, Valeyn. Just like you have yours. And I'd ask you to please respect that and trust me."

She was surprised, caught off guard by their abrupt transition into peers on an equal footing, but she nodded. "Of course. You're right. I'm sorry. I should be thanking you, not questioning you."

"No need to apologize. I'm always happy to help, my lady."

"You really need to stop calling me that," she muttered.

Ethan laughed and skilfully turned the conversation away. He pointed out taverns and various shopfronts, telling her minor bits of trivia about each as he stitched together a rough history of the boulevard for her benefit. Valeyn was impressed with his knowledge of the city. While Vale had been raised in the Iron Union, she'd had very little opportunity to walk the streets of its towns and was never given the chance to do so alone. Yvorre hadn't allowed it. Most of Vale's childhood had been spent inside Domitus, and when she was old enough to train – and after Bythe had long since lost any interest in her – she had been sent to the Shield at Hammerfall. Vale had never been able to walk the streets and simply exist like any other person, as Elyn had taken for granted in Fairhaven. Valeyn smiled as she reflected on the irony of her twin natures. Ethan turned them off the broad boulevard and led them down a smaller laneway. Valeyn was mildly surprised to see the laneway didn't conform to the strict grid layout of the rest of the city, instead it curved like the laneways of the Old City in Fairhaven.

"Now, the Archeuim Parade is one of the oldest streets in Obduratev, probably *the* oldest," Ethan said, as if reading her mind, "and by some strange act of the gods, it was never demolished and realigned with the rest of the city plan. Nobody knows why. Rumor has it that Lord Chikbor, a wealthy patron from Ciro, actually owned most of the street and was able to convince the right people to overlook it."

"I'm a little surprised Bythe hasn't intervened. This must be an affront to his need for order."

Ethan grunted a laugh. "I highly doubt your father has ever set foot here."

The street was smaller than the others and seemed to host more people. The taverns were more frequent, and lights were strung overhead in drooping arches. Tables lined the street, occupied by well-dressed men and women drinking or eating from small plates. Laughter and low chatter rippled through the small street, and Valeyn almost felt warmed by it. A small crowd of men were gathered around one table, and as she passed, Valeyn could see dice being thrown amid small piles of Darkiron coins.

"I thought gambling was against the laws," she said as they moved past the men.

"There are laws, and there are laws," Ethan said with his casual indifference that marked him as one of the wealthy. "These places exist for a reason, and no law is ever going to stamp them out. The trick is for them to exist in a way that doesn't upset too many people. That's how society really works."

"Well, I'm a little surprised the Helmsguard haven't stamped this out," she mused.

"Oh, they have," Ethan answered. "Archeuim Parade has been officially closed down at least three times as far as I can recall, and only the gods know how many times before we came here. And yet, once the complaint has been officially dealt with, the same storefronts reopen, and the same people return."

"Why don't the Helmsguard come back?"

Ethan laughed. "Oh, they have. They're all around you, Valeyn. They're just not looking to make any arrests tonight."

Valeyn shook her head but couldn't help smiling at Ethan's infectious good mood. "And who's *we*?" she asked.

"Sorry?"

"You said '*we*' came here. Who did you come here with?"

"Ah, we're back to secrets, my lady. There are things I'm not at liberty to discuss."

"Fine, keep your silly secrets." Valeyn rolled her eyes. "I'm pretty sure I can guess anyway. You and your friends coming down here for drink and women. It really doesn't take a genius to understand young male behaviour."

Ethan smiled. "Again, something like that."

They walked in silence for a time and Valeyn took in the euphoric mood that swept over her in pulses.

"I can see your point. People seem happy tonight. I'm not sure that's something that should be discouraged," said Valeyn.

"This city has been far too tense for far too long," Ethan remarked, a strange solemnity passing over him for a moment. "These people need enjoyment; they need a distraction. You can't keep people controlled for too long, and this war has been going on for far too long."

"What are you saying? Are you talking about rebellion? That'd never happen in the Iron Union," said Valeyn.

Ethan shrugged. "A year ago, I would have agreed with you, but things are changing. The houses are bickering between themselves and the people are the ones paying the price. They expect your father to save them, but they're slowly realizing that's not going to happen – and I think they're getting angry."

They rounded another curve in the road and walked toward a small bistro set into the street level of the tall building that lined the street. It was a run-down place, little more than a hole in the wall with a small, faded sign over the entrance. Small tables with assorted stools were scattered around the front. A street busker was strumming a lute at the side of the shop and several customers were enjoying their wine in the cool night air. A raised male voice demanded her attention, and she noticed two young men at a table near the entrance, talking to the serving girl. They seemed agitated and one of them had his hand on the girl's wrist. Ethan also noticed and his pace slowed as he assessed the scene. The two men laughed and the one holding the girl's wrist pulled her toward an empty stool in an obscene effort to get her to sit down. Patrons glanced nervously at the scene, but none interfered. Valeyn suffered no such hesitation.

"Wait!" Ethan ordered, placing a hand on her shoulder before she could move. "Let me handle this."

Before Valeyn could protest, Ethan moved quickly toward the table. Valeyn followed a few paces behind, adjusting the veil before her face and doing her best to assume the appearance of a helpless mistress.

"Gentlemen, are you having a pleasant evening?" Ethan announced, then turned to the serving girl with a smile. "Jasmine, you get bigger every time I see you."

The two men turned and looked at Ethan with open hostility.

"Can I help you, mate?" said the one holding Jasmine's hand. They were both large men in their early twenties, possibly laborers of some description given their looks. The other young brute slowly rose to his feet and glared at Ethan like a dog defending territory.

"No, I think I'm here to help *you*. I'm here to pay for the meal you've just enjoyed so you can go on to your next stop with a full purse," Ethan replied in an even voice.

The young woman looked at Ethan with undisguised relief.

"Thanks, mate, but I don't need your charity, so why don't you just take off?" said the young man at the table dismissively.

"Because you've got your hands on the daughter of a friend of mine," Ethan said. "Do you think it's alright to disrespect a family in this way?"

"They're alley trash, and we'll treat them the way they deserve! Back the hells off!" shouted the standing man in a predictable attempt to bully Ethan into submission, or to provoke him into a fight, where Ethan could then suffer a justified beating.

Ethan refused to rise to the bait. He lowered his voice in pitch and spoke with a calm, grim sincerity. "My name is Baron Ethan of Mac-Soldai. This family is under my protection and the protection of the house of Mac-Soldai. Think very, very carefully about the consequences of what you do next, for it will decide the course of your miserable life."

Doubt flickered over the face of the man standing. The man gripping Jasmine's hand gave his friend a thoughtful glance, then after a moment he released her and rose to his feet.

"Whatever. I didn't want her anyway," he muttered, glaring at Ethan in the manner of a beaten man still keen to save face. "I suppose you can have her if you're that desperate."

He stepped back from the table and looked about to say something else, but a hardening of Ethan's expression made him hesitate.

"C'mon, Lash. Forget it. Let him pay and let's go find some dice," said the friend, gripping Lash by the shoulder and giving him an honorable exit from an unwinnable escalation. Lash allowed himself to be pulled around a little too easily and they walked up the laneway.

Ethan stared at their retreating backs as Valeyn stepped alongside him. "And I thought we were supposed to be in disguise?" she said.

"No, *you're* in disguise. I don't need to hide down here."

"Apparently not. In fact, it seems you're a bit of a celebrity," she replied.

The door to the bistro flung open and a tall, middle-aged man strode forth. His face wore deep lines from decades of deeper worries, and quiet anger seared within his eyes.

"What happened?" the man brusquely demanded, as he marched up to Ethan with such resolve that Valeyn wondered if he intended violence.

"It's alright, Symin, it was just some ruffians. I've dealt with them," Ethan said with a reassuring tone.

Symin looked up the street and took a step toward the two men still visible in the distance. Ethan placed a retraining hand on his chest. "It's over, Symin. Do the smart thing. Let it go."

Symin glared at Ethan, then sighed and nodded curtly. "You steal the righteous vengeance from angry old fathers, Ethan, but thank you. You're a frustratingly wise man for someone so young."

Ethan grinned and shook Symin's hand vigorously. "Anything of value that I know, I learned from you, old man."

Jasmine leaped forward and wrapped Ethan in a child-like hug

"It's alright, Jasmine, they're gone, and I doubt they'll ever come back, now that they know what might happen to them."

"I didn't do anything, I promise. I just asked them to pay their bill," she sobbed, and Valeyn was again reminded of Naya and her terrible, undeserved guilt.

"I know," Ethan said reassuringly. "You've turned into a beautiful young woman. It's not your fault men like that exist."

"I'm in your debt, Ethan. Thank you," Jasmine said.

"Don't worry, Jasmine," said Symin. "If they ever come back, it'll be the last time."

Ethan raised his hands in a placating manner. "Symin, we don't want you attracting attention to yourself, and you won't be able to protect your family from a prison cell. Why don't we discuss this inside, and we'll see what we can do about increasing some security here?"

Symin nodded again then abruptly swung his cold, blue eyes onto Valeyn. "You're not a complete gentleman, Ethan. You haven't even introduced your lady friend," said Symin, stepping forward and extending his hand to Valeyn. "My name is Symin, a friend of the impolite Baron Ethan. I'm very pleased to meet you."

Valeyn hesitated only a moment, but her veil concealed her face and she'd prepared for something like this. "My name is Elyn, and the pleasure is mine."

"Oh, Ethan. You have a companion tonight. Martya's going to be jealous, you know?" Jasmine said playfully.

"We're not staying, I was only planning on calling in on your father briefly. I actually wasn't intending to make this introduction," he said, glancing at Valeyn somewhat awkwardly.

"You were going to leave her in the street while you did business with father?" Jasmine said with mock outrage.

"You're judging me? I thought you were in my debt." Ethan asked.

"That was before I realized you have no manners," Jasmine replied before stepping before Valeyn. "Please, Elyn, I apologize for the conduct of your chaperone. Would you like to come in and have some dinner?"

Ethan looked alarmed but Valeyn was feeling playful. "Why, thank you, Jasmine. I would be honored."

Symin nodded his approval and ushered them both into the small bistro.

"*Elyn*," Ethan whispered as they moved toward the entrance, "this isn't a good idea. I can move freely here, but you can't show your face."

"Well, I'm supposed to be your secret lover, aren't I?" she answered. "I assume it's very common for a secret lover to preserve her privacy with a veil, even during dinner. And besides, I'm hungry."

Despite its small entrance, the interior of bistro was surprisingly spacious, with several large tables economically packed into the space. Symin ushered them to a large table in the back then moved into the kitchen to prepare their dinner. Valeyn scanned the room, the walls were covered with various paintings and patchwork quilts that looked to be homemade. Ethan followed her gaze and smiled.

"The crafts of Symin's family. Not exactly master artists, but you can't deny there's certain talent that runs in his family. I think it comes from their bloodline. He emigrated here from north of Klyph. After Maelene's fall, those lands were hit hardest by the war. A lot of his friends chose to flee to the Federacy, but Symin's a patriot and warrior, if not a soldier. Rather than flee, he convinced many of his countrymen to commit their strength to the empire. He chose to bring his family and many of his people to the Ironhelm. I admire that about him."

"Why didn't they join the Helmsguard?" Valeyn asked.

Ethan shrugged. "It's not their way. They don't view warfare the same way we do. Every man is trained to defend his home and his neighbour, but they don't have an organised army. They don't believe in conquest. You'd almost call them pacificists, if they weren't so effective at killing their enemies."

"I have to admit, I'm a little surprised, Ethan," she said, adjusting the cushions under her so she could sit a little more comfortably.

"What do you mean?"

"All these years I've known you, I always thought you were a typical member of the nobility, and yet, you've befriended these people. Somehow, I don't think your mother would approve of this."

Ethan's smile was edged with bitterness. "Well, ironically my mother does approve of this, although not for the reason you're giving me credit for. One of the reasons Archeuim Parade continues to flourish is thanks to the . . . unofficial sponsorship of several houses. Most people down here know how this works; those two gentlemen outside certainly did. Like I said, there are rules you can bend, but there are certain rules you never want to break, especially here." He sighed and hesitated. "Valeyn, I didn't mean to bring you in here . . ."

"Ethan!" a female voice rang out.

He rose as a woman of striking beauty swept into the room and collided with his embrace. Ethan looked a little uncomfortable as the woman gripped him before placing a kiss on his cheek and pulling away to flatter him with a broad smile. Valeyn wasn't sure where to look and was suddenly grateful for the veil.

"You've been away far too long. You're lucky we still let you in," the woman teased in a thick accent. She was tall and looked to be in her early thirties. Her dark hair fell in gentle waves over tanned shoulders and she wore a pale dress that was very well suited to her feminine curves. Watching their casual intimacy, Valeyn was surprised at the unexpected pang of jealousy she felt.

"It's good to see you again, Martya," Ethan replied then gestured to Valeyn. "I'd like to introduce you to my companion, Elyn."

Martya smiled knowingly at Ethan then turned and bowed low to Valeyn. "Welcome to our home, Lady Elyn. My name is Martya and we are at your service. Please let me know how I can make you comfortable."

"Thank you, Martya," Valeyn stumbled, taken aback at the genuine display of hospitality and suddenly feeling very rude for covering her face. "I apologize for . . . this . . ." she said, pointing at her face.

"Oh, no. Please!" Martya clasped Valeyn's hand between her own, as if to prevent her from attempting to remove the veil. "Do not think of it. We understand and respect the need for privacy and discretion here." Martya smiled and shot Ethan another quick glance. Again, Valeyn felt excluded from something.

Martya called to the kitchen in her native tongue and her younger sister answered. A moment later, Jasmine emerged carrying a plate of flat bread and various dipping sauces in small, ceramic bowls. Martya and Jasmine arranged them on the table in from of Valeyn.

"Excuse me, please. I need to have a word with Symin," Ethan announced. "Ladies, would you please entertain Elyn for a moment?"

"Of course," said Martya with delight. "I'm sure we have a lot to discuss."

"Well, I won't be long," Ethan said, throwing her a cautious look, which Martya ignored.

"Take all the time you need. We're going to be talking about you," said Jasmine, taking the chair to Valeyn's left.

Ethan shook his head and muttered something to himself before walking to the bar where Symin was waiting.

"We really shouldn't tease him," smiled Jasmine, glancing over her shoulder at this retreating back, "but it's too much fun not to. He's such an easy target."

"That's only because he's a good man," said Martya. "Good men are easy to fluster because they care about what you think, bad men aren't interested in what you say about them."

Valeyn looked over at Ethan but he had his head bent over the bar, deep in conversation over something.

"How long have you known Ethan?" asked Jasmine.

"A long time. About half my life. But it's been . . ."

"Complicated?" Martya answered, then broke into a clear and beautiful laugh. "It always seems to be that way, doesn't it?"

"Yes. Although sometimes I think I don't really know him at all. I suppose, I've been a little preoccupied recently. No, that's not true, not recently. I've always been preoccupied. I guess I haven't given him as much thought as he deserves."

"Well, I'm sure you had your reasons." Martya answered, and Valeyn thought she detected an air of judgment in the words.

"Yes, we all have our reasons," Valeyn repeated. The conversation died and an awkward silence spread across the table. Valeyn struggled to think of something to fill it. "How do you know Ethan?" she asked.

Martya glanced at Jasmine and seemed to consider her words before answering. "He's been a friend of the family for some years now."

"Although we don't see him as much as we used to. That's a shame," said Jasmine.

"He was able to help us with a problem some years ago, and he's been helping us ever since. Like I said, he's a good man," said Martya. As she spoke, her eyes involuntarily flickered to the corner of the room and Valeyn's instincts urged her to follow the betrayal of that glance. Among the three young children, was one with dark red hair and a thin, aristocratic face. As the young boy looked up, he saw Ethan and his face brightened into the unfettered adoration of a delighted child. He cried out with joy and ran over to where Ethan swept him up into a blissful hug of giggles. Valeyn tried to disguise her shock but it was futile.

"Ethan's a father?" The words tumbled out before she could stop them, and both of the other women instantly stiffened.

"You're a guest, Lady Elyn," Martya answered in a slightly formal tone, "and I don't wish to be rude, but please, I ask you to respect my privacy and the privacy of my family."

"Of course, I'm so sorry," Valeyn rushed to apologize. "It's just that, it's a bit of a shock. I've known him for so long, and I had no idea."

"Well, like you said, it's possible that you really don't know him that well. You've been, how did you say it, *preoccupied?*"

The observation was a rebuke, but Valeyn was starting to understand the depth behind the judgment and that it might have been a fair one.

"That's quite enough, Martya," Ethan's voice broke the tension and Valeyn realized he was standing next to her. He gave the table a stern glance before crouching down to address the young boy, who was clinging to his leg with the unbound adoration of children. "Alright, young man, I need to have a conversation. Why don't you go and play, and I'll be along later?"

The boy nodded fiercely and ran back to his playmates with a sense of obvious pride.

"I'm sorry, Ethan. I didn't realize," Valeyn mumbled.

"It's not your fault," he sighed, as he pulled out a chair and settled in. "It's mine. It was silly of me to bring you with me tonight, I really didn't think it through. I didn't mean to burden you with this. You have enough problems."

Valeyn laughed a little uncomfortably. "It's not a burden, I just didn't know that you had a son. Why didn't you tell me?"

Ethan glanced at Martya and she looked back at his unspoken question.

"Go ahead, if you like. This impacts you far more than it does me," Martya said.

Ethan looked over at the young boy in the corner. "Jaymet is a fine boy, and I'd be proud to call him my son. Alas, that honor goes to Rayner, not me."

"Your brother?" asked Valeyn.

"Yes," Ethan sighed, taking up a piece of bread and dipping it into the sauce. "He was the one who introduced me to Archeuim Parade. It was always a favorite place of his. We used to eat here a lot back in the old days, and of course, he, uh, *befriended* Martya."

"Don't be shy about it, I'm not ashamed," smiled Martya. "You aristocrats are so pretentious with your civility and double standards. People are a lot more honest in my homeland, about many things. I was his concubine for a time."

"I see," said Valeyn, grateful again for the veil. "And then Jaymet was born. That's wonderful."

A look of disappointment darkened Martya's beautiful face and she sighed gently.

"When Jaymet was born, my brother decided he had other priorities," said Ethan.

"I see," Valeyn repeated in a quieter tone.

"Well, you know my mother. When she discovered that Rayner had fathered a son, she wasn't too happy with him, and she was even less impressed with his plan to pretend his son didn't exist. Such little secrets have a way of coming back to haunt families if they're not managed appropriately."

"So you agreed to take care of them?" Valeyn asked.

"Well, mother's political pragmatism aside, I thought it was the least we could do. I love Rayner, but I can't say I condone the way he chooses to treat people. So, for several years now, I've been checking in on them."

"More than that," laughed Jasmine. "You're part of our family now. Jaymet adores you, and to me, you're the aloof, older brother I never really wanted."

Ethan laughed and shook his head. "Yes, I have an arrangement with Symin, and I make sure they're being taken care of. But it's more than that. I've had the honor of becoming a part of this wonderful family."

"And I get to spend my days knowing that I chose the wrong brother," Martya said, looking at Ethan with a look of such unrestrained affection that Valeyn again felt as though she shouldn't be there.

She saw the way this family looked at Ethan and, in that moment, realized they knew him in a way she never had. Ethan had been her loyal lieutenant for most of her professional career, and she had ignored him. He had even offered her love, and she had rejected it. How could she be so blind to the virtues of someone so close to her?

But I'm a god. I've had far greater problems.

And yet, the self-consolation did nothing to reassure. Instead, a horrible truth assailed her. She'd been treating Ethan with the same disrespect Bythe had displayed toward her; always a distraction, never a priority. The same contempt wrapped in the same excuse. The realization was an affront and she recoiled at it.

"I'm sorry. You're good people, and I'm dishonoring you," said Valeyn.

Jasmine and Martya looked at her strangely.

"Please, Lady Elyn, don't say that," Jasmine said.

"No, that's not even my name," Valeyn answered and she lifted her hand to her veil.

"Wait!" snapped Ethan, but it was too late. Valeyn removed her face covering and placed it on the table before her. Confusion greeted her across the table and even Symin stared at her from across the bar.

"Lady *Elyn*," Ethan enunciated the alias. "Let's stop this now before you take it too far. You won't be able to undo this."

"I don't want to undo it, Ethan. I've been selfish. I've been selfish to you, even to the these ladies and to this family right now. I'm still thinking about myself, always about me, just like Bythe, and this needs to stop."

Jasmine looked worried. "Please, Lady Elyn, it's unwise to speak against Lord Bythe, even within Archeuim. He still sees all."

Valeyn smiled at her. "No, Jasmine. That's what I'm trying to say. Bythe isn't interested in our conversation tonight. My father is only interested in himself and the things that interest him. Just as I've been much the same. Even sitting here under your hospitality, I'm only seeing what I want to see, and for this, I offer you my deepest apologies."

"Your father?" Martya asked slowly, looking hard at her, then at Ethan.

"My name isn't Elyn. My name is Valeyn, daughter of Lord Bythe."

It was as if she'd drawn a weapon. The two women paled and stood up, unsure of whether to run or to fawn at her feet, but Valeyn was faster. She beat them to their feet and reached out to gently catch both women on the arm.

"Please, I tell you this as a friend, not as your god, or ruler, or whatever I might be. I want to be open with you, as you are with me.

"Well, that's that, then," Ethan muttered to himself, but nobody paid him any attention.

Symin, clearly troubled by his daughters' reactions, had begun to cross the floor, but slowed to a halt as he understood who Valeyn was.

"Are you here to punish us? If so, then take me and spare my family. They share no guilt in my business."

"There is no guilt in your business, Symin. At least not in my eyes. And I'm not here to judge. I haven't been sure about my purpose here. I'm still not sure. But I think I know where I can start. I think I can get to know my people. I get the impression it's been a long time since anyone in Obduratev has paid much attention to the people down here. No, I'm not here to judge, I'm here to serve."

Martya and Jasmine looked at Valeyn with disbelief, and a measure of respect crept into Symin's eyes.

"Ethan, the Unity Assembly has no interest in the domestic affairs of the citizenry, does it? That falls more in the realm of the Court?" Valeyn asked.

"The Assembly don't care if we live or die," answered Symin. "The Court holds the real power in this city, at least for people like us. They're the only ones I need to keep well paid."

"You're not speaking like a typical businessman, Symin. I think there's more to you than I realize," said Valeyn with a smile

"And you're not speaking like a typical god, my lady. I might have to think the same of you," replied Symin

"Ethan, I think I'd like to take a close look at the Court, starting tomorrow. Now that I have some free time on my hands, perhaps I can spend it doing some good in my father's city."

"That sounds like an excellent idea," answered Ethan.

"Then please be seated, and we'll start the meal." Symin gestured to his daughters and they moved toward the kitchen. To Valeyn's surprise, Ethan followed but Martya stopped him with a wave of his hand.

"You're a guest tonight, Ethan. Stay here with Lady Valeyn," Martya said.

"You want to cook?" Valeyn asked with raised eyebrows. "I didn't know you could."

"One more thing I've learned from Symin, not from my mother," Ethan replied. "In the Klyph tradition, they all share in making the meal, and we all share in eating it. But it looks like I'm off duty tonight."

"No," Valeyn said. "Let me also join in. Please."

Symin and his daughters shared looks of disbelief before the father answered.

"Lady Valeyn, I appreciate the offer, but this is too much. Let us at least prepare a meal for you."

Valeyn shook her head and stepped toward the kitchen. "Consider it a royal order. I have to warn you though, I'm terrible at cooking, but if you show me what to do, I might be able to handle a simple task," Valeyn said as she crossed the floor and headed behind the bar.

"Don't argue with her, Symin," Ethan said in her wake, "she's a god, which means she's almost as stubborn as you."

Symin barked a laugh and began issuing instructions to his daughters in their foreign tongue. Within seconds the room was a hive of bustling activity and laughter, and Valeyn found herself swept up in the joy of a simple domestic happiness she'd never experienced. As she set herself to work, buttering the large pans in preparation for grilling a collection of exotic meats, she decided that if she was not going to be heard by the men in power, then she would offer her help to those who truly needed her.

CHAPTER 9

"It was during the height of the Anarch – the period of terrible wars between Bythe and Maelene – that the full might of the Helmsguard was galvanized and brought to bear on a single enemy. The mining colony of Krag was refashioned into a military fortress, solely intended for the making of war, and the black-clad soldiers of the Iron Union were mustered there in the thousands. As the war against the Outland Alliance extended over decades, the lands of Hammerfall and Greenridge bore the brunt of the fighting, and felt the impact of the devastation. For this reason, Bythe ordered the construction of the Shield – an immense iron wall from Krag to the ocean – intended to prevent Maelene's armies from spreading destruction into the heart of Bythe's empire. While the Shield was largely effective, it had the unintended consequence of condemning Hammerfall to years of entrenched warfare as it held the front line of the Iron Union's defenses.

For reasons which are unknown, the Shield was never completed and the pass to the north remained unprotected. Some claim it was an intention design to herd an enemy to entrapment against the coast, while others fear it is symbolic of Bythe's waning interest in the protection of his own empire."

~Kaler of the Ageless

"Our country was named Hammerfall for a reason, as we have always been proud to endure the blows of Bythe's enemies. As such, it's only fair that we have the right of first selection of the occupied territories," declared a stout young woman with bright blue eyes and a fashionably clean-shaven head. She was Chek-Thurla, the Chancellor of the House of Amoras, and she had held the floor for almost ten minutes now, arguing passionately that the territory of Hammerfall should expand to annex the lucrative trading ports of the Federacy; territories which themselves had barely been claimed by the Iron Union. She had fierce competition from others at Court.

"And the House of Amoras has already been granted stewardship of Outpost and Wheatsheaf," pointed out a dark-skinned man who was representing the interests of Alovat and the Grand Duchy of Joana . "Are you suggesting that Hammerfall should simply keep expanding eastward indefinitely?"

"You are out of order, Chancellor Lightborne," barked the elderly Master of Ceremonies, who was completely ignored.

"Outpost and Wheatsheaf are but ramshackle towns, mere scraps thrown to us. We deserve more than this!" Chek-Thurla retorted.

"Don't other houses deserve a share in the spoils? We too have sacrificed our sons and deserve to be compensated," said Lightborne.

"And I suppose you think the Grand Duchy of Joana should occupy the Federacy, and extend your monopoly over the Union's seafaring capability?" replied Chek-Thurla.

"Krag has supplied most of the Union's real strength. We are the engine of Lord Bythe's war machine, and we are the ones who should be first in line for any rewards," shouted a thin man representing the Fortress of Krag.

The Master of Ceremonies repeated his feeble admonishment, but he was again ignored as more raised voices overpowered his. The Septine Hall descended into chaos for the third time this morning. Valeyn sighed and rubbed her temples with the thumb and forefinger of one hand. After four weeks attending Court, it wasn't getting any easier.

Ethan had begun making the necessary arrangements to have her attend the Royal Court of Lord Bythe as soon as they had returned to Domitus. The Unity Assembly had made it clear she wouldn't be returning to their chambers anytime soon, and her father had made it equally clear that he had little interest in intervening in the petty politics of his empire – as if the execution of his war against the east were a trivial thing. Valeyn knew she would eventually have to fight her way back into the Unity Assembly, but Ethan had been right; her brutal dismissal by Morbus had proven she was unprepared for the levels of manipulation these men employed, and she needed practice before facing him again.

While the Royal Court of Lord Bythe was not as important as the Unity Assembly, it was still no fledgeling arena. All of the royal houses were represented, and while military matters were never directly discussed, the political power generated by the war dominated every agenda. Ethan had agreed that – all things considered – it was an ideal opportunity for her to practice her influence. The Royal Court gave Valeyn the opportunity to influence decisions that could impact the lives of the citizens of the Ironhelm. She'd already overruled two temporary war levies on merchants and had warned the municipal councillors that any further attempts to increase taxation would require her personal approval. Such actions were no doubt earning her enmity among the councillors, but it was the welfare of her people that mattered to her more.

For this role, she'd wisely chosen to leave her armor in her apartments, opting instead for the same dress uniform worn by the other Iron Union officers, with high boots and a double-breasted tunic sealed by a silver clasp over her left collarbone. Driven by some insight – and to distinguish herself from the other officers – she specified the material be tailored in the deep emerald colors of her armor. The garment had been ready for final alterations within a day of her command.

The sharp rapping of the Master of Ceremony's staff upon the marble floor gave the small man a degree of authority, although Valeyn suspected the ensuing silence was driven more by the desire for a decision than by any respect for each other.

"Heir Designate Valeyn, Daughter of Lord Bythe the Immortal, has heard your petitions. As representative of our most esteemed lord, it falls to you to decide on his behalf," the Master of Ceremonies intoned.

A hundred eyes turned to her expectantly. Valeyn returned their gaze with a patient smile from her high seat at the end of the Septine Hall.

"Chancellors, I thank you for bringing this petition to my attention and for presenting your claims to me with such . . . tenacity," Valeyn said, ignoring Ethan's smile. "You each have a valid claim to the ports, and I'm sure each of you would use them to increase your service to my father's empire. However, as you all know, the capture of the Federacy is still a recent victory, and the front is not that far from those three cities. I feel it's premature to speak of ongoing stewardship while the war is still being fought."

Chek-Thurla's smile was smug. "Heir Designate, the fortifications of Bonehall and Darcliff have fallen with ease. Even Fairhaven has been razed to the ground, as you well know. The enemy has been pursued to the farthest corner of their lands. The settlements in Greenridge have already been ceded to us, and I merely ask for a continuation of an already established precedent."

The deliberate reference to Fairhaven's destruction irritated Valeyn, and she mentally reaffirmed her decision. "And as *you* well know, Chancellor, our forces have not yet conquered Roy. In fact, I regret to inform you that the rumors you've probably heard are true; we were pushed back from Roy when we were on the cusp of victory." A murmur of alarm rippled throughout the hall, and Valeyn waved a hand to calm the jittery crowd. "A temporary setback, I'm sure, but it underscores the point that the war isn't over. The front can turn against us, and it's not wise to count our victories until the enemy surrenders."

"My lady, please be reasonable," Chek-Thurla said with a clenched jaw.

"I *am* being reasonable, Chancellor. I'm ensuring we don't become distracted with distributing the spoils of war until after we're certain they're ours to distribute. I won't have our houses bickering while there's an enemy still to be fought."

"If that's the concern, then I propose a compromise," Chek-Thurla replied. "Divide the three ports between us. At least then we will each be satisfied that we've been treated fairly, and we can put this behind us."

Valeyn now identified her opponent's true objective in this negotiation and recognized the offer of compliance for the lie it was; if Valeyn gave in to this promise of obedience, then the threat of future disobedience would forever be wielded against her. Only a fool believed otherwise.

"No. I've made my decision," Valeyn said flatly.

"My lady," said Lightborne "I do not disagree with the Chancellor's proposal. It seems a fair compromise."

Valeyn glared at the man. "Would you question my father after he had made such a decision, Chancellor?" she said quietly. The hall fell silent.

He lowered his eyes respectfully. "Of course not, my lady. Forgive me. Your wisdom is not questioned." He bowed low and retreated into the crowd of the court as if trying to make himself invisible.

Chek-Thurla shook her head in disgust and turned her back on Valeyn. "We could only wish we had the girl's father here," she muttered in a voice which was low, but clearly intended to be overheard.

Valeyn was ready. "I beg your pardon?" asked Valeyn.

"Apologies, my lady," Chek-Thurla replied, turning back to Valeyn with the smug expression back on her face. "I was simply reflecting on the wisdom of Lord Bythe, and we all hope we may see him in Court again soon."

"Are you dissatisfied with my service in his stead?"

"Of course not, my lady. I'm happy to serve a delegate," Chek-Thurla replied with exactly the right hint of sarcasm. But Valeyn didn't need to justify her actions this time; she just needed someone to make an example of.

"Well, I'm not sure I'm happy for you to continue to serve me, Chek-Thurla. I don't think I like your tone," Valeyn looked for the two men now standing in the crowd. "Chancellors, I've reconsidered and I think you were right. Dynn and Freeport will be granted to Joana and Krag, respectively. Vigilsea, however, will not be bequeathed to Hammerfall and will instead remain under Ironhelm authority. I trust this is satisfactory."

The faces of the two men shone with pride, and they both bowed low. Chek-Thurla, by contrast, looked fit to explode.

"Valeyn, this is an insult to all who serve in Hammerfall!"

"Then consider this an insult in exchange for an insult. I won't tolerate any displays of disrespect in my father's Court, regardless of your house or your station. Loyalty will be rewarded; disrespect will be punished."

Chek-Thurla wheeled about the hall, looking for political allies, but none met her eyes. Her fellow Chancellors from Krag and Joana were looking quietly pleased with their sudden change in fortune and refused to answer her silent plea for help. Valeyn's dispensation of prizes to Chek-

Thurla's powerful rivals had stripped away their support, and the smaller houses would never dare back her without them. She had been deserted and now had little choice but to return to Greund and explain her grievous miscalculation to Xhadik, Lord of Hammerfall.

"Chancellor," Valeyn declared, "you are barred from my father's Court for three months. If you say one more word in protest, I will have you stripped of your position and order your house to provide a replacement, along with financial sanctions and a formal apology. You may now leave."

Chek-Thurla sagged, bowed low, and quietly left the chamber. A murmur ran through the crowd, and Ethan gave Valeyn an approving nod. He'd invested many hours training her in courtly debate over the past weeks, and Valeyn had learned that it was not that dissimilar to combat. Bouts were not always won by the strongest combatant, they were usually won by the person who had enough discipline and patience to wait for their enemy's mistake, along with the will to punish them ruthlessly for making it. This was serving as excellent practice for her return to the Unity Assembly.

"Are there any further petitions, for the Heir Designate?" the Master of Ceremonies called over the crowd. The remaining dignitaries at the front of court fell silent, none of them seemed willing to test Valeyn's patience any further this day.

"My lady, please!" came a voice from the back of the room. Valeyn gestured and a page stepped forward to part the crowd and usher a middle-aged nobleman to the floor before her. He had a weathered face under thinning gray hair, and Valeyn recognized his black and silver crest from the house of Cadian in the southern provinces of Mac-Soldai. He attempted a bow, but almost toppled over, and Valeyn realized he was on the edge of exhaustion.

"Guards, bring this man a chair and some water," Valeyn commanded, and within seconds the nobleman was sitting and drinking deeply from the cup given to him.

"Forgive me, my lady," he gasped. "But I've ridden here for seven nights and hoped I could make it in time for Court. I needed to speak to you."

"Calm yourself, you're here now. What's driven you here under such duress?"

"My lady, my name is Tage, I'm the Lord of Cadian, in Mac-Soldai. I've come to report an attack on our own people, on Iron Union soil."

Valeyn glanced at Ethan but he shook his head in reply. Whatever this man was about to report, Ethan had received no word of it from his family. "Then speak, Lord Tage. Baron Ethan, Lord Watch to the Heir, rules your lands and will be very interested in your tidings."

"Forgive me, Baron Ethan, but I've tried to petition your family as is the proper way, but I wasn't given an audience until another three days hence and I needed to call for help quickly, so I thought it best to petition Lady Valeyn directly."

Ethan waved away the apology. "Who has attacked you and when did this take place? Give us details, Lord Tage."

"I can't give you details on the attackers as I wasn't there to witness them. But I'd been leading a patrol along the Barrens of Silence, a completely uneventful patrol, there hasn't been any sign of bandits or nomads for coming up on three years now. We'd traversed a southward arc through the Pass of Erodus for about two days, and we didn't see so much as a footprint from any enemy. So, we completed our sweep and returned home to Karmel-Fannon, only to find it . . . gone."

"It was completely sacked?" asked Valeyn.

"Not sacked, my lady. You don't understand. It hadn't been burned or torn down. It was just *gone.*"

"What you do mean, *gone*? You're not making sense! Are you drunk?" snapped Ethan.

"No, my Baron," pleaded Tage. "Please believe me when I tell you I've not had a drop besides the water you've just given me. I've ridden seven days straight with barely time to sleep, so I might seem in a stupor, but I swear it's not through drink, sir!"

Valeyn nodded with a patient smile. "I believe you, but help me to understand, how can your manor and lands be gone?"

"I don't understand it either, but it's as if they've been scooped from the land. There's nothing but a bottomless, black hole marking the space where my home and lands once stood. Everyone is gone; my wife, my daughters . . . everyone."

Valeyn was reminded of the bizarre and twisted landscapes she witnessed within the Render, but Mac-Soldai was hundreds of miles from those places. Such a thing couldn't be possible. Then she recalled the young girl who asked Valeyn about her missing grandmother; the innocent and truthful girl who'd said her grandmother's farm was *gone*. Valeyn felt a sickness creep into her stomach.

"This pit you saw, describe it to me," she commanded.

"It's hard to put it into words, my lady. It's like . . . an emptiness. The air around the pit is ice to breathe, and a few of my household guard who strayed too close to its edge succumbed to suffocation and had to be pulled back. It's like there's nothing there anymore, not even air. The space is just . . . a void."

The Court broke into shouts, some in alarm, others accusing the nobleman of spreading lies and panic. The Master of Ceremonies tried again to silence the chamber, but Valeyn could sense genuine fear from the man. Whether or not his home had actually vanished was a separate question, for now. He certainly believed it had. Again, she glanced at Ethan, only to see her own doubt reflected in his expression.

"Your lands border the Barrens of Silence," said Ethan. "There are a lot of strange things far in the south. It's possible this is some illusion or deception from an enemy looking to take advantage of us."

"My lord, please. In all the years we've guarded your border, we've seen many strange things in the south, and peculiar magics are nothing new to my people. But this is not an illusion or a sleight of hand by some wild shaman. This is true power — a terrifying power we've never seen before."

"Then why didn't you take this matter directly to your lord? An evil of this scale should be immediately referred to the Earl of Mac-Soldai," asked Ethan.

"I beg pardon, my lord, but like I said earlier, I tried. I immediately left my men behind and rode my horse almost to her death to get to Arbek within three days. But I was overwrought with passion and when I told my story . . . and the guards suspected me of drinking, much the same as you did. They told me to come back for an audience in ten days, and when I protested, they threatened to imprison me. I had no choice but to ride here. I remembered Court would be held today and thought to bring you the news directly. It cost me seven more days and another three horses, but I'm here now. And I swear upon the helm of Lord Bythe that my story is true."

Valeyn's brow creased. "Lord Tage, I know there are similar rumors in the streets of Obduratev. I also know that I need not remind you of the grave penalties for bearing false witness before the Royal Court of Lord Bythe, so I can only assume you are speaking truthfully — or at least, speaking the truth as you see it."

"Of course, my lady," Tage responded without hesitation, causing Valeyn's disquiet to increase.

"Very well. Baron Ethan, I want you to look into this matter personally and with haste. Dispatch a relay of messengers to your household to order a full and immediate investigation into Lord Tage's account. I expect a report within six days."

"As you command, Heir Designate," Ethan replied.

"Thank you, my lady!" Tage gasped and now that his mission had been completed, his eyes glazed over as if he were ready to collapse.

"Guards, take him to the infirmary at once. See that he's given every care," Valeyn ordered.

Two Helmsguard carefully lifted him from the chair and, placing his arms over their shoulders, gently walked him from the hall. Ethan summoned an adjutant to execute the orders as Valeyn watched the nobleman led from the chamber. Whatever had happened in Mac-Soldai, it had been dire enough for this man to drive himself to the point of death to report it. She was so lost in thought that she didn't even notice the approach of Morbus until his voice broke her concentration.

"Really, Heir Designate, you give too much credence to the ramblings of a drunkard."

Valeyn almost started with surprise when she recognized the rotund man standing in the center of the room. Ethan quickly finished issuing his orders and crossed to her side.

"Minister of Intelligence," Valeyn announced, recovering quickly. "We weren't expecting you to grace Court today."

"My apologies for my lapse in courtesy, Heir Designate, but the duties of the Unity Assembly are quite taxing, and we have little time for these social events."

Valeyn tried to ignore the condescension, as rising to his carefully laid bait would only undo the dominance she had just achieved before her subjects.

"Are you here to petition the Heir Designate for her favor?" Ethan said acerbically.

"In a manner of speaking, yes," Morbus replied with a knowing smile. "But I request a word with the Heir Designate in private, if you please?"

Valeyn looked at him for a moment before nodding. His smile widened and he gestured to the door at the far end of the Septine Hall.

"We need not ask the entire Court to leave on our account. Why don't we have our conference in your father's throne room? I'm sure he won't mind if we borrow it, don't you agree?"

The room broke into a buzz of conversation and the Master of Ceremonies rapped on the floor once more. "The Court shall be in adjournment until the Heir Designate returns," he attempted to announce over the noise.

Valeyn rose and led Morbus to the end of the hall. Ethan hurried to follow and Morbus glanced at him as they walked.

"Really, Baron, I think you insult the daughter of Lord Bythe. I'm sure she has little need of protection from a man like me."

"She has every need of protection from a man like you," Ethan replied coldly.

"Baron Ethan is my advisor as well as my guard. He may join us," said Valeyn.

Morbus shrugged. "As you wish, my lady. I'm not sure why you're so nervous. I only want to talk."

Valeyn didn't reply. She signalled the two Helmsguard before her, and they pulled the black doors open, saluting her as she passed through them and closing them behind the party. While she'd seen her father's throne room many times in her life, it seemed that every time she beheld it, she was seeing it for the first time. The room was vast, as if it had been designed to accommodate a legion of soldiers standing alongside one another. Shadows covered the depths of the great hall, making it almost impossible to judge the size of the room. Black pillars adorned with immense iron masks flanked the walls and stretched high into the dark recesses of the unseen ceiling above. Every inch of the room had been designed with one intent – to make the visitor feel small. It was very typical of her father.

"Well, we're here, Morbus. What do you want?" Valeyn snapped, dropping any pretense of civility as the doors clanged shut behind them.

"I admire direct language, Valeyn," he answered. "I hope you don't mind me addressing you by name? I assume we're speaking informally now?"

"Address me however you please but get on with it."

"As you wish." He stepped over into the center of the throne room and looked up at the immense throne. "Impressive, isn't it? You remember how he looks when he's sitting there? Incredible."

He looked at Valeyn for a reaction, but she refused to indulge him. After a moment of awkward silence, he returned his eyes to the throne and continued his speech. "It's said he forged this himself, using his own mastery over the metals of Kovalith to craft a mighty seat that would match his glory. Can you imagine that? What sort of person places so much thought and effort into making his chair?" Morbus slowly mounted the steps before the throne. "It's all a bit much, isn't it? Like everything about your father, it doesn't serve any practical purpose; it's just designed to intimidate. It's not even very comfortable."

With a surprising act of audacity and agility, he leaped and pulled himself onto the throne, wiggling back and settling into a comfortable position before looking down at Valeyn. "Do you think you'll sit here one day?"

"You're out of your mind, Morbus," Ethan said. "If I call the guards now, you'll be arrested for blasphemy!"

"Really?" Morbus asked, then clapped his hands twice. Before anyone could react, a service door opened at the far side of the chamber and a Helmsguard stepped through. He paused and looked between Valeyn and Morbus with obvious confusion before snapping to attention. "I'm thirsty, guardsman. Bring me grapewine," Morbus ordered from his seat on the high throne.

The guard saluted with his fist across his chest then wheeled about and retreated through the service door.

"What were you saying, Ethan?" Morbus sneered. "They'll arrest me? Have me hauled up before Bythe? Or will they simply do whatever the hells I order them to do?"

The guard returned with a goblet in his hand. He stood before the throne and bowed his head, offering the cup to Morbus, who took it, sipped, and winced theatrically.

"Really, guardsman, has this bottle been opened for a month? Never mind, this will have to do. Dismissed." He waved the guard away and smiled down at Valeyn as he took another sip. "You can't really blame them. As if they'd know the difference between grapewine and grainoil. Now, Valeyn. Do you know how long it's been since our great Lord Bythe sat where I am now? I honestly couldn't tell you. You had an audience with him recently, so you tell me. What do you think of him? Do you really think he cares who's using his furniture?"

"I think you're showing a dangerous level of disrespect toward my father. Do you think he can't turn his attention here if he chooses? You have no idea of his power, so I suggest you get off his throne now," Valeyn warned.

"As always, you recall your father through the eyes of the child you once were. Your father hasn't been omnipotent for years, if he ever was. In fact, the last time he showed a fleeting interest in this world was when he thought he'd sired an heir, and once that was a disappointment, he retreated into his citadel again."

"He cared enough to acknowledge me in public, or have you forgotten that?"

"Oh, yes, I admit that display was a little surprising. I'd wagered Snyed a fair bit of Darkiron that he wouldn't even show up, let alone recognize you. That was irritating. And then he appointed you to the Unity Assembly. Really, Valeyn, did you think you could just walk in there like you belonged? Surely you're still not that naïve?"

She eyed him carefully with a growing suspicion. "No, I wasn't expecting a warm welcome."

"And you weren't expecting me at all, were you? I could tell by the look on your face. That was rather priceless. I apologize for the dramatic entrance, but I really couldn't help myself, and of course, you understand why I had to sideline you the way I did? I can't have you interfering with my plans. It's nothing personal. Well . . . maybe just a little personal."

Valeyn stepped forward and met his eyes. "How long have you been one of the Prodigals?"

Morbus's laughter echoed through the empty room, but Valeyn waited patiently for him to answer. "Such a dramatic name, isn't it?" he said at length. "I wonder who came up with it? It certainly wasn't anyone I know, but it works very well."

"Were you a traitor even when you served Yvorre?" she demanded.

"I feel I must address two points there. First of all, I am no traitor. It is not treason to fill the vacuum left by gods who have gone mad. In fact, only a traitor would stand by and let his countrymen suffer. Secondly, I was not an active member of the Prodigals when last we met. No, it took a betrayal far greater than Yvorre's to open my eyes to the hypocrisy of those we serve. But you'd know all about that, wouldn't you, Ethan? We have a lot in common."

"I don't have anything in common with you," Ethan answered.

Morbus shook his head like a disapproving teacher. "Incorrect, my young Baron. Like me, you were assumed a traitor in the view of our beloved Lord Bythe. You were dragged up here in chains, brought to the very spot where you now stand and made to beg for your life. You were ordered to prove your innocence even though you were probably guilty of nothing worse than having poor choice in women. But unlike you, I wouldn't meekly crawl back to my masters to lick their boots once they'd decided I was again worthy of their attention."

Valeyn could sense the genuine anger emanating from him and appreciated how much the experience had scarred him. "So it's revenge you want?"

He smiled down at her. "Trying to belittle me, as always, Valeyn? Are you trying to make me feel small and petty just because I've finally seen things that you can't? I don't deny that revenge plays a part in my desire, but no, it isn't why I'm doing this. Can't you see? Your father is mad. He's lost all interest in this world."

"He's still in command of his empire," Valeyn replied.

"For the time being. But your father will fall. Especially now he's confessed to copulation with our hated enemy! You're all the evidence we need to prove his hypocrisy. Now it's only a matter of time before we bring him down, and when that happens, all of the proud houses will fight each other over the remains. The Iron Union will rip itself to pieces."

"Unless a leader has already taken power before that can happen?" she asked.

"Succession planning isn't treason. In fact, this sort of thinking will save your father's empire from his own short-sightedness."

"And let me guess who you have in mind to succeed him." Valeyn asked, gesturing to Morbus as he sat comfortably on the throne.

His eyes narrowed as if he were sizing her up, and his playful demeanour dropped. "Well, that's an interesting question, made even more interesting by your return. You see, as much as I desire to sit here, I'm willing to admit it doesn't *have* to be me."

"What are you proposing?" Ethan asked warily.

"Simple pragmatism, Ethan. Surely you can appreciate this. Valeyn, we don't need to be enemies. In fact, we can help each other. By now you know that I control the Unity Assembly, which means I control the armies of Bythe. This makes me one of the most powerful men in the Iron Union, maybe even *the* most powerful. And while that puts me in a very strong position to assume power, I don't deny that it presents another set of problems. For instance, I'm not sure how well the people of the Union will accept me, and while controlling the Helmsguard will grant me a large amount of power over our citizens, it would be a lot better if they approved of their new leader."

"So, in other words, your problem is that nobody likes you," said Valeyn.

"How cute," Morbus grunted. "I suppose I don't have your feminine charms, girl, but be under no illusions — I'm perfectly ready to supplant your father when the time comes. Your unexpected return, however, has presented us with an opportunity we had not anticipated."

"You want Valeyn to support you in overthrowing Bythe," Ethan said.

"We ask that Valeyn exercise good sense and understand how events are going to play out in the very near future. Your father is going to fall, one way or the other. If you support us, we'll ensure you are very well rewarded." Morbus patted the armrest of the throne to underscore his point.

"You're saying you'll let me rule if I support you?"

He chuckled. "Well, you'll rule in a manner of speaking. You'll certainly be the official leader of the Iron Union. You'll hold Court, as you've become quite accustomed to doing, you'll keep the masses happy, along with most of the nobility. You will live a life of comfort, prestige, and importance. It's a very generous proposal."

"But the real leadership of the Iron Union will sit with you and your conspirators," said Ethan. "Valeyn will just be the public face for you to hide behind."

"You expect me to serve the Prodigals as a figurehead?" asked Valeyn.

"You make it sound so terrible. It's a very fair offer, and one where we both benefit. I'm honestly not sure what there is for you to consider."

Valeyn laughed. "I will never serve you, Morbus. This is my father's empire and I'm his rightful heir. Why should I hand this power over to you?"

Morbus shook his head sadly. "You still don't understand, do you? You hold no power. The promise of transition is a delusion. The time of gods is over, Valeyn. The Desecration is upon us. You have to accept this. The people of Kovalith will no longer blindly follow the whims of their gods once your father is gone. We're going to rule ourselves for better or worse. Let me speak plainly. You will never replace your father. We will not tolerate a life of servitude under another god, whether it be Bythe or you or any of the others. I'd sooner destroy the Ironhelm than let that happen."

Valeyn's mind ran through the possibilities. She could sense no brazen deception from Morbus, and despite her revulsion for the man, the offer was somewhat rational. An alliance with the Prodigals would solve many problems and avoid open conflict. But to betray Bythe? She was quiet for a moment, then decided.

"I stand with my father. I stand loyal to my duty as a member of the Helmsguard, as should you, Minister."

Morbus slapped his palm against the arm of the throne in frustration "Stupid girl! Why would you oppose us? Think about this. When your father dies – *when*, not *if* – and *when* I'm sitting here, you'll need to run a lot farther than the Fareaches to make sure you're safe this time."

"Be careful with your threats, Morbus. I have every right to kill you simply for sitting on my father's throne. Don't push me."

Morbus leaned forward and his eyes were ablaze with grim excitement. "Then do it, Vale. I don't want to die, but I'd gladly sacrifice myself to you. This city is already on edge, and such a murder by the daughter of Bythe would be the spark this city needs to tear everything apart. The guards would be here in moments and it would all start to end. So, do it, you cowardly little bitch!"

Rage swept through her, but Ethan placed a hand on her arm before she could act on the impulse.

"Not now. He's ready for this. If you kill him, it'll go badly for us," Ethan warned.

She clenched her fists and pushed her fury back down. Ethan was right. There was little doubt that Morbus would have prepared for this confrontation, and if she killed him, steps would be taken to ensure it was public knowledge before his body was cold. He would become a martyr.

"Yes, listen to your lover, girl. He seems to have a lot more sense than you," Morbus taunted, seemingly a little relieved that he was going to survive after all.

"Shut your mouth! It might still be worth it," Ethan growled before turning to Valeyn. "Relax. Don't be baited by him. You still have leverage. He wouldn't be asking for your help if he didn't need it."

Valeyn nodded and looked back at Morbus. "Ethan's right. For all your talk about the Desecration, you have no power to overthrow my father. You need me for that. How would you do it without me?"

"That is an excellent question," replied Morbus with a slow smile. "Perhaps I'll let my associate answer that one."

"Elyn," said a cold and familiar voice.

Valeyn turned slowly. Ferehain stood behind her. The hood of his flowing, black robes was lowered, revealing his porcelain skin and dark hair framing a thin face. He was flanked by two other figures. The first, Valeyn instantly recognized as Exedor, although the shock at seeing him alive was almost lost among the overall confusion of the moment. The third figure was another slender Ageless dressed in the emerald-green robes of the Entarion. Possibly Aleasea? But with the dark hood raised, it was impossible to be certain. Ethan turned to raise the alarm, but Valeyn touched his shoulder.

"No. Not yet. Stay behind me," she said and walked slowly toward the intruders. "What are you doing here, Ferehain?"

Ferehain's dark eyes found hers and Valeyn could see a change in them. He had never been affectionate toward her, but now she could sense something else. A ruthless determination radiated from him, and she was instinctively on guard.

"I have been in contact with the Minister for some time now. The Royal Inquisitor has been very helpful accommodating this."

Exedor smiled and offered a short bow. "It is pleasing to see you again, my dear. My employment arrangements have changed in recent months, and although my new supervisor can be harsh, I have to admit, the benefits are exceptional."

"I thought you were dead," said Valeyn.

Exedor smiled. "The benefits are *very* exceptional."

Valeyn looked past Ferehain to the figure in green. "Aleasea?" she asked, but the figure didn't move. She returned her gaze to Ferehain. "I thought you returned to Fairhaven to help the Alliance. What are you doing here?"

"Fairhaven is destroyed, and the Alliance is defeated. You know this," answered Ferehain.

She looked at the three of them and could sense raw power. *Kai* infused with other elements she couldn't place, but the overall effect was intensely potent to her senses.

As if reading her thoughts, Ferehain spoke. "Ask the question."

"What have you done with The Tower?" she asked.

Ferehain look at her dispassionately. "I have claimed The Tower. It is now mine and I will use the tools of the gods to end this war. I will succeed where Maelene failed."

"The Imbatals?"

"They are also mine now."

"The Tower, and all that is in it, was bequeathed to me, Ferehain," Valeyn said carefully.

"And you chose to cast those gifts aside. I have simply claimed the power you discarded and made it my own."

Valeyn thought for a moment, drawing on every diplomatic tactic Ethan had taught her. She somehow knew they were all in terrible danger, but didn't know why. "I didn't say I'd renounced my claim on The Tower, Ferehain, just that I needed to help our people."

"Let us not play games. Your actions spoke for you. You left The Tower and did not return. Do not blame me for acting when you walked away."

"I'm helping end this war."

"No, you have betrayed your people to join the enemy, as I have always known you would."

"I haven't betrayed anyone."

"Do not lie to me, Elyn. You have been recognized as the Heir Designate to the Iron Union. You stand here in the very throne room of your father and refuse our offer to act against him. You are his blood. You are him. You are my enemy and you always have been, from the first day I saw you."

Valeyn could sense the situation deteriorating. She looked again to the figure in green "What do you think of this, Aleasea? Surely, you don't believe that I've betrayed you."

Still, the figure in green said nothing. The black recesses of the robe seemed to mock Valeyn's questions.

"What's wrong with her?" Valeyn asked.

"Aleasea was a beautiful idealist, but such views cannot hold in the cruel world. I have been forced to utilise her strengths in a manner I find unpleasant, but in the end, I was given little choice."

"Ferehain, what have you done?" Valeyn could feel the sense of dread increasing, as if she were being led closer to a trap about to be sprung.

"I have come to discuss the question posed by you only few moments ago. How indeed, will Bythe be destroyed? You clearly lack the will, if not the power, and Morbus on his coveted throne has no ability to realize his desires. I will destroy Bythe the Deceiver and the Iron Union and every last remnant of his memory on Kovalith. I have already begun."

"The attack at Roy?" asked Valeyn.

Ferehain shook his head. "Oh, Elyn. I am disappointed but unsurprised. You never were a bright student. The assault on Roy was simply the latest in a series of steps I have taken to undo your father's empire. I had thought you would be aware of the others by now, but perhaps you are not as powerful as I assumed."

Valeyn knew in that moment that any rational parts of his mind had been subsumed by whatever power he'd attained in the Render and that the time for diplomacy had passed. "Don't assume anything about me or my power, Ferehain. Give me the time—"

"Time is your enemy. Time will undo the largest of mountains just as it will the greatest of gods. Time is the enemy of all your kind. It sends the gods mad. Did you know that Aleasea once had power over time, but it was taken from her lest she also descend into madness herself?" He swung his hand like a pendulum, a strange expression on his face.

"What are you talking about?" Valeyn demanded.

"Tick . . . tock," he said in a monotone.

"You're not making sense."

"Tick."

Tock

The clack of machinery could now be heard in time with his voice.

Tick . . . tock.

Valeyn tensed and Ethan looked at her in dismay. From the dark recesses behind the throne, three large figures walked into the light with an unnatural gait.

"Ferehain? What is this?" she asked in a warning tone.

"I have seen the futures through Shin's Oraculate. I know the Desecration cannot be prevented, but it has also shown me how Bythe and his daughter can be defeated. I will not blindly follow the Oraculate as you did. I will test it for deception before committing my plans."

"Valeyn, be ready," Ethan said, as the closest Imbatal turned its impassive white hood to look at him.

"Now it's my turn to be disappointed in you," said Valeyn, with a little confidence returning. "Are you threatening me with these? Don't you remember how easily I dealt with the original?"

"We're unarmed," warned Ethan

"I no longer need a sword to deal with these creatures," she said and extended her open palm toward the closest of the clockwork demons. She focused on the hundreds of gears and metallic pulleys that gave life to the abomination and willed them to stop moving. The creature refused. She refocused her mind and pressed harder, reaching out with all her father's *kai*. The Imbatal paused and a shrill grating sound came from the creature as it shuddered and resisted her.

"What have you done to them?" Valeyn asked as she struggled for control over the monster.

"I have altered them based on my recent observations," Ferehain said. "I must give you credit, Exedor. Mercurion's attempt has proven most instructive. I concede that I should have listened to you earlier."

Valeyn began to understand the depths of the peril they faced. The new power of Ferehain combined with the knowledge possessed by Exedor meant that Valeyn was exposed on almost every front. The remaining two Imbatals began to advance on Ethan, and she knew she was out of time.

"Sound the alarm!" she ordered and sprinted toward the first creature. While their resistance to her *kai* might have increased, she was relieved to find their reactions were still slower than hers. Valeyn was upon the first Imbatal before it could reach Ethan. She grabbed the forearm of the creature and pivoted to pull it off balance, but before she could send it crashing to the floor, it countered by pulling its arm back and breaking her grip with a swift blow from its free hand.

It seemed their reactions were *barely* slower than hers.

Three against one. Near-impossible odds, no matter how experienced the fighter.

Valeyn dimly recalled the first time Vale met Elyn, defending her from three murderous thugs. Ethan was calling for guards, but Valeyn knew they would be too slow. Her only hope was to draw the attention of all three Imbatals and ensure they were focused on her. Moving quickly, she kicked out at the nearest creature and felt its metal breastplate buckle beneath its white robes as it fell back and skidded across the marble floor, crashing against the throne where its body seemed to snap.

Strong arms seized her from behind, restraining her own arms in a vice-like grip as the third Imbatal positioned itself before her. There was a sound like unsheathing metal and a long blade extended from its forearm. The creature pulled back its fist, preparing to impale Valeyn through her head. Unable to free herself, she forced every fiber of her will into one supreme mental effort as the blade sailed toward her. Her power was enough to slow the blade as she twisted her head aside. The weapon scraped her cheek and smashed into the hooded face of the Imbatal behind her.

Valeyn wasted no time. She struck the extended arm and smashed the elbow joint, which allowed her to rip the weaponised forearm from the creature that had just tried to kill her. Pulling the blade from the face of the dead Imbatal, she turned back to face her attacker. It was already moving at her and Valeyn barely had time to avoid the second blade as it extended from the remaining arm. She sidestepped the creature and swung her makeshift weapon at the head of her attacker, feeling a satisfying thump as the weapon dug deep. It stood for a moment, ticking and whirring spasmodically. Adrenaline surged through Valeyn as she lashed out with her bare fists, beating the Imbatal to the ground until it was nothing more than smashed chunks of metal and bloodless flesh under a stained white robe.

Valeyn drew deep breaths as she scanned the room for any more threats. There were none.

"Perhaps a little more work is needed?" said Exedor with a shrug. "Their heads certainly seem to be a weak point."

Ferehain said nothing. He was staring at Valeyn, seemingly absorbing every detail. She felt violated by his gaze.

"I warned you, Ferehain," she snarled as she advanced on him. To her surprise, he didn't move or prepare to defend himself as she approached. He simply continued to analyse her movements with the same unwavering stare. She pulled back her fist, swung at that cold, dispassionate face, and he blocked her strike with his palm. Strain appeared on his face but he continued to withstand her force, and – much to Valeyn's surprise – she found she was unable to overpower him. They remained in a stalemated tableau for a moment. Ferehain's eyes found hers, and a burning hatred assailed her.

"How I would dearly love to test myself against you right now. Ever since that first day you despoiled my home I have longed for this moment."

In that instant, Ferehain looked ready to strike, but before he could, a distant rumble echoed throughout the chamber. Strength flared in Valeyn's heart as she felt her father's potency stirring deep within the Ironhelm. Bythe had sensed Ferehain.

With a grunt of exertion, Ferehain forced Valeyn away from him and also stepped back, looking about the room as if expecting Bythe to appear. It occurred to Valeyn that she had never seen Ferehain nervous before, even for a moment.

His face settled into the familiar mask and he spoke almost to himself. "I must be patient, and I must be disciplined. Now is not the time for rash improvisation, as much as it might satisfy me." He looked at Aleasea and Exedor. "I believe we have learned what we came to learn. Aleasea, it is time to show these people the magnitude of the peril before them."

Aleasea's robes billowed in the familiar Ageless way and she seemed to glide forward.

"Aleasea, please!" Valeyn shouted. "Listen to me. What's happened to you?"

The green-robed Ageless didn't answer. She moved forward and crouched before the throne, lowering her hand to the floor. Guards were filing into the room and crossbows were drawn. The rumbling was increasing in volume. Ethan was giving orders to block the doors and prepare to contain the intruders, but Valeyn knew such efforts were futile.

"No, Aleasea," Ferehain said over the noise. "Not while Bythe still lives. We will move eastward. That facility is far more vulnerable."

The throne room was now buzzing with shouts and orders, but Ferehain acted as if he were alone with Aleasea and Exedor. He reached within his robe and before anyone could react, the three intruders blazed with light and were gone.

•　　•　　•

"I want the Watch Officer arrested at once!" Morbus continued in his tirade in the chamber of the Unity Assembly. "I want him hanged! This is completely unacceptable. How can the Ageless strike in the heart of the Ironhelm without detection? Do we have traitors in our ranks?"

Valeyn watched Morbus and couldn't help but admire the performance. The rage, the shock, and the indignation, all designed to deflect attention from the one man who deserved it. Mere minutes had passed since the attack, and Valeyn was still trying to understand what had happened. She was off-balance and Morbus knew it.

"The intruders vanished using some sort of magic unknown to us. It's almost certain they used the same method to gain entrance. Leave the poor Watch Officer alone," said Habistich.

"Is that supposed to comfort me? I thought we were reliably informed that the Ageless were no longer a threat after they were betrayed by one of their own. Now we find them here days after you return. Is this a coincidence, Valeyn?"

It was a clever tactic, instead of attempting to defend himself from Valeyn's impending allegation of treason, he attacked first, positioning her as a potential traitor so her own counteraccusations would look desperate.

A lie is most convincing when it is barely a lie.

Morbus had learned Yvorre's lesson well.

"This isn't the Ageless," said Valeyn. "The Ageless are all but destroyed, and even at their full might, they never had this level of power. This man has renounced the Ageless and now stands alone."

"Wonderful," Snyed muttered sarcastically. "So, this *ex*-Ageless terrorist has now developed the power to simply appear wherever and whenever he pleases, with an army of Yvorre's nightmare creatures at his command? How long before we're all murdered while we sleep?"

"I don't think it's that simple. If Ferehain could kill us like that, he would have tried it already. No, I think there are limits to what he can do, especially when my father protects us. In fact, I'm certain," said Valeyn

"Your opinion isn't reassuring," muttered Snyed. "Do you have anything else to tell us, or is this yet another consequence of you refusing to share all you know?"

Morbus stared at her and it was a challenge. *Tell them! Roll the dice and see what I have planned for you.*

Valeyn glanced at Ethan and read his face.

No.

There was no telling how many allies Morbus had, but she was certain that every one of them was ready for her accusation. If she denounced him now – without evidence – it was impossible to guess the consequences. Disbelief at best, civil war at worst. Besides, Morbus could wait. Ferehain was the threat. Once he was dealt with, Morbus would have no one to protect him.

"Given that I was the target of his attack, no, I wasn't expecting it. And I can't believe this has to be explained to you, Snyed," snapped Valeyn.

"Alright, everyone, calm down," said Sarele. "Valeyn, you need to tell us all you can about Ferehain and about this Tower. We can't have any more lies of omission this time. The risks are far too great."

Valeyn sighed. "I've told you everything. I swear it. The Imbatals were created by the gods Romona and Nishindra. They were designed as a weapon to be used by my mother against my father. They were given to me, but I rejected them. I left them behind."

"Why didn't you destroy them?" demanded Sarele.

"Because at that same time, I was poised to capture Fairhaven," answered Ethan. "And once she'd intervened, she agreed to return to the Ironhelm, not back to The Tower."

"I didn't know that Ferehain would remain in The Tower, and I certainly didn't think he could take control of it. If I knew this I never would have come here." Valeyn thought of Aleasea's unmoving form and a sickness crept into her stomach.

"And your Royal Inquisitor, Morbus?" Sarele asked slowly. "How did he come to be in the employment of our enemy?"

Morbus sighed and drank the remains of his grainmalt in a single mouthful. "I'd had some contact with him in the Render, but then I heard nothing after he had reached The Tower. I assumed he was dead."

Sarele glared at him for a moment but said nothing more. Valeyn had noticed Morbus was holding back the full truth; that Exedor had been a Prodigal, like himself. The fact that he refused to admit this proved to her that many of those present weren't aware of the extent of his plot.

"Alright, let's sort this out," said Dox. "What does this mean for our campaign in the east? Should we pull our forces back?"

"It doesn't mean anything. All this talk about the Desecration and the end of everything. We've never seen any god display that much power, not even Bythe. He's bluffing!" said Snyed.

"No. I'm sorry, but I don't think he is," said Valeyn quietly.

"And why do you say that?" asked Habistich.

"There were other items in The Tower, powerful Artefacts from the gods that Ferehain now has access to. He can use these in ways I can't predict."

"Even so," continued Snyed, undeterred, "we have ten thousand troops in the field across half the known world. Ferehain can't match us. He doesn't have an army that size."

"He doesn't need one. He can use those Imbatals to strike us where we're most vulnerable at any time, just like he did in Roy," said Valeyn

"And the Outland Alliance can do the rest of the fighting for him," concluded Ethan.

The room fell silent as everyone considered what they'd heard.

"Dear gods, this is bad," said Dox.

"I'm afraid it's even worse than that," Valeyn said. "The Tower was constructed on a direct link to the power that created Kovalith itself. Ferehain believes the Desecration has started. This means the gods are returning and they'll want to take all of their power – their *kai* – from the land. They want to destroy us."

"The Desecration. You have brought it upon us," spat Udrax.

"No, I didn't," she replied, exhausted and exasperated. "I've tried to keep this world together while everyone else has been determined to tear it apart. I'm tired of trying to convince you. You wanted full honesty from me? Well, there it is. Don't complain now that you don't like what you're hearing!"

"I'm sorry, Valeyn. You can't expect us to believe this Ageless has the power to destroy everything? That's just not plausible," said Sarele.

"If he found a way to tap into the forces that built this world, then I don't think there are any limits," said Valeyn.

"But what does the Desecration have to do with his plan?" asked Sarele.

"I don't know," said Valeyn.

"This is blasphemy and I will tolerate it no longer!" shouted Udrax. "Bythe is our protector. He created the Ironhelm and he will not see it fall. You should all be shamed for your lack of faith!"

He opened his mouth to launch another outburst but was interrupted by a distant ring of an alarm call. In an instant, everyone was on their feet. The guards drew weapons and Valeyn instinctively scanned every inch of the room – bracing herself for another appearance of Ferehain or his Imbatals, but the room remained undisturbed except for the distant sound of the alarm and the rising sound of voices and rushing feet.

"Find out what's happening," Morbus ordered and a guard quickly vanished through the door.

More voices could be heard, followed by the welling sounds of distant shouts and cries. Valeyn opened her mind and listened to the sensations around her. It seemed as if the entire city was writhing in unrestrained panic. A sense of terror and disbelief rippled from thousands of people in the streets below. Something terrible had happened.

"Sirs! Look eastward," the guard shouted as he rushed back into the room.

Everyone in the room hurried to the windows and looked down into the streets. Valeyn could feel the panic continuing to rise. People seemed to be gathering on the street below, as if watching something. But what?

We will move eastward. That facility is far more vulnerable.

She recalled Ferehain's words and immediately scanned the city. From this vantage point, she could clearly see the eastern side of Obduratev and yet nothing seemed amiss. She scanned the streets in puzzlement.

"What the hells is the matter with everyone?" snapped Snyed. "Guard, what's going on?"

"Eastward, sir!" he repeated.

Valeyn looked to the horizon and saw it. To the left stood the tall, proud sister-spire of Illustrux reaching into the sky and marking the northeast corner of the Ironhelm. But to the right, where the spire of Pientas should have been, there was only a brown smudge on the horizon. The smudge seemed to be expanding as Valeyn watched, and she understood it was a dust cloud — an impossibly large dust cloud, as if something mighty had fallen. Valeyn closed her eyes.

"What's happened to the spire?" one of the junior ministers asked.

"It's gone," Valeyn said, almost to herself. "Ferehain has somehow collapsed it."

The room broke onto a cacophony of shouts. The panic in the streets below infected the room above, and for a moment, sheer chaos reigned within the highest tower of the Iron Union.

"He can't have that much power. He just can't. It's not possible," muttered Sarele.

"It's the gods. It's the Desecration. It must be!" shouted Habistich.

"No, it's not the Desecration." Valeyn said as she turned away from the scene and walked back into the center of the room. She thought of the reports of destruction that had been filtering through. She thought of Tage, desperately trying to convince her to share his belief in an outrageous story. Complete obliteration, simply too fanciful to be believed.

"The assault on Roy was simply the latest in a series of steps I have taken to undo your father's empire. I had thought you would be aware of the others."

Valeyn knew that such an act of destruction was beyond the Ageless. It might even be beyond Bythe. A terrible realization dawned on her.

Ferehain had unlocked the secrets of The Tower and was deliberately unravelling the foundations of the world. The Desecration was no longer the problem. If Valeyn's fears were true, Ferehain could now threaten the soul of Kovalith, and such leverage would give him power over the gods themselves.

BOOK TWO
REPRISALS

CHAPTER 1

"When Maelene's actions in The Tower inadvertently brought about the Etherian and commenced the Desecration, untold damage was wrought upon our lands. Kai from every god was ripped from our world and returned to them as a sign that our people were ready to be judged. And while the bleeding from this injury was quickly halted by Maelene, the damage could not be reversed without direct intervention by the gods.

In a structurally weakened world, acts which should have been inconceivable were suddenly possible. And, like a frayed tapestry, the complex weavings of the lands could then be unravelled by one with the knowledge and the means to simply pull the right threads."

~Kaler of the Ageless.

Valeyn's party pushed through crowds trying to pour out of the open gates. The refugees were packed together, covered in dust and wild-eyed with panic as they fled for their lives. Orders shouted to control the mob were swept away among the tumult. A thin wedge of soldiers pressed through the crowd and cut a path for Valeyn. Panic hung in the air like the dust obscuring her clear view. The proud spire of Pientas was gone, and the debris left in its wake hung everywhere. All about her were the cries of people. Some were injured, others clearly dying. At the side of the boulevard, a woman called out for her children. Tears cut through the dust on her face, and her eyes were swollen and red. Valeyn looked away and tried to block it out. Her senses were drinking the pain emanating from every soul in the street, and it all but overwhelmed her.

As Valeyn rode closer to the center of the city, the crowd grew mercifully thinner, but the extent of the destruction worsened. The beautiful buildings lining the street now displayed the scars from the cataclysm that had befallen only a few hours earlier. Edifices were cracked and, in some cases, completely collapsed. Some were speared by large chunks of black metal, remains of the citadel flung across the city in all directions. Pockets of soldiers moved about, clearing the bodies from the roads and lining them in some form of grotesque order, but the soldiers were few in number – most had been in the citadel when it was destroyed.

The boulevard was now rent with cracks, and the closer they rode to the center, the more the road impeded them with crevasses and uneven steps. Finally, Valeyn called for a halt. For some reason, she was reminded of the Render and felt very uneasy.

"Ethan, tell the men to set up command here. Save every life they can. That's their only priority. Understood?"

Ethan nodded and shouted orders to his subordinates. Without delay, the soldiers broke formation and began setting up a command post. Medical supplies were unloaded from carts and the beginnings of a makeshift infirmary were established. Order was slowly set against the chaos, Valeyn hoped it would be enough.

It had been no more than a few hours since the citadel had collapsed. Valeyn had immediately commandeered a battalion and led them to the city at an almost dangerous pace. Others were no doubt following. The Unity Assembly were almost certainly drawing up plans to defend the Iron Union against this latest threat – Morbus and his allies feigning surprise and concern – but Valeyn knew none of them would be thinking about the citizens. That was *her* duty now.

"Any sign of Ferehain?" Valeyn asked.

"Nothing yet. If he's still here, then he's at the center of it," Ethan replied, nodding at the boulevard as it twisted deeper into the broken city.

"With me, Ethan," she said, and he fell in line behind her without a word.

She picked her way across the broken road and moved deeper into the city. All about her were broken people pulling themselves from broken buildings, but she couldn't afford to think about them. She'd done all she could to help. Now, she was needed elsewhere. She could feel something at the center of the city, something that simply should not be there. As they picked their way closer to the ruins of the citadel, Valeyn could sense the despair giving way to panic once more. A break in the ground rose before them, and over it clambered two young men, neither of them glancing at Valeyn as they sprinted down the slope toward her.

"You there!" she commanded but it was as if she hadn't spoken. Both men shot past her and continued their headlong dash before Valeyn could open her mouth again. Ethan watched the men retreat, glanced at her, then looked at the rise ahead of them. She knew what worried him.

"Stay well behind me," she ordered Ethan before carefully picking her way up the slope. As she crested the rise, something set each of her preternatural senses alight.

Before her lay a scene of complete devastation. A massive, gaping hole at the center of the city where the citadel had stood only hours before. Metal and wood were strewn out across the space like hundreds of giant sticks thrown about by a careless child.

Buildings leaned inward as if they were in pain, and what had once been a carefully ordered grid of perfection was now an unrecognizable mess.

But this was not what had seized her attention. From the center of the hole, a dome of nothingness was rising. It was like a cloud, but it resisted any attempts to be defined by Valeyn's eyes. It seemed to be of every color, and of none. It was shimmeringly bright, and yet whenever she looked at it directly, there seemed to be nothing beyond a vague, gray depth. It gave off a feeling of something completely unnatural, as if it were something that absolutely should not exist in a natural world. Valeyn abhorred it instinctively.

Slowly, Ethan joined her and stared at the scene in puzzlement.

"What is it?" he asked.

Valeyn clenched her jaw. "I think this is what Tage was reporting to us back in Court."

"Tage? He said his home had been destroyed."

"No, he said it was gone, replaced by emptiness."

Ethan looked down at it with slight revulsion. "Do you know what it is?"

"Not exactly, but I recognize the power. This comes out of the Render. It's linked in with the fabric of Kovalith."

"It feels . . . wrong somehow. I can't explain it," said Ethan.

"I know," she answered.

Valeyn glanced around, looking for any sign of Ferehain or one the Imbatals, but she found none, only the emptiness of the strange mass before her.

"It is an *absence* of *kai*," said a voice, and Valeyn wheeled around with her sabre drawn. A small man stood on the broken road behind her wearing plain clothes and an unremarkable face under short-cropped hair. He looked to be somewhere in his thirties, but she knew he was far older — he was not even of this world. He wasn't even looking at her. Instead, he paced the rim created by the broken boulevard and looked about him strangely, as if he were misplaced inside a dream.

"An absence of *kai*," the man repeated, seemingly talking to himself.

"Who are you?" she demanded but the man ignored her. Instead he picked his way down the slope a little uncertainly, then peered into the mass of dirty light as if it held something inside for him to see.

"Answer me!" she ordered, but still the man said nothing.

"Valeyn, are you alright?" asked Ethan.

It was then, Valeyn realized she hadn't been speaking aloud. The stranger's words had been echoing inside her being, and she had been instinctively answering him the same way. It was like the voices she'd been hearing with increased frequency. Was she going mad? Or did those voices belong to others?

She looked at him again and forced herself to see him for who he truly was. She looked past the illusion generated by the confines of Kovalith and instead focused on the essence of the man, the immortal energies swirling around him, mauve in hue, and she found she knew him.

"Lubalt-Teble," she called out, and he glanced back at her.

"Wonderful," he spoke aloud with a brief nod. "Some questioned if you'd even recognize your kin or hear their calling. I admit, I was one of them."

"Lubalt-Teble?" questioned Ethan, looking at the man in disbelief. "This is not him. Valeyn, this is just a man."

She looked hard at the unremarkable figure tracing a path around the anomaly. "No, this is him."

Ethan smiled and risked a few steps down the slope to better look at the man. "Lubalt-Teble was supposed to be a god of love and seduction. He was said to have lain with hundreds of women to understand the art of lovemaking. This man looks like a bookkeeper."

The man's expression betrayed a level of amusement as he continued inspecting the light. "I was interested in your fascination with sex and the preoccupation it casts over your kind. I admit I was not entirely successful in my goal, those biological sensations were enchanting, yet I could never quite understand the addictive hold it takes on you."

"I find it impossible to believe that a man as plain as you could have seduced so many women," said Ethan.

He turned and fixed Ethan with blue eyes which were suddenly quite cold. "Whatever made you think my acts were consensual?"

A wave of revulsion swept through Valeyn, and the little man suddenly seemed quite dangerous. "What are you doing here?" she asked.

"I think you know the answer to that, dear Valeyn."

She moved down the slope to place herself in front of Ethan. Lubalt-Teble finally turned and gave her his full attention. "My, you are truly impressive," he said. His eyes drank in her body and the look seemed to taint her. "A child of this world. Who would have thought it possible?"

"You heard the call of The Tower?"

"I did," he shrugged. "But the truth is many of us had already begun the journey back here. Some of us had become aware of your creation and decided this little experiment had finally run its course, and it was time for it to end."

"If this is the Desecration, or whatever people want to call it, then why are you doing this? Have you sided with Ferehain?" she asked.

"Oh, we've done nothing of the sort. Do you think we lower ourselves to alliances and bargains with our own creations? We gave this world life; we don't need to bargain with it. You need to understand the natural order of things if you're going to take your place among it." He took a step closer and looked up with blue eyes filled with malice and calculation. "Tell me,

Valeyn, have you taken men in this world? I'd very much like to hear about it."

She was about to strike him when a voice stopped her. "Leave the child be, your obsessions of the flesh are truly sickening."

Valeyn looked above and beheld an impossible sight. A woman stood suspended in the air. She was heavyset, with dark skin covering her strong physique. Long black hair cascaded over her body, which was covered in a flowing blue dress.

Lubalt-Teble smiled. "Ah, this is something of a family meeting, isn't it? Valeyn, do you recognize your father's sister?"

"Pia?" Valeyn responded automatically.

"Goddess of the oceans," Ethan added, looking up at her with wonder, yet Pia looked about as if they weren't there.

"Where is my brother?" Pia asked Lubalt-Teble.

The rapist god turned away from Valeyn and seemed to will himself into the air. He grew in size as he floated up to stand next to Pia.

"Who can say what is passing through his addled mind? But he'll be here."

They spoke without looking at each other, as if their physical forms were superfluous, and Valeyn realized they had reverted to their unspoken language.

"What's happening?" Ethan whispered and for the first time in her life, Valeyn heard fear in his voice.

"Pia! Goddess of the sea! We praise you!" A voice cried out from beyond the crest, causing Valeyn to hurry back up the slope. Six people were gathered on the ruin of the boulevard, staring at the suspended forms of the gods with rapture. More were emerging from the ruins and walking slowly toward the group.

"Get them back, Ethan," Valeyn said. "They shouldn't be here, nor should you."

Ethan looked up at Pia as if she were an apparition. "Pia was killed by Lord Bythe over four hundred years ago. That's why the seas are cursed against us. She can't be here — not unless the Desecration has finally come."

Valeyn gripped Ethan by the shoulders and looked deep into his eyes. "Please, be strong Ethan. I need you. Get these people to safety. I have a feeling something terrible is about to happen."

Ethan's face hardened and he nodded. He glanced up at the floating figures with a strange mix of dread and hatred. "Do what you need to do," he said, then hurried toward the rapidly growing crowd, shouting orders for soldiers to join him.

Valeyn turned back to Pia and Lubalt-Teble. Both were fixed in the air, completely indifferent to each other and to the people beneath them. They looked casually about the space around them as if pre-occupied. Valeyn reached out with her feelings and focused on the two of them floating in space. As she did so, it seemed as if a veil lifted from her vision and she understood that the empty spaces of Kovalith were merely extensions of the same *kai* used to construct everything else. She strengthened her mind and mentally *gripped* the air around her – it responded. She lurched abruptly forward and stopped a few feet above the ground. She closed her eyes and repeated the mental exercise, again willing herself a few feet higher into the air. Shouts reached her ears, but she forced herself to ignore them. She pulled at the air again and this time rose dangerously high. Looking down, Valeyn knew a fall from this height would probably kill her, but for some reason she was unafraid. It was as if her body thought she was on the ground and falling was impossible. She chose not to explore the rationale behind her newly found absence of self-preservation.

Lubalt-Teble nodded down at the dome of perverse light that Valeyn could now see was beginning to slowly grow. "We were never quite sure how the *ovoid* would appear. It's fascinating to behold, isn't it?"

"It's unmaking the world. This isn't right. You're not supposed to be doing this now, you're supposed to wait until judgment is passed," said Valeyn.

"What do you mean by '*you're*' not supposed to be doing this?" asked Pia. "You do not consider yourself to be one of us? This is disappointing, although it is also unsurprising."

"And we're not doing this, well, not directly. Maelene's disciple has proven himself to be remarkably inventive," said Lubalt-Teble. "Although our arrival has probably assisted your friend's effort. The *kai* underpinning this world has become very unstable now that we're back. I suppose we could help in some way, if we were inclined."

"Then do it!"

"We are not interested," snapped Pia, looking at something on the horizon.

"Not interested? People are dying. You cared enough to create this world, you have a responsibility to defend it."

"She's so much like Maelene, isn't she?" said another voice. Valeyn turned to see a tall man with a lined face under a mane of swept-back, silver hair. Valeyn didn't need to notice the fine clothes to recognize Basalt the Wander. One by one, the gods were gathering, and Valeyn's feeling of disquiet grew.

"You were all once like her. You simply choose to misremember," said Pia.

"Where are the others?" asked Lubalt-Teble

"I don't know," Basalt replied with the same distracted air. "I feel that some are here, yet others haven't arrived."

"And where are those who are here?" asked Pia.

Basalt shrugged. "Revisiting their past glories, I suppose. Perhaps taking a final look before it is gone forever? I cannot understand why. This all feels so different now. I no longer see the appeal."

Valeyn looked down and noticed the crowd had grown larger. She could make out Ethan's men trying in vain to disperse the people. She decided to use the skills Ethan had taught her; words of mortals against the vanity of gods.

"Listen to me," Valeyn commanded in the silent language she instinctively knew. The three heads slowly turned in unison and stared at her. "I understand why you're here. You believe the Desecration has begun, that Bythe and Maelene have summoned you to cast your judgment on the world, but this isn't the case. Nishindra tricked my mother into awakening The Tower and bringing about the Desecration. This is a deception; you've been summoned too soon."

"A deception?" Pia asked.

"A mistruth told to gain advantage," Lubalt-Teble said.

"Of course," Pia replied with a vague expression of amused bewilderment. "Such things were possible in this place. We enjoyed such games with them, did we not?"

Basalt shrugged with a disdain that only increased his arrogance. "Diminishing ourselves to such a level was unbecoming of us. What is to be gained by denying ourselves our awareness?"

"I seem to recall a certain happiness," Pia said. "There was joy in simply existing from moment to moment, unburdened by knowledge of what was to come. One cannot truly feel happy if one eternally dwells on the problems of tomorrow. This place allowed us to experience that peace."

Basalt shook his head but didn't answer.

"While I wasn't here to witness you personally, the scriptures say you enjoyed yourself most of all, Basalt," said Valeyn. "Maelene tells me that you were haughty and full of exuberance for this world while you walked within it."

Basalt raised an eyebrow as he considered her. "Do you seek to embarrass me? We all partook in the pleasures of this place, but you do not understand what lies beyond. When you join us in the Etherian, you will better comprehend your true nature."

"You will see that this is not who you are," Pia added.

"Nishindra drew us to this place, and it was he who convinced us to dwell here for a time, but it did not suit us," said Lubalt-Teble.

"It sullied us, corrupted us with base desires. I no longer remember this place fondly," said Basalt.

"I understand, but that's not really the issue here, is it?" said Valeyn, pointing to the crowd beneath them. "Look at the people you created. Listen to them. They worshipped you. They still do."

Chants and prayers could be heard below as the crowd grew larger and louder, but the three gods above them seemed not to notice.

"We have heard this argument before, child," said Basalt. "Your parents used it quite eloquently."

"And Nishindra, most of all, and yet, he is not even here," added Lubalt-Teble.

"Nishindra tricked Maelene into summoning you. In a way, he's tricked you. You're not supposed to be here."

"They were the rules of the game, as I recall," answered Pia, looking again to the horizon.

"In any event, it matters not," said Basalt. "Many of us had already decided the time for judgment had come. Kalte and Ceriv were among the first to return. Nishindra's gambit was simply the final argument."

Valeyn thought furiously for a reason that would somehow sway them. "You also agreed to honor the wishes of Bythe, my father. I can tell you he wouldn't agree to this. These are his people, and he'll defend them."

Pia broke her gaze from the horizon and smiled at Valeyn. "We may hear your father's views for ourselves. He is here."

A crack seemed to rend the air and for a moment, all was dark. The crowd below screamed, certain that another attack had begun. Within seconds, the daylight returned, but it somehow seemed dimmed as if obscured by something. The screams of panic quickly turned to cries of surprise and awe at the shadow cast by the unmistakable bulk of Bythe. He hung suspended in the air above them all, even over the other gods, mighty and towering.

Valeyn was shocked. Trumpets rang below and the crowd fell to their knees in a wave of supplication. Slowly, Bythe turned his mighty armored head and looked down at the four gods waiting for him. Even from such a distance, Valeyn could feel the power of his gaze and she sensed judgment.

"Brother, you are as dramatic as I recall. I have missed you," Pia said without a change to her cool expression.

Valeyn compared Bythe's towering bulk with the dark-skinned woman. According to the legends, Pia had sought to claim Alovat and much of the Grand Duchy of Joana as part of her oceanic kingdom. She had lured Bythe into a negotiation at the beaches of Joana, with a plan to drag him into the ocean where he would drown under the weight of his iron. But Bythe had seen through her deception, and the legends say he dragged his sister by the hair, deep into the arid deserts of Hammerfall, where she stood, staked to the ground and left to slowly die of thirst and dehydration over twenty years. Pia had cursed her brother with her last words, commanding the ocean to forever be his enemy. But if there were any trace of bitterness within her, she certainly didn't show it today.

"What is the meaning of this incursion? I did not summon you." Bythe's voice rumbled within his helm.

"The Etherian was called by Nishindra," said Lubalt-Teble. "We're now prepared to judge the Forge, our creation."

"Unacceptable," said Bythe. "I demand time to complete my argument."

"You no longer see things clearly, little brother. The madness has taken hold, and you still play at your games of power and importance, as you always have. But take heart, this will pass when you return to us," said Pia.

"I have no desire to return to you," Bythe replied. "My only desire is to prove the righteousness of my way. I have almost achieved this"

"We are tired of this game," said Basalt.

"That is an excuse. You are only tired now because you know you have lost. You wish to move on. I will not allow it. I will prove the dominance you once sought. I will have victory."

"Victory over what, brother?" Pia asked. "This world was a fleeting distraction for us, and it no longer holds sway over our attention. You have used it to further your petty need for recognition. We have eternities of existence to ponder. Basalt is correct. This place was always beneath us."

"You constrain yourself with your mortal form, Bythe. You should relinquish it and re-embrace your true nature. You will see things much more clearly when you do," said Lubalt-Teble.

"Your jealousy is as obvious to me as it is unfitting. You seek to thwart me as I stand on the cusp of triumph, and I will not permit it."

"You will not have a choice," said Lubalt-Teble.

"You dare to threaten me?" Bythe's voice was a low rumble and his body floated closer. Lubalt-Teble's subsequent step backward was as instinctive to him as it was instructive to Valeyn.

"Calm yourself, brother," interrupted Pia. "We did not come to fight you."

"Indeed, you did not. None of you had the power to match me on this world, you are certainly no match for me in these shadows of your former forms."

Valeyn looked hard at the figures before her and her perception shifted. The three gods looked somehow thin, as if she were viewing them through a veil of mist.

"You can't touch us, can you? You're not really here. You lost your mortal forms and when you did, you lost your power to interact with this world," she said.

"You have such a mortal intellect," said Lubalt-Teble in a tone thick with condescension. "We agreed to such terms when we created this place," said Basalt. "But we still sustain it. Our energies give this place the soul it needs to thrive, and while we can no longer directly interfere with this world, we can simply end it, if we choose."

"You understand that would kill everyone," said Valeyn with forced restraint.

"And we created everyone," said Pia. "None of this would exist were it not for us. We have the right to destroy that which we create."

"But that isn't right."

Pia looked at Valeyn with genuine pity. "Poor girl. You have yet to experience the glory of the endless lands beyond the stifling confines of Kovalith. Once you do, you will understand that your mortal concepts of right and wrong simply do not exist. They are but rules created for a game which we tired of centuries ago."

"Our energies are not infinite. You will learn this soon enough. This world requires a soul, and we have all lent a part of ours in order to give it life. We must decide if this creation merits continued existence or if our energies are better used in other endeavours. The time has come for us to judge," said Basalt.

"But you're not here to judge, are you? You've already made up your minds! You're taking the soul from this world!" Valeyn snapped.

"You see clearly, daughter," said Bythe. "However, their desires are irrelevant. They cannot pass judgment without the full Congress, who have not yet gathered."

Lubalt-Teble shrugged and gestured to the mass of light lingering where the citadel once stood. "The Congress matters little. It would seem the judgment will be made with or without us. The disciple of Maelene has uncovered the secret of undoing our *kai*. Once this takes hold, Kovalith will simply unravel. It will eat away at the existence of this world until there is nothing left."

Valeyn watched the ball of strange, pulsing light. As it expanded slightly, the rubble of a nearby wall collapsed and fell into the sphere, where it dissolved instantly. "So, this isn't your doing?" she asked.

"We have not granted this rogue Ageless any such power. He has discovered it for himself," remarked Pia in a voice not without respect.

"What sort of power could Ferehain have discovered?" Valeyn asked.

"Any sort of power can be achieved, providing you're prepared to hurt enough people to gain it. This Ferehain would appear to have become quite driven in his vendetta against you, Bythe," said Lubalt-Teble.

"And I suspect, you as well, Valeyn," Pia added.

Valeyn looked back at the light and her feeling of dread increased. "Can't you stop it?"

"As you quite rightly observed, we are no longer of this world. We no longer hold direct power here," said Lubalt-Teble, glancing down at the people gathered beneath them. "But if I'm being honest, I can't say I want to do anything."

"I think the real question, Valeyn, is can *you* stop it?" Basalt asked with a look of curiosity.

The sphere was growing larger and had already reached the cusp of the crater which had marked the perimeter of the citadel. Valeyn watched as it slowly corroded everything it came into contact with, dissolving rocks into particles of light, which then joined the ever-growing ball of energy. The scene held a strange sense of ethereal beauty.

"Father, what can we do?" she asked Bythe.

Bythe did not answer, instead his impassive mask continued to face the three gods before them.

"Father, please," Valeyn repeated.

"That does not concern me," Bythe answered.

Valeyn looked at him with suspicion "You said you wanted time to save this world."

"I require time to complete my conquest of your mother's creations. Once I have proven myself over the last god who stood against me, my purpose will be fulfilled."

"But, Father, the Union . . . your people . . . they'll be killed by this!"

"Then they will die in my name, and it will be a fitting tribute."

Valeyn paused as she tried to comprehend what she was hearing. Recalling Ethan's advice, she chose her words carefully.

"Father, Maelene is gone. There's no one left to fight. I understand your need for victory, but what's the point if your empire burns in the process?"

"My empire is a reflection of my greatness. If it burns in victory, then it will be a pyre in my name."

"But the people — they look to you for protection."

"The people are no different to my other possessions. The board must be cleared eventually. The game will be over, and I will have triumphed without the descent into madness."

A commotion erupted from the crowds beneath them. Valeyn looked down to see the wall of light had broken past the cusp of the crater and was moving toward the gathered people. Guards were trying to move the crowd away from the threat, but the people seemed transfixed by the gods above them.

Pia looked at Valeyn with a measure of sympathy. "Valeyn, I tell you with certainty — you cannot save this world. You must learn to detach yourself from these beings. They are simply not real. None of this is real. You will understand this once you join the Etherian."

The wall of light was gradually increasing in speed and Valeyn realized it would reach the gathering withing minutes. She looked around for Ethan and found him shouting commands to his men in a vain attempt to move the people back.

Why aren't the people running? Sickness struck her as the answer became obvious. Her gaze swept over a crowd of men and women, desperately prostrating themselves in prayer. *They expect us to save them.*

"Strange beings, aren't they?" remarked Lubalt-Teble. "They won't even save themselves in the face of certain destruction. They blindly look to us for protection. How can you seriously argue a case for these people, Valeyn?"

A terrible scream broke from below. A Helmsguard soldier had moved to test the wall of light with his sabre, and everyone now watched as his body was slowly undone. Panic erupted from the crowed as people finally comprehended the peril. People were pushed aside as others began a blind run for safety. Some shouted imploringly at the sky, begging the gods for deliverance from the threat, and the wall of light continued its inexorable path toward them. Ethan was screaming at the people, begging them to leave, but there were just too many of them.

"No. No," said Valeyn, backing away from the gods before her. "I can't accept this. I won't.

"Well, what can you do, Valeyn? Can you wield the abilities of the gods? What are your limits?" Basalt asked, and she understood there was something of a challenge in his question.

"Yes, what can *she* do?" sneered Lubalt-Teble.

Valeyn swung her fist at the repulsive man. His face barely had time to register surprise before it collapsed inward and his entire form seemed to fold up under her blow. The other gods merely watched without emotion or expression as Lubalt-Teble's body vanished from the air.

"Daughter, you will not act in this way without—" Bythe began but Valeyn turned her back.

"Shut up," she snapped and willed herself to move to the ground as quickly as possible. To her surprise, her feet were on land in an instant, but she didn't waste any time thinking about this. A wall of the *ovoid* loomed before her. Now that she was closer, she felt something unnatural emanating from it, as if the fabric of the world were screaming in protest against its existence. The sickly light continued its path toward her, but she stood her ground, turning her feeling inward, searching for any secret or skill that she could employ against this terrible thing.

There was nothing. Valeyn had inherited elements of her parents' *kai* — her mother's influence over nature, her father's craft over metal — and fused them in a moment of physical power against Imbatal. While her proximity to other gods seemed to be unlocking something greater within her, nothing in her makeup seemed capable of overcoming the existential scale of what now confronted her.

"I . . . I can't do this," she confessed. She looked up at her father and the two remaining gods. "Help me!" she screamed, but if they heard her, they made no move to reply.

Cursing, she turned away from the *ovoid* and sprinted to the crowd. Most of them had now fled but there were still dozens of people, too old or too afraid to leave.

"Help me, Valeyn!" cried a middle-aged woman, struggling to get to her feet with a lame arm. Others saw Valeyn and took up the desperate plea. People started moving toward her, as if her mere presence would protect them. Guards moved in swiftly and Valeyn soon found herself behind a wall of armored men. Ethan ran to Valeyn's side, his helmet was gone and his red hair unkempt.

"I can't get them out," he said breathlessly. "There's too many and it's coming too quickly. What should we do?"

Unfamiliar faces implored Valeyn for help, begging her not to leave them. Valeyn shook her head. "I can't abandon them," she replied.

Ethan nodded grimly and looked at the approaching wall of destruction before turning back to address his men. "Soldiers of the Ironhelm. Servants of Lord Bythe. Stand your ground with your life. Our lord is watching us. Make him proud and satisfy your obligations before him."

The bellowed responses from the soldiers was clear and final. It was nothing short of inspiring, their courage moving, and Valeyn felt sudden rage at the deceit.

"No." She looked up again at the gods above them and closed her eyes. She reached out with a tendril of feeling and latched onto something. The world around her began to melt and sway. Though foreign, it now made sense to her. Acting purely on instinct, she opened her eyes and took in the panicked crowd before her. She absorbed their screams and cries for forgiveness and closed her eyes again. The screams heightened and then took on a muffled, distorted tone, as if she were hearing them underwater. All sense of direction vanished for an instant, then the ground was at her feet – but she was standing upside down. She opened her eyes and the world spun back into the right position, causing a swell of nausea. Clear daylight assailed her and the grand edifice of Domitus loomed skyward.

"Valeyn? What did you do?" gasped Ethan.

They were back in Obduratev, standing in the great square before the citadel. Valeyn knew that she had done this, but the knowledge was already slipping from her mind. She couldn't keep her thoughts together.

The air filled with cries; screams of panic, surprise and joy. Black-clad citizens stared at them in disbelief. Guards flooded into the square, assuming an ambush, but then halted in confusion at the sight of dozens of refugees now assembled in the square.

"My gods, you saved us, Valeyn!" said Ethan.

She staggered away from him, looking for some clear air. The ground seemed to be shifting and she felt like throwing up. Exhaustion rushed from nowhere and assailed her in waves. Ethan's hands caught her, and she felt herself toppling into his embrace.

"Don't worry, I've got you. Everything's going to be alright," he said, as she felt consciousness begin to drift. Her last, distant thoughts were of the unusual fear in his voice as he shouted for help.

CHAPTER 2

Dear Father,

Wheatsheaf is finally free from the Helmsguard. We reclaimed the town a few hours ago. The enemy had retreated with barely a fight. It looks like the sheer devastation from the war engines left a problem for the Iron Union: they had no structures or positions to rally behind once they found themselves in full retreat. It served them right.

In fact, the past few weeks haven't been much more than a straight march through Greenridge as the Helmsguard scurried from Darcliff to Fyrn and then to Stonekeep in a vain effort to find a defensible position for their inferior numbers. More and more soldiers have joined up with us at each liberated town, our force now triple what it had been at Roy.

The Helmsguard eventually decided to make a stand within the walls of Stonekeep, but they held the fortress for less than a day before realizing I was manoeuvring troops into an encircling position, which would lead to a capture of their entire army. I almost had them all. I came so close, father, but we had to let them retreat. I wish you could have seen their fleeing backs.

And so, they retreated further to Wheatsheaf, but now we've chased them out of there as well. I'm going to keep chasing them, Father. I'll do it until they're out of the Outer Wild, and I'll keep going until they'll never be able to hurt us again. Don't fear for me, just be proud, please.

Love,

Captain Jason of Fairhaven

Jason had spent the past hour securing the western docks to ensure there would be no surprise visitors from the water before returning to the command post in the Wheatsheaf town square. In a matter of weeks, they would advance on Outpost and then finally drive the Helmsguard from the Outer Wild. The evil days that had once forced Nadine and Elyn to flee for their lives were over. According to all reports, Outpost had been spared the ravages of the war engines and it remained largely intact, although it was reported to now be an eerie shell of the bustling town Nadine used to speak of so frequently. Although Jason knew that it would never be her home again, its regained liberty was important to her. Her family had made their fortune there, and the Iron Union had taken that from her, just as it had taken her father and their daughter.

As Jason returned to the town square, he noticed it was the only part of the town with a decent number of people. They were mostly soldiers, of course, but there were many civilians among them. There were no children to be seen, only men and women had remained behind, presumably those who had nothing to lose or little left to live for.

Warmaster Zain stood next to Kaler at the edge of the square, overseeing the soldiers of the new Outland Alliance as they set to the business of restoring order to the town under their new occupation. Jason looked over the collection of men and women in various colored uniforms, the pale blue of Fairhaven now only occasionally seen among the mix of Marfort's green and the grays of Darcliff and Bonehall, but more frequent were the un-uniformed men and women from Roy, the Federacy, and dozens of other places. They had all joined the swelling army of their own free will and there'd been no uniforms to give them. On one level, it unsettled the part of Jason that had been schooled by Captain Lewis, yet on another, it seemed fitting for an army comprised of free people from the east. No suits of black iron for them. Why not let their individualism show?

Warmaster Zain greeted Jason with a curt nod as he approached. They'd never be friends — Jason had realized this a long time ago — but they seemed to understand each other, even if they didn't always agree.

Kaler also inclined his head in his typically impassive manner, but Jason still found comfort in the gesture.

Zain brushed his dark hair back. "Any trouble?"

Jason shook his head. "All quiet. I've left a unit there anyway, but I don't expect anything."

"The iron people have never been good on water," Zain agreed.

"How are things here?" Jason asked, casting his eyes over the square. People formed ordered lines, waiting for their turn to register their names and details before being sent to the supply tent at the end of the square where they'd receive medical care, food, and whatever basic provisions could be found for them.

"They're a sorry lot. I'm not sure if any of them even know who we are or what's going on. They don't seem to understand that we're freeing them."

"Years of occupation will do that to you," said Jason.

"They're clinging to us. It's almost as if they want us to replace the Helmsguard. How can you just give up your independence like that?" Zain said with a touch of disgust.

Jason shrugged. It was as alien to him as it was to Zain, yet he couldn't help feeling a degree of sympathy for these people.

"You should not judge so harshly, Warmaster," said Kaler. "It is natural to seek security, even at the price of freedom. It is indeed how the Ageless were able to assume such authority over you for centuries. Do not consider yourself to be superior in this regard."

Zain gave Kaler a strange look but only shook his head in reply as he returned his attention to the crowd before him. "Anyway, we'll have these people processed before sundown, then we'll start searching the town for those who didn't come forward."

Jason nodded. "How many spies do you think we'll have?"

"In a town like this, for as long as this one's been occupied? I'd say at least a hundred, probably more," Zain sighed.

"It's not the spies that worry me, it's the partisans," said Jason. "We can't leave them at our backs, we'll need to find every single one."

Zain and Kaler exchanged a glance, before the Warmaster returned his attention to Jason, seemingly ready to resume an old argument.

"Captain, we've had this discussion before, and my position has not changed. We're going no further than Outpost."

"You don't command my army, Warmaster," Jason said without emotion.

"But I do command *my* army, Captain, and I will not send even one of my soldiers into Helmsguard territory. It is one thing to defend ourselves, it is another thing entirely to invade. We did not come here for this purpose."

"In either case, it may not be wise or even possible," said Kaler. "I remain increasingly concerned by what I hear from the west."

Jason grunted. "You mean the stories of devastation? Wild storms of power ripping apart the land? I would have thought the Ageless, of all people, would keep a sensible head when it comes to rumors."

"Indeed, I do. Which is why I never dismiss nor accept any information without a critical assessment based on my own experience. Only a fool would do otherwise," Kaler replied.

Jason chose to ignore the barb. It was probably well-deserved. "Then what does your analysis tell you?"

"That the Desecration is not a thing to be dismissed, and that while my own gifts may not be at the same level as the Ishantir, I can sense . . . a disparity from the west, as if the *kai* of this world is somehow off-balance."

"And so, the stories we've been hearing might be true," said Zain. "It would explain a few things. As much as I'd like to believe that our victories have been well-earned, our enemy has fallen back far too quickly for my comfort. I've been waiting for them to spring a trap, but that's obviously not going to happen."

"That could mean they simply over-extended their capacity for war by chasing us into Marfort, and we've punished them for their carelessness," said Jason. "It's a common mistake, especially among inexperienced commanders."

"Or it means there's something very wrong within the Iron Union," said Zain. "We still haven't been able to explain the destruction of the war engines and those clockwork demons. Where did they come from and who is commanding them?"

"All the more reason to push forward! If this is true, if the Helmsguard are in disarray, then this is the perfect time to take advantage. It might not come again."

Zain shook his head. "There is too much uncertainty. The soldiers will soon need rest. We've come farther than expected in a shorter time than planned. And much of our strength has come from people who want to drive the Helmsguard from our lands, but not to venture forth into theirs. This requires careful planning. We don't want to make the same mistake the Helmsguard did by stretching too far too quickly."

"Fine. We rest the men once we take Outpost, and we plan the next stage of the offensive."

"I say again, it is not an *offensive*. Besides, there are far too many unknowns for my comfort," said Zain. "If there is an unseen hand at work, then it is a powerful hand for it to control a force of Imbatals. I will not send my soldiers into the midst of such a force until I know more of its ambitions."

"So why did you come, Zain? To send the Helmsguard back across the border without punishment for what they've done? To send Bythe a clear message that he's free to walk in here and destroy our lives without risk of any reprisal?"

"There have been reprisals. We've routed his army and beaten him back," Zain replied.

"So, that's it? A man invades your home and threatens everything you have, and you just chase him out the door and hope he doesn't come back the next day? We have to make him pay for what he's done to us. We have to make sure he never does this again!"

Kaler raised a palm in a conciliatory gesture. "Captain, there is a great difference between defending one's home, and invading the home of another, even if such an act is justified. The Violari had petitioned for such aggression during the long years of the Anarch, and while the Ageless were very successful at repelling invaders from our lands, we discovered the prolonged invasion of the Iron Union was far more challenging."

"Perhaps the Ageless just lacked the motivation," Jason answered.

"Or perhaps you have too much?" said Zain, turning to face him squarely. "Vengeance is driving you, Jason. I can see it. By the gods, I understand why. It makes you a powerful man, a man worth following.

And men will follow you, because they'll see their own rage mirrored in yours. But your pain isn't their pain. It can't be. And how far are you going to push them to see your own pain satisfied? When that happens, are you still leading them, Jason, or are you just using them?"

The honest appraisal stunned Jason and he was momentarily taken aback. Confusion swirled within and melted into frustration at his inability to answer the direct truths that cut through his bluster. He felt naked, as if realizing everyone had always understood he was just a young boy from Fairhaven, still desperate to prove himself to everyone.

"Perhaps Warmaster Zain is simply a coward?" Jason's words came without thinking. They were the petulant reflex of a defeated child, and while Kaler's expression darkened into alarm, the Warmaster only shook his head in the manner of a patient, older brother.

"I know you didn't mean that, Captain, so I'm going to ignore it," Zain replied.

The response only enraged Jason further, for when aggression won't open a door, the impotence of that anger becomes claustrophobic. He wheeled about and sought escape from the two men who saw through him, violently barging his way through soldiers, as if daring any of them to challenge him. None did. He turned and strode blindly down a side street, grateful for the solitude it offered.

"Is it true?" asked Romona, as she appeared beside him. "Do the men follow you out of shared rage? Does this overrule their fear of death?"

He shook his head, as much to ward away her presence as to answer her question. He accomplished neither.

"You will answer me, Jason. I did not return you to life out of sentiment. I wish to understand you. If you are not comfortable with this arrangement, I can return you to death's embrace."

The threat of death was delivered with the same calm innocence that marked each of her statements.

"I don't know," he answered. "Probably, for some of them."

"And this shared rage is your sole reason for existence now? You simply wish to visit death upon others?"

"I don't want to kill everyone, just one man, and anyone who stands between us."

"And Valeyn? What if she chooses to stand between you and Baron Ethan? Will you turn on her?"

Jason's jaw clenched. He'd avoided confronting this question, although he knew it was almost inevitable.

"If she sides with my enemy, then she's made her choice. I just want the chance to kill him."

"If that is all that you wish, then I am certain this can be provided for you. Are you certain that you do not wish for more?"

"Yes," he lied and turned his face away from her. He'd tried to avoid thinking about a life beyond Ethan, but as he marched alone down the streets of Wheatsheaf, he began to realize he'd never really expected to survive beyond that confrontation.

For the first time in months, he felt the ache of his absent wife.

·   ·   ·

"Sarele, we need the help of your house. Give us control of whatever men you can spare. Our people are at risk, and we have to help them."

Sarele's handsome face darkened as she considered Valeyn's plea. "I can't do that, Valeyn. You're simply asking too much."

Valeyn straightened on her couch where she'd spent most of her time over the past three days. "I'm the Heir Designate and your god, I can order you," Valeyn warned.

Sarele's face lit with amusement. "The gods don't seem to be in control of their own empires anymore, Valeyn. You can order me all you want, but I can't deliver you soldiers that I don't have. They're under the command of Morbus and Snyed now."

It had been a frustrating period of recovery for Valeyn, and one she couldn't recall with lucidity. Ethan had told her how the Acolytes had been the ones to take care of her, ordering the Helmsguard with an authority nobody had expected. Valeyn had been returned to her apartments where even Ethan had been forbidden entry for two more days. Valeyn could recall the ministrations of the Acolytes, but wasn't sure if they'd been at all helpful other than watching over her while she'd recovered. Once she had, it had taken her little time to ask Ethan to find his mother.

"You can order your men back," Valeyn countered.

"Yes, I can, and I can then face Morbus's long-awaited accusations of treason. Wheatsheaf has fallen and within days, your old friends will be marching on Outpost. If I attempt to recall my troops now it will give Morbus and Snyed the excuse they've been waiting for to strip my house of any power we still hold in the empire — that's if I don't spark a civil war in the interim. I'm sorry, Valeyn, but you'll forgive me if I don't follow the advice of the politically naïve."

Valeyn sighed. "You've seen what's happened at Arbek, to your own people. I know you care about them. This is happening everywhere. Ferehain has begun striking out all over the Union and I'm getting reports of refugees heading in by the thousands. They're looking for Bythe's protection, and we need to offer it."

"And why isn't *he* offering it?" Sarele asked.

The two young Acolytes standing at the rear of the chamber gasped and began muttering a quiet prayer of forgiveness to a god who clearly wasn't listening. But it wasn't blasphemy. Valeyn knew that it was actually a very good question. Where was Bythe? Why was he standing by while Ferehain slowly undid all his work?

"Mother," Ethan interjected, "Valeyn makes a valid point. We need to help our people. Surely, we can do more. Perhaps Symin could help us? He's indebted to us in many ways."

Sarele gave her favorite son a measured glance. "What are you suggesting?"

"Symin has networks throughout the cities, we already know this. If you can spare some of the household guard to help manage these refugees, I can see to it that Symin can provide somewhere for them to seek shelter. The man's a patriot, he'll help us."

Sarele looked torn between admiration for her son's initiative and its conflict with her own sense of self-preservation. Finally, she gave a curt nod.

"I'll see who I can spare, but you make sure you get Symin to agree first," Sarele answered before turning to Valeyn. "It would help if we understood when we could expect some more direct support from your father."

Valeyn rose to her feet, which were reassuringly steady after three days of unuse, and politely gestured them to the door. "You don't have to worry about that, Sarele. I intend to ask him that question right now."

Minutes later, Valeyn emerged from the Secret Paths and into the vast halls of Bythe's chambers. Striding past his catacombs of acquisitions, she marched down the polished marble steps and into the room where she had met with him. It was empty. Only the vast landscape of Obduratev lay out before her on the glass. The room was silent.

"Father!" her voice echoed around the cavernous space before silence flooded in once more.

"Bythe!" she screamed. "Where the hells are you?"

The light seemed to dim in the chamber and a low rumble replaced the echoes of her cry. The large doors at the far end of the room swung open and slammed violently against the white walls. Bythe marched forth and headed toward her with a speed that was startling. The dark god stopped inches from her face, which was turned up at him in a shield of anger and defiance.

"Take your helmet off and look at me!" Valeyn demanded.

She didn't even see his hand move as his armored gauntlet struck her across the face. Valeyn cried out and collapsed onto one knee. She hadn't felt such pain since before she had become a god, and yet she thought it was somehow fitting that only her father could hurt her now.

"Never speak to me in such a way," Bythe demanded.

Rage lingered behind his words and Valeyn felt fear. Pushing aside the need to apologize, to seek his forgiveness and approval, she instead wiped her mouth and looked at the blood smearing the back of her hand. Slowly rising, she thrust it at him.

"Is this how you express your love, Father? Is this what you want? My blood? Here, take it. Hurt me."

He caught the extended wrist in a painful grip, but she remained defiant, refusing to cry out.

"I want you to act appropriately. I want you to act like my daughter, capable of all things," he warned.

She tried to pull away, but his fist was like steel. Growling in anger, she let her rage push aside her fear and smashed against his wrist with her free hand, freeing herself from him. Bythe grunted in the first expression of weakness she had heard from her father, and his retaliation for such an expression was all the more terrible. She was suddenly unable to breathe, and it took Valeyn a moment to comprehend that her father had lifted her by the throat. The world then shook and she was lying against the far wall, Bythe slowly walking over to where he had apparently thrown her. She tried to summon the will to rise but her body wouldn't respond.

"I have killed gods for far less than what you have done to me here, girl. Do not test me," he said.

She pushed herself to her hands and knees and stayed there for a moment; exhausted and defeated. "What do you want from me?" she asked.

Bythe's mask looked down at her and for a moment, it seemed as if she could peer through the black eye-slits and sense the man beneath. "I want your obedience."

Valeyn tried to stifle a sob but failed. The single cry echoed across the room, mournful and pathetic. "You already have it. I would give you anything, can't you understand that?" she whispered

Bythe seemed to hesitate, as if completely unprepared for an assault of honesty. He stepped away from her and moved uncertainly to the massive window over his empire.

"I . . . no longer think as I once did. There are times when I . . . fear . . . that I am not the same god I once was."

The admission was unsettling to her. She slowly stood and wiped the blood from her hands. "Father, please. Talk to me."

Bythe was silent for a moment, when his words eventually came, they carried a softer edge.

"We all came to this place to learn something of ourselves. At least, that is how I remember it. And one by one, fell into madness. Most of my brethren desired to leave — they were ill suited to this place — but I chose to remain."

"Why?"

Bythe looked out the window and his response was slow, as if he struggled to recall. "I had created all of this — my empire. I could not abandon such perfection."

Valeyn walked over to stand next to him. "But there was more, wasn't there? You created your people."

"We all had a hand in creating the life on this world, but your mother and I took a particular interest in guiding the people we had made."

"You wanted them to live."

Bythe was quiet for a moment. "Yes. I remember. We did not want them to die. We did not want their lights to go out as if they had never existed. We wanted to lead them, to help them grow. I demanded . . . *we* demanded the others give us time to build this world into something that deserves existence"

Valeyn knew she had to tread very carefully. "And yet, it led to war. This can't have been what you wanted."

"Maelene would not see things correctly. The madness took hold of her too soon, and she strayed from the path of order into the wild recesses of her mind."

"I have met my mother, and I believe she simply saw the world in a different way than you."

"I once believed that . . . and yet I no longer feel that way. My mind has strengthened."

She placed a small hand on the immense arm of her father. It felt cold and hollow. "Father, do you see? The madness has influenced you as well. You pushed your view so intensely you led the people you swore to protect into war."

"War can breed strength. Strength is needed for children to survive. I know you understand this."

"Yes, but war can destroy and kill needlessly."

"You speak like the child you no longer are. War is a truth. There will always be conflict."

"But look at this." Without understanding how, she reached out with her *kai* and altered the image on the window. It changed to look out over the broken ruins of Stonekeep, then it swept to a scene of the town of Outpost, with its burnt-out buildings resembling the charred skeletons of human lives. "Look at what you've both done. This war has raged for too long. It's taken everything from me. It needs to end."

"That may be true, but it is now irrelevant. The war is all but over."

"The war is far from over, Father. Your forces . . ." She stopped and corrected herself. "*Our* forces are in retreat. Ferehain's weapons have taken a toll, and we've had to pull back. You're losing your grip on the Outer Wild. Don't you know this?"

"A trivial detail. The last remnants of Maelene's alliance will not reach these walls before the Desecration takes them. I have already won. Now, I am ready for this to end."

"End? But what about the people you wanted to guide? The war isn't over, Father. In fact, it's the opposite. Your war has escalated out of control. Ferehain has unlocked the secrets of The Tower. He was the one who collapsed Pientas. I think he has enough power to challenge even you."

She concentrated again and the image shifted to show a wall of white energy. It moved slowly along a wall of dark metal, twisting and dissolving the iron and stone wherever it touched. Soldiers positioned along the wall were fleeing before it's relentless onslaught. Some fired crossbows into the mass, but it was like shooting at floodwater and the missiles simply vanished into the dirty white light.

"This is the Shield. You constructed this to keep our enemies at bay. It took you centuries to build, and he's undoing it in a matter of hours. Look at what he's now capable of, Father" she said, but Bythe seemed unmoved.

"Maelene's lapdog secretly fears me with every fiber of his being. He may play tricks with our creations, but he will not attempt to claim the Ironhelm from me. You have nothing to fear from him while I am here."

The words were oddly comforting to her.

"I want to believe you, but he's growing more and more powerful. Everything is changing."

"Indeed," answered Bythe. "You are also changing. You are assimilating the *kai* of my brethren and wielding it instinctively. This is how you were able to transport yourself from Pientas. That act was impressive. Your potential could be unlimited, given enough time."

"Then grant me that time. Help me. If we stand together against the other gods, I could learn their gifts. I could counteract whatever Ferehain has done. I could even manipulate all the *kai* and stop the Desecration. Don't you see, Father? I could be the answer!"

"No." Bythe's judgment was sudden. "If you try such a thing, you will fail. Mark my prophecy, daughter; despite your growing power, Valeyn will never save this world."

"But he's tearing apart your empire. He's unravelling all of Kovalith. You've seen this. Why don't you stop it?" Valeyn asked

"I will not!" Bythe snapped in frustration and Valeyn recoiled. Bythe lifted his metal glove and it glowed with a dark, reddish hue. He seemed to stare at it for a moment before it gradually faded. "I dare not. I spent overmuch in my efforts to conquer your mother's lands and in my efforts to find you. I still have great power to defend myself, but there is . . . little else left to me now."

Valeyn no longer needed to try to read her father. It was as if she could now almost touch his mind. It was a storm, rising and falling like the eddies of wind, and yet she could feel the heart of his disquiet.

"The Godfire," she murmured. "The power at the heart of the war engines. That was your *kai*? You sacrificed it to build those terrible weapons?"

"I sacrificed the last of my essence to end this war. It cannot have been in vain now."

"You're dying."

"I can never die. I will never die. You see the world in such limited ways. I conserve the power I have left to sustain this form. I will see the end. I will stand at the Desecration and I will prevail before the others." His voice rose in pitch slightly, and Valeyn could now recognize the tinge of madness return to his speech. Her father was gone. There was now only a tyrant in his stead. She stepped back from him.

"Then why bring me here at all? Why didn't you just leave me in peace in the Fareaches?" she snapped.

"I do not know. Perhaps I yearned for you in a moment of weakness? Perhaps the madness did indeed touch me. But I am clear of mind today, and I have no need of you now!"

A bell rang in the distance and Valeyn snapped the window to again show the Ironhelm beneath them. Smoke was rising from the northwest corner of the city, and she willed the image to go there. The wide boulevard was littered with the bodies of dead Helmsguard as a shopfront burned. There was a glimpse of white in the street beyond, and an Imbatal's tall form came into view with an almost casual gait. Blood stained the pristine white of its robes but Valeyn knew that this was not from any injury it had sustained. It cast its blank face from side to side, searching for another victim.

"Look at this!" Valeyn pleaded. "Ferehain's killing our own people. Help me, Father. Make a stand for your followers. Come with me and fight for them!"

Bythe was silent for a long time as his black iron mask considered the white mask before him.

"No," he said at last. "I will not risk it. I must prevail in the end. I will stand above them when the time comes. I will not fail before them — not again."

She wasn't sure what he meant by his last statement, but she didn't have time to wonder. "So, you really don't care at all, do you?"

Bythe slowly turned his head and she felt the cold weight of his black stare. "Valeyn. I am not who you need me to be. I never have been."

Valeyn looked at him and felt tears starting to well. Turning her head, she fought back against them. She'd be damned if she was going to give him that victory too.

"Well, I'm sorry we disappoint each other," she grated the words and left the room as quickly as she could, deciding the tears wetting her cheeks were the last she'd shed for him.

CHAPTER 3

"After years of steady advancement through the Outer Wild, the collapse of the Helmsguard was as surprising as it was sudden. The unpredictable nature of Ferehain's attacks, combined with the eruptions of the ovoid across the western lands, sent the carefully organised structure of the Iron Union into disarray.

Bereft of their supply lines and with communication now sporadic at best, the various Helmsguard units found themselves isolated from central command and forced to respond to whichever threat was most imminent. Soldiers occupying the Federacy were forced to return to Hammerfall and contend with the panic caused by the dissolving lands of their countrymen. Units intended to reinforce the invaders were diverted to defend Greund and Rhaskitov after three separate attacks from the Imbatals. As panic beset the citizens of the Iron Union, the Helmsguard had no means, nor desire, to continue a war against the Outland Alliance. Indeed, the very foundations of the Iron Union were now threatened by the slow corrosion unleashed by Ferehain. And as the gods offered no absolution, despair gripped the people of the Iron Union."

~Kaler of the Ageless

Jason had never before seen the ramshackle town of Outpost, birthplace of his wife, but Nadine had spoken of it often. He knew it had never been a beautiful place, yet as he now walked through its streets, he could tell the past few years had taken an even greater toll. For every occupied house, the next two were empty, boarded up or falling into disrepair. Weeds choked the silent, rubbish-strewn alleys he passed, making the near-empty streets seem strangely festive by comparison. Their army had ridden into the town a few hours earlier, scattering the meager assortment of Helmsguard who had stayed behind to provide the illusion of a defense. It was the same pattern that the Outland Alliance had encountered for weeks; the Alliance would advance in greater and greater numbers, and the Union would evaporate before them. The celebration at this victory was far greater than any other – for the first time in years, the Helmsguard were no longer part of the Outer Wild. They had been driven out.

But Jason took no comfort from this apparent endorsement of his tactical brilliance. He knew that Zain was right; something was wrong within the Iron Union. He didn't know what it was, but the problem gnawed at him. He left the men to enjoy an hour of well-deserved entertainment and used the time to be alone with his thoughts.

"Why do you not celebrate with your men?" Romona asked as he walked. "Do you not wish to join in their happiness?"

"I don't share it," Jason snapped as he turned a corner and walked down another street which was depressingly identical to the others. He didn't know where he was going, but he knew he wanted to be alone. The slightly ethereal form of Romona followed at his side.

"You feel your work is not done?" she persisted.

"Of course my work isn't done. The people who did this to me are still out there. They still need to pay."

"You have beaten them. Is that not payment enough?"

"I haven't beaten them, something else did. I haven't had an impact."

"And so, it is not enough for your enemy to lose, you must be the one to have hurt them in some way. Is such a trivial detail really so important?"

Jason stopped and decided he'd had enough judgment

"Is this a limitation of the all-knowing gods? How can you not understand this? Justice isn't a *trivial detail*. I deserve this. They took *everything* from me!"

Romona smiled with a sense of immortal patience.

"Not everything. You still have much, if you had but the courage to recognize it."

Romona faded and beyond her, Jason saw a figure he instantly recognized. Long, blonde hair betrayed the identify of his wife. Yet the subtle tilt of her head and an indescribable shift of her posture were the telltale signs that only a husband would instinctively see – his wife was in tears. In that moment, his anger vanished, and the vulnerability of his wife consumed him.

The double-storied home of her childhood stood before her, abandoned and dilapidated by years of neglect. Its tiled roof had several holes and a crack ran down the front wall, threatening to cave the entire structure inward. The windows had been shattered from fire at some point, and the surrounding black smoke stains gave the impression of grieving eyes staring back at her in accusation. This place had seemed like a castle in her youth. Now it lay small and derelict, little more than a discarded memory.

He quietly walked over to Nadine and stood beside her as she stared at the house. She didn't turn her head as Jason approached, but he knew his wife sensed him.

"It's so small," she sniffed. "Far smaller than I remember."

"They always are," Jason said.

"This was supposed to be a good day. I thought this would be a glorious homecoming after so many years. But it isn't. I feel terrible. Why?"

Jason sighed and risked placing his hand on her shoulder, and when she didn't flinch, he squeezed it gently.

"You still miss him."

Nadine's lip quivered and she began to cry again. For a moment, she was like a girl, the small child who used to play in these rooms while the giant voice of her father echoed large through the cavernous house.

"It isn't fair. I still want him to be here," she said in a thick voice. "I hate them for what they've done to us. I hate them."

Jason extended his embrace and drew her into him.

"I know. I know," he whispered.

Although he felt the same, it somehow seemed wrong to admit it, to further indulge her black thoughts. They stood there for a few moments longer, each lingering in the comfort of the other's silence before the demands of their worlds would reach out and drag them back into a mass of noise, confusion, and pain. Eventually, she separated from him and they started skirting the perimeter of her old home, as if assessing it from a safe distance, but refusing to go in.

"I always thought that returning would make me feel better. When will it be enough?" she asked absently as they approached the rear of the house.

Jason said nothing. He knew that silence was best.

"I've finally done it. I've pushed them back and taken back my childhood, and for what? Look at it. My home is ruined. It's never coming back. He's never coming back. What do I do now?" She bowed her head as if to cry again, but this time she took a deep, steadying breath – not a quivering sob – and released it. "This darkness has got to end, Jason. It just can't sustain itself. We need to find a way to climb out of this pit or it's going to consume us both."

Jason turned away and walked over to rest his palm on the whitewashed stone of her home. It was once a proud structure, but it now stood fractured from time and abuse. He struggled for an answer, the rage, frustration, and guilt all mixing within him and stalling any articulation of his feelings.

"Jason," Nadine warned, and he turned instantly. She was pointing inside. "I saw something move. I think there's someone in there."

Jason drew his sword and motioned her behind him. "We haven't accounted for everyone yet, there are bound to be partisans hiding out." He moved toward the back entrance.

"What are you doing? Don't go in there alone. Call for a unit."

From nowhere, frustration surged through him. *Call for a unit? I'm so weak that even my wife thinks I can't even defend her home against some filthy vagrants?*

She said something else, but he couldn't hear her. His heart was racing and relived sensations flooded his mind. Thoughts of Captains Haft and Dagmar and the way they'd looked at him with contempt. The deep knowledge – the hard truth – that he'd never be as strong as Captain Lewis. These thoughts plagued him as he ventured into the dark of the house. Yet he didn't know why.

The room had once been a kitchen but now was barely recognizable as such. Dust and soil covered the rotten timber floorboards and beams of light illuminated patches while casting all else into a deeper gloom. Nadine's call for soldiers reached him, but she seemed a long way off. He scanned the room patiently, looking deep into the dark recesses of the corner. There was something in there. Abruptly, the darkness seemed to move. He looked up and realized he'd been looking at the folds of a deep emerald cloak, concealing a human shaped figure.

"Aleasea?" he asked.

He wasn't sure how he knew it was her, but he didn't doubt his instinct. Perhaps when he cast back her hood during their flight through Haere-Est, he'd learned to recognize her. But he knew she stood before him now, just as he also knew that something was very wrong.

"Aleasea?" he repeated. "Are you alright?"

Again, she didn't answer. Jason remembered the day he had broken that sacred law and dared to look at her face; she'd been injured and needed his help. If he hadn't acted, they might both have died. He stepped forward and carefully sheathed his sword.

"Aleasea. It's alright. You're safe now. Kaler is still with us. He can help you."

He thought he saw her head move but he couldn't be sure. He wasn't even completely sure it was her, but he needed to know. The Ageless were allies, and most of all, he needed to prove to everyone that he wasn't a coward. He had to prove it to himself. He edged across the kitchen slowly, until his hands were inches from the dark hood. It seemed to stare back at him with dejection and he was reminded for an instant of the first time Ferehain had stared at him in the alley.

Run, the feeling screamed at him.

Coward another screamed back.

He reached up and pulled at the green hood, breaking the spell of darkness and allowing Aleasea's deformed face to snap toward his. Jason cried out and stumbled back, tripping over something and landing on his rear in the dark. Aleasea continued to stare out blindly, her milky eyes moving slowly back and forth as if she wasn't sure he was there. Her once-beautiful, porcelain features were distorted grotesquely, her golden hair ragged and patched with white scalp visible everywhere.

"Jason!" Nadine's voice reached him, and he heard her footfalls approaching. He wanted to warn her but couldn't. He was frozen in horror.

Why?

Nadine's cry broke his terror and he looked up to see his shock mirrored on the face of his wife. She was staring at Aleasea with her hand raised to her own cheek in mirrored anguish, and Jason understood her expression wasn't fear, it was sympathy.

A laugh cracked his thoughts and Jason looked past his wife to the tall man in a black frock coat casually entering the kitchen behind her. He had never met Exedor, but somehow Jason recognized him on sight. Stories of Bythe's Royal Inquisitor had spread far, and yet, it was more than that. Jason looked into the dark eyes of the refined, middle-aged man and knew his name as if he'd spoken it. As if the mental abuse he'd just been enduring – all those insecure thoughts that had driven him inside – had left the Inquisitor's fingerprints on his mind.

"I take it you know each other," Exedor said without looking at Jason. Instead, he toured the kitchen as if inspecting it, disdain written clearly across his thin face. "Nadine, I have to admit, I'm a little disappointed. As the leader of the Outland Alliance, I knew you came from nobility. Well, nobility such as you define it in the Outer Wild, but even so, I expected the standards to be a little higher. Is this really the house you grew up in?"

Nadine glared but refused to indulge him with an answer.

"I understand it's seen better days," Exedor continued, "but still, I expected more than this. Now, your husband on the other hand . . . I'd not be surprised to learn *he* grew up here. But then, I'd not be surprised if he grew up in a pigpen. He is a soldier after all . . ."

"What are you doing here, Inquisitor?" snapped Nadine.

Exedor looked at her directly for the first time, smiling at her fire. "Allow me to correct you. My name is Exedor, formerly the High Constable and Royal Inquisitor to Lord Bythe the Immortal, currently rendering my services to . . . another employer. We haven't been formally introduced, although I've heard a lot about both of you. You may or may not have heard of me. It hardly matters. I think you have far more pressing questions on your mind right now."

"What have you done to Aleasea?" Jason asked through gritted teeth.

Exedor followed his glare to the wretched figure in the corner. She had retreated, as if confused and scared by the commotion around her. Exedor crossed the room and looked at her thoughtfully. "She was very beautiful, wasn't she? Believe me, I took no joy from this. Not like me at all. Perhaps

I'm getting sentimental with age, or perhaps experiencing death has brought about a change in me."

"You're an animal," spat Jason.

"Oh, it wasn't me," Exedor continued, never taking his eyes from Aleasea. "My employer is responsible for most of this, I simply added the finishing touches, under his instructions, of course."

Jason had heard enough. He wanted nothing more than to smash this man's arrogant smirk until it broke, along with the rest of his face.

"Jason, no!" Nadine shouted, but he wasn't listening. He was already on his feet and striding directly toward the thin man. Jason knew he could easily overpower him and when he did, this tough-talking bureaucrat would beg for forgiveness over what he'd done.

But Exedor glanced at him and Jason noticed the man's dark eyes were now a strange shade of red. In an instant, his confidence bottomed out like water rushing out of a shattered bucket. He stumbled and sank to his knees, fear and uncertainty crippling him.

"I have been given a unique gift, Captain Jason. I can see weakness in people. For instance, I can see your uncertainty, your guilt; weaknesses that undermine your own confidence and capability, and ironically, reinforce themselves as a result. You almost reek of it."

He looked down at Jason, tilting his head with curiosity. "I was born with that ability. To be honest, it always confounded me that others couldn't see what I could. It allowed me to cultivate a fair amount of influence within the Royal Court of the Ironhelm. But it was Lord Bythe who recognized this gift and weaponised it."

Nadine carefully stepped between them. "Leave him alone."

Exedor laughed. "And now his wife comes to his rescue? I see where his lack of self-confidence comes from."

"I'm not afraid of you, Inquisitor," Nadine snapped.

"No, you're not. You're a strong one, I grant you that. You fear no man," Exedor agreed, turning his glowing eyes onto her. "But you're afraid of yourself. You're afraid of who you might become without your father to guide you. You actually thought you could save him by remaking yourself in his image, which would mean those who killed him had failed."

Tears began to well in Nadine's eyes. "Stop."

But Exedor was merciless. "Don't you see? This is a deception. He's dead and you are not him. He's never coming back, and there's nothing you can do to change that. You can't mitigate it or compensate for it in any way. He is simply gone!"

"Stop!" she cried and sank to her knees beside her husband. Jason put his arm around her, as if he could shield her from the pain she inflicted on herself.

Exedor looked over the two broken people and yet, his face was devoid of victory. He considered them for a moment, then lowered himself to a crouch, viewing them levelly as his red eyes returned to a natural dark-brown.

"You both need to overcome this. There is far too much at stake now. Valeyn needs you," said Exedor.

Jason thought he'd misheard the sentence and looked at Exedor with genuine confusion. Exedor returned the expression with a frustrated glare.

"I don't have time to walk you through this. I've already tarried here too long. Valeyn should never have returned to the Ironhelm. She's walked into a trap."

Jason's jaw clenched. "What have you done?"

"Again, you lay the evils of the world at my feet. No, I haven't set a trap for her. Yet it seems I'm probably the only one who hasn't. She has no idea of the danger she's in."

"Valeyn can take care of herself," said Jason.

"Not from this. She should never have turned her back on Ferehain. That madman's ambitions will be the end of us all, and even those I once called allies are blind to this. I have no love of the gods, but it seems I'm now forced to plan a very dangerous move."

"Ferehain is one of us," said Nadine.

"Ferehain has done this," Exedor snapped, pointing at Aleasea. "He is no longer your ally, and he has become far too powerful for anyone to oppose, even Valeyn. I have been enjoying his hospitality of late, and you can believe me, he has changed considerably. Bythe is still the only one he fears, but I worry that restraint will soon be removed."

"I don't think I'll take you word on anything, Inquisitor," Nadine replied. "I have no doubt that you're only here to send us into a trap."

"Ferehain means to rip the Iron Union apart, but in doing so, he will destroy all of Kovalith. He is as mad as the gods he claims to oppose. The Iron Union is going to fall, and Valeyn will need you."

"Valeyn left us to be with the murderer of our child," Nadine shouted.

Jason closed his eyes as her words resurrected painful memories. "She told me she was going to the Ironhelm to confront Bythe. She's going to end this, Nadine."

"Is she? How do we know she isn't helping Bythe?" she retorted.

"Something's wrong with the Helmsguard, we both know that. Our victories have been too easy. If Valeyn had joined Bythe and set her powers against us, then I don't think we'd have gotten out of Roy. No, something's wrong, and whatever it is, it's turned Bythe's attention away from us."

"Valeyn is going to need help," Exedor interrupted. "This entire world is being remade and whether you like it or not, you are both connected to the events that are about to unfold. Your choices – your action or inaction – will have an impact either way."

"I'm sure Bythe can help Valeyn better than we can," said Jason.

"I suspect Bythe is dead, or if not, he soon will be. Valeyn will take up the throne, but she will find the Iron Union is no friend. As I said earlier, there are many plotting against her."

"You mean your allies, the Prodigals? You want us to help Valeyn fight against your allies?" said Nadine.

Exedor inclined his head.

"You expect us to believe you're working against your friends and not simply sending us into a trap? I thought you hated the gods. Why do you now want us to help one?" Jason asked.

Exedor smiled ruefully. "I agree it is ironic that we have been placed in this position. Perhaps there is a way for each of us to achieve our goals, but the chance is narrow and the risk is immense. And I must be clear; you will despise the path I send you down."

Jason was taken aback by the honest admission and for a moment, he wondered if there was some truth to what he was hearing. "And what path is that?"

"I have been tasked with the job of raiding Ironhelm targets to sow terror and despair within the Iron Union. I deliberately chose to attack Krag and the surrounding military installations around the Shield. I have done this so you might have a clear path into the heart of the Iron Union. If you strike out quickly and seize Krag, I can guarantee you will then have an opportunity to strike into the very heart of the Ironhelm. But you must act now. Timing is crucial."

As if reading Jason's mind, Nadine intervened. "Don't be absurd. I don't believe you, and I certainly won't follow your advice. If you've come here to kill us, then just do it, but I'm not going to be manipulated into leading more of our people to their deaths."

"Please, give me some credit. I don't expect you to believe me, and I certainly wouldn't have believed *you* if you told me you did. I came here to tell you what you need to do. The motivation to do so will be quite different."

Approaching footfalls sounded from beyond the kitchen window. Exedor looked out at the sound with curiosity, his brow slightly furrowed, before glancing at Aleasea and then nodding as if they were part of an unheard conversation. He looked around the darkened room, staring past Jason and Nadine, searching the shadows for something else.

"Of course, I should have known one Ageless would be drawn by the presence of another," Exedor said to the darkness.

The purple-robed form of Kaler emerged from the darkness and moved to stand between Exedor and the two figures on the floor. "I do not know what you have done to Aleasea, but I can promise you that you will not leave here alive."

"Be careful, Kaler," Jason warned. "He has . . . tricks."

"I can sense the stain of Bythe throughout him and while he might find a way to best me, even an Inquisitor cannot stand against the entire unit of soldiers outside. There is no escape."

Exedor nodded. "You are quite correct, Ageless. One Inquisitor cannot possibly overcome dozens of armed soldiers, along with a member of the Violari. I have been sent on a mission by your old master, Ferehain."

Kaler's stoic features remained unmoved, but Jason caught a flicker of emotion, and Exedor clearly sensed it.

"That's right. You're almost as farsighted as he is. He has this somewhat annoying ability to scry things from afar. In fact, there's every chance he is sensing what I'm doing even now, which is why I'm out of time," said Exedor.

"I thought you said that Ferehain sent you here," said Jason.

"Not here, specifically. He certainly wouldn't approve of the conversation I just had with you, which is why I have to eradicate all traces of it. Fortunately, the work he has set for me does exactly that."

"Stop speaking in riddles," snapped Nadine.

"Ferehain also ordered me to start spreading the chaos that has been infecting the Iron Union beyond its borders. I chose to use this opportunity to meet with you, but unfortunately it also means that your old hometown must now become my target. I cannot leave any trace for him to detect. And I certainly cannot leave this place unharmed."

"You are not leaving," Kaler stated in a matter-of-fact tone.

Exedor smiled. "As I said earlier, one Inquisitor cannot stand against you all, but I'm afraid you're facing more than just one Inquisitor."

He gestured and the green-robed figure of Aleasea abruptly lurched forward.

"Aleasea. Can you hear me? asked Kaler, but she gave no response. Instead, she shuffled awkwardly to stand next to Exedor, her vacant eyes scanning the room but acknowledging nothing.

"Aleasea, look at me," Kaler demanded.

"And now you begin to comprehend your dilemma, Ageless," said Exedor. "I didn't know the truth about her at first, but I'm guessing that you do."

"Aleasea," Jason called, adding his voice to Kaler's appeal, but it was equally futile.

"Had I known, back when we were in the Render, that I had the most powerful of the Ageless under my control, things might have gone differently. Ferehain, on the other hand, was armed with knowledge greater than mine, and he certainly didn't waste the opportunity."

Exedor nodded at Aleasea and Jason felt an odd sensation, like an unseen blanket had been wrapped around him. He had a sudden urge to move but found he couldn't. Panic gripped him momentarily as he fought against the unseen force. Forcing himself to calm, he noticed that Nadine and Kaler were also completely still, and that only Exedor and Aleasea were moving. Jason's mind flicked back to Fairhaven, when he had fought alongside Aleasea against Imbatal, and he remembered her unique ability to manipulate the flow of time to slow her enemy. Yet that act seemed almost trivial compared to this display of power. Exedor gestured at the kitchen wall and Aleasea turned to head toward it. Within seconds, the stones crumbled, as if worn by a thousand years, and light flooded into the kitchen.

"A little dramatic, I admit," said Exedor, he led Aleasea out into the yard, "however I need you to appreciate the situation you're in, so please, indulge me."

At least two dozen soldiers were waiting outside, and Jason silently willed them to strike Exedor down, but they didn't. In fact, none of them moved.

They can't move.

A creeping horror inched into his stomach as he began to comprehend what Exedor meant. Something had been done to Aleasea. She was displaying a level of power he had never seen, and Exedor's gifts were somehow enabling him to wield it.

Exedor and Aleasea moved to the center of the overgrown yard and paused. The Inquisitor cast his eyes over the tableau of frozen soldiers and smiled, glancing back at those within the house.

"Impressive, isn't she? But this isn't what you have to fear. Ferehain is going to rip Kovalith to pieces and the only resistance against him will be Valeyn. But she is also going to fall before him, that is certain. You will be her only hope, as well as ours."

Exedor glanced at Aleasea and another unspoken command passed between them. She walked clear of him and stood alone. For a moment, she simply remained there, staring at the ground in silence, then without warning, she threw her head back and cried out. The agonising sound rose in pitch and filled Jason with a sense of despair. Even Exedor took a step back. Jason noticed the man's cool exterior seem somehow fractured, and a strange expression lay on his face as he glanced away from Aleasea's torment.

She fell to her knees as if wracked by some deep, internal agony. Placing her palms on the ground to steady herself, Jason first thought she was going to be sick, but wisps of steam began to rise from the dirt under her touch, and he saw the soil was bubbling. A single ray of bright light shot up from the ground, and the unnatural sensation in Jason's gut grew stronger. He knew he was witnessing something perverse; a corruption not just of Aleasea, but of the land itself. The splinter of light was joined by another, then a third, and within a minute, a dozen strands of dirty light were polluting the air in a shimmering haze. Aleasea was swaying on the ground, dangerously close to the light and it seemed as if she were leaning toward it, perhaps willing herself to topple in. At that moment, Exedor moved quickly to pull her to her feet, guiding her almost gently away from the danger. He leaned in to speak quietly into her ear, and an instant later they vanished from sight.

As soon as they left, Jason was able to move again. Chaos erupted as the dozens of soldiers were also freed to react to what they'd witnessed. Only Kaler remained still, but his eyes were fixed on the light before them, disbelief written on his youthful face. The dozen streams of light began to coalesce into one solid band, causing it to begin its inexorable growth, slowly dissolving the existence around it. Several soldiers were approaching the light with weapons drawn and Kaler reacted swiftly.

"Captain, order everyone back. Evacuate this entire area," the Ageless commanded.

Jason heard the fear in Kaler's voice and it made him obey without question. He shouted commands and his men fell back to the end of the street. The pulsing light seemed to silently mock their retreat.

"What am I looking at, Kaler?" Jason asked.

"Summon Warmaster Zain. We must take counsel immediately. It appears the Inquisitor was not lying about the peril facing this world." Kaler answered, his eyes fixed on the scene before him. "We now must determine the truth of the rest of his warning."

•　　•　　•

The street was filled with rubble. Chunks of black rock from the surrounding buildings were scattered over the once-pristine boulevard, the structures themselves now lurched awkwardly skyward like broken monuments. Countless bodies lay among the ruins; most of them were Ironhelm soldiers, broken forms lying at unnatural angles, but there were civilians among the dead. Innocents. Valeyn had lost count of the number of times she'd sworn vengeance. She took a breath and adjusted the emerald plates on her armor, carefully tightening straps which had worked loose and realigning the greaves on her legs. The ritual was a routine one, ingrained in every solider from their youngest age to ensure they were always protected, and yet it had always served to soothe her mind.

This was the fifth attack in two days. Ferehain had increased the frequency and ferocity of his assaults to the point where he clearly felt confident enough to strike the Ironhelm at any time. The Helmsguard were now on constant alert and the cities locked down. A permanent haze of smoke lay over Obduratev like a shroud of mourning, as Ferehain's unrelenting attacks left the city constantly ablaze somewhere. She hadn't slept in days and exhaustion now eroded her strength. Even the new power gained by the presence of the gods hadn't been enough to sustain her. Of course, this was his strategy; by attacking the city, he attacked her. And Ferehain now assailed Valeyn without respite.

She completed her ritual and glanced over her shoulder at the soldiers running up the boulevard. Within moments, Ethan was at her side, assessing the slaughter with identical dismay.

"My gods," Ethan murmured.

Valeyn didn't answer. She wondered where the gods were among all of this. Were they watching from above, smiling at the pure insanity unfolding beneath them, smug and content that their preconceived conceits were now proven true? A crack rent the air and a fresh cloud of smoke rose behind the buildings to their left. Valeyn drew her sabre.

"Wait for us, Valeyn," Ethan said, placing a hand on her arm.

She refused to take her eyes from the column of rising smoke. How many people were dying in that moment? How many daughters were being slaughtered before the horrified faces of parents while she waited and thought and strategized.

"No," was all she said before she was gone, clearing the rubble-strewn street within seconds and racing toward the fire. She turned off the boulevard and into a side alley from where the smoke rose. A store was burning, and the body of a middle-aged shopkeeper lay on the road, blood running through the cobblestones under her feet.

Tick. Tock.

The murderous synchronicity of a clockwork heart defiled her ears. An expressionless white mask considered her as fresh blood ran from the blade on its arm. Valeyn acted. She flew at the creature with her sabre. The

Imbatal backpedalled and raised its blades in defense, parrying her blows with an efficiency she hadn't anticipated. It deflected her last strike with its left forearm, then swung a vicious counter blow at her head with its right arm. The blade screamed straight at her forehead and she barely moved aside in time. She felt blood running over her left eye from the gash it had made. She was momentarily stunned. How had Ferehain managed to increase the speed of these creatures since their last battle? Then the obvious realization dawned on her.

They're not moving faster. I'm slowing down.

"That is correct," said Ferehain as if he had read her thoughts. He was standing above her, almost casually, on a stone balcony overlooking the alley. His long black cloak billowed in the still air and his hood was removed, revealing a face devoid of emotion.

Before she could respond, the Imbatal seemed to detect her distraction and turned the situation to its advantage, rushing at her in a flurry of strikes. Valeyn was now the one to backpedal, furiously deflecting the blades, each strike coming quicker than the one before.

"Your own clockwork heart is slowly running down, as cold and as artificial as theirs. And the gods will not save you." Ferehain's voice drifted down to her as she fought for her life.

Valeyn missed the next strike and it deflected off her green pauldron, which mercifully held. "Ironic, I would think," continued Ferehain in an almost disinterested tone, as if he were a detached teacher lecturing a class. "But then again, perhaps not. After all, you were the one who defeated Imbatal by wearing him down. I now simply use your own strategy against you."

Forcing every fiber of her will to the fore, she focused on the machine before her and willed the metallic components into entropy. It fought her but she pushed back, crying out at the effort until the satisfying sound of failing gears reached her. The Imbatal voiced its unnatural death rattle as she viciously swung her blade and severed its head.

Breathing hard, she wiped at the blood running over her left eye and glared up at Ferehain, preparing to launch herself at him without another word.

Tick Tock.

A second Imbatal appeared further down the alley and a terrible scream rang out; a woman's scream filled with primal grief. A third creature could now be seen behind the other, cutting away at something, blood staining its white robes. Exhaustion flooded Valeyn but she pushed it away. There was no choice. She gave Ferehain a final, murderous glance, then leaped down the alley toward the creature. Ferehain didn't react.

She reached the first Imbatal and resumed the same dance. Valeyn slashed at the creature, who parried her blows before returning in equal measure. She knew she was weakening, and for the first time in years, knew that the possibility of death was very real.

But can you truly die now? Your power grows in the presence of your kin, why do you not embrace all you can be?

The unknown voice invaded her mind. Or was it her own voice? Was this more of the madness? She tried reaching for the Etherian's power but didn't know where it lay or how to wield it. Her actions at Pientas had been instinctive, but now whenever she tried to recall the new *kai*, it felt like something was wrong. She deflected the Imbatal's blades and thought of Shin dying before her.

But will you take your place in the Etherian like Shin, or will the chains of Kovalith pull you down? You are born of this world, your fates are inseparable.

She ran at the Imbatal, shouldering it in the chest and sending them both crashing into the dirt like felled trees. Rolling on top of the demon, she smashed at it with her bare fists, breaking up the metal plates and gears beneath her. It also grated like the first, then fell still.

The next Imbatal, seemingly sensing the demise of its comrade, ceased its slaughter and turned slowly in her direction.

Tick. Tock.

Yet another Imbatal stepped out of the burning store behind her and Valeyn's head swam for a moment.

You can't do this, can you? This may be the end. How does it feel to finally confront death, Valeyn?

She rose and collected her sabre, holding it unsteadily as the two remaining creatures advanced at her from opposite sides. They paused as the sound of pounding feet reached them, and both creatures turned to appraise Ethan's men as they poured into the alley. Valeyn swore under her breath and attacked the Imbatal ahead of her, knowing the other at her back could be dealt with by Ethan's men. Her vision blurred as she spent her last efforts to destroy this latest threat. The cries of men dying sounded distant behind her, and she listened for Ethan's voice, hoping he wasn't among the casualties. She knew there was something familiar tugging at the edge of her mind, but she couldn't place it.

"No!" Ethan cried and Valeyn spun. Fear gripped her throat and she expected to find him lying bleeding at the foot of an Imbatal, but he wasn't. He was staring at something in the ruins; at the strangely familiar rubble, at the rubble of Archeuim Parade, at the bodies of Martya and her son.

Ethan shouted something inarticulate as he stumbled toward the two corpses, seemingly oblivious to the danger around him, and for an instant, Valeyn remembered Leon. Pain spiked in her back and she fell to her knees, knowing the Imbatal had stabbed her from behind; but strangely, it now seemed irrelevant. Ethan stood before her, his face a portrait of pure misery as he cradled the dead child. Behind him, the last of the Helmsguard were brutally dispatched by the second Imbatal, and Valeyn now waited quietly for the end.

"Wait." Ferehain's command barely carried over the noise, yet both of the Imbatals obeyed instantly.

He walked across the alleyway, stepping over the bodies of the Helmsguard and letting his black cloak trail over their corpses. Finally, he stood over Valeyn and looked down at her with his constant, impassive stare.

"We knew it would one day come to this, did we not? On that very first day I beheld you following me down an alley like this one, I knew I should have ended your life at that moment." Ferehain lowered himself into a crouch so their faces were level. "Did you know I felt that instinct? On that day, where we first looked at each other, I somehow knew, even then, that you should not live. I had the sudden impulse to kill you and your friend, Jason, as you both cowered before me. It would have been so easy, and I could have averted so much pain." He offered her a cold smile then stood. "But I doubted my own wisdom. I had listened to the counsel of Aleasea and allowed sentiment to weaken my resolve. I told myself that it was discipline that stayed my hand, but it was not, it was weakness. I was indecisive and you were allowed to live, to grow in power and to poison us all."

"Ferehain, we were allies. I saved you from Exedor. You're distorting the truth."

"No, we were never allies. It is true that I put myself into positions of weakness, but I see now that this was your doing. I allowed you to lead us into the Render. I allowed myself to be influenced by Aleasea out of sentiment. Had I listened to my own counsel from the start, none of those events would have transpired. I hated you from the first moment I saw you, and I was a fool to ever ignore that truth. I turned my back on you, and look where this has ultimately led us."

"Why, Ferehain?" she whispered. "Why kill these people? Kill me, if you have to, but why kill innocents?"

"There are no innocents, Elyn. You know this. These people chose to follow your father. They still serve him and defend him and kill in his name."

"And what about them?" Valeyn cried, pointing to Ethan as he wept over the bodies of Martya and her son. "Do you now take pleasure in the murder of children?"

"I no longer take pleasure from anything. You have driven the last vestiges of such feelings from me, and there is only hatred left. You and your father have taken everything, and now you both know what it is like to have everything taken from you."

"I've already lost everything, you arrogant bastard! You didn't need to do this to Ethan!"

"Your lover made his choice, serving both your father and you. He must now pay the price for his decisions. Those who continue to serve the gods will not be forgiven or excused."

Valeyn shook her head with a sense of resigned disbelief. "You've become a monster."

Ferehain looked down at her with a flash of puzzlement. "As have you, Elyn. As have all gods. I am simply returning your behaviour in equal measure, holding it up for you to see. Your outrage at this treatment is all the justification I sought."

"You're wrong," Valeyn muttered and shook her head, but her words sounded like defeat and Ferehain recognized the surrender.

"No. I am right, and your death proves it. I admit, this is more satisfying than I could have expected. You always took pride in your friends, flouting this as some kind of evidence of your virtue. Well, my dear Elyn, where were they when you needed them in the end?"

Valeyn lowered her head and closed her eyes. She was tired of everything and now she just wanted it all to end. The air grew cold and a low rumble reverberated in her ears.

Is this death?

The rumble grew louder and Valeyn opened her eyes to behold a sight she'd never seen before. The alley was growing dark. Ferehain was looking at something behind her, and his expression fixed in a rictus of pure, irrational terror.

"Unhand my daughter."

Bythe's command boomed through the alley like a tangible force, and Ferehain stumbled back. Valeyn turned to see the massive frame of her father striding up the alleyway. The Imbatal that had stabbed Valeyn instantly turned and leaped at Bythe, both blades extended toward the new threat. Bythe didn't break stride as he swung his massive iron hammer, swatting aside the Imbatal as if it were an insect and smashing it into dozens of pieces.

Ferehain shouted a command and the remaining Imbatal stepped forward, cautiously assessing the incoming force, but it looked like a rabbit pondering an avalanche, and Bythe swung his hammer a second time to send the demon to oblivion.

Bythe advanced on Ferehain, who was retreating toward the entrance of the alleyway.

"Face me, coward!" Bythe commanded, and Valeyn felt terror at the pure fury in his voice.

Ferehain looked about frantically, then made a series of gestures.

Tick, Tock.

One by one, a dozen Imbatals appeared on the rooftops above them, and Valeyn dimly understood the magnitude of the perfect trap Ferehain had set for her. She was never meant to leave the alley. The Imbatals leaped from the roof, directly pouncing on her father and preventing him from closing the gap on Ferehain. For a moment, Bythe's black armor vanished under a mountain of white and Valeyn could only watch as her father was overwhelmed. Valeyn willed herself to her feet and took an unsteady step toward the mass of clockwork machinery, trying to understand what she could do, knowing she had to try something. An Imbatal flew from the tumult and rolled across the cobblestones, followed by another. A black shape rose in the midst of the white, and the Imbatals seemed to drip away from Bythe like melting snow. His red kai burned with a searing intensity and to Valeyn's eyes, he looked consumed by a towering pyre. With a growl of rage, he swung both fists in a fury, smashing at the figures around him and breaking them as if they were dolls. Within a dozen seconds, there were only five of the creatures left, and they were now retreating cautiously before the mad god's onslaught.

Bythe turned his unseen face to them and all five of the creatures stopped, their clockwork hearts frozen. Valeyn could sense a perverse satisfaction from her father as the creatures grated and squealed horribly at the trauma wracking their unnatural bodies. They seemed to collapse inward, and all fell in a pool of thick, yellowish liquid pouring from their own wreckage.

Bythe surveyed the alley, seemingly looking for Ferehain but he was gone. Then his black eyes fell upon her and they looked at each other in silence for a moment.

"Are you harmed?" Bythe finally asked.

Valeyn was momentarily stunned by the question. "I ... I'm alright. But what about you?"

Bythe didn't answer. Instead, he scanned the alley, and Valeyn could see the red *kai* slowly receding into his black form.

"Maelene's disciple has fled," he finally replied. "As I said, he is weak. He does not possess your strength. You must remember this."

"Thank you ... for saving me."

Valeyn wasn't sure if he heard her. He was slowly looking about as if his gaze were penetrating the walls around them. A noise behind Valeyn reminded her of Ethan. She turned to watch him lifting the body of Jaymet, his face devoid of expression. In that moment, she truly saw him for the first time — not a nobleman or a soldier, but a man who had lost a surrogate child. Just as Elyn had lost her father in the street so many years earlier. She wanted nothing more than to reach out to him, to hold him and give him the support he desperately needed in that moment.

"Valeyn. Come. I need you."

Bythe's voice jolted her, and she turned back to her father as if commanded.

"The Ironhelm will be safe, for a time, but you must come with me," Bythe instructed.

Valeyn looked again to Ethan but he was moving away from her, cradling the body of the young boy carefully in his arms as if he were afraid to wake him.

"Give me a moment, please," she asked.

"Your companion and your compassion must wait. Your place is with me. I ask that you trust me."

Valeyn had never before felt such conflict. The ache of Vale's unmet needs against the unreconciled pain of Elyn's suffering. For a moment, she wished she were two people again, she wished Valeyn never existed.

"Forgive me, Ethan," she said, as she turned to follow her father.

Ethan didn't respond.

CHAPTER 4

"The tragedy of Aleasea is a tale rarely told among the Ageless. Among the first and the most gifted of Maelene's creations, Aleasea quickly established a deep empathy with the lands and people of Kovalith. Her desire to understand the world swiftly granted her an immense knowledge of the natural laws that governed it. Of all her interests, it was human life that excited her above all others, and she found this passion mirrored in Ferehain, another of Maelene's first generation of Ageless. Together, they studied all facets of human existence, and the emotions that underpinned them. After unsuccessfully petitioning Maelene for the right to create a child, they nonetheless decided to proceed in secret. And while the birth of their daughter was hailed as miraculous, Maelene only wept upon hearing the news. For as she had predicted, her Ageless could not sustain life of their own, and the young daughter of Maelene and Ferehain quickly grew ill and died. To spare her Ageless any more grief, Maelene removed some of their gifts, including any ability to create life. For Aleasea, her mind was altered so that she forgot how to influence the natural laws of Kovalith, although shadows of these abilities still remained.

While Ferehain fell into a depression from which he never fully recovered, Aleasea chose to press aside all who had wronged her and renewed her love of the people of the world.

It is said that Aleasea's compassion was her greatest strength, however it was a strength that could easily be turned against her by someone now totally devoid of empathy."

A circular cordon of soldiers had been formed roughly fifty yards away from the light, but Jason remained inside, along with Nadine and Kaler. Warmaster Zain strode through the lines and paused only briefly to consider the scene, before approaching them. For a moment, all four stood in silence, watching the light almost with admiration. It was growing and had begun to slowly dissolve Nadine's childhood home. They watched the roof tiles corrode into dust as the light touched them. Brick by brick, the house began to topple, and the potential of this destruction was understood by the witnesses.

"What is this?" Zain finally asked.

"This is named the *ovoid.* It is the tear of existence, the very absence of *kai,*" answered Kaler. "This is what is left when the power of the gods is removed from our land. It is a self-feeding, self-sustaining corrosion, that will release the *kai* binding Kovalith and in doing so, destroy all it touches."

"And how do we stop it?" asked Zain.

"I do not know," replied Kaler. "I fear it cannot be stopped. Kovalith is an unnatural creation. The *kai* is the life force of the gods that sustains it. The *ovoid* is not actually something to be stopped. It is, in fact, an absence of anything."

"And how do you stop nothing?" Jason asked quietly.

"I don't accept this," said Nadine. "How can our existence be so fragile? There must be a way to counteract this. If Aleasea can do this, then someone must be able to undo it."

"I have never before seen anything like this. This is power on the scale of the gods. No Ageless has ever had this level of skill, not even Aleasea. I cannot understand how this is possible," said Kaler.

"Ferehain," said Nadine. "He went into the Render and something's happened to him. He's found an army of Imbatals, and he's done something to Aleasea."

Jason turned to Kaler. "You knew him. You were his protégé. Can he do this?"

Kaler was silent for a long time, and Jason knew he was debating the extent of his answer. Years earlier, Jason would have been punished for asking such a question – possibly even executed – but now the Ageless were a spent force, and secrets seemed a meaningless indulgence. Finally, Kaler sighed, and it sounded like a surrender.

"We knew of The Tower, deep within the Render. This was thought to be the most powerful Construct created by the gods and one integral to the creation of all of Kovalith. If Valeyn took Ferehain there, then he might have access to the knowledge with which the world was made and so could be unmade."

"Exedor said Valeyn didn't keep an eye on Ferehain," said Jason.

Kaler nodded grimly. "And that would explain what we are witnessing."

Nadine rounded on Kaler. "How could Valeyn let this happen? She's meant to be stronger than Ferehain. Why would she leave so much power in his hands?"

"It's my fault," Jason said quietly. It all made sense now. "Valeyn saw that I was going to die back in Fairhaven. She knew I . . ." He paused, as if unsure he should voice his weakness. "She could see I wanted to die. She used The Tower to intervene, but she was alone when she came to us. She must have left Aleasea and Ferehain behind, and Ferehain took advantage of the opportunity."

Nadine stared at him for a moment, but he couldn't meet her gaze.

"This is not your doing, Jason," Kaler interrupted. "Nor is it the fault of Valeyn. Ferehain is responsible for his own actions. His views became increasingly severe after we lost Maelene, and still we followed his teachings. He was a strong leader in times of war and there were many of us who believed he should have led us in favor of Veroulle. But his actions after the Temple's destruction were a sign we should have heeded. His taking of black robes, a warning we should not have ignored. It pains me deeply to admit this — he was as a father to me once, but deep in my heart, I know he has fallen just as I know we are witnessing the fruits of his madness."

"Can you stop him?" asked Zain.

"He wields the power of gods now. If even Aleasea could not stop him, then I hold as much chance as you."

"And so, it seems we have our explanation as to what plagues the Iron Union," muttered Zain. "An attack from Imbatals and this sorcery? It's little wonder they can't stand against us."

The last traces of Nadine's home collapsed inward and a nervous buzz rose from the surrounding soldiers. The column of light was stronger now and growing slightly faster.

"And Ferehain is now going to unleash this weapon upon us? Why?" asked Nadine.

Kaler shrugged. "There will be a logic beneath his madness, but I cannot guess what it might be."

"Exedor says we need to go to Valeyn," said Jason.

"Exedor is a liar," replied Nadine. "It's far more likely his real plot is to lure us into a trap."

"Liar or not, this power is very real," said Kaler, staring fixedly at the light, "and if Exedor can wield it as we have just seen, then nobody is truly safe."

"What about Bythe?" asked Zain.

"Exedor seems to think Bythe is dead, or soon will be," answered Jason. "Valeyn might have overthrown him. Or maybe Ferehain has. Either way, we know the Helmsguard are in trouble, and this makes me believe that Bythe is also."

Zain nodded. "So it seems this Ferehain is now our real concern. But we are not his enemy. I see no reason to take any action."

"You'll feel differently once one of these appears in Marfort," said Jason, nodding at the *ovoid*.

Zain shrugged. "Then let us deal with that if it happens, not before."

"And what if this was our only chance to deal with it? What if later is too late?" said Jason.

Zain looked at Jason but didn't answer. Jason realized he'd never seen the Warmaster unsure of himself before.

"Valeyn would be the only force capable of stopping Ferehain. It does make sense for us to help her if we can," said Kaler.

"It could also be a trap," repeated Nadine.

"Indeed, that is a very real possibility," Kaler agreed. "But I believe it is a greater risk to refuse to aid her. For if Valeyn falls and Ferehain is supreme, then there is truly no hope left."

There was silence as the group digested the grim but unassailable logic.

"I believe I should go to her," Kaler said at last. "My skills will be of use."

"No," said Jason. He'd made his decision. "Exedor said Valeyn would need her friends. I don't think this is about power, it's about something else. If somebody needs to go, then it should be me."

"Regardless, I could help," Kaler said, sounding offended.

Jason smiled and placed a hand on Kaler's shoulder. "If this is a fool's errand, then let me be the one to suffer it. You'd be putting yourself in danger for no good reason. Stay. Your skills are needed here as well."

Nadine turned to her husband with a strange expression on her face, as if she were caught between an argument and an embrace. "Jason, no. If Valeyn needs you, why hasn't she sent word?"

Jason shrugged. "Maybe she can't? Maybe she's been captured? I don't know."

"Or maybe she's sitting on the throne alongside her father and laughing with Ethan over what they've done to us. Maybe this is just the final insult, a trap to bring you before them so they can rub your nose in it."

The venom behind her words surprised Jason. He stepped closer and saw the tears betraying her stern expression. "I know you don't mean that. You love Valeyn."

"No, I loved *Elyn*!" Nadine cried, thumping Jason's chest. "She was sweet and caring and kind. I don't know Valeyn. I definitely don't see Elyn in her."

"I'm not sure Elyn would recognize you either. You're hurt. You remind me of Elyn after Leon died."

It was a risky thing to say, but it was the truth and had to be spoken. Nadine looked at him silently for a moment.

"Maybe you're right. None of us are who we used to be. Maybe we're all just supposed to end badly. I hate Ethan, and I think I hate her," she said.

Jason embraced his wife and she didn't resist, sobbing deeply as the months of guilt and rage now poured out.

"And now she's going to take you from me," Nadine's muffled voice came from his chest and Jason felt tears dampen his own cheeks. He didn't know what to say. A hollow reassurance would be a lie, and he wasn't going to let a lie violate the first truth they'd shared in months.

Kaler stepped forward and looked at them both. "Very few people have the strength to hold true to themselves in the face of despair, and there is no shame in surrendering to it. But those who can defy grief are the ones who can bring hope to their world. My heart tells me this is the very support Valeyn will need." He paused for a moment, clearly hesitating over his next words before finally diving ahead. "I cannot withhold this counsel; my instinct tells me that Elyn will need both of her childhood friends. I do not trust Exedor's motives, but I still believe his advice is sound."

Nadine nodded, wiping her eyes. "I know," she said. "Which is why I'll be going too."

Jason and Zain shared a look of dismay, but she silenced them both with a wave of her hand. "Jason, you can't convince me of the importance of your mission without also convincing me that I should be part of it."

"Absolutely not," said Jason. "It's one thing for me to go. It's another matter entirely for you."

"And why? Because you've already tried to throw your life away twice, and you think the third time will work? Is that what this is really all about?"

Jason's mouth worked silently for an answer, but his wife wouldn't let him avoid this.

"No, you've had your say so let me have mine. We have to try to put everything behind us now — all of it. There's far too much at stake. What do you really want?"

"Ethan," Jason said quietly. "If you come with me, would you let me kill him when the time comes?"

Nadine closed her eyes and drew in a deep breath. "Jason, I hate him as much as you do, for my daughter and for my father, but this is bigger than my need for vengeance. It's bigger than both of us. You need me with you if for no other reason than to prevent this from devolving into a personal vendetta."

Jason couldn't fault the argument, so he tried an alternative. "But you're our leader now. You can't leave our people."

"And you command our army, yet you think you can go," Nadine shot back the obvious rebuttal.

"Shane and Geordine are more than ready to step up, and you have the Warmaster. I'm going alone, or with a few men—"

Nadine's laugh cut him off before he could continue, and she looked at him warmly. "Oh, Jason, stop it. You can't go stealthily into the enemy's lair like some hero in a story. And what are you going to do once you get there? Knock on the gates and ask permission to see the ruler of the Iron Union because you're old school friends?"

Jason looked embarrassed. "Well . . . I'm still working out the details."

"You need me with you. We need to go in there with strength and force a dialogue. The only way this works is a formal parlay between leaders, not a fireside catchup between friends. Then we might have a chance to see if we can help her."

"She's right," agreed Zain. "You're a brave man, Captain, but this is a job for diplomats rather than fighters. Your approach is far too risky. If you're caught, you'll just be thrown in a dungeon, if you're not killed outright. You'd never reach her."

Jason felt a surge of frustration at the truth — at the revelation that his plan was so clearly a suicide mission. *Is this all I really want?*

He suddenly felt so tired. Tired of the war. Tired of his unrelenting anger. Tired of hating. He wanted it to end, and yes, he knew death would certainly bring that. But his wife was refusing to give up, and he knew she was much stronger than him in so many ways. He looked at her face – worn prematurely from war and the tolls of its tragedy – and loved her again, and in doing so, drew strength from her.

"Fine," Jason said. "So what does this mean? Are we going to press into the Iron Union after all?"

Zain grimaced. "I still haven't changed my view; I don't see the need to press our luck. However," he looked into the growing light of the *ovoid* and frowned, "I admit there are things here I don't fully understand. So if our existence is at stake, I'll follow the wisdom of those more experienced in the ways of gods."

Kaler nodded. "We should commit half our forces to the offensive, keeping the rest at Outpost to guard supply lines. We don't want to make the same mistake our enemy made by overextending too quickly."

Zain withdrew a well-creased map from his robes and studied it. "A smaller army may be able to strike out across Hammerfall, move south of the Shield and assail Fortress Krag directly. If Exedor was telling the truth and he weakens them first, then it's possible they won't be in a position to resist a quick attack."

"Seize Krag?" asked Jason.

"It is one of their most prized installations. Taking it would certainly command their attention," said Kaler.

"And if the Inquisitor spoke truly, and their forces are weak from within, this could also give us a unique opportunity to use an invading force in ways we had not previously considered," said Zain, seeming to warm to the idea.

"Once we've gotten their attention, we petition the Helmsguard for a negotiation between leaders," finished Nadine.

"How do you know Valeyn will respond? Maybe they'll just get some diplomat to waste your time while they plot a counterattack." said Zain

"If Valeyn is in command and if she needs us like Exedor says, then she'll seize the opportunity," replied Nadine.

"And if Exedor was lying and this is a trap?" asked Zain.

"Then we might be there a while," muttered Jason.

"In that case, I suggest we come up with a fallback plan," said Nadine. "Warmaster Zain, I think I have a job for you."

Zain bowed his head obediently as Nadine started to outline a plan that would either save her army or ensure its destruction.

•   •   •

Valeyn followed her father into the throne room and the massive doors slammed behind them. The chamber was empty and silent, save for the tread of Bythe's feet across the black marble floor. Every soldier they had encountered on their return to Domitus had prostrated himself upon Bythe's command. Even the priests had been ordered to yield when they had rushed to attend him. Their god would suffer no worshippers this day.

"There was a time when this was all I desired order and authority. And then I achieved it, but that all seems so long ago." Bythe's voice was different. It still had the intensity of command, and yet uncertainty lingered on the edges of his words. "There are times . . . when I cannot understand how it all came to this . . . times when I recognize that I did not intend any of this to happen. I hope you can believe this, Valeyn."

"Are you making excuses, Father?"

His helmet turned and his dark eyes looked at her in silence for a moment. "Perhaps I am. This was all a game to us once. When we first came here, this was intended to become a manner of sport for the rest of my kin, but it was never so trivial to me."

He walked to the throne and for a moment, Valeyn expected him to sit. Instead, he rested his massive gauntlet on the arm of the throne, looking at the cold steel as if deep in thought.

"I was weak, Valeyn, in the Etherian. I was among the smallest of us. It is hard to describe this to one who has not witnessed existence beyond this world, but within that place, my voice among the gathering was not as strong as the others. Once we were here, in the confines of this world, we were equal. But beyond that, I found that my drive and ingenuity gave me a purpose my brethren did not possess, or even understand. I could be far more powerful than them in Kovalith."

"You wanted to be better than them? Was all this really just about your ego?"

"No, you do not understand. It was more than that. My ambition drove me. I achieved more here than any other god, save for your mother. Like me, she was driven by fire and determination in her own way, and for that, I truly loved her."

"You speak more about my mother than you do about me."

"You are right." He was quiet for a long time, his outward form unmoving, and yet, she could sense turmoil within, as if her father struggled against himself. "I have been so preoccupied with my war — with my games and my petty goals — I did not remember why I chose to stay within this world. I should have seen you for who you are, but I did not. I chose not to."

"It . . . it's alright," she quietly replied. The natural response. The lie.

"No. It is not. I see this now. I recall a time when I wanted the existence of these people to mean something. When I wanted to watch them grow. I believe . . . something happened. Maybe they did not grow into the people I wanted them to be. Maybe my expectations were misplaced. Selfish? I do not know."

"Well, even if that's true, that's in the past. At least now we have time to fix this."

"There is no time, child. I have been a fool and it is only at the end that I finally understand this."

Valeyn felt strange hearing his confession. She wanted him to stop talking. She was desperate to stop the words she knew he was going to say.

"Father, you're not going anywhere. These are your people; they still need you."

"No, Valeyn. They are your people now, not mine. They have not been my people for a long time. While they may fear me, I can see they love you. You have reached out to them as I once did, and they have responded to you in my place. In the end, this is far more valuable. I want you to lead them when I am gone."

Bythe abruptly sank to his knees then rested his bulk against the base of the throne. Dread filled her.

"Are you hurt?"

Bythe shook his head. "Those creatures cannot harm me. Only I can truly harm myself, and I have done myself more harm than I realized. So much hurt, in so many ways. I knew the time of the Desecration was nigh and I was desperate to win this war, desperate also to claim you as my prize, as a trophy to my peers when they returned. You must never forget, daughter, that our gifts in this world have limits. There is always a price to be paid for our deeds, and I created weapons that were the greatest this world will ever see."

Valeyn understood. "You created the Godfire."

Bythe's frame seemed to heave as if he were unloading a burden. "That power was the very end of me, Valeyn. I have been clinging to life ever since. I wanted you to return to me as evidence of my victory, but I now see the folly in such selfishness. Your love for the people under your protection — it reminded me of the god I once was. We wanted the people of this land to grow, and you are the ultimate expression of that. I realized this, too late. You have made me realize how much I have lost. I no longer deserve this throne. I no longer deserve to sit here when judgment is given.

This world must be redeemed or condemned by its true children. You are one of those children. You are my child."

"Please, stop talking like this."

"Valeyn, there is no time. Our brethren are here. They will judge you now. They will judge everyone. I fear they will judge Maelene's disciple and find his actions to be just. If he succeeds in undoing my work, it will prove this world unworthy. I wanted to fight for this world, to stand for it, and yet I see I cannot do this. I have fallen into madness and corruption, like the others. I have failed. You must not."

He rested himself against the foot of the throne and raised his hands to the twin horns on his helmet. With a violent twist, he broke the seal at the collar and slowly pulled the helmet away, letting it fall to the ground where it shattered.

The face beneath was old; thin and lined with centuries of worry and countless thoughts. His forehead was strong and bright eyes shone out from beneath a commanding brow, and yet the eyes seemed afraid. They were the scared eyes of an old man who had reached the end of his authority and had nowhere left to go. They cast about the room with a hint of panic, before settling upon Valeyn, and when they did, warmth flooded them.

"Valeyn, I am so sorry for what I have done to you."

Valeyn moved close to him. The tears rose and streamed down her face yet she tried to hold her composure. Words simply would not come.

"You are the very best of me, and indeed, the best of your mother. Please remember this."

Valeyn placed a trembling hand upon her father's face. "How long do we have?"

His smile gave her the answer her ears would not hear. They looked at each other, alone among the immense emptiness of the throne room.

"I envy Leon," said Bythe. "I envy the years he had with you. To raise you as his daughter and to shape you into the perfect woman you are today. I wish I had given you this."

"Father, don't . . ." she answered but her voice was breaking.

"Why do we let these moments pass us by forever? Why don't we recognize them until they're far away from us?"

"Stay with me for a while longer, please,"

His sharp eyes faded and the fear returned to them for a moment before his eyelids closed.

He was gone, but she held onto his unfinished promises, searching still, for the father who never was.

CHAPTER 5

"Our god, the immortal Lord Bythe, has transcended this life and passed into the lands of the Etherian, where he will watch over us for all time.

Do not grieve, for this was foretold. Lord Bythe would often speak of this day, and of his desire to move beyond the confines of the physical, where he would be free to protect each of us from the evils which beset our lands. This is a day of rejoicing.

He has given us his daughter, Lord Valeyn the Immortal, fully recognized and accepted as his rightful heir. Lord Valeyn returned to us at the preordained hour to take up her place alongside her father and assume his burden. Lord Valeyn now sits on the throne and the mantle of our protection now falls to her.

We know she will not fail us."

~Royal Coronation Proclamation of Udrax the Oppressor,
High Priest of the Iron Union

Valeyn looked out the window of the immense Imperial Carriage. In the distance, a tower of the *ovoid* polluted the sky, and she tried to judge how quickly it was growing. They seemed to be everywhere now, continual reminders of the Desecration driving the people of the Iron Union into a constant state of panic. Driving *her* people. The Shield was all but destroyed; centuries of work now gone in a matter of weeks. And now, Fortress Krag had fallen to the Outland Alliance. She turned her gaze to the impressive edifice built into the shoulders of two mountains and wondered how it had been possible?

Vale had seen Krag as a child. Her tutors had drilled her with the tales of its glory, how it had once been a mining colony, quickly transformed into a factory of war to repel invaders from the Outer Wild. The deep pits from which vital ores were extracted from the land were still in operation, and the smelters and forges had been repurposed to dispense an endless supply of arms to the generations of soldiers who lived there.

And somehow it had been taken. She glanced again at the report before casting it to the seat beside her. Somehow the Outland Alliance had known it was vulnerable, that the Helmsguard had been redeployed to deal with the devastation caused by the *ovoid*. How had they known? And who would lead such an assault? Veroulle? Or perhaps one of the warmongering captains from Bonehall?

The report was strange for its ambiguity and also for its counsel. Although Valeyn understood it was unwise to disclose too much intelligence in writing – especially when interception by the enemy is a very real possibility – it also carried the strong recommendation that Lord Valeyn the Immortal may wish to assess the situation personally.

Morbus was already there in his capacity as Minister of Intelligence, and Valeyn had no doubt he was behind the strange request. This only unsettled her further. He'd been keeping a very low profile in the weeks since she ascended the throne, and the continual threats facing the Ironhelm meant she'd yet had no chance to expose and denounce him as a traitor. This visit would be the perfect opportunity to do so.

So why was he inviting it?

The Imperial Carriage slowed to a halt and Valeyn sighed. There were too many questions and dwelling any further without more information would simply tax her mind for no benefit.

She had only to glance at the door and one of the attendants immediately moved to open it. More attendants scurried about to connect a metallic ramp to the lip of the doorframe, which would allow her to descend from the carriage without exertion. A priest bustled forward and began chanting a ritual prayer to Valeyn – their god and protector. As had happened countless times before, the minor priests took up their positions and began chanting in response. All about them, soldiers paused and snapped to attention. The retinue rankled Valeyn, but she knew there was nothing she could do about it. She had tried to stamp out the practice altogether but had been unsuccessful – strange that a god can seemingly do anything but command followers to cease their worship. At least she'd been able to convince her soldiers to remain upright in her presence, a request that took a lot more effort to enforce than should have been necessary.

She walked down the ramp as the chants from the priest rose in crescendo, and the clap of a hundred fists striking metal breastplates rang out across the field. The carriage looked more like a metal fortress supported by eight massive wheels and twice as many horses. Indeed, the squat, armored turret that served as her private chamber could easily seat six people, and that wasn't counting the antechambers that held her priests and attendants.

A carriage.

The thought of riding in a casket designed for the elderly or infirm had insulted her, but Udrax would not accept her riding on horseback. Apparently, she was no longer a warrior in the Helmsguard. She was now above all of them, and her people should be reminded of this, even by the manner in which she moved about her empire.

She glanced about, looking for Ethan, and found him dismounting his horse a few yards from the carriage. He quickly checked the animal with the unconscious concern Valeyn found endearing before handing the reigns to a squire and crossing to her. They hadn't had much time alone since her father's death, and each knew the other was grieving their own private loss. Without openly stating it, they knew they were unable to console each other, but both understood they could fill their shared emptiness with work. Duty was the perfect consolation; it was the only one available.

"Comfortable trip?" Ethan asked, nodding at the opulent vehicle and ignoring the scalding gaze of the priest, who was outraged at such a lack of deference.

"Don't start or I'll take your horse on the journey back and make you ride in there like an old man."

Ethan shrugged. "Fine by me, I just don't think your new friends would let me inside."

She ignored the veiled reference to the new distance between them and walked toward the assembly of waiting dignitaries, the round form of Morbus clearly visible at the center. To his credit, he had the good sense to bow as low as the others when she approached, yet even this rankled Valeyn, as it denied her an excuse to be displeased with him.

"Lord Valeyn the Immortal, we praise your name and—" a junior noble greeted her but she cut him off with a wave of her hand.

"I've no time for worship. Just report!" she snapped. The young officer paled as if she had sentenced him to a painful execution, and Valeyn inwardly groaned. If she had previously been frustrated by her lack of influence, it now seemed she had too much. Either way, it seemed a lot harder than ever to get things done.

"Forgive me, Fersis, but perhaps I might be better suited to this task." Morbus interjected smoothly, placing a hand on his shoulder and gently pulling him back. "I am prepared to brief you, Lord Valeyn, if you so wish it."

Valeyn met his gaze but grudgingly admitted there were perhaps some advantages to a man who had no desire to grovel before her. "Go ahead."

Morbus launched into a dramatic but accurate description of the situation. "It is as we suspected The Outland Alliance has somehow managed to advance far deeper into the Iron Union than originally believed, no doubt using the cover of Desecration to mask their advance. They have curiously chosen to bypass Greund and Rhaskitov and instead, mounted an audacious yet successful assault on the Fortress of Krag."

"How is that possible?" Valeyn asked evenly.

Morbus nodded solemnly, and she sensed he enjoyed knowing something she didn't.

"How indeed? Normally, such an attempt on our greatest military installation would have been laughable. But with the Shield in tatters and Hammerfall beset with these lesions of the Desecration, it is not surprising they managed to get this far without serious resistance."

"How did they take Krag?" she snapped. She knew Morbus was drawing this out — that it was another piece of theater — but there was also something else. He was leading her somewhere.

"Well, that is an excellent question, my lord," he answered. "It would appear that Krag suffered an attack by Ferehain's Imbatals no more than three days before the Outland Alliance arrived. Your men fought valiantly, but the gates had already been breached days before and had not been repaired in time. Additionally, the command staff had been decimated and the defenses already in disarray when the Outland Alliance surprised them. It appears to have been a very well-timed operation."

"*Ferehain's* Imbatals?" she asked, the accusation in her question clear to both of them.

"Yes, my lord. Is there something you'd like me to explain?" he replied, meeting her gaze evenly.

Morbus was calling her out once more, daring her to expose him. And it was almost time. All she needed was justification, and even a tenuous implication in Krag's fall would be enough.

"In due time, Minister. For now, you may continue," she answered.

"As you wish, Lord Valeyn. My sources tell me their commanding officer is a young Captain Jason, from Fairhaven," he looked at her and she could see the triumph deep in his eyes. "I believe you're familiar with him, my lord?"

Valeyn tried to mask the shock and the questions that immediately flooded her mind.

Jason has taken Krag? Why is he doing this? Is he moving against me? Does he know that I'm in command now?

She stared at the stone battlements in silence, weighing a thousand variables in her mind.

"Well, in any case, he is the one who has requested a formal parlay. Oh, and someone else, let me see," continued Morbus, turning to a piece of paper pulled from within his robe and studying the notes with a furrowed brow. "Some new leader of this Alliance. A young lady by the name of . . . Nadine."

It was as if he had struck her, and she couldn't help but stare at the round bureaucrat in disbelief. "Jason and Nadine. They've both asked to speak to me?"

"Yes, my lord." His grin was almost comical but Valeyn knew he was taunting her, hoping for an irrational reaction. She thought of Ethan's teachings and calmed herself. If Jason and Nadine were both here, it could only mean that they were trying to reach her, and this was a good thing. In fact, it was a *very* good thing – an opportunity she had never even considered.

"Nadine of Fairhaven is now the leader of the Outland Alliance?" Valeyn asked.

"Well, it's hard to fathom the organisational structure of that rabble, even back when they were led by the Ageless, but it seems she is in a position of some authority now. At least, that is how she signed the request to parlay. For what it's worth, my intelligence network confirms that the armies of Marfort and the Federacy seem to be following her orders, otherwise I would never have entertained her request."

Valeyn considered the possibilities. If Nadine was trying to establish communication, it must be an attempt to establish peace. An alliance between the Iron Union and the Outer Wild had never been achieved in the history of Kovalith. Jason and Nadine could even help her fight against Ferehain and remove Morbus. She tried to keep her excitement in check.

"Valeyn," Ethan said quietly. She turned and met his look of complete shame.

"Oh, Ethan," she whispered.

"Valeyn, I shouldn't be here. After what I did . . . Jason will want his revenge."

Ethan was right. Jason had tried to kill him the last time they met. There would be no peace negotiations if they knew Ethan was here.

"It'll be fine. Just go to the command tent and stay out of sight. If I need you, I'll send for you," she said. Ethan nodded and turned away. She watched his retreating back for a moment before realizing Morbus and his entourage were waiting on her.

"Take me to them," she ordered.

A wave of surprise rippled through the surrounding dignitaries, and Morbus laughed as if she had just made some witty remark. "Oh, come now, my lord," he rumbled. "You're not serious?"

"I want to meet with them," she answered in an even voice.

"And what sort of message would that send? That our Lord Valeyn the Immortal, the last god and protector of Kovalith, can be so easily manipulated? This is beneath your station."

"Nevertheless, it is my will."

"Then let me go in your place with a diplomatic delegation. We can relay the communications to you. This filth should not be given the honor of a personal audience. Think of your own reputation."

Valeyn could see what Morbus was doing. He knew she was desperate to be reunited with her childhood friends, and he was going to use this to challenge her judgment in a very public fashion. She was tempted to order his arrest that instant, but she knew this would also play into his narrative as the victim of an unstable god.

Patience.

"As I said, it is my will, Minister. Do not question it." Her voice was steady and without anger, but the statement still sounded more like an explanation than an order. She hated him.

Morbus raised his palms as if he were a parent negotiating with a difficult child. "I'll make the arrangements, but I'll be coming as well, along with a delegation."

Valeyn opened her mouth to protest but something in his expression stopped her. Of course he knew she wanted to meet them alone. But if she made this request now, he would make it look like an act of madness — or worse, potential treason. Realizing the futility of her position, she changed her mind. "Of course, Minister. I expect nothing less."

Morbus bowed low, but not low enough to conceal his small grin, and he turned to his ever-hovering, sycophantic entourage. Valeyn brushed him from her thoughts and focused instead on the distant fortress.

Jason. Nadine.

It felt like it'd been years since she'd seen them. She realized that in some part of her mind, she'd started to believe she'd never see them again. The excitement she felt was a sensation she'd almost forgotten, and she ached for the reunion. But why were they here? The counterattack into the Iron Union had taken everyone by surprise, but this was now only heightened by the revelation that her friends were responsible. Nadine had always been level-headed and Jason had grown into a brilliant leader. Neither of them should have approved of an aggressive strategy with so much risk. Valeyn recalled the last time she'd seen Jason, with sunken cheeks under the eyes of a man ready to die, and she felt herself shiver. She tried to push aside the suspicion that he might still be that man.

·   ·   ·

It took far longer than expected to make the necessary arrangements for the negotiation. The delegation from the Outland Alliance had been reluctant to agree to the terms set down by the Iron Union, and a full day and night passed before a compromise was reached. In the end, Valeyn had to intervene and offer to ride out with her retinue first — a move met with the carefully manufactured outrage of Morbus. Both sides agreed on an escort of thirty-six soldiers — no more — plus six delegates for negotiation, although Valeyn seriously doubted that Jason and Nadine had any delegates with them at all.

The following morning, Valeyn rode out on a bay stallion, surrounded by black iron soldiers. The desert air was crisp, and steam formed on her breath as she rode to the meeting point, an unremarkable spot on the open plain before the fortress. She took up her position, seated at the center on one side of a makeshift table surrounded by fourteen mismatched chairs. Morbus took the chair to her right, and five more of his diplomats and adjutants filled the others. Moments later, the gates of Krag parted and a line of brightly colored figures filed out. The Helmsguard snapped to attention as the enemy soldiers crossed the wastes. Valeyn hadn't needed her keen vision to recognize the familiar uniforms of the Outer Wild, but when her eyes fell on the men wearing the bright blue livery of Fairhaven, she felt an unexpected pang of homesickness.

You're the leader of the Iron Union now.

The thought was a rebuke to childish sentiment. She knew she'd need the discipline. As if the gods were listening, the lines of solders shifted and Valeyn's heart jumped as the familiar forms of Jason and Nadine suddenly appeared. It took every fiber of her will to restrain herself from leaping to her feet.

Morbus gave a command and three delegates moved forward to meet the approaching party. Valeyn watched with frustration as insincere pleasantries were exchanged with pointless formalities. Jason looked at her and in that moment the world around them simply ceased to exist. In the light of that glance, she was back at Fairhaven, a young girl anxious about her uncertain future, mercifully oblivious to what was to come, taking comfort in the presence of her closest friend. Then Jason's face hardened into resentment and the memory broke, leaving only the cruelty of the present. Nadine's face was unreadable. She looked older, small lines now visible at the corners of her eyes, yet it was something in her gaze that undid her youth. Nadine looked at Valeyn as if they were strangers.

She shook her head briefly and tried to focus. A delicate tightrope stretched before her and she knew she would need every ounce of skill to cross it. "Enough, Morbus. Bring them to me," Valeyn commanded, rising to her feet.

Moments later Valeyn stood across the table from her oldest friends. As expected, they brought no retinue other than their guards, who stood several feet behind. A thousand questions flooded her mind. *Are you alright? What about your parents? Are the Ageless still with you?*

"Councillor Nadine and Captain Jason, I present our immortal protector and most-highest master, Lord Valeyn of the Iron Union, last god of Kovalith," said Morbus.

"Good morning, Lord Valeyn," said Nadine, and the cold greeting erased Valeyn's questions.

"Councillor. Captain," Valeyn answered. She wanted to hug them both, but she merely nodded to each of them in turn.

They sat and endured a momentary uncomfortable silence.

"I see you've taken your father's colors," said Jason, nodding at Valeyn's armor. "What happened to the green? I guess that didn't go down well with your new friends?"

"I wore the green for a while, but when my father died and I was appointed to the throne, it . . . well . . . it no longer seemed fitting," said Valeyn.

"I see," Nadine replied, the judgment in her voice unmistakable.

"The Lord Valeyn does not explain her decisions to you," Morbus snapped.

"It's alright, Morbus," Valeyn waved her hand absently. "It's obvious we have a history, so let's deal with that. Councillor Nadine and Captain Jason were my friends in childhood. I hope we can all use this as a starting position for our dialogue."

"Elyn was my friend. You're not her," said Nadine. Jason was silent.

"Alright," said Valeyn, trying to think of some way to recover the advantage without becoming adversarial. "Then let's start. Why is the Outland Alliance here?"

"The Outland Alliance is defending herself from the unrelenting and unprovoked attacks from the Iron Union," said Nadine.

"You've taken Krag. This is not defense; it's an invasion of Iron Union territory," observed Valeyn.

"It's a counteroffensive. One made necessary by your most recent invasion of our land with your war engines," said Jason. "Surely you remember what your army did?"

"That wasn't my army—" Valeyn stopped herself as she felt the members of her delegation shuffle in their seats. "They were the orders of Lord Bythe, my father. He is no longer in command. This gives us an opportunity to discuss a change in policies."

"Indeed," interjected Morbus, "and if you surrender your army unconditionally, we may allow you to negotiate some terms in your reparations to us. This is the one time we will make such a generous offer."

"Morbus—" began Valeyn but Jason's laugh interrupted her.

"Surrender? We've taken the prize of the Helmsguard right from under your nose, and you think we're going to surrender?"

"You may have taken the fortress, but you do not have the forces to keep it, my young captain. Within days we will deploy enough soldiers to retake Krag, and then you will not receive any concessions or mercy from us," replied Morbus.

"If that were true, then why haven't you done it already?" asked Nadine. "Where are your Helmsguard? Are they occupied elsewhere?"

For the first time since the meeting began, Valeyn doubted her old friends. Could it be that Nadine and Jason were allied to Ferehain? Did they plan the attack of the Imbatals to clear Krag's defenses? Had this all been carefully designed? Was Morbus manipulating them? She leaned back in her chair as if to give herself a little more space to think. "Alright, you asked for this meeting. What do you want?"

"We want to discuss the terms of an armistice," said Nadine.

"Absolutely not!" snorted Morbus. "You will surrender now, or you will be killed when we reclaim the fortress. Those are the only options available to you."

"Do you speak on behalf of your Lord Valeyn?" asked Nadine.

"He does not," Valeyn answered. She met Nadine's eyes across the table and an understanding flourished between them.

Armistice.

Nadine was asking her to end this conflict. And not just this battle. She was asking Valeyn to help end the entire war. Centuries of bloodshed could cease. What random chances had conspired to place both childhood friends in such a position? Or was this more than chance?

Don't get ahead of yourself, Valeyn. Take this one step at a time. She took a breath and steadied herself. "An armistice is a bold suggestion, Councillor. There are many powerful people on both sides of the conflict who would stand in opposition to your proposal."

"That's true," said Nadine, nodding. "But the most powerful person from the Iron Union sits before me, and I would like to know her position before discussing the preferences of others."

Morbus motioned to a guard and mumbled an order into his ear. There was something very peculiar about the exchange, but Valeyn knew she couldn't question him in the middle of the negotiations.

"You're wrong, Councillor," she answered, "when you said that I'm not Elyn. I remember her as vividly as I do Vale, and I remember how much we both wished for peace when we were younger."

"Then you agree to an armistice in principle?" Nadine asked.

"Lord Valeyn, we should recess a moment," interrupted Morbus, but Valeyn took pleasure in ignoring him.

"I'm inclined to agree," continued Valeyn, "but I think I'm making my advisors nervous, so we should probably discuss your intentions to withdraw from Krag before we go too much further."

"We're not leaving Krag until we have an agreement. One we can trust," Jason said bluntly.

Valeyn paused and considered her words before looking sincerely at both of them. "Jason. Nadine. If we come to an agreement, then you'll have my word. I hope you can trust me that much?"

Nadine returned Valeyn's empathic plea with a stare that had been bled of all emotion. "When Maelene met with Bythe to discuss peace, she was betrayed and imprisoned. When the Outland Alliance tried to negotiate with the Iron Union, my father was also betrayed and murdered. Are you going to tell me I'm being too cautious, *Lord Valeyn*?"

Valeyn tried to form a reply, but Jason spoke, and any hope of reconciliation shattered. "Bastard!"

Valeyn followed his stare and saw Ethan, frozen in place midway between the command tent and their table. Her breath stopped. The fate of everything she strove for was balanced in a single moment. Morbus exploited it.

"I sent for Baron Ethan in your name," he said. "I know how useful he's been to you in matters of diplomacy and judged he could best serve the Iron Union by standing at your side in this hour."

Fury boiled within Valeyn. She turned to the overweight Minister but noted the triumph in his voice. She was trapped and he knew it. Jason rose to his feet with the slow, deliberate movements of a man bent on finality.

"Jason, please." Valeyn also stood, her voice was a low warning.

"He murdered Nadine's father. He killed our daughter," Jason answered in a tone that was equally low and dire.

Valeyn looked into Jason's eyes and spoke carefully. "There isn't a day that goes by that Ethan doesn't regret his actions at Fairhaven. He wasn't himself. My father's influence, his anger . . . spread far deeper than any of us knew."

"You're defending him," Nadine said in horror. Her words became an accusation, an immutable statement of fact that divided them.

"Captain Jason, are you threatening harm against Baron Ethan?" said Morbus with feigned surprise. "You've travelled here under the conventions of parlay."

"I demand justice for my daughter - a father's justice. That outweighs any diplomatic rubbish!" Jason hissed, his eyes never leaving Ethan.

The delegation began to buzz with concern. Valeyn knew she had to act quickly before the situation lurched beyond her control.

"Guardsman!" she snapped. "Remove Baron Ethan from the field and confine him to the command tent."

"No!" shouted Jason.

Within one instant, the course of the world was altered. Several things seemed to happen at once, one upon the other, each affecting the other, until there could be only one outcome, and not even a god could will it otherwise.

Nadine reached up to Jason. Her hand gripping him by the arm in a futile attempt to restrain him with reason, but he pulled away. His gaze was set on his enemy, and he would not let anyone prevent him from fulfilling his mad destiny. He leaped the table and reached for his sword. The scene descended into chaos. Men were shouting and people broke from the table in fear. Helmsguard moved in and drew their own swords.

Valeyn shouted orders for her men to stand down but they were ignored. Ethan was fixed where he stood, seemingly torn between retreat and dignity. Jason had drawn his sword and had started to run directly at his enemy. It was suicide; sheer impulsive insanity. Valeyn acted. She reached out with her unnatural speed and gripped him by the arm, pulling him back. Jason growled and swung his sword without looking at his assailant. The blade cut through the air at Valeyn's head, but she refused to release him to death, and braced for the impact, turning her face away. Pain fired through her cheek as the blade opened the side of her face. The shock of the strike snapped her head back and her vision reeled, but she tightened her grip on Jason and refused to let him be swept away into the current of madness he so clearly craved.

The shouts became screams of rage. Valeyn knew they would kill him now. He had sealed his own fate, and hers. Blinking through the blood, she pulled ruthlessly on Jason's arm and sent him crashing to the ground. His sword flew from his hand and Valeyn willed it to her, where she held it against his neck, glaring at him from her face masked with blood.

"Stop!" Her voice boomed over the field. Everyone froze. Valeyn scanned her soldiers, as if daring anyone to defy her. None did.

"He is not to be harmed," she announced. "Sheathe your weapons."

"Jason! Stop this!" Nadine cried out, but – knowing better than to try to reach him – held her place.

Slowly, the Helmsguard did as they were ordered, and Valeyn started to relax.

"Ethan! Return to the tent, now!" Valeyn commanded, and he quickly obeyed with his honor intact.

"No!" Jason cried and struggled to free himself from her grip. Valeyn pulled on his arm and his cry turned into a scream of pain. She decided she'd break his arm if it meant saving his life. Placing her boot on his chest, she pinned him to the ground effortlessly and wiped the blood from her eyes.

"Jason! What's wrong with you? Do you want to die?"

"Yes!" he yelled. "Just let me take him with me."

"And what about Nadine? Do you want her to die too?"

Jason opened his mouth but paused. Something akin to clarity washed over him, and for a moment, it seemed as if he had no idea where he was.

"What about your people?" Valeyn pressed on. "You're here to negotiate a peace for all of them, not to settle a private vendetta, no matter how justified your grievance might be."

Shame emanated from him as the gravity of his recklessness became clear.

Valeyn sighed as she sensed his sanity return. "Now swear to me you'll put this aside until our business is concluded."

But before Jason could answer, slick laughter interrupted him. Morbus stepped forth, applauding Valeyn with absurd theatricality. "Bravo, Lord Valeyn. Your sense of humor is a quality we missed in your father."

Valeyn turned her black look on him. "What the hells are you talking about, Morbus? None of this is a joke!"

Morbus paused as if she'd slapped him, a well-rehearsed look of surprise growing on his round face. "My lord, forgive me, but you cannot be serious?"

Valeyn knew she should be careful with her words — she knew this was a trap — but she was also furious, and power often permits a person to indulge their worst impulses. Valeyn proved to be no exception.

"Just shut up, Morbus. I can see what you're doing. I won't let you ruin this chance for peace!"

Morbus looked grave and turned away, directing his next words at the delegation of lords, as if pleading his innocence. "My lord, you have just accused me of a most grievous crime, and I'm shamed. May I ask, do you have any evidence to support this?"

His words echoed hers from all those years ago, when Vale had trapped Morbus with his own angry outburst and had him removed from command. Valeyn took a moment to reflect upon the patience of vengeful men.

"I don't need evidence, Morbus. I'm your god. Respect my will."

"Well, of course, Lord Valeyn. Your will isn't in question. However, forgive my blasphemy, but I wonder if your judgment hasn't become corrupted by these . . . infidels, who have clearly conspired against you? They come here under the banner of peace, friends of your other self, Elyn. She was the bastard aspect of Maelene, was she not?"

"My prior life is not your concern!"

"Oh, but it is, Lord Valeyn. Forgive my impudence again, but you are not like your father. You face challenges he did not. Part of you was raised among the enemies who have come here. They know this, and they seek to use your childhood as a weapon against you."

"Silence, Minister!" she snapped.

Morbus gave her a calculated pause, as if he were considering speaking further, then reluctantly lowered his head in an exaggerated gesture of submission against his better judgment.

She turned back to Jason and pulled him to his feet. "Let's get back to the table and finish this!"

But another voice spoke.

"Apologies, Lord Valeyn, but the Minister has a point," said Bellatruv from the grouped delegates. "They've come here under a flag of parlay only to try to assassinate one of your own lords in front of you."

There were murmurs of assent from within her lords, and she didn't need to look at Morbus to know he was wearing a smug grin.

"This wasn't an assassination. It was an act of passion in a moment of madness," Valeyn answered.

"It hardly matters what the reasons were," Bellatruv continued. "The fact is, he broke the truce and tried to kill one of us. Any of us could have been killed by him. Doesn't that concern you, my lord?"

"Of course, your safety matters to me. But none of you were in any danger while I was here."

"Our safety aside, he *struck* you, Lord Valeyn. You stand before us bleeding by his filthy hand. No. Such desecration cannot be tolerated. Death is the only penalty," said another young ambassador.

"Nobody is going to die today. I won't have another negotiation end in bloodshed. Is that clear?" Valeyn's frustrated retort was too emotional, and her delegation recoiled before her, their confidence in her draining with every word she uttered.

"Please, gentlemen," interjected Morbus, his hands raised in rational conciliation. "The Lord Valeyn has given us her preference for no bloodshed, and we must respect that."

Preference? Valeyn noted how Morbus had subtly diminished her order to a suggestion, open to negotiation, and in doing so, had diminished her. But any attempts to argue with Morbus – who had now brilliantly positioned himself as the voice of reason – would only strengthen perceptions of her emotional volatility.

"But clearly, these negotiations are over, Lord Valeyn," Morbus continued. "A stay of execution is already an enormous display of diplomatic goodwill in the face of such treachery. We will not execute these prisoners without further process, but they will remain prisoners under Ironhelm law. We certainly cannot entertain the continuance of negotiations after they brazenly broke the laws of parlay. Surely, you agree?"

It wasn't a question. Every single face among the delegation now eyed her doubtfully. Even some of the Helmsguard were glancing at her with an unusual lack of discipline. There was only one answer to his question.

"Of course, Minister," she replied.

Morbus clapped his hands and the Helmsguard immediately moved in. Jason grunted in protest as he was hauled to his feet, but Nadine didn't make a sound, she simply stared at the woman who was once her friend.

"Confine them to apartments in Domitus," Valeyn called out, almost as a futile afterthought. "They're to be treated as diplomatic ransom, not as criminals."

Again, Morbus paused dubiously before slowly nodding his head. "If you judge it best, my lord. Although I cannot agree that the Captain is no criminal."

"Just see it done!" she snapped. Morbus turned away without a reply.

Valeyn tried to think of a way to salvage the situation but it was lost. Jason and Nadine were her prisoners, and nothing could change that now. Any attempt to free them would only make the situation worse. She needed time to plan her next move. She desperately needed Ethan.

Guards escorted Nadine and Jason away from the table and in the direction of the Ironhelm camp. They didn't resist. But before they were led away, Nadine paused and fixed Valeyn with a cold smile. "And so, another attempt at peace ends in our betrayal. It was stupid of me to assume anything had changed. Congratulations, Lord Valeyn. It seems that you're very much your father's daughter."

Nadine was then ushered away, and Valeyn was left to contemplate the brutal truth of her words.

BOOK THREE
RESURRECTION

CHAPTER 1

"Leadership and veneration are intersecting ideals, often conflated, yet distinct all the same. One does not always follow the other, and it remains a mystery why some are granted the benefit of unquestioning obedience, while others are permitted no such luxury.

It is possible that Lord Valeyn was simply weaker than her father, and did not have the desire, nor the power, to control the Iron Union.

It is also possible the unprecedented threats facing the Helmsguard were a challenge insurmountable to any leader.

Or perhaps Valeyn was the undeserving recipient of the pent-up frustration of a people who had, for centuries, secretly chafed under a leader they had professed to love. A frustration which was swiftly and ruthlessly exploited by an opportunistic ruling nobility.

No matter the reason, Lord Valeyn's failure would change the fate of the Iron Union forever."

~Kaler of the Ageless

"That was foolish of you, Ethan. How could you allow yourself to be manipulated in such a way? Why would you believe that Valeyn had called you before a man who had sworn to kill you?" Sarele's words were the condescending judgment instinctive in every disapproving mother.

"I'm sorry," Ethan murmured, as he shook his head. "My head wasn't where it needed to be. I shouldn't have been there at all."

Sarele sighed and looked aside. She was sitting on the edge of a large leather chair in the Library of Pertaakan, high within Domitus. Ethan sat on the couch opposite while Valeyn stood next to the large fireplace at the far end of the spacious room. It had been their first opportunity to speak openly about the arrests. Now that Valeyn understood exactly how much influence Morbus wielded, she hadn't dared to broach the subject with anyone until she was safely back within the inner chambers of Domitus. She now knew there were spies everywhere.

"Ethan," Sarele continued, "I know you're upset about Rayner's son; I am as well. But you need to keep things in perspective. There are greater matters at stake. He wasn't our family. He was illegitimate."

Ethan's glare was cold. "You're saying he was bastard? His name was Jaymet. He was real. He was your own grandson, not that you ever bothered to see him. Does that really mean nothing to you?"

Sarele's own weapon had been turned on her, and for a moment, her face flooded with shame.

"It's alright, Ethan," Valeyn interrupted. "It's not your fault. I was in the best position to see what Morbus was doing, and I missed it. We need to focus on what we do now."

"We need to move against Morbus, and quickly," said Ethan. "Mother, it's time. The House of Mac-Soldai is powerful. It's time to use that voice."

Sarele's expression hardened, but Valeyn could sense the conflict beneath.

"I can't," Sarele said.

"No, you can. You just won't," replied Ethan.

"I don't have enough support at the Unity Assembly. I can barely hold my seat there."

"But you have enough influence with the houses, and we hold the largest army in the Union. We can threaten them with force."

"That would lead to open war between the houses, Ethan," said Valeyn. "There has to be a better option. We can still outmaneuver Morbus. I've done it before."

"What other options are there? We're out of time. Morbus has been slowly weakening us from within and now that Bythe is dead, he's going to act. You can't even denounce him now, he's ready to resist you. He's been ready for a long time," Ethan asked.

Valeyn began pacing the rug before the fireplace, head down as she tried to order the problems in her mind. "Jason and Nadine may have given us the opportunity we need. People are tired of war and this new threat of the Desecration has made the old wars irrelevant. If I can negotiate a peace with them, even an alliance, it could turn the political winds in our favor."

"No doubt that's why Morbus was so keen to have them arrested and discredited," agreed Sarele. "It's a good idea, certainly preferable to risking bloodshed between the houses."

"We still don't know why they took Krag. It might have been a trap," said Ethan.

"That's a good question, but fortunately it's one we can answer," replied Valeyn. She crossed back to the mantle over the fireplace and struck her fist against the large brass bell that hung suspended over the woodwork. The door opened and an officer entered the room, Valeyn gave an order for the hostages to be brought to her.

"I don't think it's a good idea for me to be here," said Ethan, adjusting his uniform as he rose.

Valeyn nodded and both Ethan and Sarele walked to the door.

"Careful, Valeyn," Sarele said as she paused on the threshold. "Morbus will be waiting for the chance to accuse you of conspiring with the Outland Alliance."

"What's the alternative? I do nothing and let him execute them for his own political gain? This a risk, but I have to take it."

Sarele nodded then closed the door behind her.

Minutes later, four Helmsguard led Jason and Nadine into the library. They were both now dressed in garments of dark silk, intended to be an act of diplomatic hospitality, but Valeyn could see how poorly the clothes suited both of them and rued the clumsy error of judgment.

"Wait outside. Leave me with them," Valeyn said to the guards.

The soldiers hesitated before one of them spoke. "My lord, we have orders to protect you—"

"I'm not in any danger, soldier, and I'm getting tired of explaining myself!"

The four soldiers bowed low and immediately left, closing the door behind them.

"Well, well," said Jason, as he casually walked over to the couch and sat. "It looks like our jailer has finally made the time to see us. What took you so long? I guess running an empire is a busy job."

"Stop it, Jason," Valeyn snapped. "You know I didn't want this."

"Do I?" Jason replied. "I don't think I do. I don't think I know you at all anymore."

"You tried to kill Ethan! What the hells did you think was going to happen?" Valeyn snapped.

"That I could count on some loyalty from an old friend, maybe?" Jason answered.

"Oh, grow up, Jason! Do you think I can stand by while my *old friend* tries to murder a member of the nobility right in front of me? There are rules that even *I* have to follow."

"Rules?" Jason rose from the couch and walked to stand before Valeyn. He was shorter than her, but his anger made him a domineering presence. "He killed Paeter. You remember Paeter, don't you? You knew him longer than I did. He was your best friend's father. Hells, he even saved your life back in Outpost! And you defend his murderer?"

Valeyn sighed and looked at Nadine, who had turned her back to them and walked to stare into the fire.

"Nadine, you have to believe me — I hated Ethan for what he did. But you also have to understand that Ethan also hates himself."

"So that makes it alright?" asked Jason. "He feels guilty about murdering an innocent man so we should all just let it go?"

"It's war, Jason. Nobody is innocent. You know that. Paeter had planned his own trap for Ethan, and Ethan prepared his. He offered Paeter the chance to surrender and Paeter refused. The outcome was always going to be tragic, one way or the other, and everyone who walked out onto that field knew it in their own way."

"He only won by using a traitor. One of us. How can you side with him after what he did to our home?"

"Did Ethan burn Fairhaven, Jason? Or was that your decision?"

"He left me no choice!"

"And he says the same thing about you! Don't you see? This hatred has spiralled between the two of you, and somehow I feel that I've been part of it. Paeter's death, Fairhaven, it might all have been different if I'd done something else."

"Are you in love with him?" Nadine's question was a shock, and Valeyn had no idea what to say. She'd avoided asking herself the question, and now that somebody else was confronting her with it, she found she'd prepared no refuge.

"I don't know," she mumbled.

"Of course, you know," Nadine answered.

"So, you're in love with the man who killed our daughter," said Jason, disgust lingering beneath his words.

"Stop it, Jason. I know you're hurting, but Ethan didn't kill your child," answered Valeyn.

"Then who did? Who's to blame? Is it me? Is that what you're saying? The gods know, *she* blames me." Jason pointed a finger at Nadine. "But really, this is all because you two are in love. That's the reason my life had to be ripped apart. You're to blame! You and your lover!"

Valeyn was stunned by the accusation. Even Nadine had turned to look at her husband, naked pity clear on her face.

"You say you don't recognize me, Jason?" said Valeyn, "Well, I don't think I recognize you either. You're not the young man who Elyn used to adore. You're dark. You're looking to kill and to die. You and Ethan are men I've loved in different ways, and I hate what this war has done to both of you. I just want it to stop."

Jason collapsed onto the couch, his face ashen. He stared at the floor and when he spoke, it was barely a whisper. "It's my fault. I provoked him."

"What are you talking about?" Valeyn asked.

"I knew he loved you and I used it against him. I knew that you – that Elyn – used to love me, and I taunted him with it, so I could make him angry and lure him into a trap. And it worked. I thought I was so clever. I had no idea what I was starting."

Valeyn looked at him and Nadine stepped away from the window

"Paeter died. Our baby died. Why did I have to make it so personal? Why didn't I just surrender? It all could have been different."

"Jason, stop. You don't know that. You'll never know. Stop looking for blame. It doesn't help," said Valeyn crouching in front of him.

Nadine quietly rounded the couch and sat beside her husband, taking his hand. "Jason, I don't blame you. Not anymore. You're right, I was angry at you for a long time, but I was angry at everyone. Sometimes, I still am. But it's pointless now. What's done is behind us. I'll mourn my father in my own way, in my own time, but I know he'd want us to move on. He had no time for vengeance."

"I still hate Ethan," said Jason.

"I know," said Nadine. "But we can't live like this."

Jason sighed and tears ran down his cheeks. "I wish I knew how to forgive him, but I don't"

A knock sounded at the door and an officer with four Helmsguard soldiers entered the room. Valeyn glared at them.

"What's the meaning of this intrusion? I left orders I wasn't to be disturbed," she said.

The officer looked straight ahead when he spoke, avoiding Valeyn's stare. "My apologies, my lord. I've been given orders to bring the prisoners to the throne room for immediate trial."

"Who gave you these orders?' she asked, already guessing the answer.

"My lord, the orders have been issued by Minister Morbus on behalf of the Unity Assembly."

Valeyn grunted a laugh. "Of course. Well, I countermand those orders. The prisoners stay with me. You're excused, Squire."

The officer paled but didn't move. He licked his lips nervously, as if searching for the right words.

"Didn't you hear me, Officer?" Valeyn snapped. "Is there something else?"

"My lord, I have been given orders that I am to follow to the letter. I have been explicitly told that these orders are not to be overruled by anyone — not even by you."

Fury rose within her. Morbus was now directly sowing insurrection, but this was too much, even for him. She had him now.

"Squire, this is insubordination," she said calmly.

"My lord, please. I have been told that it is insubordination to disobey these orders. I respectfully ask you to spare me this crisis and address this directly with Minister Morbus," he answered, still staring directly ahead. "Please, my lord."

Valeyn willed herself to calm. It wouldn't do any good to torture these poor men, they weren't the source of the problem, and besides, Morbus's overreach had now given her the solution.

"You have orders to escort them to the throne room?" she asked.

"At once, my lord," he answered.

"Well, it just so happens I'm in the mood to pay a visit to Lord Morbus. Let's all go together, shall we?"

"Of course, Lord Valeyn," the officer replied, visibly relieved.

Valeyn fumed quietly as she led the procession down the massive hallway of the citadel. Morbus had clearly overplayed his hand by ordering soldiers to disobey her, and yet there was an odd feeling within her, a sense of disquiet. She knew something was wrong. This was a very stupid thing to do, and Morbus was far from stupid.

The shrill sound of horns heralded her arrival and the massive doors of her throne room opened as she approached. The sight before her made her pause at the threshold. Morbus was lounging comfortably upon the throne, an arm draped lazily across the armrest. Udrax, Snyed, and the rest of the Unity Assembly were scattered around the room, their faces unreadable as Valeyn regained her composure and entered. The clip of her boots on the black marble floor echoed across the chamber as she slowly walked to stand before Morbus, who looked down at her with a smirking face. Ethan and Sarele entered the room behind her and both paused as they took in the possible implications of the gathering.

"So, tell me, Minister," Valeyn asked, almost conversationally, "by which means would you prefer to be executed?"

Morbus's smile widened. "Oh, my dear child. You were always a good soldier, I grant you that, but you were never particularly good at reading the room or seeing the big picture, were you?"

Valeyn glanced around at the other men. So many faces, some stoic, others hostile, a few ashamed, none of them friendly. Even Habistich avoided her eyes.

"So, what is this then? A conspiracy? A treasonous plot to overthrow the throne?" she asked the room.

"It's a trial, Vale," answered Morbus. "A trial of your friends and of you."

"You're insane, Morbus," she growled. "And I've had enough of your games. Guards, arrest him!"

Nobody moved. Valeyn again looked around the room, this time at the Helmsguard who stood like statues in their alcoves; soldiers loyal to Morbus.

"No, Vale, you're the one who's insane. Or at least, you're on the way to madness," answered Morbus. "We all know it, or at least those of us who aren't blinded by fanatical worship."

"You mean the Prodigals?" answered Valeyn.

Morbus laughed. "Yes. The *Prodigals*. We can say the name out loud if you like. It doesn't really matter anymore. It's no longer a secret like it was under your father. You see, Bythe went mad. We all saw it. Anyone who bothers to glance casually through the recorded scriptures can see they all suffered it one way or the other, and now we see it in you."

"I won't tolerate this, Morbus."

"No, I don't expect you will. That itself is part of this discussion. Bring the prisoners forth!" he shouted to the guards. Nadine and Jason were roughly bundled in front of the throne."

"Stop! That's an order!" she shouted, but the solders didn't acknowledge her.

"I'm afraid the time of the gods and their daughters is at an end. People are tired of their endless wars, and it's time we finally had peace," announced Morbus as Jason and Nadine were each led to separate platforms flanking either side of the throne.

"Peace? And you're going to deliver it, are you? You're going to achieve what others couldn't?" asked Valeyn.

"In one form or another, yes, I am. Now that the true gods are gone, we can finally set about repairing this world."

"You're forgetting about me."

Morbus chuckled to himself. "I said the *true* gods, Vale. Come now, let's be honest. We all know you're not one of them. You were born here, mortal and imperfect like the rest of us, but unlike the rest of us, you reject your place. You seem to think that you're better than us, that you deserve to rule over us. That doesn't exactly seem fair, does it?"

Snyed called out from across the room. "We only followed you because we didn't have an alternative, but now we do. You're going mad, Valeyn, just like your father and the rest of the gods. It's time for a better way."

"Have *you* all lost your minds? Even if you somehow managed to negotiate peace with the Alliance, the Desecration is here! Morbus can't protect you from the end of the world!"

"But I can," Ferehain's voice cut across Valeyn's as he slowly emerged from the darkness behind the throne, followed by the shrouded form of Aleasea, Exedor, and a number of Imbatals.

"My gods, Morbus. You want to hand him the throne? What are you thinking?" Valeyn whispered.

"He has done what you could not," answered Ferehain. "He has found a way to save this world."

"So, after that speech about rejecting the rule of gods, you're still going to replace one god with another?" asked Valeyn, gesturing at Ferehain as she addressed the Assembly. "Do you really think Ferehain is going to help you make peace with the Outland Alliance? He's no longer one of the Ageless, and he's not exactly trustworthy. You have no idea who you're bargaining with."

"There will be no negotiated peace with the Alliance. That's your approach, and it's as insane as you are!" snarled Morbus. "Our proposal is a change in management of the Iron Union, with a far more direct approach against our enemies."

Ferehain seemed to be completely disinterested in her. He walked over to Jason and stared at him intently, as if analysing a puzzle. Valeyn suddenly felt uneasy.

"What do you want, Ferehain?" Valeyn called out.

Ferehain continued to stare at Jason for a moment longer before slowly turning his attention to her. He walked over to stand before her, his sharp eyes were as fierce and as cold as the first time she'd ever seen them in the chambers of Sanctuary, only now there was the strange lilt of a zealot within that look, and Valeyn began to understand he was no longer that same man.

"I want this to end, girl," he said, with the calm inflections of a patient teacher. "It is ironic that it was you who placed the means to achieve this in my hands. But perhaps not. Perhaps it is ordained? After all, is that not the one consistent trait of all gods, that one way or the other, they find a way to destroy themselves?"

"Ferehain, I'm going to ask you one last time, for the sake of Aleasea, Veroulle, and all the others, please stop this. We've had our differences, but we've always been on the same side."

"We have never been on the same side. I have always hated you. This is simply the end that I have always foreseen — a world without the gods — and that includes false gods like you."

"I still have more power than you, Ferehain. Don't test it," said Valeyn.

Ferehain's mouth curved into a patient smile. "We will see." He continued walking over to where Ethan now stood and fixed him with the same curious look.

Morbus cleared his throat in a strange way and drew her attention. "Your true place has always been in this room, hasn't it? Or at least, that's what you've believed on some level. Only now, I have found a way to take it from you."

Valeyn took a slow and deliberate step toward him. "You're overstepping, Morbus, and you're forgetting yourself. Don't think that allying yourself with Ferehain will protect you as it did with Yvorre. You're just finding another master to grovel before."

His face darkened. "I'll never grovel before you, Vale, and I won't grovel before any god. I'd rather die."

Valeyn smiled. "I intend to help you there."

"Yes, prove me right, Vale. Despite all the talk of change, you're no different from your father. Show us the edge of your blade and put us in our place once more."

Valeyn hesitated and glanced across at the gathered assembly, then at Ethan. It seemed to her that he was imploring her to slow down, to think and use diplomacy rather than action. Ferehain was merely watching the exchange. Something was wrong. She turned to Snyed.

"On what grounds are you supporting this insurrection?" she asked.

"We've been working on this for quite a while, young lady. Your father was growing weaker, and we'd planned to move against him. Your arrival mixed things up a little, but not that much. In many ways you've made it easier. The transition upset a lot of people and we've been able to exploit that.

"Your grievances were with my father; I'm not him."

"You're close enough," he sneered.

She looked across the faces in the room. "You have not answered my question, so I ask you again. On what grounds do you lead this insurrection?"

Morbus gestured to Jason and Nadine. "These two are leaders of our declared enemy, and you consort with them. Your little performance at Krag has swayed the few people left who we needed to convince. Not even a god is above treason."

She played the only card left, even though she knew it would corner her into one course of action. "I am a god, my will is absolute. It is impossible for me to be treasonous to myself."

"You've been treasonous to us, to your people! You were always weak, Vale. We all knew it. We used to laugh at you when you were an officer. Bythe's bastard daughter. The girl nobody wanted. You were always a joke to the rest of us."

"Be careful, Morbus. Ferehain can't protect you from me."

"At least your father was strong. I mean, for all his faults, we respected his consistency and his complete ruthlessness. You, on the other hand, want to be loved. In fact, you want it so much that you invite your friends here to support you. You're like an unloved child desperate for acceptance. Now we all understand why your father despised you!" sneered Morbus.

That was enough. Valeyn acted. With her sword free, she crossed the throne room in an instant, plunging her weapon deep into the man's round chest. Pain registered on his face as he struggled through his last moments, but not fear or regret. Only a grim sense of satisfaction emanated from him as he slumped sideways into death.

The room was still, only the slow dripping of blood from the edge of the throne onto the floor broke the silence. After a moment, Ferehain stepped forward and glanced up at Morbus's corpse.

"And so it is. The gods will always rule through force and violence. They will never change, not even those who claim otherwise."

Valeyn turned to face him. "Stop these games. I'm putting an end to this."

Ferehain raised an eyebrow. "And how are you going to do that. Are you going to use more violence against me? Will you forge your rule in blood, just like the other gods?"

Valeyn looked at the blood on the floor and paused. Ferehain had a point. She knew she couldn't murder her way through this and still claim she was different to Bythe. There had to be a better way. Or was this hesitation just another sign of weakness?

Or are you simply going mad?

She wasn't sure if the voice was in her head or if someone had spoken aloud. Ferehain smiled as if reading her confusion. "But I do agree with you, we should put an end to this now."

How do you intend to achieve this?

Ferehain's head snapped around at the sound, and Valeyn understood the voice was now audible to all, that it was a familiar voice, the voice of a curious god.

"Our judgment is contingent upon the release of our *kai* should we judge it so. Who are you to assume control of this, Ageless?" A young woman in a white dress was standing in the dark recess of the throne room, where no one had been a moment earlier. She walked forth on bare feet with a serene expression, uncaring of the guards who drew sabres against her. She walked in front of Jason and shook her head. "I have been watching this one. He intrigues me. I cannot say that I approve of your treatment of him, Ageless."

"Romona," Ferehain said, unsuccessfully trying to cover the surprise he clearly felt. "So, you have finally come."

"I have been here for some time. I have always been a curious one. Oh, so curious. As I said, I am curious how you intend to bring about this ending you speak of, for I am fond of death and of endings."

"I hold the *kai* that underpins this world, and I control all of it. This is what your brethren desire more than anything."

"You have appropriated this prize. You now hold it ransom?"

"Indeed, and I can release it to you, should we reach agreement."

"And yet, you are full of bluster and deceit. You do not control all the *kai*, not while the daughter of Maelene and Bythe lives. She changes and grows more powerful in our presence, is this not a worry?" Romona said, gesturing to Valeyn.

Ferehain smiled. "A mere detail, but you are right. This is something I should address before we proceed."

He turned to face Valeyn and she raised her weapon. Her mind raced as she fought to make sense of the situation.

"Don't try this, Ferehain. You said you wanted to put me on trial. If you attack me now, you will die."

"I want to put the daughters of Bythe and Maelene on trial. You – Valeyn – are a façade, a forgery. And I will prove it."

He glanced at Exedor and Valeyn felt a sharp pain split her mind. She cried out as she tried to hold onto her thoughts.

"Hello, my dear. I trust you're happy to see me again?" said Exedor as his eyes darkened. "It's time we finished the little talk we started back on the beach at Tiet. You remember, don't you?" Valeyn became aware of two voices in her head, both Elyn and Vale. She squeezed her eyes shut and tried to calm her thoughts. She knew this was only in her mind.

"We discovered the great and powerful Valeyn was not as stable as she thought she was. There's a crack in your mind, and I can find that crack."

Valeyn trembled but refused to fall to her knees. She opened her eyes and glared at Exedor.

"The only crack you'll find will be the one I put in your neck. Stop this. I know it's just an illusion."

"No, it is not," said Ferehain and extended his hand. "It is true, the Desecration has enhanced your power to the point where you can mimic the abilities of other gods. I suppose, in theory, you could save Kovalith. I imagine this thought has occurred to you. But this change has also destabilised you. This was my intention, and I admit, I have been relishing this moment for some time."

A nimbus of green and red light hovered around her for a moment, and then it was as if the split in her mind was suddenly wrenched violently in two. The pain flashed through her being and pulled the air from her lungs, robbing her of any ability to cry out.

The naked bodies of Vale and Elyn were thrown across the room in opposite directions, where they each slammed violently into a wall.

"No!" Ethan cried out. Jason and Nadine were stunned, and their disbelief was mirrored on the faces of the Unity Assembly. Only Ferehain was unsurprised.

"And so, we come to the final betrayal, and the truth is exposed for all to see," Ferehain said. "You are not truly one of the gods, merely a forgery, an aspiration, a pretense. And now this has been proven."

Romona looked down upon Elyn and Vale impassively as both women struggled to their feet in disbelief. They were now both young women aged in their early twenties, both with identical features, only Elyn's dark eyes distinguishing her from Vale's blue.

"Elyn?" Nadine asked. "Elyn, is that you?"

Elyn didn't answer, she glanced around the room as if seeing it for the first time

"You have undone our work. How have you achieved this?" asked Romona with no more than mild curiosity.

"That is the question, is it not?" replied Ferehain, flourishing a twisted metal object in his hand which now pulsated with a green and red glow. "You might remember this, Romona. I believe it was your creation when you were attempting to harness the *kai* of this world. Exedor had this for a time, and now I have found a way to prefect it. Like all gods, it was only a matter of time before Valeyn would grow careless with her power, and she did not stop to consider how her rapid growth might come at the expense of disciplined control."

Vale was breathing heavily, Elyn could sense her trying to force herself to calm and fight down the sense of panic that was rising.

As if ordered by an unheard command, two of the Imbatals marched forward, seized both Vale and Elyn by the backs of their necks, and propelled them both to the center of the room before Ferehain. At a nod from him, the two creatures forced both women to their knees with the slightest application of pressure to their spines.

"Cover them up, for the god's sake!" shouted Ethan.

"I do not believe the gods care about their state of dress," answered Ferehain. "In any event, they can come down and make such a request themselves if they feel uncomfortable. Until that happens, I am assuming leadership of the Iron Union and denouncing Valeyn as a false god, undeserving of the throne. Do any on the Unity Assembly object to this?"

Ferehain glared with satisfaction at the pale faces of the timid men he had cowed so completely. "Very well, as there are no dissenters—"

"I object." Sarele's voice rang over Ferehain's and all were silent. Ferehain turned and looked at her with calculation in his eyes.

"Lady Sarele of Mac-Soldai, mother of Commander Ethan, you are the sole objector and are overruled."

"Nevertheless, I will not stand by and let this happen. I will not recognize you as leader of the Iron Union. And you!" she turned to the gathered men of the Unity Assembly. "You disgust me. We've had our differences, but I would have never believed you all capable of such cowardice."

"Such insults are meaningless," said Ferehain. "You son is a conspirator and is also facing trial for his actions. You are removed from the Assembly."

"You will not touch my son!" Sarele shouted in a display of pure maternal rage. "Not unless you wish to cast your new empire into open war! I will send every man against you, and I will see your new city drown in blood if you do this."

"Arrest her," snapped Ferehain.

"Wait!" shouted Snyed. "You're arresting *us* now? That's not how it works, Ageless. We *make* the rules, we aren't held to them. I have no love for Sarele, but we don't just arrest her because she's a pain."

Ferehain hesitated, clearly unprepared for the defiance his ignorance had started.

"Ethan, let's go," Sarele said, turning for the door.

"Stop them," said Ferehain.

Guards moved forward and the Assembly broke into cries of anger and confusion.

"Wait!" shouted Ethan. "I surrender myself for trial, but you have no grounds to hold my mother. She is free to leave under the law."

Ferehain opened his mouth but Snyed spoke over him.

"That's right. You're off the Assembly, but you need to leave, Sarele. The Unity Assembly wants no quarrel with the House of Mac-Soldai."

Sarele stared at Ethan in alarm, torn between her own freedom and the safety of her son.

"Go, Mother," Ethan said, nodding at the door. "But if you finally feel compelled to act, then you know my advice."

Sarele dropped her eyes and left the room. Every eye seemed to follow her exit, as if everyone understood the stability of an empire might now rest upon the conscience of one powerful woman.

·   ·   ·

Elyn pulled the sheet around her shoulders and looked across the room. Everything seemed strange to her eyes. After years of existing as Valeyn, that being had now been brutally cut from her life, and now she was simply Elyn once more. Valeyn was gone, and somehow Elyn knew she wouldn't ever come back. Yet she wasn't afraid.

It was strange, she knew she should be. She knew the young Elyn of Fairhaven would have been terrified at her current situation. She was captive, held at the mercy of a man who hated her, completely uncertain of what to do or what would happen. Yet, she wasn't afraid.

She made eye contact with Vale and her twin nodded in return.

"*Elyn,*" Vale said in her mind. "*I'm with you.*"

"*And I won't leave you,*" Elyn replied.

A band of strength passed through their shared connection. She felt older now, much older than the young woman who had bonded with Vale back in Fairhaven, and she knew Vale felt the same. Elyn's old fears and anxieties bubbled in the back of her mind, but they seemed to be silly, childhood preoccupations. The world seemed much smaller now.

She wasn't sure how long it had been since Sarele had left them, but it couldn't have been more than an hour. Habistich had insisted on the guards finding them clothing, and Ferehain had eventually relented, more from apathy than conviction, but he'd refused to let them leave. Elyn suspected he probably wasn't sure what to do next, but he seemed to be in complete control for the moment.

"*Do we provoke him?*" Vale asked in Elyn's mind. "*Try to gain some advantage?*"

"*Maybe, but not yet,*" Elyn replied. "*Let's wait. He controls the board, and we're at a disadvantage. Let him make his moves, then we'll see how we can respond.*"

Vale silently agreed. Elyn then noticed Romona was watching both of them and understood she could hear their exchange. Elyn and Vale had been speaking in the language of gods. Had they always done this? Elyn wasn't sure, but it felt natural to her now. Her gaze fell on Jason and Nadine and her heart leaped. It was Elyn – not Valeyn – who now saw her old friends from childhood, and it was Elyn's eyes that now filled with tears at the unexpected surge of emotion. Nadine's hand went to her mouth and Jason instinctively stepped forward.

"Halt!" snapped the nearest guard, drawing his sabre. "Step back prisoner."

Jason stopped but kept his eyes on Elyn.

"Elyn!" he cried. "Is it really you?"

Elyn smiled. "Yes, Jason, it's me. Had you forgotten what I looked like?"

Jason's grin broadened and he attempted to take another step, but two more guards moved toward him with their weapons drawn. Jason paused and glared at them both.

"I just want to talk to her. What's the harm in that? We're not going anywhere."

"Step back or we'll—" the solder began, but Romona's serene voice cut him off.

"You will do nothing. I have followed this man for some time, and I wish to judge him myself. I would have him speak to his friend."

The guard looked at Ferehain, who was watching Romona.

"You would judge him?" Ferehain said quietly. "Very well, they may speak."

The guards stepped back and Jason rushed across the floor, wrapping Elyn in a hug that was almost violent in its intensity. Nadine quickly followed and once her husband was finished, gave Elyn a hug that was almost as passionate.

"My gods, Elyn. I can't believe it. I thought I'd never see you again," said Nadine.

"Neither did I," replied Elyn as her tears dampened Nadine's shoulder. They held their embrace for a long time before finally separating. Nadine and Jason both looked at Elyn from head to foot.

"You've grown. You're a woman now," said Nadine.

Elyn smiled. "I know. I can feel it. Although, I'm curious to know how I look."

"You look great," said Jason. "You look like Elyn."

Jason helped Elyn lower herself to the floor and then the three of them sat together, as if they were back in Fairhaven.

"Are you alright? What happened to Valeyn?" Ethan asked.

"I don't know. She's gone, I think," said Elyn.

"How can she be gone?" asked Nadine. "I thought your reconciliation was permanent?"

"So did I," said Valeyn. "It seems that Ferehain's been able to bend the rules of this world. All gods had their weaknesses. I guess Valeyn's was fairly obvious when you think about it. Ferehain just needed the right tool, and Valeyn was the one who gave it to him."

Jason's brow furrowed as he looked at the space between Vale and Elyn.

"If we could get you close to her, do you think you could reconcile again?"

"I don't think so, Jason. Whatever part of us formed Valeyn . . . it's missing. Ferehain erased it."

"Can we get it back?" asked Jason.

Elyn sighed and shook her head. "It's gone. Valeyn's gone. She's not coming back. I just know it."

"I told you she was weak. Valeyn was never going to transcend into the Etherian." Elyn didn't need to turn her head to recognize the vile voice of Lubalt-Teble as he strode into the room. The guards turned in surprise and drew their weapons again, but stood down at a signal from Ferehain. Romona didn't look at the new arrival, but Elyn knew they were aware of each other.

"So, this is the great Ageless leader who will reckon with the gods? This should be amusing," Lubalt-Teble sneered as he glanced at Ferehain.

Jason and Nadine looked at the god with alarm, but Elyn touched them both reassuringly.

"Ignore him," said Elyn. "He's just a braggart. He can't hurt you."

Nevertheless, both Nadine and Jason continued staring at the god as his dismissive gaze swept over them.

"Nadine, Jason, why did you come? Please, you must tell me," asked Elyn.

Nadine tore her eyes away from Lubalt-Teble and lowered her voice. "Exedor came to us. He said you'd need us."

"Exedor?" Elyn repeated with a sense of disbelief. She looked up to find Ferehain staring at her. She didn't know if he could hear them, she supposed there was little she could do about it.

"He told us Bythe would be dead, that you couldn't hold the throne, and that you were in serious danger. He basically predicted everything we've just seen," continued Nadine.

"It was a trap," Elyn said.

Jason nodded. "We thought that too, and maybe it was. But still, I'm glad we did it. Seeing you again . . ."

Elyn felt a wave of gratitude and shame wash over her. "Then I've probably led you to your deaths. It was all for nothing. I should never have come back here."

"Hey, stop that!" chided Jason. "We came here ourselves. We came here for you. I'd do it again if I knew that it meant we'd get to see you again."

Nadine placed her hand on Elyn's. "He's right. You returned from The Tower to save Jason when he needed you. Do you think we'd do any different?"

Both her friends looked at each other, then over at Vale. Ethan had been permitted to speak with her, and he knelt beside Vale with deep concern on his face.

"So, are you free from her influence?" Jason asked, nodding at Vale.

"Her *influence*?" Elyn answered.

"Yes. Vale's influence; the daughter of Bythe," said Jason.

"Jason, I'm the daughter of Bythe. So's Vale. We're still the same person. She's no more evil than I am."

Jason levelled a hard look at Ethan. "I meant what I said earlier. I hate him, and if Vale's at his side, then I'm sorry. I know she's your sister, but I can't accept her either."

"Jason, please. She's not my – I need you to try to let go of this, for me, if not for yourself," said Elyn. Jason only continued to stare at Ethan in reply.

"Why will you not do this?" asked Romona.

"An excellent question," said Exedor, walking over to join Ferehain next to the throne. "They are a strange people, aren't they? Self-centerd, arrogant, and blind to the needs of others. Valeyn was a very appropriate deification of their values."

"I disagree. There is a sense of nobility to them." Pia's voice drifted from where she hovered in the darkness of the chamber above. Every mortal in the room looked up to see the form of Bythe's sister looking down at them.

"Then perhaps this could form the basis of your judgment?" suggested Exedor. "You wish to judge this world, then why not judge those before you?"

Romona's smile was one of childish fascination. "Yes, that is an excellent idea. You have singular talents, Inquisitor. I would have you question these people for us. I believe we should judge them."

Ferehain looked at Exedor in silence then turned to Romona. "And this would satisfy you?"

"Indeed, it would," answered Romona.

"Then let us proceed," Ferehain announced.

"Yes, let's get this over with," said Lubalt-Teble as he ascended to join Pia in the darkness above. Only Romona chose to remain on the floor. The air suddenly felt thick and a darkness seemed to descend on the room, as if a blanket had been thrown over the citadel, trapping all light and air within. And then Elyn felt them. There were others in the room — strong forces hovering above them. Faces were coalescing in the darkness above, twisting and distorting. She could sense them more than she could see them, some she recognized, others she had never known, but she felt a kindred connection with all of them. The throne room became so filled with the feeling of so many presences, it almost became suffocating. Snyed and the rest of his cronies now looked above them anxiously. Twenty-three faces now appeared in the space above them, all cold and uncaring.

Ferehain looked up and addressed them unflinchingly. "Let us now come to the meaning of this Desecration. You wish to reclaim the *kai* of this world, however this force is now unquestioningly under my control."

"What do you want?" asked Ceriv in a faint whisper.

Ferehain scanned the faces of those above him. He saw the rough faces of Dahz and Narak, the rounded features of Kalte, he saw Basalt and Pia and Ceriv, and frustration creased his brow.

"Where is Maelene?" he asked.

There was no answer.

"What do you want?" another deep voice echoed the first.

"Why is she not here? Where is Bythe the Deceiver?" Ferehain asked.

"They aren't here, Ageless," said Shin, materialising into the form of an old man with bright blue eyes. "We don't answer to each other, and as I told you once before, we certainly don't answer to you."

"Why are they not here?" asked Ferehain, seemingly unsettled for a moment. "Of all of you, they both were most invested in this world. They should be here for the Desecration."

Shin shrugged. "Maybe they lost interest after being here for so long. Things are different when we return to Etherian; perspective is restored. Whatever you have planned, you're going to have to do it without them as your audience."

"We have enough to form the Congress. Proceed," ordered Khanem, a god remembered for his obsession with the rational logic of the Kovalith. A god who had not lasted long in this world.

"Very well," Ferehain muttered. "You have come to judge this world, to see if it is worthy of a continued existence or if your *kai* should be restored to you."

"That is correct," said Pia

"And now that I am the master of all the *kai* within Kovalith, I may, indeed, permit one of these outcomes," said Ferehain.

"You are an arrogant one," said Romona with her usual innocence.

"Indeed, he is," agreed Shin.

"We should kill it," snarled Narak.

"But you cannot," answered Ferehain, "or you would have done so already. You cannot fully reenter Kovalith or you would have done so already, and I suspect that even if you wished to, my interference has now made this impossible for you."

The silent glares of the immortal faces seemed to serve as confirmation.

"What do you want?" asked Lubalt-Teble.

"A world free from the influence of the gods. I want your sacred bond that you will all leave and never return."

"Impudence!" snarled a voice from above and the sentiment was taken up by several others, yet Ferehain was unmoved.

"This is unsatisfactory," said Pia. "The soul of Kovalith is ours, and many of us wish it to be returned. It is not acceptable for you to stand in the way of this."

"Then I suggest we bargain," answered Ferehain.

"You propose a negotiation?" asked Romona.

"I have already set about unmaking this world. You have seen this. I propose that Kovalith be remade in a new, pure form. It will be a smaller world, a less complicated one, and a world that will require far less power to sustain it. You may take most of your *kai* and leave only a portion to sustain the world that is left."

"A renewed world that you will rule?" asked Pia.

"You will not concern yourself with this new world. You will have your *kai* and be gone," snapped Ferehain.

The gods fell silent again for a moment.

"This might be acceptable," said Lubalt-Teble. "I'm tired of this place and I want to be rid of it. Let's make this bargain."

"I see no problem with this," said Pia.

Wait," said Romona. "Kovalith may still be worth preserving in its entirety."

"Nonsense," grunted Dahz. "This place was unbecoming of us. It drove us to base urges which are best forgotten. Let us be rid of it."

"All the same, we have rules to follow, remember?" said Shin.

"Nishindra, you place far too much emphasis on these things. Let us be done," insisted Pia.

"He is correct," said Romona. "We have set the laws and now we must follow them. To do otherwise is to break the rules of order and invite chaos to infect our existence once more. Do we wish to return to the turmoil of Eald?"

"The case must be argued for the soul of this world. Order must be followed," said Khanem.

"So be it," answered Pia with a sigh.

Ferehain nodded. "Very well. We have a suitable selection of people from this world with which we can form that judgment. Romona has taken an interest in this one," said Ferehain, motioning to Jason. "You seek to understand these people, then let us use your own favorites as our test."

"Very interesting," said Romona, looking intrigued. "Yes, let's do this. I'd like to understand more."

"They are repugnant and uninteresting, but very well," sneered Lubalt-Teble.

"Proceed," agreed Pia.

Ferehain nodded at Exedor, and the Royal Inquisitor motioned to two Imbatals. The clockwork demons marched over to Elyn and Vale and hauled them both to their feet, escorting them to the center of the throne room before forcing them back to their knees. Exedor walked over to where Vale kneeled before one of the Imbatals. He paused and stared into her upturned face for a long moment. Vale returned the stare, seemingly unwilling to satisfy him with an unprovoked response. Without a word, he turned from her and walked purposefully over to Elyn, stooping to collect her chin in his hand and raise her face to meet his.

"And here she is," he hissed quietly, "the poisonous viper who slunk into your midst so many years ago. Nobody but Ferehain could see you for who you were, and nobody could predict how much damage you would cause except him."

"I did nothing but help Ferehain."

"You would believe that, and you would have all the gods believe as such, but this is simply not true. Your presence in Sanctuary set in motion a series of unstoppable and inexorable events that would eventually bring destruction. Sanctuary is gone, even Fairhaven itself is burned to the ground, and I lay this blame squarely upon you."

"That's absurd," replied Elyn, looking past Exedor to confront Ferehain directly. "I didn't do any of those things. You were there."

"Yes, I was there," answered Ferehain, "and I remember only too well how those events came to pass. The destruction of Sanctuary came about only because you placed yourself within its heart. You, the child of evil, put your own self-interest above the rest of everyone else."

"You took me there yourself," replied Elyn. "You took me to see Maelene when she returned to you."

"Only because I – like the others – had been deceived by Yvorre; your mother who had become corrupt and mad, like all gods are destined to do, as you were destined to do, before I relieved us of that fate. I wished you gone from the moment you set foot in Sanctuary. I could smell Bythe's vile poison in your veins, and yet Veroulle overruled me, to his own doom. Had you been euthanised as I wished, then the mad plans of Yvorre, Bythe and Nishindra would never have been pursued."

Elyn looked at her tormentor with defiance. "You're misremembering things, Ferehain. Try to paint me as evil all you like, but I'll never believe you. I was innocent back then. I was just as much a victim of the gods as everyone."

"A victim?" Exedor pounced on the word. "I seem to recall you admonishing your mother for her victimhood back in The Tower."

Exedor swept his arms upward and the black recesses of the throne room above began to shimmer. A ball of silver liquid appeared and began to twist itself into a mirror of sorts.

"Bythe was fond of these artefacts, was he not?" asked Exedor rhetorically. "An ability to cast his gaze as far as he liked, but to see only what he wanted to see. But Nishindra, your Oraculate was truly the greatest of creations. We cannot pretend to have mastered it entirely, however I have skill enough to get what we need."

The shimmering window coalesced into an image. Maelene was struggling with Valeyn in The Tower, trying to wrest the green and red energies of *kai* from her. The image of Valeyn spoke and her words carried throughout the throne room.

"*Just accept who you are, accept who you aren't,*" Valeyn shouted at her mother.

"You seemed very sure of yourself in that moment. You were no victim of anyone; you accepted your nature. You made that very clear," said Exedor.

"That was Valeyn," answered Elyn. "You're accusing *me* of evil. Elyn. Valeyn was a god. Yes, she was powerful and sometimes violent, but that wasn't who I was back in Fairhaven. Back then, I was just a girl. I was innocent."

"If you're looking to accuse someone as a dark and twisted murderer, then you've picked the wrong person," said Jason. "Elyn was the kindest soul I knew."

Exedor looked from Elyn to Jason for a moment, and when he spoke, he shattered their confidence.

"And what about Nathan?"

Elyn felt a jolt of guilt in the pit of her stomach. It had been a long time since she'd thought of the young man who tormented her relentlessly in Fairhaven, in part due to the trauma of the memories, but mostly because of what she'd later done to him.

"*What happened to the smart mouth? Remember when you said I couldn't handle a woman? How about I prove it to you right here?*" Nathan's voice echoed around the room and Elyn looked up in horror and saw herself standing next to the river in the Old City in Fairhaven. The city was under siege from the Northmen and fires burned in the distance. Nathan was lingering over her shoulder, his hands already on her body. Then she turned to face him, her expression one of ruthless fury, and Nathan immediately began to wilt under her stare. His mouth opened and closed silently, and a smile of malicious satisfaction slowly spread across Elyn's face.

"And what say you now?" asked Exedor. "Do you recall that this was among the first things you did, once you had a taste of power?"

"That's absurd!" shouted Nadine. "She was only defending herself. Nathan was a monster!"

"And so, the innocent Elyn decided to become a monster herself, at her first opportunity," Exedor countered.

"This was your doing," Elyn grated at Ferehain, refusing to look at the terrible scene playing out before her. "You'd tricked me earlier. You set me up."

"And did Ferehain also set you up when you murdered the wild man Jarren, the man who killed your adopted father, Leon? Was that not the first time you realized your strength, and your very first act was to murder somebody? What a reflection of your character this is. Elyn, going through life weak and defenseless, believing she is virtuous, only to have her ruthless nature revealed the moment she is finally granted the strength she so desperately sought. And once you became Valeyn, did your thirst for violence stop, or did you continue to kill those who offended you, those who were far less powerful than you, like the unfortunate Morbus here?"

Elyn wanted to argue further, but her words felt weak. Justified or not, she couldn't refute the accusation of what she had done to Nathan. But before she could speak, Exedor continued.

"No, on the night in Sanctuary, Ferehain had already sensed your evil, and he did nothing more than to reveal your true nature, to yourself as well as to the others, but it was Nathan who paid the price," said Exedor. "And you did not even bother to see what had happened to him, did you? You left Fairhaven that very next day, another broken life in your wake, so much like a god."

"She didn't kill him," argued Jason. "He was still alive when she left."

"But his mind was broken. He never spoke again and when he died later, he was nothing more than the echo of a man. No, it would have been far more merciful had Elyn killed him that night," said Exedor.

"You're being cruel to her, Inquisitor," said Vale. "You know very well that our father's rage was poisoning us."

"Poisoning? Yes, I might actually agree with you there," Exedor replied "Nevertheless, everything that happened afterward, all stemmed from Elyn and her selfish plan to realize her own power and ambition. Had Elyn not existed, had the people of Fairhaven been left to carry on as they had before she entered their lives, Fairhaven and all of her people would still stand today."

"Elyn didn't destroy Fairhaven," Jason interrupted.

"No, that would be you," Exedor said as he turned to regard Jason severely for a moment. "And I will come to you in a moment, but for now, I will address your point. Fairhaven was destroyed by your actions, which were in response to orders from Bythe to do whatever was necessary to reclaim his daughter. He crafted weapons of terrible destruction and did not care who was slaughtered in order to gain what he desired. Again, had Elyn and Vale never come to Fairhaven, these atrocities would not have been committed."

"You're making no sense," said Elyn.

"I agree, this reasoning is counterfactual," said Khanem. "You cannot place blame on somebody based upon a series of hypothetical non-events."

"Then I will make my reasoning plainer," snapped Exedor. "As Vale just stated, Elyn was poisoned by Bythe and committed murder without a thought. But more than that, this entire race has been poisoned by the gods. The madness of the gods is a sickness which has spread throughout the people of Kovalith. This world cannot be saved in its current form. Only by reshaping this world in a better mold will the sickness be cured."

"And Ferehain's remade world will support this?" asked Pia.

"My new world will be created free of any influence of the gods. It will be a smaller world, designed for those who are as yet untainted by the infection running through this one," said Ferehain.

"And for the rest?" asked Romona.

"You may take them," answered Ferehain.

"You're talking about genocide," said Nadine, a slow horror dawning on her face.

"No. I speak of saving those who deserve to be saved and recognizing those who have made their choices to the contrary," said Ferehain.

"And what of the rest of the people?" asked Romona, looking at Jason. "If we and our offspring have created such problems, then so be it, but why should the innocents of this world suffer also?"

"What innocents do you speak of?" asked Exedor with acerbic cynicism. "Are you referring to your pet, Captain Jason?" He strode over to where Jason stood.

"Are you going to accuse me of killing too? I'm a soldier in wartime. Of course, I kill, and I don't apologize for it," snapped Jason.

"No, I do not accuse you of violence That is your trade and you are unsurprisingly very good at it," replied Exedor, turning his face upward once more and willing his Oraculate to shift. "But let us speak of your own endemic hypocrisy."

The image coalesced into a scene that made Nadine gasp. It was Jason, his face stained by dirt and tears, looking down at the body of his infant daughter. Elyn glanced up at the image and felt the blood drain from her face. Jason's expression was a mask of pure despair.

"Exedor, why are you doing this?" Elyn asked incredulously.

"I am revealing Captain Jason for the man he truly is. The mere shell of a man. A man who goes through life, naïvely believing that his masculinity equips him for any challenge, only to have that same strength turned against him. You were unable to save your daughter, and how did you respond to such a revelation? With pure, masculine rage. With an unfettered desire to kill and to die. You burned Fairhaven to the ground, rather than let the man who killed your child claim a meaningless victory. You displaced thousands of people, and then had the hypocrisy to lead the suicidal exodus you forced onto them."

"I was trying to save them," Jason answered in an unsteady voice as the image swept to a scene of Fairhaven's burnt ruin. Wisps of smoke rose from the charred skeletons of houses Elyn once walked past every day.

"No," answered Exedor. "Even at the ends of Kovalith, you still found no respite from your hatred. You are still filled with rage at Baron Ethan, even now. You blame him for the death of your daughter. You are poisoned with hate, even though you know this is irrational. You are no different from the hateful little Elyn, looking to revenge herself on the world."

Jason couldn't take his eyes away from the scene. The man in the image had been pulling the blanket up to the dead baby's chin to protect her from the cold, thinking of how beautiful she would have been. Tears ran down Jason's face and his breath came in sharp bursts.

"You bastard," Nadine gasped. "How can you do this?"

"Captain Jason may yet thank me. I am giving him the opportunity for justice."

Exedor turned away from Jason and walked across the room, his black cloak billowing around him in an almost predatory fashion, until he stood before Ethan.

"Baron Ethan, so good to see you again," Exedor smiled before raising his voice to address his divine audience above. "Perhaps our greatest example of human filth and corruption lies with this one. This man is like his enemy in so many ways. However, unlike Jason, you are the *victim* of unrequited adoration, not the cause of it. The greatest irony, of course, is that you cannot even see how Vale used you."

"That's not true," said Ethan. "I know Vale depended on me."

"Depended on you? Yes, you're much like a reliable horse that always gets Vale to the place she needs to be," Exedor shot back.

"You've tried to break me before, Inquisitor, and failed," said Ethan. "I know my place. I'm a soldier and a nobleman."

"Ah, yes, a nobleman. Such a noble family. Noble enough to keep a bastard hidden among the slums of the Ironhelm. And now, much like Captain Jason, you know how it feels to lose something. Now that you are confronted with the death of a surrogate son, perhaps you understand the magnitude of your deeds. Perhaps not."

Jason and Nadine glanced at Ethan with unreadable expressions.

"But do we pity this man?" Exedor raised his voice to the gods above, his speech marching into full stride. "A man who now appreciates the depths of despair only because he finds himself within her cold embrace? Or do we judge him by his actions?"

The Oraculate shifted once again and settled on a terrible scene. Ethan stood on a trench-riddled field outside Fairhaven facing six figures; three cloaked Ageless, the traitor E'mar, Councillor Morag, and Paeter, Nadine's father.

"Oh, no," mumbled Nadine, raising her hand to her mouth instinctively.

"Yes, a nobleman and a soldier. So noble that he planned and performed one of the most brutal of executions I have ever seen, and from me, that is high praise."

"Stop this!" shouted Jason, fury contorting his face. "Make it stop. Now!"

Nadine was shaking her head, turning in to Jason as if he could shield her from the memory. Above them, in the Oraculate, the scene played out ruthlessly. The Ageless fell first, victims of E'mar's treachery, then Ethan signalled to his soldiers, who forced Paeter and Morag to their knees before stabbing them through their backs. Both Vale and Elyn watched the execution, Vale lamenting the actions of Ethan, Elyn mourning the death of Paeter. They both knew that Morag and Paeter has planned their own trap and that Ethan had acted within a degree of self-defense, but such acts of war were a terrible thing to witness.

Ethan was ashen. He stared blankly at the floor before him as if in shock.

Exedor approached and spoke in a low voice. "Do you have anything to say in your defense? Anything at all?"

Ethan shook his head. "They were my actions. I take responsibility for them."

"And yet your actions were brutal," said Exedor.

"I was . . . driven. I felt compelled to find her," said Ethan.

"Compelled? By whom?"

"Bythe," whispered Ethan.

"So Bythe was to blame, was he?" asked Exedor, but again directing the question to the audience in the manner of an obscene showman. He paced the floor as if deep in thought, before finally speaking. "I am a man of unique influence myself, Baron, and I am somewhat gifted in the art of speech. Would it surprise you that I have discovered the most powerful words in human language. They are the words you hunger for right now. Words that can deliver you from your pain, guilt, and regret." He leaned close to Ethan and spoke in an exaggerated stage whisper, loud enough for all to hear. "It wasn't your fault." He chuckled and walked away, shaking his head as if lost in his own thoughts. "It wasn't your fault, Baron. That's what you want to believe, isn't it? You want to be absolved of your guilt and pain, and deep down, you know these simple words can give you that peace."

"I remember him, I remember his eyes, his command . . . driving me to this," said Ethan.

"That was part of it, no doubt," replied Exedor, "but there was also your base jealousy, your pettiness, your outright desire to win. These desires drove you. Bythe's influence was merely the catalyst you sought."

"Stop torturing him!" shouted Vale. "It's clear he regrets what he did!"

"Perhaps he does, but is that only because he now feels the pain he so willingly inflicted upon others?" asked Exedor. "And does such self-serving contrition really mean anything?"

"No," interrupted Ferehain. "And it matters not. I believe we have made our case. These people are monstrous by nature, and as we have repeatedly seen, the influence of the gods merely compounds their horrific nature. Just now, we have heard them blame Bythe for their depravity, for their complete lack of humanity to each other, and this makes my case. The gods have poisoned this world with their madness, and once that infection takes hold of these people, it drives them to a level of evil that even the gods could not imagine."

"I remain unconvinced," said Romona.

"Very well. I will provide a demonstration. A final judgment of these people." Exedor turned to Jason and Nadine. "And I will give you both a gift — one that you have wanted for some time. I will give you Baron Ethan."

He made a gesture and two of the Imbatals moved. One of them seized Jason, the other gripped Ethan, and both propelled their respective prisoners to the center of the throne room. Exedor adjusted his black cloak, then walked over to where Morbus sat impaled on the throne, blood now covering the floor in a dark red pool. He gripped the hilt of Valeyn's sabre and pulled it effortlessly from the corpse, which slid from its position of mock authority and splashed into the mess on the floor. Leaving a crimson trail in his wake, Exedor walked over to where Jason stood and offered him the hilt of the weapon.

"Take it," he commanded.

Jason hesitated, then carefully extended his hand, as if expecting a trap at any moment. Once the sword was securely in his possession, Exedor and the Imbatals retreated, leaving the two enemies alone in the center of the throne room.

"Jason, no," Elyn called.

"Don't do it," pleaded Vale.

Jason looked at the sword in his hand, then at Nadine. She was staring at the floor, her expression invisible.

Exedor moved closer, looking at both men with the same, grim smile. "Well, now we come to it, don't we? The true test of your character, my young captain," Exedor said in a quiet voice. "What are you waiting for?"

The sabre trembled softly in Jason's hand. He looked at the blade, then at Ethan with a dark hunger.

"He gives you what you wanted. Will you not take it?" asked Romona.

Jason held Ethan's gaze for a moment longer, then forced his eyes away. "No. I won't do it, as much as I want to. Elyn wouldn't want me to do this."

"No!" said Exedor as he moved to stand in front of him "This is your decision and you do not hide behind others." Exedor forced Jason to meet his eyes. "This is your true judgment, and it is the worst kind of judgment for one with conscience."

"You have no idea what he did to us," Jason said.

"I know you have driven yourself to the point of madness, not because of what this man did, but because you fear your own response to it. You replay the past and dream countless possible futures, trying to answer the question of what you should have done. And down every path you find nothing but shame for having not taken a better road."

"Stop it," muttered Jason.

"These thoughts are pointless!" He gripped Ethan by the back of his neck and thrust him at Jason like a sacrificial offering. "What will plague you most in the quiet moments of your long years ahead? Do you fear the creeping guilt of killing a remorseful man? Or do you fear the guilt of knowing that your forgiveness was really just an excuse for weakness?"

"I've made a decision. I won't kill him," snapped Jason.

Exedor barked a sharp laugh "You're a slow learner. A man does not prove himself by simply making a decision, he proves himself by living with it! Which are you prepared to live with?"

Jason looked at Ethan, and his eyes turned cold. "I know it was war. I know you regret what you did. And I wish I could forgive you, Ethan, but I can't. I hate you. I'll always hate you." Jason raised his sword above Ethan's neck and with a swift action, brought it down sharply. "But I'm done with you," Jason said as the sword swung to the ground and clattered harmlessly onto the cold stones. Silence filled the room and Ethan looked disbelievingly into the eyes of the man who had spared him. "I'll never forgive you for what you did, but I can live with myself. I'm not sure you can. That's the end of it. Get him out of my sight."

"Your prosecution was not as compelling as I had believed it would be," Ferehain said, looking hard at Exedor.

"I apologize, my lord. My powers of persuasion are not what they once were after you beat me to the point of death," replied Exedor with little contrition.

A ripple of consternation emanated from the figures assembled above, as if an unheard conversation was taking place.

"I've seen enough," announced Lubalt-Teble. "Give this little sorcerer what he demands and let us be done with this place forever."

"No, this demonstration gives me heart. These people are not as corrupted as this black one would seem to judge. I do not believe we should accede to his demands," said Romona.

Anger darkened Ferehain's face, and he stared at the gods with an almost maniacal defiance. "Do you think you can stop me? You hold no leverage over me while I hold mastery over what you desire."

"It doesn't matter what you think," said Nishindra. "We've got rules and we need to follow them."

"A Congress by majority must be reached, and thus far, you have failed to convince us," said Khanem.

"We require more time to understand your argument and make our decision," said Pia.

Ferehain looked as if he were going to explode with rage. He looked about the room, seeking an outlet for his frustrations. He looked at Elyn and Vale, then from Vale to Ethan, and the cold smile returned to his lips.

"Very well, confer like the bloated and meddlesome bureaucrats you have become. In the meantime, I will demonstrate the meaning of will and resolute action," said Ferehain and he reached into his cloak to withdraw a curved blade as his malicious gaze fell on Nadine. Jason moved to stand before her.

"Don't you touch her," Jason warned, but Ferehain only smiled as he walked toward them.

"You're such a coward," said Elyn and Ferehain's smile fell. He turned his head slowly.

"What did you say?"

"You heard me. You're a coward. Weak. Look at you. You stand before gods, and all you can think about is tormenting two mortals far weaker than you. Is this how you prove yourself?"

"*Elyn, no!*" Vale warned.

They were suicidal words; but she knew she had to take his focus for Jason and Nadine to have any chance of survival.

"*Keep quiet,*" Elyn silently replied. "*It's me he hates; it's always been me. Let me make some good of it.*"

Ferehain had turned away from her friends but was now walking toward her with menace in every slow step.

"Everyone knows how much you were terrified of my father. I watched you run from him," Elyn continued. "But it goes beyond Bythe, doesn't it? You never had the courage to lead. You complain about Veroulle, but you always did as you were told, because you feared him."

"Elyn, I suggest you hold your tongue," said Exedor. She ignored him

"You were weaker than Aleasea. Didn't that insecurity burn you? Look at what you've done to her. You've crippled her to keep her under your control. Are these the actions of a strong man?"

Ferehain stood over her, a looming presence over the young woman, but she rose to her feet and stared up at him defiantly

"But one thing I've always wondered. On the day you failed to protect Maelene from Bythe, were you really overpowered by the enemy – a brave lone survivor like you say – or did you simply hide until the fighting was over? Were you just a coward then, as you are now?"

It was a brutally calibrated attack, one worthy of Exedor, and Elyn could sense she had hit Ferehain in the deepest recesses of his being, all that made him strong had been ripped away and exposed for all to see. Elyn had never before seen such hatred directed at another living soul. His blows were terrible. The pain didn't even register at first, but when it did, it was dreadful. She had no idea how many times he struck her. The dull shock of his fists was interspersed with the cries of Vale, Jason, and Nadine as she felt her ribs snap and her legs go numb. She fell back on the cold floor, looking up at the faces of the gods, who were looking down at her with complete indifference.

"Stop!" Vale cried out. "You're killing her."

Ferehain nodded, breathing heavily from the exertion of his rage. "This is long overdue."

"She's right, you are a coward!" shouted Nadine.

"Kill her!" snapped Ferehain, pointing at Nadine with his eyes still fixed on Elyn's crumpled and bleeding form

"An excellent tactic," said Exedor, stepping forward. "But I implore you not to waste this gesture with a private execution like poor Morbus endured. A very public execution of the leader of our enemy will send a very strong message and will further cement your leadership over the people in your new world. I can arrange for a Royal Termination immediately."

Ferehain's breathing slowed and his composure seemed to return. He glanced at Exedor for a moment as if unsure what he'd said, then considered the advice. "Very well, see to it. I want it done today. I want to remind the gods and men of this world what swift and unyielding will can do," he said, glancing up at the beings above them.

Exedor bowed low and motioned to two of the Helmsguard. The armored men gripped Nadine by her arm and led her to the door. Jason could only look on helplessly under the watchful supervision of the Imbatals.

"I will take the Baron and the Captain to the holding cells—" began Exedor, but Ferehain cut him off.

"Send them to the catacombs and assign them to our best Inquisitor. Bring word to me only when they begin to beg for the release of death."

"And these two?" Exedor asked, motioning to Vale and Elyn. "Should I take them also?"

"No. Leave them both with me," he said, staring down at Elyn as she began to drift from consciousness. "She thinks she is strong. They both do. They think that because they stood up to their father, they have now faced the worst of the world. But Bythe was a different enemy. Despite his strength, he still loved them in his own way. I have no such limitations." He sank to his haunches and reached out to brush the hair away from Elyn's bleeding face. "No, I will hurt them in ways their father never could."

CHAPTER 2

"Details of the rise of the Prodigals and their subsequent role in the downfall of the Iron Union remain unclear. Lord Bythe's increasing inattention had created discontent among the houses as well as opportunities to expand their administrative power. While this conspiracy was purely opportunistic and bureaucratic at first, the collection of powerful men quickly began to dream of much bolder endeavours. We know that the admission of Minister Snyed to the plot was the first step in escalating these dreams into a tactical plan – albeit still a plan of subterfuge, as none of the Prodigals had yet identified a means to challenge the power of Bythe directly. It was not until the ambitious Bureaucrator Morbus inserted himself into their midst that they were guided to an unlikely ally; one with a radical plan to reshape a new world and the power to execute it.

It is highly unlikely the Prodigals would have turned to Ferehain had they truly understood the depths of his own madness – a truth they sadly discovered too late."

~Kaler of the Ageless

Jason allowed himself to be led down the vaulted corridors of Domitus. There were Helmsguard at either side of him and another two escorting Ethan several feet ahead. At any other time, he might have been awestruck by the majesty of the citadel as its scope and magnificence were gradually revealed to him on their long journey to the catacombs, but he barely noticed.

Nadine's about to die.

Jason's every instinct was to free himself, to do something, anything. He knew he was capable — that even with the manacles, it was possible to surprise his two captors then attempt an escape. But to where? With every turn in the corridor, he hoped for a revelation that would solve his plight, but instead, every turn only revealed more complications; additional soldiers standing guard or suspended walkways over perilous drops. Yes, he could try to escape, but every outcome would result in certain death. Still, wasn't that preferable to a slow and lingering death in a dungeon? Each passing moment presented a choice, and every choice teased death against the ever-retreating promise of a future opportunity. His mind raged with frustration.

He glanced at Ethan and wondered. If Ferehain was truly seizing control of the Iron Union, then it stood to follow that Ethan was in as much trouble as Jason. All thoughts of hatred and guilt had fled. All that mattered to him was Nadine, and he knew he would gladly accept the help of anyone – even Ethan – if it meant her life could be saved.

They rounded another corner and approached one of the large, square platforms used to traverse the height of Domitus. Jason has seen them when he was first brought in. Their engineering was as fascinating as it was alien to him, and some part wondered what *his* engineer, Sedren, would think, but at the forefront of Jason's mind was the recognition of an opportunity. They were about to be isolated on the platform, no more than four guards for the two of them. As they ushered him onto the platform where Ethan waited, their eyes met, and in that instant, they understood each other's intentions. Jason knew that Ethan's skill in combat matched his own, and if Jason initiated the escape, it was possible that Ethan could handle his share. He measured the height of the railings on the platform and estimated the amount of force it might take to send a man over the edge. It was possible to use his body weight alone, and if it was done quickly, they might be able to surprise all four guards. Then they would be alone on the platform for how long – a minute, maybe less? He had to assume they'd be discovered almost immediately, but if they could somehow take control of the platform, they might be able to outrun their pursuers . . . or at least gain a head start or fine a place to hide while they worked out their next move. It was an enormous risk, almost certainly suicidal, but he knew it was the only chance he'd get. The last Helmsguard boarded the platform and shut the safety barrier with a clang. Jason sighed and closed his eyes in preparation. This was his last chance. If he died, so be it.

"One moment, soldiers."

Jason recognized the voice before opening his eyes to see Exedor hastening toward them. The lead soldier opened the gate and stepped out to meet the Inquisitor with a closed fist across his chest.

"I'm relieving you. Hand the prisoners over to me. I will handle their interrogation personally."

The soldier glanced at his comrades before returning to Exedor.

"Inquisitor, we heard the order."

"The order was to assign them to our best Inquisitor. That is me."

"But," the soldier argued, "we were ordered to take them to the catacombs."

"And I am ordering you to hand them to me. I am still the Royal Inquisitor," Exedor replied.

The soldier hesitated and Exedor took a step closer to him, his eyes darkening as he did so.

"Are your loyalties not to the Iron Union? Who is this Ferehain who now claims to sit on Bythe's throne? He is an Ageless, our sworn enemy. Do you now follow the advice of the Ageless so unquestioningly? Are you a soldier or just a mercenary?"

The soldier's face fell into uncertainty and he glanced again at his comrades, seemingly desperate for support.

"War is upon us, and you had best be certain you are on the right side. I suggest you remove yourself from this predicament and let me assume your burden."

The soldier seemed relieved at the offer of an honorable solution and nodded to the others as they quickly vacated the platform

"Sir, do you need an escort?" asked the soldier.

"Thank you, but that won't be necessary. I am more than capable of handling two prisoners, but give me the keys to their manacles."

The soldier did as he was ordered and stepped aside as Exedor shut the gate and the platform began to descend. As soon as the soldiers were out of sight, Exedor handed the keys to Jason.

"We have little time," Exedor murmured.

Jason took the keys and within seconds had worked Ethan free from his restraints. He waited for Ethan to return the favour before turning to Exedor.

"What the hells are you playing at?" Jason demanded.

"Exactly what I told you back in Outpost. I was very clear that you would despise the path I sent you down, yet you decided to walk it."

Jason tried to follow Exedor's logic.

"You planned this?"

"Planned? That suggests I can control the actions of others. No, I didn't plan this, but I knew the fate Ferehain intended for Valeyn, and I knew she would need allies. No, more than allies — she'd need friends who would die for her."

"So you manipulated us to come here, knowing we'd be captured. You've sent Nadine to her death!"

"I have done nothing of the sort. I cannot control the actions of Ferehain. I only do what I can around the edges to avert the worst disaster possible for all of us."

"That's not going to help Nadine!" Jason snapped.

"And I warned you both that the risk was immense and the chance for success was narrow. You both made a choice in full knowledge of those risks, and that's why you're here. As I said to you before, accept your decisions and live with them."

"Are you saying it's over?" Jason asked, fighting to keep the despair from creeping into his voice.

Exedor looked up at the towering chasm of Domitus for a moment before answering. "The chance for success is even more narrow now, than it was before, but that chance still remains. I sense that all hope now rests with the two of you."

"You're highly placed with Ferehain. We can use that. You can slow him down and buy us time while I get my family to act," Ethan said.

"I suspect I've just burned all my capital with Ferehain. He witnessed my interrogation of you, Jason, and he already suspects I cannot be trusted.

His suspicions will be confirmed when he learns you are missing, which may be at any moment. I must arrange for you to be away from here immediately."

Jason readied himself to argue but Exedor motioned him to silence. The platform was slowing.

"Walk behind me with your heads down as if I've broken you," Exedor hissed.

The platform jerked to a halt and Exedor opened the gate. Jason was thankful there were no soldiers or officials waiting to enter, but there were several moving through the corridor beyond. He obeyed Exedor's directions and walked sullenly behind him, keeping his face downcast. He held his breath, waiting for a shout or a command for them to stop, but none came and they continued walking down a corridor which seemed to go on interminably. After a number of minutes, Jason waited until the corridor before them was empty before daring to raise his head. He gripped Exedor by the elbow and forced him to stop.

"I'm not leaving without Nadine."

Exedor looked down at Jason's hand as if it was filthy, then sighed and shook his arm free.

"I expected as much, although I do not support this. Your best chance for survival, and our best chance against Ferehain, is for you both to leave here right now. Yes, your wife will be sacrificed, but her name will live on as a martyr to your cause, and you can avenge her."

Jason felt rage and raised his fist. He wanted to pound the face of this smug man, but Exedor's eyes began to darken and Jason felt Ethan's restraining hand on his shoulder. He dropped his fist and shrugged himself free of Ethan.

"You're inhuman," growled Jason.

"Inhuman? I am completely rational!" he enunciated the word as if Jason were a child. "You are a Captain of the Outland Alliance, the husband of their leader. You can personally turn the tide of this war, but only if you live. No, what is irrational is for that chance to be lost out of emotional sentiment."

Jason looked away and considered the options. He knew Exedor was right. Escaping once was a miracle, escaping twice would be tempting the judgment of the gods. But then, the gods were already judging him.

"If it helps you with your decision," Exedor continued, "I have looked into the mind of Nadine, and I know she would understand. She would probably even agree it is best to leave her behind."

"I'm sure she would, but there's a lot we don't agree on. We're married."

Exedor shook his head and turned to Ethan.

"And Baron Ethan, we need to get you to rally the support of the House of Mac-Soldai before Ferehain can seize power. I presume I can count on your level head, at least?"

"Soon enough, but first, we need to get Nadine," Ethan answered.

"This has nothing to do with you," Jason snapped. "I meant what I said earlier; I'll never forgive you. Don't think you can absolve what you did to us by helping me now."

"I know that," Ethan replied, "but I'm still going to help."

Jason forced down the rebellion of his pride. He knew he needed Ethan if he was to have any chance of rescuing Nadine.

Exedor rolled his eyes. "I risked everything to help two fools who simply want to hand themselves back into captivity; but as I said, as much as I disapprove of this sentiment, it is not entirely unexpected. I was delayed in freeing you as I needed to ensure Nadine was diverted to a holding cell of my choosing."

"Then why were we even arguing?" Jason demanded.

"Because your foolish lack of judgment exposes us to immense risk. If Ferehain suspects me, which I'm sure he does, then he may have taken precautions. He might have even set a trap. And I cannot simply walk you both in there without arousing suspicion. I have already overplayed my hand to your captors, and they are probably spreading word as we speak."

He paused before a door and fished a key out of his pocket. After waiting a moment to ensure they weren't observed, he opened it.

"Jason, get inside. Baron, come with me," said Exedor.

"Why am I going in there alone?" Jason asked.

Exedor sighed and stepped close to Jason. "I'm going to say this once. We have minutes, maybe an hour, before your absence is discovered and we are all hunted down. I wish for us to leave immediately, but I will attempt to free your wife, against my better judgment. However, if you wish me to free your wife, and also take the time to explain my preparations, then we might as well head back upstairs and deliver ourselves to Ferehain right now. It'll be simpler."

Jason opened his mouth but realized he had no reply to the argument. Satisfied that he had made his point, Exedor gestured to the open door.

"Now, if you please?"

With a shrug Jason moved past Exedor and into a cramped chamber that was clearly being used as a storeroom. Wooden crates were stacked against one wall, with three more scattered about the small space. He rested on one and turned to face the door.

"I trust I don't need to remind you to keep quiet," Exedor said before closing the door and turning the key.

Jason waited for an eternity in the dark storage room, which was lit by a tiny window high in the wall. Footsteps came and went past the door, and more than once Jason tensed in anticipation of one of them pausing over some tell-tale clue Jason imagined he'd left outside to betray his hiding place. Eventually, a pair of footsteps stopped before the door, but Exedor's voice dispelled Jason's fear.

"We've returned. Please don't try to kill us when I open the door."

The door opened and the figures of Exedor and Ethan moved in quietly, closing the door behind them. Ethan placed a sack on the floor with a clattering sound, then opened it and began removing pieces of black amour.

"I couldn't get you a full suit, but this should pass a casual inspection," he said as he laid out a breastplate, gauntlets, and a full-faced black helm. Jason noticed Ethan had changed into a black officer's uniform without any evidence of his noble standing. It took them several minutes to dress Jason in the unfamiliar armor. At last, Ethan picked up a black travelling cloak out of the sack and used it to cover the missing parts of the disguise. Ethan looked at Jason and shrugged.

"It'll do. It'll have to. I just hope there aren't any eager Quartermasters looking for an excuse for an inspection, because you're violating about seven uniform codes they'd spot at a glance."

"I'll manage," Jason answered

"Alright, let's go," Ethan said to Exedor.

They left the storeroom and followed Exedor as he led them deeper into the lower levels of the citadel. Jason couldn't help marvelling at the comfort of the Helmsguard armor. For all its bulk, it was surprisingly light, and it only took him a few minutes to find he could walk in it with confidence.

After several more minutes of walking down ramps and through increasingly darker, windowless corridors, they entered a narrow office occupied by three people: a Helmsguard soldier, a middle-aged man at a desk, and Nadine, seated on a bench behind an iron gate.

Jason bit his lip under his helmet to avoid looking at her as he marched into the office behind Ethan.

"Greetings, fine men. I am Exedor, Royal Inquisitor to the Ironhelm, here to claim our beautiful young prisoner."

The clerk barely glanced at Ethan, ignored Jason completely, then settled his drooping eyes on Exedor.

"I don't have any orders on this, Inquisitor," he said.

"Of course, you don't. I'm the one in charge of the execution. Do you think I'd trust this to any of the staff? I want it done today, not next month. I've made the arrangements for the Royal Termination, and I'm ready to transfer her. Release her to my custody," Exedor ordered.

Ethan tensed and readied himself to fight as the clerk eyed Exedor in silence, before shrugging and grunting at the guard. The soldier obeyed and unlocked the door. Jason played the role of the passionless Helmsguard and quietly moved into the cell to escort her out, but when their eyes locked, it took every inch of his will to resist pulling her into his embrace. As if understanding his conflict, Nadine drew her eyes away from his and strode out of the cell, placing merciful space between them.

"To where do I mark the transfer?" asked the clerk in the universally bored tone of an administrator.

"The Domitus stockade. It will be the perfect place for such a public spectacle. I hope you'll make the time to come and watch. It will send a powerful message to all enemies of the Union," Exedor replied.

The clerk shrugged in a manner that indicated his complete apathy, and merely focused on ensuring the journal was correctly updated. Exedor turned and walked out of the room without bothering to check if his entourage was following. Ethan followed the cue and Nadine proved herself to be excellent at acting, following just as casually. Only Jason remained in the office, slowly realizing that improvisation didn't come as naturally to him as he watched them leave. The clerk glanced up at Jason with irritation.

"And?" he said.

"Nothing, sir. Sorry," Jason mumbled and hurried after his companions who were already several feet down the corridor. They marched in silence for several feet before Jason judged it safe to speak. He desperately wanted to call out to Nadine, but he knew that was a luxury neither of them had time for.

"How are we getting out?" Jason instead asked Exedor.

"Through the front gates. We continue to hide in plain sight. I believe I can continue to talk us past the guards, and Baron Ethan has the means to get us out of the city once we clear the citadel," Exedor softly called back.

"And then?" asked Jason, suspicion creeping into his voice as he wondered what Exedor and Ethan had planned.

"Worry about then later," Exedor snapped. "We're not out of here yet, so it's *now* that should still concern you."

As if the words were a prophecy, the shrill clang of alarm bells rang in the heights of the citadel. Seconds later, the alarm was echoed in the halls below. Ethan's face hardened as he gave Exedor a knowing look.

"We're discovered?" asked Nadine.

Ethan scanned the corridor behind them for a moment. "No one's coming after Nadine, so that alarm is probably just for me and Jason."

Exedor nodded. "However, they'll look to secure Nadine immediately, so I judge that we have minutes, at best."

"So we fight," said Jason. "I need a sword!"

Exedor glanced at him with a such a look of condescension it was almost sympathetic. "No, Captain, one does not fight. In that situation one dies. Follow me."

Exedor hurried ahead of them, scanning the hallway's flanking black colonnades until he found what he was looking for. He bent into a recessed alcove adorned with the horned helm of Bythe and seconds later the back wall folded inward to reveal a dark passageway.

"Get in, quickly!" he snapped, glancing down the hallway in each direction.

Jason waited until Nadine was through before following her. Seconds later, Exedor followed and sealed the entry. The dim passageway ahead curved downward and was lit by recessed lights glowing in the walls every several feet. Jason felt dizzy as he looked at it.

"Where are we?" he asked Exedor, who was brushing past him to move to the head of the party.

"Given the front door is no longer an option, I've been forced to improvise again. These are called the Sacred Paths. We're really not supposed to be here. Our wonderful Lord Bythe would have had us killed if his priests discovered us soiling his passages with our presence. However, he's dead, and given the current management want to kill us anyway, I conclude there's little downside in taking this risk. Now follow me," Exedor answered before walking down the curving passageway.

"Will they look for us here?" Nadine asked.

Exedor shrugged. "It's hard to say. The Helmsguard would never search these halls while Bythe was alive, even if they knew about them, which is unlikely. However, Ferehain has insight into this power, and it's possible he knows about this place, in which case it's only a matter of time before he searches for us here. Either way, it's a moot point, this is our only option now, and if they find us here, we die."

Nadine fell silent and the party followed Exedor down the descending passageway. Jason was reminded of Sanctuary and understood there would be some mystical property to their passage, but he also remembered that Ferehain helped build Sanctuary, and that meant these paths were probably already known to him. It was difficult to judge how long they spent descending the passage; to Jason, it seemed like twenty or thirty minutes, with each minute stretching into hours. However, one blessed relief had been the absence of any pursuit. By now, the entire citadel would be on high alert, probably along with the rest of the city. Jason thought it was now prudent to start asking the obvious question.

"How are we going to get out?" he asked Exedor.

Irritation flashed on Exedor's face at the question, but he answered over his shoulder. "These passages lead out of Domitus, some of them stretching deep into the Iron Union. We'll follow them as far as we can and see where they lead us."

"So, you don't know where we're going?" Jason pressed.

Exedor sighed. "No, Captain, I do not. If this plan does not suit you, feel free to suggest an alternative. Or if you prefer, I'm sure one of these exits will drop you into the hospitality of the Ironhelm. Avail yourself of one."

Nadine glanced at Jason and shrugged. Exedor was right, they really had no other option besides the path he now led them on. If it was a trap, it was still better than the alternative.

"Yes, please, do shut up," Exedor snapped, as if reading Jason's thoughts.

Jason was trying to think of a suitable reply when a noise behind him drove the petty impulse from his mind.

"Wait!" he hissed, and the party immediately came to a halt.

Nadine's blue eyes scanned her husband's face and she immediately understood. Ethan and Exedor's countenances were of puzzlement and irritation, respectively.

Jason held up his hand to ward off their question and waited, eagerly testing the silence. For a long time, there was nothing, then there was a sound, faint and pulsing, cresting and falling over the waves of silence above them. The familiar ticking sound of a clock. Nadine recognized the fear dawning on her husband's face. Ethan's expression turned from confusion to dread as he also recognized the lethal sound.

"Go!" Jason shouted at them, taking off his metal helmet and throwing it aside.

They ran. All four of them sprinted down the narrow passageway, Jason bringing up the rear, occasionally risking a backward glance to see if a white figure pursued them. After several minutes of sprinting headlong through the tunnel, Nadine and Exedor began to stumble as the adrenaline started to withdraw its temporary support. Catching her foot on a flagstone, Nadine tumbled to the ground and rolled a short distance. Ethan wheeled about and caught her descent, gently helping her to her feet as Jason came rushing up to her. She waved both of them away but stood with her hands on her knees for a moment, breathing deeply to get air back into her lungs. The ticking sound was louder now, echoing down the passageway behind them, rhythmic and relentless. Jason could clearly make out the sound of boots on stone in perfect synchronicity.

"We're not going to make it," he said, looking over at his wife.

"Well, don't even think about staying here to try and buy us time. You won't even slow him down," Nadine gasped between breaths.

Jason glanced at Ethan, who shook his head in confirmation.

"Exedor," Jason said, "can you get us back into the Ironhelm?"

"We passed an entrance half a minute back," Exedor answered, pointing back toward the sound of the approaching creature.

"Great," Jason muttered. "And if we keep going, how long until the next one?"

"Perhaps a minute, maybe an hour," he replied.

Although it raged against his primal instincts, Jason knew what they had to do.

"We go back. Move!" he ordered, no longer a man plagued by rage and guilt but a natural captain once more, and everyone obeyed without a word. He led them up the passage, the echoes of the Imbatal's boots now so clear it sounded as if the creature was around the next bend. They arrived at another recess in the wall and Exedor moved in. Ethan and Jason stood blocking the corridor in an act that was as gallant as it was futile. Hours seemed to pass as Jason stood fixed in that position, the ticking of gears and clap of footsteps pounding in his ears. Something moved in the dim light at the far end of the corridor.

"It's open," Exedor called.

"Is it clear?" Jason asked.

No answer came.

"He's gone through," Nadine called.

Jason swore and glanced at Ethan, who nodded.

"Go, Nadine!" Jason ordered.

Nadine knew better than to argue, and within seconds she vanished through the door. Jason glanced over his shoulder to watch her go, and when he looked back, he was staring at Imbatal. It looked at Jason as if it recognized him, halting and cocking its head sideways as it assessed the fugitives before it. Jason wondered if the Imbatals shared memories, or if he was just new prey to this creature.

"Now you," Jason ordered Ethan. "Find Nadine and secure her."

"Yes, Captain," Ethan answered then was gone.

Jason was unarmed but he knew it didn't matter; a sword would help as much as a broom, and there was no way to stop this thing. The Imbatal seemed to arrive at the same conclusion, and a long blade brutally snapped out of its forearm. Jason spent a moment sizing up his enemy, then turned and ran. The Imbatal's ticking sound remained consistent, but the footsteps abruptly quickened and Jason knew it was in pursuit. The alcove gave way to a large door leading to a corridor. Jason bounded through and found himself in an open space in a dark room with light filtering through wooden slats in the roof and walls. The three figures of his companions were visible in the gloom. There was no one else around.

"It's an ore shed," Ethan said, anticipating Jason's question. "We're out of the citadel, but still within the walls of the square."

"Outside!" Jason snapped.

Exedor had already seen to his exit and stood at the door, the rest of the group rushed to follow. The bright afternoon sun beat on Jason's brow, forcing him to shield his eyes as he scanned the tactical situation. To his right lay a hundred yards of open ground leading to the citadel walls. A small service hatch set in the wall lay open, leading to the city beyond. It was designed to transport ore carts into the citadel and Jason judged they could easily make it through. To his left lay at least a dozen more ore sheds in ordered rows, an ideal hiding place from the Imbatal, at least for a moment. A terrible reminder of Nadine's failed attempts to hide from Jarren on the day of Ascension invaded his mind, but he pushed the thought away. Heavy footfalls behind Jason reminded him of the unyielding deadline for his decisions.

"Run to the wall, get through the hatch!' Jason commanded.

Nadine hesitated and Exedor looked at him disbelievingly.

"But he'll see us," Nadine argued.

"Please, trust me," Jason said.

Nadine said nothing more, she broke from the cover of the ore sheds and ran as quickly as she could across the open space to the wall. Ethan didn't hesitate, he simply followed the order. Exedor seemed torn between staying with the group and taking his chances by himself. To his credit, it only took a second to decide the balance of probabilities lay in his favor if he had accomplices at best, or human shields at worst.

Jason watched them run then looked back into the gloom of the shed. The Imbatal was slowly extracting itself from the cramped confines of the tunnel, righting itself to its towering seven-foot height before staring down at Jason. He counted five seconds, five agonising seconds, as the Imbatal began to stalk toward him with that stilted, unnatural gait, then

Jason ran again. He ran as hard as he had ever run in his life, sprinting desperately for the service gate, praying to whichever god or goddess who still cared enough for him. Timber cracked as the Imbatal crashed through the shed's smaller doorframe and gave pursuit. Nadine and Ethan had already reached the hatch, and Nadine was stooping over to fit herself through, with Ethan preparing to follow. Exedor was seconds behind them, Jason much farther behind. He didn't look back. The deep thumps of the Imbatal's strides seemed almost casual in their pace, but he knew it was gaining with impossible speed. Jason felt the terror and he let it drive him. An unintelligible cry came from his lips as he increased his pace to the point where his legs burned. The service hatch rushed at him as quickly as the Imbatal closed the gap behind him. He had no time to duck his head. He threw himself at the hatch and hit the dirt as the air exploded from his lungs. Ethan's hands gripped his forearms and pulled him through the hole, dragging Jason to his feet. The Imbatal barely slowed before it followed Jason through. Lowering itself into a crouch, it launched itself at the hatch like a catapult ball, smashing into the stonework and cracking the surrounding wall as it shuddered. And then it stopped. Its shoulders wedged tight into the surrounding bricks and its knees tucked up awkwardly underneath, it found itself suddenly unable to move. It paused for a moment, shifting its head from side to side as if trying to understand the predicament, then it tried to reverse itself from the hole it had made, but only succeeded in scratching at the dirt with its feet. Pausing again, it regarded Jason with its blank eye slits, then tried to slash at him with its trapped arm but could only fan its blade in the air. The ticking sound increased in intensity and the Imbatal seemed enraged. The scene would have been comical, had it not been so deadly.

"You seem to have a knack for outwitting automatons," said Ethan, recalling Jason's successful tactics against the war engines.

Jason nodded wearily. "These things will follow you relentlessly. And the only thing an Imbatal can't do is call for help."

A crumbling of the wall made them all step back. The Imbatal had started to rub its forearm against the entrapping stonework, slowly worrying the hole to allow it more leverage. Even as they watched, the creature began to rock back and forth with greater and greater momentum.

"It'll be free any second," said Jason.

"Then I suggest we should be somewhere else," answered Exedor.

Jason scanned the surrounding streets, thankfully deserted from the ongoing attacks, but none offering him a guarantee of safe passage. He hesitated, then glanced at Exedor.

"Where were you trying to take us?" he asked.

"To the sanctuary of Baron Ethan's family," Exedor replied.

"It's too far in the open street," said Ethan. "But I have an alternative. Follow me."

Jason glanced at Nadine who returned the uncertain expression, but the further crumbling of stones behind them seemed to answer their unspoken question.

They followed Ethan as he led them at a quick pace down the nearest alleyway to their right. They turned frequently, ducking into service alleys which lead to open boulevards, then crossing into opposite alleys and starting the process again. Within a minute, Jason had lost all sense of direction and had to trust that Ethan wasn't simply leading them back to Domitus. After minutes of this, Ethan held up his hand and slowed to a halt.

"Alright. That should be far enough to shake Imbatal from our trail. Now we walk. Hopefully, we won't earn a second glance where we're going but follow my lead and be ready to run at my signal."

With that, Ethan adjusted his cloak and turned casually into the adjoining boulevard, motioning for the others to follow him. The street was broad and sparsely populated with traders tending to their storefronts or citizens moving quietly in groups of two or three. A sense of oppression lay heavily over them all, as if the entire street was tense and ready for something terrible. As Ethan predicted, nobody wanted to look at his party as they moved quietly past them. In fact, it seemed as if everyone was intent on minding their own business, as if the mere acknowledgment of another person would somehow invite danger onto all of them. After several minutes, Ethan led them into a side alley named Archeuim Parade. The alley was deserted and large sections of it lay in ruins. It was obvious that a raid had taken place not long ago as many of the shops were now deserted and boarded up. Ethan led them around the curved alley, skirting chunks of rock that lay in the path, and approached a small bistro, which was also boarded up. Ethan glanced up and down the alley to ensure they weren't observed, then knocked firmly on the door. He waited a long time and when nobody answered, knocked again.

"It's Ethan. I have friends and I need help, please," Ethan called through the glass window in the door. Shadows moved in the frosted gloom and the door opened to reveal the face of a young woman who should have been beautiful but seemed already stained by untimely grief. She scanned the group blankly then looked at Ethan.

"Who are they, Ethan?" she asked in a flat voice.

"Fugitives. The Helmsguard will be looking for them and they need a place to hide."

"I'm sorry, Ethan, we can't," she replied and started to close the door.

"Wait," Ethan said, placing his hand in the doorframe. "I'm a fugitive now as well. Things are bad. I need help."

"Let them in," said a male voice, and the young woman obeyed.

The four people moved quickly inside the bistro and Ethan bolted the door behind them.

"Jasmine, prepare something for our guests," said a middle-aged man who was seated at a table in the darkened room. He rose as Ethan approached and the two men embraced.

"Symin, I'm so sorry to come to you like this," Ethan said.

"Don't be absurd, Ethan. After everything you've done for us over the years, how can I not help you when you're in need?" answered Symin.

He gestured to a table and three of them sat, Exedor deciding to keep a safe distance near the door. Symin gave him a wary glance but said nothing at the display of ingratitude.

"I had nowhere else to go. I'm sorry. They'll almost certainly be watching my family, I can't risk taking them there now."

"Where's Valeyn? Is she alright?" Jasmine asked as she returned to the room, placing a platter of sliced fruits and a jug of water before them.

Ethan's face fell. "No, she isn't."

He briefly recounted the events of Ferehain's insurrection and the separation of Valeyn back into Elyn and Vale.

"He can kill gods?" Jasmine asked in horror.

"I don't know. He's powerful, smart, and now has access to the most powerful weapons the gods created, so it looks like there's very little he can't do," said Ethan.

"Where is she now?" Jasmine asked.

"I don't know that either," Ethan answered. "She's being held captive."

"Let me see what I can do," said Symin, as he got up and walked to the rear of the Bistro.

"Symin . . ." Ethan began but Symin simply dismissed him with a wave of his hand and called to the back room. "Fen! In here now, please."

A young man with dark features emerged from the back room and gave the visitors a quick look before turning his attention to Symin.

"Yeah, chief?" he asked in a thick accent.

"Something's happened at the citadel. Rustle the pack. Find Quix. Run up an eye."

Fen nodded at the incomprehensible lingo and vanished. Jason turned a glance on Ethan, who shook his head at the unspoken question. Exedor wasn't as subtle.

"I see now, you are the Black Chamalas," he called out with a smile. "Well, well. I congratulate you, sir. I must admit, your little smuggling operation was always frustratingly elusive to us. I really should have thought to look for you here, hiding among the nobility in plain sight. Again, I congratulate you."

Symin's eyes fell on Exedor and his stare was cold. "And who the hells are you?"

Exedor inclined his head in a mock bow. "My name is Exedor, formerly in the service of Lord Bythe, now currently seeking other employment opportunities."

"An Inquisitor?" he bellowed, rounding on Ethan. "You brought an Inquisitor to my door?"

Ethan held up both hands, looked murderously at Exedor, then to Nadine and Jason, before replying. "Easy, Symin. He's not an Inquisitor any longer. He's helped us escape and condemned himself to death by doing so. I can't speak to his motives, but I think he deserves a chance."

"Why, thank you, Baron. And all I needed to do was to destroy my career and risk my life to earn this goodwill," Exedor replied in a hard voice.

"I don't care. He can't be trusted to not turn us in the minute is suits him," spat Symin.

"He helped us too," Jason admitted, then told the group of Exedor's warning at Outpost.

"I'm not sure that was help. Sounds like he led you into a trap," Symin answered when Jason had finished.

"Of course it was a trap. But it was as much of a trap for me as much as it was for you," Exedor snapped. "Most of all, it was a trap for Valeyn. She was in the center of the snare, and she couldn't even see it tightening around her."

"So, you sent us into the snare with her?" Nadine asked.

"No, I gave you a choice. You willingly walked into the trap. You know you did. But you did it to help her, that's what friends do. I simply manipulated your better nature — that's what I do. And now I sit in the trap with you. I hope that makes you feel better?"

Nadine was silent for a moment then nodded. "Yes, that's fair. We knew the risk and we took it, but that doesn't answer the question. What did you expect us to do?"

"Yes, Inquisitor. Explain yourself or I can guarantee I'm not letting you leave this alley alive," snarled Symin.

Exedor smiled at the threat, then sighed. "Oh, very well. What does it matter anyway? Bythe made me his Royal Inquisitor, but I've always despised the gods, all of them, after what they did to . . ." His voice trailed off and an unsettled look covered his face before he shook his head slightly. "When the Prodigals made contact with me, I didn't hesitate. After all, with a Royal Inquisitor as an ally, there was no limit to what they could accomplish. Then I was taken captive by Ferehain, and I came to understand him and how dangerous he was."

"So why didn't you warn the Prodigals instead of coming to us?" asked Jason.

"I tried, but they wouldn't listen. The fool Morbus was blinded by greed and his petty revenge on Vale. They have lost perspective, or perhaps they simply have not had the benefit of my firsthand experience with Ferehain. Either way, they do not understand what they are dealing with, and when they do, it will be far too late."

"And so you turned to us? What sort of plan was that?" Jason asked.

"It was a plan born out of equal parts desperation and necessity. It was hardly my finest work. Once I foresaw that Ferehain's ascension to Bythe's throne was inevitable, my plan, as loose as it was, was to bring you together as enemies of a common foe," Exedor said, motioning to Jason, Nadine and Ethan. "The Outland Alliance combined with the influence of the house of Mac-Soldai can still stand against the forces that Ferehain controls."

"You're talking about splitting the Iron Union. That would be civil war," said Ethan.

"I'm talking about the complete destruction of the Iron Union if we fail to act. If civil war is the price of seeing tomorrow, then so be it!" Exedor countered with a rare display of temper.

"It's not up to Ethan. I'll never ally myself with that man," said Jason.

"I thought we were past this." said Exedor.

"I said I wasn't going to kill him. That doesn't mean I'm going to fight at his side!"

Nadine placed a hand on her husband's shoulder and spoke to Exedor. "It's an academic point, anyway. Our army is weeks away in the east. What made you think we could help Baron Ethan, even if we were inclined to?"

"Because I know our theatrics at Krag were simply a diversion and your army has been moving westward for over a week now," said Exedor.

Nadine's face fell in surprise, and Ethan looked at her with an almost identical expression. Symin barked a curt laugh.

"Is that true?" asked Ethan.

Nadine nodded at Exedor. "Well, you didn't expect us to walk into the heart of the enemy without a plan to walk out, did you?" she said.

Exedor returned the gesture with a nod of his own. "You think like an Inquisitor, Councillor."

"Captain Zain is an excellent tactician. It was his suggestion to take the army through Joana, where the devastation was greatest, while I distracted you all at Krag," said Nadine. "I take it he's been successful?"

"I believe so, if this morning's intelligence is to be relied upon," replied Exedor. "I'm told there's a force of over three thousand soldiers advancing two days east. Obviously, I told the officer that it was an absurd piece of misinformation and immediately had it destroyed."

"Why isn't the Helmsguard stopping them?" asked Ethan in disbelief.

"The high command has been in disarray for the past week since the Prodigals began their insurrection. It's doubtful any reports are being responded to, if they're even getting here at all," said Exedor.

"My gods," said Ethan, turning from the others and walking across the room. "An army of men can stroll across our lands, and we're powerless to stop them. It's really come to this. Everything is finished."

He walked over to the far corner and Jason saw for the first time that there was a makeshift shrine in the shadows. Flowers covered a stool that had been covered in the deep purple cloth of the Klyphian tradition. Upon the stool lay a necklace, a ring, and other feminine reminders of a woman who had clearly passed away recently. Then Jason's eyes fell upon a small tunic and pants, the only keepsakes of a small child. Jasmine also rose from her seat and walked to where Ethan stood. Placing a hand on his back, she spoke gently.

"Ethan, come away. We have had this discussion before. This was not your fault."

"Then why do I still feel like it was?" he answered.

"Baron Ethan, you do not have time for self-pity," Exedor scolded, the disdain clear in his voice. "Your house is strong, you can seize power, but you must act now. Go to your mother. Your family still controls the largest single army in the Union. Tell her to mobilise them, link up with Warmaster Zain, and move against the madman who has stolen the throne!"

"My mother has no affection for Snyed, but an alliance with our enemies?" Ethan said with incredulity.

"A temporary alliance of necessity," Exedor replied. "The Unity Assembly will come around to your banner once you make your move. There's no other way, Ethan!"

"And what's the point? Vale's probably dead. Even if I succeed, the Iron Union will be ripped apart. Everything I care about has been taken from me. What's the point?" Ethan murmured as if there was no one else in the room.

Nadine glanced at Jason, then rose and slowly crossed the room to stand at Ethan's turned back. "Not everything is gone — not yet. There's still a lot you can salvage," Nadine chose her words carefully. "I know a lot has been taken from you, and you might lose more. But no matter what happens, if you're still breathing, you can rebuild and reclaim a life. It will be a different life, but a life all the same. But you have to choose it, or you can wallow in the misery of what's been done to you . . . this is what I had to decide after you came to us at Fairhaven."

Ethan looked around at her and in that moment, something seemed to pass between them, not a forgiveness nor a reconciliation, but a simple recognition of the harsh reality that fate had placed upon both of them.

"I think you're a stronger person than I am," he said quietly, shaking his head.

Nadine had just opened her mouth to continue when the curtains at the rear of the room parted suddenly and Fen entered, crossing to Symin. The two men conferred quietly before Symin rose from his chair.

"Something is happening in the Domitus square, it seems that Elyn and Vale are still alive, but there is to be some sort of demonstration," Symin said.

"An execution?" asked Ethan.

Symin shrugged. "I don't know, but it's happening now."

Jason, Ethan, and Nadine looked at one another, each of them clearly sharing the same thought.

"You are all of you insane if you think you can prevent this," said Exedor. "This is no doubt a plot to motivate you into a suicidal attempt to do just that. Ferehain's Imbatals will be waiting for you, and this time you will not escape."

"I have to agree with him," said Symin.

"I don't care, I won't just hide here," said Ethan.

Jason thought for a moment. "If this is a public demonstration, there'll be an audience?"

Ethan nodded. "It'll be smaller, but these spectacles are designed to draw a crowd."

"Then you and I can risk it, providing we don't get too close. Nadine, you stay here," commanded Jason, her Captain once more.

"No," Nadine argued. "It's a trap, like Exedor said, or it's an execution, either way there's no benefit to you going."

"If it's a trap, then I'll avoid it, if it's an execution . . ." Jason's voice trailed off and he struggled to fight the inevitable grief as he thought of little Elyn. "If it's an execution, then at least I'll bear witness . . . and then we'll avenge her."

"And I can do no less for Vale," said Ethan.

"I take it you'll excuse my absence," said Exedor. Everyone ignored him.

"I'll get you both a change of clothes," said Symin.

Minutes later, the two young men were walking back up the large boulevard that had given them an escape earlier that day. Symin's clothes were comically large for both of them, but they were adequately hidden beneath equally oversized cloaks. Unlike during their trek earlier, the street now buzzed with a vibe of excitement, dread, and anticipation. People had caught word that something was happening outside Domitus, but they seemed unclear about what it was. Jason was far too cautious to risk asking anyone directly, and Ethan seemed to hold similar concerns; the danger of leaving a trail of witnesses who could later be questioned was far too great. Jason allowed Ethan to silently lead him through the city. Their path was meandering and often circular, clearly intended to expose anyone following them, but if there were people shadowing their footsteps, Jason saw no sign of them.

Eventually, Ethan concluded they were undetected and led Jason onto a main boulevard, which was now crowded with people moving in the direction of the citadel. Jason adjusted his hood and fell in step with two men moving alongside him.

"I'm tellin' ya, it's happenin'" said a short, overweight man closest to Jason.

"You're full of it," said the man next to him. "They'd never turn on her. She's Bythe's daughter."

"Yeah, but she ain't Bythe, is she?" said the first. "She's some kinda half-breed. Or a bastard of Maelene, the witch-goddess. The army was never gonna accept her."

"Don't be a moron. Who would be in charge?"

"The army, I guess? There's some bloke I never heard of. Apparently, he's calling the shots now."

"Rubbish!" replied the taller man. "What's happened to Lord Valeyn, then?"

"She's dead. They had a trial and he executed her. Happened in the square half an hour ago apparently."

"Don't believe it!"

"Well, you'll see it for yourself in a minute."

Jason and Ethan shared a worrying glance and quickened their pace. They gently forced their way through the throng as they entered the square. Jason felt Ethan's hand on his arm, and he glanced at Ethan to see him nodding toward something behind them. Jason carefully glanced over his shoulder to see black, armored Helmsguard standing guard inside the citadel walls, their faces fixed on the crowd, scanning the people as they entered. Pulling the hood of his cloak further over his brow, Jason turned his face away from them and tried to blend in with the rest of the crowd as best he could.

"Maybe this was a bad idea after all," Jason murmured.

"Maybe," Ethan concurred, "but I need to know what happened to Vale. Stay in the crowd and just do whatever they do."

The push of the crowd became stronger as they were herded closer to the citadel. It was claustrophobic, but Jason realized he could no longer see any of the Helmsguard through the mob, which meant they could no longer see him. They had been slowly shuffling forward for long minutes when the crowd began to jostle and stir. People were starting to push back in the opposite direction, leaving the square hurriedly. There were shouts of protest, shoves, and countershoves, and for a moment, Jason feared he was about to be caught in the midst of a full-blown riot. The people who were pushing back past him seemed angry or upset. A young woman openly wept as she pressed her way past Jason, seemingly desperate to flee whatever confronted her, and Jason felt his stomach sink. He almost forgot himself and prepared to press his way through the crowd when he heard Ethan swear. It was an uncharacteristically ignoble sound, causing Jason to pause and follow his gaze. The departing throng had created a break in the mob, and through the gap, Jason could see what had horrified Ethan. Two scaffolds had been erected on opposite sides of the square, and each of these harboured a mirrored monstrosity; one held the form of Elyn, the other of Vale. They were each tied to a frame, their naked forms hanging limp in the late afternoon sun. The long hair of each woman hung like a shroud over each face, their heads lolling over their breasts, their bodies covered with vicious purple bruises and dried blood. But what horrified Jason even more, was the crude sign attached before them, the words painted in deep scarlet: Behold, our Desecration.

Jason felt himself stop, the shock and the rage fighting for control of him. His vision began to blur and then he felt himself begin to move without willing it. He would take down her body. He would stop this, or he would kill as many people as he could before he died in turn. Ethan's hand gripped his shoulder and then the young Baron's pained face filled his vision.

"No, Jason. Please. Not here. Not here."

Jason wasn't quite sure what was happening, but he allowed Ethan to guide him back a few steps. Jason looked at Ethan, waiting for him to say something, but Ethan only looked back at the obscenity, pools of tears forming on his high cheeks. He drew in a breath, then turned to face Jason.

"You have my support. You have my word. Every soldier my mother commands will be yours . . . every coin we have . . . everything will be given to you and your wife. They will pay for what they've done. Ferehain will pay. I will gratefully purge everything we own to make that happen."

Jason only nodded in reply. He couldn't take his eyes from the unmoving form of Elyn, while Ethan stared respectively at Vale. For the first time, Jason found himself feeling empathy for the man he had once sworn to kill, fury and justice uniting them as brothers in a moment of final and complete resolution.

CHAPTER 3

"While the military powers of the Iron Union were focused on fighting Ferehain's forces, little thought was given to the people of the Ironhelm during its last days. The terror of those faced with the complete breakdown of existence was almost too profound for comprehension. Instinctively, most of them turned to the gods for salvation, as they had so clearly returned and were no doubt prepared to reward those who had been loyal. One can only imagine the betrayal these people must have felt as they slowly understood their gods had no ear for the prayers offered to them.

And so, those who found themselves abandoned by their gods, remembered the one who had cared for them. And to them, Valeyn became the single light to give them comfort at the end of all creation."

~Kaler of the Ageless

Elyn blinked and tried to focus her vision. Sensations assailed her. The sun seared down onto her naked form and her skin burned. The ropes on her wrists and ankles bit into her flesh. The impressions were strange, painful yet somehow distant and removed. She looked across the square and saw Vale hanging limp from a scaffold. Elyn knew she was still alive. Ferehain didn't want a quick and clean death — not for her. She needed to suffer. She needed to be degraded in front of everyone; the gods and the mortals alike.

How long had she hung there? She had no idea. It had felt like days. Maybe it had been.

She cast her mind back, trying to recall what had happened. Her mind seemed clouded now, constrained again by mortal perceptions, and it was difficult to try and focus. Exedor had left the throne room, leaving her with Vale, and with Ferehain. And that's when it had begun. While Elyn had expected punishment, possibly even torture, she hadn't expected Ferehain to do it personally, and she had underestimated the passion buried deep within the twisted man.

The beating of both Elyn and Vale had been brutal. He used nothing more than his hands, no magical artefact, no weapon, only the savage brutality of a man's fists. And he beat them both in silence, as if it were a private – almost intimate – ritual for himself alone. The pain had driven the breath from her body, and the only control she found was over her own cries of pain, for she knew they were the sounds Ferehain sought. Each grunt, every reflexive cry, was a small victory for him. He rained his fists upon the unprotected flesh of Elyn then Vale in equal measures, his face a mask of twisted and grotesque hatred.

And all along, the gods had stood watching. Their own silence a terrible judgment of the unworthy god before them.

Finally, when Elyn thought she might at last slip into the blessed relief of oblivion, he stopped the physical beating and began the humiliation. He offered his prisoners no clothing, but ordered them marched into the square, where he had their scaffolds quicky erected and their naked and beaten forms displayed.

He had stared at them both with such quiet satisfaction. No words were required. Both Elyn and Vale knew what his look conveyed. He had beaten them. He had won. And his final act was to destroy Valeyn's legacy by desecrating the illusion of Valeyn for all to see. The Ironhelm would finally reject Bythe's bastard daughter as the fraud she had always been.

"Elyn."

Vale's thoughts reached out to touch Elyn's mind, and for an instant, she was reminded of Fairhaven and of the day a timid, young Elyn had reached out into the unknown to touch the mind of her twin, before everything had changed irrevocably.

"I'm here," Elyn replied.

Their minds touched in a way that was familiar and instinctive, and yet it was also different; it was far more intimate. Their minds had once been one, and now they were apart. It was as if that feeling of complete intimacy still remained between them. Elyn didn't need to ask if Vale was alright. They could feel the physical hurts of each other, the trauma each had suffered at the hands of Ferehain, and yet they could also sense the other's unyielding mental strength. They were separate, but they were no longer the same young girls who met at Fairhaven. They never would be again. Their eyes locked across the square and they said nothing further. No words were needed. They each knew what was expected of them, and each knew what was bound to happen. Yet Elyn felt strangely serene, as if she were somehow invisibly shielded from the knowledge that should terrify her.

The hours had passed like this, innumerable and interminable. Day slipped into night, just as Elyn and Vale slipped into consciousness and out again. The crowd had steadily grown. What had started as a timid gathering of a few dozen people had now grown to a mass of hundreds. At first, the crowd had been raucous and uncouth — a typical mob baying for blood as entertainment, a mob demanding the punishment of someone for the crime of simply being in a higher class. But among them were those who had reacted with horror and disgust; those who had turned away, but had later returned with others. And when the fickle natures of the mob had become bored by the absence of a violent spectacle, they had left to be replaced by solemn mourners in greater and greater numbers. While Ferehain had doubtlessly intended the exhibition to be a humiliation, Elyn could sense it had instead become something of a vigil. The night was lit by candles, and Elyn became comforted by the tiny lights as she drifted in and out of consciousness in the dark.

The dawn came slowly for her, protracted by the ceaseless lapses in and out of sleep. It seemed like the day had already passed when the first rays of sun illuminated the square, but when the rays struck Elyn's face, she was surprised to see the square had filled with people now stretching out beyond the citadel walls. The Imbatals still stood guard around the platform, but during the night they had now turned outward, facing the crowd, seemingly knowing that the greatest threat now came from behind them.

"*Do you feel it?*" Vale asked.

Elyn woke from her torpor. Her throat was dry and she craved water, but she steeled her will and pushed the feeling aside; it was only physical. Opening herself, Elyn sent forth a wave of emotion, no longer a timid tendril of feeling, and drank in the sensations of the city. She felt the grief of those gathered in the square, the despair, frustration, and rage that simmered underneath their calm and supplicant postures. Then she reached out further and felt the tingling pinpricks of a million souls scattered throughout the Iron Union. Once such an act would have been unthinkable, it would have terrified her – but now it felt as natural as extending her arm. It no longer frightened her. Nothing frightened her anymore.

"*I can feel it,*" Elyn replied and glanced over at Vale with a smile, which she returned. They both knew it was very close to the end now. They just had to be strong for a while longer.

Elyn turned her face to the east and waited. The sun began to rise slowly and when it did, the rays were no longer bright, but brown and sullied by smoke, the smoke that was rising from the east, growing thicker as the sun rose higher. People in the crowd began to notice, and the respectful silence of the vigil became increasingly fractured by pockets of anxiety.

Elyn felt another stab of intense pain that threatened to pull her into blackness, but she resisted. Her mind teetered on the edge of waking thought, but she knew she needed to remain. Her work wasn't done — not yet.

"You struggle on the brink of death," said a female voice.

Elyn opened her eyes to see a young woman with long, fair hair staring up at her. The six Imbatals immediately snapped their heads around in unison at the appearance of the newcomer.

"Hello, Romona," Elyn said. The words were a rasp and Elyn realized that she hadn't actually spoken for over a full day and night. The young goddess looked up at her with the ever-present expression of blank curiosity.

"You are in a unique position, Elyn. To hold death at bay and to yet linger in the twilight of its shadow. I envy you greatly."

Elyn laughed and Vale echoed the sentiment from across the square.

"I think you over-estimate the appeal of my situation," Elyn replied.

The Imbatals began to advance on Romona but then paused abruptly, their blank faces cocked sideways. It seemed they were confused by her presence.

"Ah, my children," said Romona, as she turned and approached the towering figures. "I suppose I am something akin to their mother. This was the closest I could achieve to the state which you willingly now place yourself in." She looked over the closest creature, staring into the blank slits in the hood as if trying to peer into the soul of the creature beneath. She sighed deeply. "What has this Ageless done to you? He has missed the point entirely, yet that is not surprising. You were never intended as weapons of war; you were meant as a path to something beautiful."

"Have you come to judge us?" asked Vale.

Romona shrugged. "My judgment has already been given; the others are deciding as we speak." She nodded at the approaching smoke. There were sounds now, the unmistakable clangs and shouts of combat, growing steadily louder. "But this may change things somewhat."

"I imagine it could," agreed Elyn.

Behind them, the massive doors of Domitus opened and a contingent of twelve Helmsguard marched out in formation, in their wake strode Ferehain, his cloak billowing behind him as he descended the steps. The shrouded form of Aleasea trailed behind the group. He crossed the square and walked directly to where Romona stood.

"I have been patient long enough. It is time," Ferehain said.

"You concept of patience is a strange one, Ageless," Romona answered. "However, I believe our decision is imminent, irrespective of your eagerness."

"Ferehain!" Snyed's voice boomed across the square and the broad man stormed out of the citadel entrance with several other members of the Unity Assembly in tow. "What are you doing out here? We need you back in the command room!"

"You can report to me here, Snyed. What is the status?" Ferehain answered.

Snyed glanced at Elyn before deciding to continue. "It's as we feared — an attack by the Outland Alliance and some allies. They've managed to infiltrate the east gate and they stormed in at dawn."

"And how did they achieve access to the city?" Ferehain asked.

"They've got Helmsguard fighting alongside them. We've got traitors," growled Snyed. "You should never have let Baron Ethan escape. He's far more dangerous than you gave him credit for."

Ferehain cast his eyes over the gathered mass, ignoring Snyed's hypocritical change in advice. "It does not matter. Why are these people still permitted to congregate here? Begin arresting them, or executing them," he said.

"We have bigger problems, Ferehain!" Snyed snapped in frustration. "I need every man to help put down the rebellion. If you start a riot here, you're going to make things a lot worse for us!"

Ferehain's brow furrowed as he considered the predicament. "It is simply the remains of Captain Jason's army plus a few turncoats. Surely you can deal with them."

"It's also the House of Mac-Soldai! Do you have any idea how many soldiers they control? If that traitor Ethan has managed to rally the entire house against us, they could overrun this city by nightfall and hold it for a long time. And to make it worse, there are reports that some of the houses in Court are openly declaring loyalty to Lord Valeyn. Troops from Alovat are said to be on the way!"

"Lord Ferehain, this is getting out of hand. If we do not act swiftly, the Iron Union could be plunged into civil war," said Dox.

"Then recall your units from the field and bring them here quickly. Must I direct you in everything?" Ferehain snapped.

"Our communication lines have been cut by the chaos you unleashed, Ageless! Half of my commanders have gone missing after your insurrection, and we haven't had time to replace them with loyalists. I can activate maybe one fifth of my army right now!"

Ferehain turned from them. He wasn't listening anymore.

"You gods believe you can toy with anybody. You feel you have the right to do whatever you please. Your arrogance will be your undoing," Ferehain said.

"As will yours," Romona answered.

"Then perhaps an example is called for." Ferehain gestured to two of the Imbatals and they stepped forward. "Grant Romona the oblivion she craves. Let her see if the second experience is any more profound than the first."

The Imbatals didn't move. Ferehain glanced at them.

"Kill her!" he repeated. Again, they stood as if they were statues.

"They will never harm me, Ferehain. I created them," Romona replied with a slight smile.

A distant crash sounded from beyond the citadel wall, and the crowd began to roil in fear. The citadel doors reopened and disgorged a stream of armored soldiers marching at double-pace toward the source of the sound.

"Ferehain!" shouted Snyed over the noise. "What's the matter with you?"

Ferehain didn't take his eyes from Romona's as he addressed Snyed.

"Take the soldiers and defend the city as you please. I have greater matters to attend to."

Snyed's incredulity was almost palpable. "*You're* the one with power. Do something!"

Ferehain didn't answer. He simply glared at Romona as if carefully considering his next move.

Snyed shook his head. "You told us you had the power to protect us, but it turns out you're just another lying god. Valeyn was right. We were fools."

He turned to leave, and had he waited a moment longer – or perhaps glanced over his shoulder – he might have seen Ferehain raise his fist. He might have wondered at the meaning of the strange gesture. Elyn didn't need to wonder — she could sense what he was doing before it happened. Life on Kovalith extends from *kai*, and Ferehain now controlled almost all of it. With little more than a gesture, Ferehain seized the threads of *kai* that ran throughout Snyed's body and simply pulled them out. It was doubtful that Snyed even knew what had happened as his lifeless body slumped to the ground.

"Yes, you were fools," Ferehain said as the rest of the Unity Assembly fled from him in panic. "Blinded and weakened by your own fear and ambition. Such petty men."

"You seem very willing to kill — almost eager to do so. How are you any different from us?" Pia's voice carried effortlessly over the tumult. Cries of shock rang out from the crowd.

Elyn looked up to see twenty-three figures assembled in a circle above them; Lubalt-Teble, Pia, Dahz, Narak, and nineteen other gods.

Bythe and Maelene still weren't among them.

"Finally," said Ferehain, "you deign to grant me an audience. Have you reached your decision?"

The gods hovered above the mass in the square, indifferent faces cast in different directions. Some considered the people beneath them, others were focused on Ferehain while Pia, Basalt, and Kalte seemed more interest in the battle beyond the citadel walls — a battle that was edging closer with each passing second. Pia looked over the conflagration for a moment, then shifted her focus to Ferehain.

"This world unites against you," Pia said.

"A minor insurrection, one of no consequence. It will be crushed before nightfall, another example of the wild and corrupted nature of these people," answered Ferehain.

"I think not," said Dahz in his gruff baritone. "They fight with purpose."

"And with honor," joined Narak. "We would have approved of such mettle."

"Your argument was that these people are corrupted and beyond salvation, that they should be erased and created anew," Pia said, then paused as she glanced back at the conflict, then at the gathered crowd in the square. "And yet they do not seem to agree with your assessment of them. Many of them have rejected you."

"More than that," said Nishindra. "They're even putting aside their differences to unite against you. Half of this city still adores Valeyn after everything you've done to discredit her."

"The more you assert your viewpoint, the more the people of this world resist it," intoned Khanem.

Ferehain's face grew cold.

"So, you are ruling against me." It wasn't a question.

"These people are capable of growth, of learning from their mistakes. Perhaps they can be redeemed," said Romona.

"They won't be redeemed. If you don't side with me, I'll destroy them!" snapped Ferehain.

Elyn heard Ferehain's rare use of informal speech and understood how close he was to breaking.

"Then that shall be your decision, not ours. We will not consign them to an eternity under you," Pia replied

Ferehain turned and walked a short distance, deep in thought and seemingly eager to recover the deteriorating situation. At length, he paused and turned to face the gods above him.

"If we do not form an agreement here, then you will not retain your *kai*, and your creations will die. You will achieve nothing."

"The *kai* may return to us in time," said Pia. "We do not really know, but we have all of creation and existence to explore this new question. We will not bargain with you, Ferehain. You do not understand these people as clearly as you believe. They are not poisoned. They have rejected you, as they have also rejected us."

"Our judgment is somewhat ironic, in that their defiance of us has proven them deserving of our support," said Khanem.

"Then we all lose. This world burns. So be it," said Ferehain. He spoke to himself as if handing down his own judgment.

Elyn knew this was no longer a bluff. This was a man who was standing on the edge of a precipice and whose only choice was to surrender his pride or to jump. She knew his decision.

"Ferehain. Stop. Please!" Elyn gasped but her throat was dry and she was unsure he could hear her. Even if he could, she doubted he would ever listen. But Elyn knew this would be the last time she would have this opportunity. There were no more chances after this. She turned to Aleasea. "Aleasea, please! After all we've been through, you can't let this happen."

The dark green hood seemed to turn in her direction and, for a moment, it felt as if Aleasea was looking at her, attempting to recall a young girl from Fairhaven.

"Judgment is given," intoned Khanem. "Kovalith will remain and its fate will be left to the determination of those who dwell here."

As if the matter was settled, the gods pulled back from their positions above them and retreated into the sky, where they remained faintly visible, like massive shadows silhouetted against the bright blue curtain above. Another series of crashes rent the air, followed by the sound of advancing men beyond the walls. Elyn could sense the battle had reached the citadel.

Ferehain's defenders must have been in full retreat. The crowd began to edge forward, a mix of sympathy and fear overruling self-preservation.

"Valeyn," a woman's voice cried out. "What does this mean?"

"Valeyn, help us," called another.

"We need you!"

As if emboldened by one another, the calls became louder and greater in number. Ferehain turned to look at them, then at Vale and Elyn tied to the scaffolds, and it seemed that he'd forgotten they were there.

"Valeyn," cried a young girl as she climbed up onto the platform. She was no more than ten years old, and she looked from Vale to Elyn with fearful uncertainty. "Valeyn, are you alright?"

She stepped toward Elyn and the Imbatal closest to her swung around. With one savage blow, it extended its arm and drove the blade into the young girls chest, pushing her body back into the crowd as it stepped forward menacingly. There was a moment of strange silence as the crowd seemed to struggle to comprehend what they had just witnessed — as if they thought the casual murder couldn't have really happened — before they exploded with a rage that was both primal and unrestrained. The Imbatals reacted immediately; all six of them snapped into combat readiness and prepared to face the riotous mob. People began to swarm onto the platform, and Elyn braced herself for what was about to happen.

"Slaughter them," Ferehain shouted over the noise, and the creatures stalked forth in their jittering, unnatural gait.

"No," Romona said quietly and the Imbatals froze in place. "You will pervert my work no longer. Let them have peace."

The crowd hesitated for a moment, seemingly waiting to see what the creatures would do. A man cried in rage and leaped onto the Imbatal who had murdered his daughter. It toppled to the ground under his weight, offering no resistance, and the mob quickly closed in on it like ants covering discarded meat. Another Imbatal fell, and within seconds, all seven of them were tumbling under a wave of human fury.

Ferehain watched the scene, turned, and raised his fist as if he were about to strike Romona, but the will suddenly seemed to leave him, and he diminished for a moment.

"This is pointless," he said. "It is time to end it all. Let the gods' justice be done. Let them all witness."

"Ferehain, please. You don't want to do this. Think of Fairhaven and everything we shared there. Please don't erase that," Elyn pleaded.

He glanced at her then smiled. "Yes, Fairhaven. That would be most fitting."

Ferehain walked away from them all, beckoning sharply to the hooded form of Aleasea, who responded in a manner that now seemed weary. She gestured broadly and the empty space before them seemed to part like a curtain. The scene beyond was broken and ruined and achingly familiar to Elyn.

Fairhaven.

The two Ageless walked through the portal and into Fairhaven, yet the door didn't close behind them, it remained open as if Ferehain were inviting pursuit, or at least witnesses to what he was about to do.

"*He wants everyone to watch as he burns Kovalith*," said Vale.

Elyn nodded as she felt the first hands start to loosen her bonds and gently remove her from the scaffold. A large man took her over his shoulder and eased her to the cold tiles of the citadel courtyard.

"Get her water and clothes, quick," came a familiar voice.

Elyn opened her eyes and saw the large form of Symin hovering over her, barking occasional orders to other men in the mob.

"*Ethan's done this*," said Vale.

"*He's a clever man*," answered Elyn, "*and very handsome too. Do you think he'd be interested in me?*"

The wave of humor rippled between their joined minds, and Elyn found herself smiling even as they were about to lose everything. Vale was brought alongside her, and they were both carefully dressed in light cloaks, more for the preservation of their dignity than anything else. Both Vale and Elyn found the gesture amusing.

"*We stand on the edge of oblivion and worry about modesty,*" said Vale.

Elyn shrugged. "*I know there's poetry in being naked in death like you are in birth, but I'd rather look decent,*" she replied.

"Would you like me to see if they also have a hairbrush around?" Vale asked with a smile.

Elyn laughed then gripped her side where it hurt. Symin returned and bowed low before them.

"My Lord Valeyn," he said, refusing to acknowledge the absurdity of pretending they were still one entity. "Can you walk?"

Vale and Elyn shared a look and unspoken words passed between them.

"Yes, we can walk, but that's not the priority. Where are Jason, Nadine, and Ethan?" asked Elyn.

Symin quickly recounted what had happened. How Ethan had returned to his house and flown into a rage. How Ethan had ordered Symin to activate his network of spies and saboteurs immediately. How he had never before seen a man filled with such absolute and final conviction as Ethan declared that the entire might of the House of Mac-Soldai would link up with the Outland Alliance and march on Domitus at sunrise, and that Symin would use every man to assist from within.

Elyn was going to ask about Jason and Nadine, when the clamour at the opening of the square increased. She turned to behold a sight she would have never thought possible; a column of Helmsguard was entering the square, carefully taking positions along the left-hand wall and establishing a defensive permitter, but along the right hand wall ran soldiers wearing colors of green, gray, and the light blue of Fairhaven. Together, the two units encircled the courtyard but kept a watchful eye on the seething mob before them. A group of three Helmsguard advanced on the portal to Fairhaven, but struggled as if they were trying to force their way into a driving storm. After several attempts, they retreated and took up a position several feet away, watching the entry with suspicion.

"*They can't follow him,*" said Vale.

"*No, but we can,*" replied Elyn.

"Elyn!" Jason's voice carried from across the courtyard and seconds later she was swept into the strong embrace of her childhood friend. Another set of arms encircled her from behind and she didn't need to look to know that Nadine had joined the embrace. For a moment, the chaos around them subsided, and Elyn relaxed into the comfort of her closest friends. She did this completely, knowing it would be the last time. Gently, she extracted herself from their grip and looked at them both. They were both talking excitedly, but she wasn't listening to their words. She simply took in the beautiful faces of Jason and Nadine, the people who had been with her for the best and worst moments of her life. It was time to say goodbye to them.

"Thank you both so much. You've done more than I could imagine. You saved us," said Elyn.

"Don't give us too much credit. It wasn't that much of a fight. Half of the Helmsguard either deserted or joined us once they saw Ethan's banner. I have to admit, he was useful. I'm almost glad I didn't kill him."

The glib remark still carried the edge of bitterness, and Elyn placed her hand on his shoulder.

"You did the right thing. For all of us, but mostly for yourself. I'm so proud of the man you've become."

Jason shrugged away the compliment in the way all soldiers do.

"Anyway," he said, "Ethan's men are securing the citadel, and Zain is setting up a perimeter. I think it's over for now."

Elyn shook her head. "I'm afraid not. Ferehain's returned to Fairhaven. He's going to use the remains of Sanctuary to try and destroy Kovalith."

"Can he really do that?" asked Nadine.

"I think so," said Vale. "With everything he learned at The Tower, it's almost certain."

Jason and Ethan shared a look.

"Alright," Ethan said to Jason. "See how many men you can spare and give me ten minutes to do the same."

"Wait, both of you," Vale said.

"You won't be able to follow him," added Elyn. "The door is a bridge built on *kai*. Only those of us who can manipulate *kai* will be able to cross it."

"So, why's it still open?" asked Jason.

"He wants you all to watch," said Vale.

"And he's inviting Vale and me to follow," said Elyn.

Ethan snorted and shook his head. "He thinks you'd follow him? What an arrogant bastard."

Vale glanced at Elyn, and they both rose to their feet.

"We have to," Elyn said.

All three of the companions looked at Elyn and Vale with complete bewilderment.

"You can't be serious?" said Nadine.

"You can barely stand, Elyn," said Jason. "And besides, you're not Valeyn anymore. What are you going to do, talk to him? No, you're staying here and I'm getting you a medic."

"I'm dying, Jason," said Elyn.

Jason's face drained of color and Nadine stepped forward, gripping Elyn by the arm.

"What are you talking about? You're not dying. Sit down, for the gods' sake. Jason, get that medic!" Nadine ordered. Jason moved to obey but Elyn held up her hand.

"It's too late for that. The life that nurtures me, the *kai*, it's fading. Something's broken."

Jason looked at Vale as if she could somehow help, but Elyn's twin only shook her head.

"Ferehain's beating should have killed her," Vale explained. "We survived only because of our shared strength. But Elyn's injuries are too great. It's only a matter of time."

Ethan turned to Vale, his brow furrowed with worry.

"Are you . . . ?" Ethan began but Vale shook her head

"Elyn took the beating for all of us. Her sacrifice saved me and saved you all from Ferehain's wrath."

"I'm not going to waste that sacrifice by slowly dying here, not if there's a chance I can do something," said Elyn.

"And I'm not leaving her to face him alone. We're going together," added Vale.

"Fine, alright," Jason muttered as if trying to make sense of what he was hearing. "Let's go."

Elyn smiled but held her tears back. "You can't go through the gate — it won't let you. I'm sorry, Jason. You can't protect me this time. You need to let me go."

Ethan's shock mirrored Jason's.

"Vale," Ethan said, "you can't stop Ferehain. It's suicide. Please don't do this. Stay with us."

Vale finally looked at Ethan with the open love he deserved. Without a word, she stepped close and gently kissed him.

"I do love you, Ethan," Vale whispered. "And I'm sorry. You've always deserved better than me. I'd like nothing more than to stay here with you, but I need to do this. It's my duty. I know you understand that."

Ethan opened his mouth to argue then stopped himself. The maelstrom of frustration and grief was evident, restrained only by his respect for her. He shook his head and looked down. Elyn took Nadine and Jason by the hand and the three of them stood together in silence for a moment before they embraced for the last time.

"I can't believe I'm going to lose you again," said Nadine.

"You'll never lose me. I've been proud to know you both. Just promise me you'll love each other and remember me please."

"We could never forget you, Elyn," Jason replied in a voice thick with grief.

A crack rent the air and the ground beneath them shook. Elyn pulled away from her friends and wiped at the tears that threatened to obscure her vision. The people gathered in the square began to murmur, the fear sweeping toward Elyn in waves. Vale and Elyn both glanced at the portal, then at each other.

"I'm sorry, we need to go now," Elyn said.

They were still talking, but Elyn wasn't listening. She couldn't. She knew that if she let herself listen to their pleas, she'd never leave. Neither would Vale. And while she wanted nothing more than to spend her last moments in the comfort of her closest friends, she wouldn't let that selfish desire rob them of their chance to live – even if that chance was almost impossible. Elyn and Vale turned from their friends, took each other's hand and walked silently through the crowd toward the shimmering portal — the door leading back to Fairhaven, where they knew it would finally end.

·   ·   ·

The tower of ugly light speared skyward. Both Elyn and Vale walked down the ruined streets of Fairhaven, skirting the discarded refuse and weeds which now choked the small, winding streets of the Old City, until they entered the city square. The beam of the *ovoid* now consumed the space where the Temple had once stood. The town was utterly desolate, like a fractured memory that couldn't be fully recalled. Vale and Elyn both shared a moment of sadness as they watched the old stone bridge crack, then collapse into the River Claiream as the *ovoid* consumed it.

"*I remember sitting on that bridge with Jason and Nadine,*" said Elyn. "*You know, I think I was happy here once.*"

"*I remember it,*" answered Vale. "*You had some good times here.*"

Elyn sighed. "*Let's go.*"

They turned their backs on the light and walked out toward the outer ring of the warehouse district. They didn't need to search for him — they could feel his malevolence burning like a beacon in the fog. They passed under an archway that had been built into the Old City wall and into the wider streets beyond. Elyn looked at the distant watchtowers overlooking the barracks and recalled the night she'd been dragged before the wrath of Captain Lewis for staying out past curfew. Vale laughed as she sensed the memory.

"*I can't imagine the punishment I'd have gotten for pulling something like that in the Ironhelm. Captain Lewis went easy on you,*" Vale said.

Elyn smiled. "*I didn't think so at the time. But you're right, he was a good man.*"

They walked without another word, sharing Elyn's memories as they made their way to the place where Ferehain waited. Elyn steeled herself as they rounded a bend in the road that brought the marketplace into view. Ferehain stood in the center of the road, his black cloak fluttering in the gentle breeze as he stared at the ground, seemingly deep in thought. Elyn looked about and found Aleasea, her hands placed in the dirt in a strange posture and her face still obscured by her green hood.

"I hoped you would follow," said Ferehain without looking up. "Have you come to try and make peace with me, now that you have won? Have you come to try and avert the consequences you have wrought on this world?"

"We've come to talk to you. We know you don't want to do this," said Elyn.

"This is where it began for us, isn't it? Where it really began; the day your surrogate father was killed. That was the day my suspicions were confirmed; the gods had touched you. I was sure it was Bythe himself. I did not know how I knew, but I knew I was right."

Elyn looked over the marketplace and needed nothing to prompt her memory. She remembered Leon lying there, his blood leeching into the dirt as she tried in vain to wake him. But the memory no longer hurt her, instead she recalled it with a sense of regret, as if watching from a great distance. Standing among the ruins of the worst day of her life, Elyn realized she no longer feared the past.

"What have you done?" Vale asked in a voice that was now eerily identical to Elyn's.

"The gods are so fond of their rules. Kovalith was crafted around anchors for the *kai* to balance it against the *ovoid*. Most of this stemmed from The Tower, of course, but as Kovalith grew and expanded in size, they needed to establish such anchors to sustain this world. You know this is where we established Sanctuary."

"You're going to unbalance Kovalith by destroying Fairhaven's anchor under Sanctuary," said Vale. "You're a monster."

"I could have done this from The Tower, but then you gave me the idea of returning to Fairhaven instead. I thought it was more fitting."

Elyn and Vale both looked at the *ovoid* and saw it shimmer and fluctuate violently.

"And if you destroy this, Kovalith will tip into the *ovoid* completely?" asked Vale.

Ferehain grunted a laugh. "*If* I destroy it? Do you think I would offer you a chance to change my mind? It is already done. You have simply come to bear witness. I want you to understand that you have also lost. Then I will kill you before I join you in death."

They both knew they didn't have much time. Elyn was getting weaker with every passing moment. Elyn drew a breath and chose her words carefully.

"But you don't need to do this," Elyn said. "You have a choice. It's not too late. No matter what you've done, we can still fix it, together."

"But I do not want to fix it!" Ferehain's voice snapped and he moved faster than either woman could follow, closing the space between them in an instant. He must have struck them; both Elyn and Vale shared the sense of confusion as they both lay in the dirt watching Ferehain loom over them. They both focused on what needed to be done.

"Please try to remember. You once stood for what was right. You protected people. You cared about this place more than anything," said Elyn.

"Yes, that was a long time ago, before you corrupted it. Before you, your father, your mother — all of you — squabbled to destroy everything I valued," replied Ferehain. He gripped Vale by the front of her robes and lifter her to eye level. "You – the disgusting image of your father – you have always been beneath my contempt." He flung her into the dirt, slamming the breath from her body. "But you," said Ferehain, as he stepped over to Elyn, slowly lifting her until her face was inches from his. "You always tried to prove me wrong. You even tried to subvert my place and discredit me in front of my own people. I have never forgotten this."

Elyn knew that his accusations were false, that they were now distorted through years of rage and hate, but she wouldn't allow herself the distraction. She focused her mind.

"Please, you and I have always shared a connection. You reached to me in Sanctuary, and you protected me. I know you think you've fallen too far, but I know you can come back to us. I know you care."

Ferehain laughed. It was shrill and raucous and carried the ring of madness. "You poor, simpering girl. How little you understand people in the end. You think I care for you? I never cared. If you want to look into my heart at the end of all things and know what it holds for you, know there is nothing but derision, nothing but contempt, nothing but pure, cold hatred!"

"But Ferehain," gasped Elyn, as she finally locked eyes with him, "I haven't been talking to you."

Where Valeyn had once spoken with a single voice, Vale and Elyn now spoke with two; Vale's defiance had distracted Ferehain, while Elyn's compassion reached for Aleasea. Ferehain paused and his face dropped into a contortion of anger and confusion, his head whipped around to see Aleasea, her hood lowered and her eyes slowly regaining clarity. Tears marked her cheeks and as they did, the tracks of Ferehain's injuries were beginning to fade.

"Aleasea! Heed me!" Ferehain shouted, but she didn't seem to hear him. She was staring at Elyn. They were remembering a time long ago, when Elyn had been young and frightened and alone beneath Sanctuary.

Aleasea had opened herself to Elyn — had shown her the young girl who had been filled with hopes for a better world before the centuries had worn away her ambition. There was no connection with immortal power, but a simple bond between women that Ferehain could never have considered, nor detected, nor ever understood.

Elyn reached out and gently placed her mind against Aleasea's. The strength of Elyn's gaze was both intense and intimate. For a brief moment they both caught a sensation of an ancient woman filled with pain and weariness. Then Elyn drew the despair into herself — a single act that mirrored Aleasea's kindness from so long ago — and when Elyn withdrew her mind, the black despair left with it. Elyn looked at Aleasea and to her relief she saw compassion on her face. On some level, Elyn knew that whatever she had taken from Aleasea's soul was fatal to her. Elyn felt satisfied with the trade.

"What have you done?" snarled Ferehain. He wheeled on them, sensing the connection and feeling fear for the first time in centuries. His eyes widened as he finally perceived their trap. "You planted the idea of Fairhaven in my mind. You planned this."

He pulled back his hand to strike Elyn in a blow that was certainly intended to be fatal, but Aleasea's voice stopped him.

"That is enough."

Her words erased the malice in the air and Ferehain seemed unsure what to do. He turned around and withdrew the vile Anticipus from his robe, thrusting it at Aleasea's face like a weapon.

"Do not make me use this," he threatened, but Aleasea waved her hand and the artefact vanished in a flash of light.

"You will not," she answered smoothly. "In fact, you will never harm me again."

He looked at his empty hand in disbelief, then at Aleasea as she slowly walked toward him.

"I do not wish to fight you," Ferehain warned, but Aleasea's smile was heartfelt.

"Oh, Ferehain."

Vale and Elyn didn't even see Ferehain move as he launched his attack on the woman he once loved. All they saw was his body – frozen mid-strike – paused awkwardly in a position inches from her.

"You have done your job far too well," she said. "You have restored my power and enhanced it beyond what Maelene intended. What hope do you now have against me?"

She nodded and Ferehain was flung into the air, tumbling into the dirt far away from her. Elyn was reminded of a cat toying with a helpless mouse, and she almost felt pity for Ferehain.

"It is over, Ferehain. This must end," Aleasea said as she casually walked toward him.

Ferehain rose to his feet, shaking his head like a man who could not accept the sunrise.

"No. It's too late. It can't be stopped. Not even you can stop it now."

Aleasea paused and looked at the rippling tower of *ovoid* and the tremors of the Desecration began to shake Kovalith for the last time.

"No, I cannot. This is beyond even me," Aleasea said.

"Ferehain. Please stop," the voice of a young child floated down from above.

"Naya," Ferehain said as he looked skyward.

The silhouette of a child was now visible against the sky, and behind her were the larger shadows of two last gods — a broad-shouldered man and a woman with long hair. Bythe and Maelene. Ferehain stared at the young girl who had reminded him of his own daughter from so long ago, then back to Aleasea, and for a moment, it looked as if he had wakened from a dream.

"All we can do now is ensure we do no further harm to this world," said Aleasea, as she closed the space between them. Ferehain looked at her with an expression that was almost bewildered. In that moment, all of his hate seemed to fall from him, and the two faced each other as the oldest of friends.

"How did you hold onto your conviction after all that happened? I never wanted this, my love. I wanted to be noble, like you are. I wanted to protect this world from the people who would harm it. I only wanted to protect you."

"You can protect us now," Aleasea replied.

She took his hands in hers. They stood like that for a long time, each studying the face of the other, a face they had both known for centuries. Fear and uncertainty crept into his expression and there was something almost innocent about him in that moment. At the end of Ferehain's grandeur and ambition and power, all that was left was a broken man at the end of his dreams. He looked again into the eyes of Aleasea and spoke to her for the last time.

"Why couldn't we have our child? Was that too much for us to ask?"

She took him into her embrace and held him there. She held him as the world trembled along with his sobbing body. And she held him as she took his life force, and as the wreckage of a once-great man faded from sight and left existence forever.

Aleasea stood alone for a moment, and neither Elyn nor Vale said a word. Both could sense her private grief, and neither would intrude upon it, even as the world trembled beneath them. At length, she sighed and favored both of them with a warm smile that made Elyn feel as if she were a girl again.

"Elyn, Vale. I cannot express how I feel to see you both again, but I regret that we do not have the time this reunion deserves."

There were no words or explanations needed, both Elyn and Vale now instinctively knew what they had to do. They each now had unity with a parent's *kai*, but where this had once been an uncontrolled and rough split, it was now clean and total; Elyn now wielded Maelene's power, and Vale controlled Bythe's.

"Ferehain had me infect Kovalith with this malady, and I may be able to undo it, however I will not be able to repair the damage I have done," Aleasea said.

"We know," said Vale.

"Leave that part to us," said Elyn.

The ground shifted violently, and a distant crash marked the sound of a building collapsing. Aleasea looked at them with concern as she understood what they were proposing.

"The anchor of *kai* under Fairhaven has been destroyed, if you try to replace this, it may strip you of all your power," she said.

"Then we'd better get started," said Vale as Elyn nodded next to her.

Aleasea stepped forward and raised her arms. Closing her eyes, her expression hardened into a mask of concentration. At first, there was no reaction and the trembling of the ground continued, but slowly the tower of light began to flicker and waver, like a candle reaching the end of its wick. A grunt of pain escaping Aleasea's lips was the only indication of her intense effort. The *ovoid* began to diminish in size and then in brilliance, as Aleasea extended her hands as if she were physically forcing it back into the ground. Vale and Elyn both closed their eyes and cast their heads back. Fountains of light erupted from both women, as the green *kai* of Elyn and the red *kai* of Vale poured into the damaged ground left in the wake of the *ovoid.* The immortal life force flowed from each of them as they both surrendered it. There could be no return to godhood. Both Elyn and Vale cried out as they emptied their beings of everything. When Elyn and Vale felt the last pulses of *kai* leave their bodies, only then did they wilt and open their eyes. The column of the *ovoid* was smaller now, but it was still there. Aleasea looked over at them with exhaustion set deep in her eyes, but where there should have been a sense of victory, there was only a look of defeat.

It wasn't enough.

The light began to edge forward again, and the ground started to shake even more violently, as if their actions had only invigorated the corrosive disease eating away at the roots of the world. Elyn felt the pull of her *kai,* as if it were trying to drag her down into the world. She forced herself upright, resisting the temptation to simply let go and become one with everything.

"I am sorry," said Aleasea. "It is as I feared; our power was simply not sufficient."

Vale turned to the collection of impassive shadows against the darkening sky.

"Help us! Don't you care about this world? Give it your power!" Vale shouted to the gods.

"How can you stand by and watch? I thought you wanted Kovalith to live." accused Elyn.

The eyes of the beings above them glowed like stars, but their faces remained shrouded in darkness.

"Kovalith will remain and its fate will be left to the determination of those who dwell here," said Khanem. "Such was our judgment. We will not condemn this world, nor will we aid it."

"Damn your judgment!" snapped Vale. "You can still save us. Follow our example and repair the damage."

"You ask us to give even more of our soul to sustain this world?" asked Lubalt-Teble. "You demand too much. Be thankful that we don't take back what's ours."

"You have a strange sense of fairness," said Aleasea. "If Kovalith falls then your souls will be restored. You are not noble beings."

"The judgment remains. Kovalith must stand or fall on merit. We will not interfere," said Khanem.

"Father?" asked Vale, but the shadowed form of Bythe didn't respond.

"Do not appeal to my brother. His *kai* alone could not help you in any case. The damage is too great," said Pia.

"I'm sorry, but our judgment is made. We can't interfere, even if we want to," said Nishindra with a hint of regret.

"Then there's another way," Elyn said.

Aleasea looked hard at her.

"One god's *kai* isn't enough, so what if we sacrificed Valeyn's entire soul? Vale and Elyn's souls? Could that restore the balance?"

Despair swept across Aleasea's face as she comprehended. "Such an act *might* save Kovalith, but it would destroy you both," she said.

Elyn smiled weakly and took Aleasea's hand.

"I'm dying, Aleasea. You know this. There's nothing to be gained by trying to save me. And if my death might make a difference, then I want to do this."

Aleasea glared up at the gods in silent accusation then dropped her stare in defeat.

"And what of you, Vale?" Aleasea asked. "Are you also willing to sacrifice yourself in this way?"

Vale nodded without hesitation. "Valeyn couldn't save Kovalith, but maybe the two of us can. Who knows? Maybe it was always meant to be this way."

"You once told me to discover my own wisdom," said Elyn. "I'm sorry, Aleasea, but I know this is the right thing to do."

"I also once said that you are my child no longer. Today I am reminded of that, but it saddens me deeply."

They embraced and Elyn wept briefly into the arms of her surrogate mother before she pulled herself back. She turned and met Vale's eyes. They knew what they had to do. The river of *kai* was still pulling at them both, begging them to follow the current into the foundations of the world and become one with it. They knew that all they had to do now was simply let go, to surrender into that flow, to stop resisting, to stop and to finally rest. They joined hands and smiled.

"*Are you ready?*" one of them said.

"*Yes*," replied the other.

"Wait," a voice called from behind them. The voice was deep, but no longer ominous. It carried authority but also compassion. It was the voice of their father. A tall man with broad shoulders was now approaching. Gone, was the black armor of iron, leaving behind an older man in the grandeur of age. White hair swept back above his heavy brow, and sharp eyes were set in a weathered face.

"I will not allow this," Bythe said as he approached, looking over both his daughters with the casual authority of every father.

Vale had to stop herself genuflecting, and even Elyn felt the compulsion to bow, but instead of fear, the man before them now projected something else; a thoughtfulness and empathy that had been absent from the armored man Valeyn had met.

"It is good to see you both with such clarity at last, and I am so very sorry this moment has come so late," Bythe said.

"Father," Vale said with a small smile touching her lips. "It's . . . alright. We want to do this."

"No, Vale. I have been freed from the madness of this world and, I now understand . . . you were right. You tried to teach a truth to an ungrateful father. I must atone for this arrogance, but at least, you have taught me how."

"What are you saying?" asked Vale.

Bythe looked over his daughters and his face softened. "I will do what you propose. I will spend my *kai* in your place. The soul of Bythe will be more than enough to save this world."

Shock washed over Elyn and the twins looked at each other in bewilderment.

"Father . . . no. This isn't right," said Elyn.

Bythe smiled. "No, child. What isn't right is for my daughters to right the wrongs of their father. What isn't right is for the gods to linger at the expense of their children. Once gods create a world, they need to remove themselves from it utterly, for it is the only way their children will grow."

"But we don't even know if this will work," said Elyn.

"We created this world with fragments of our souls. I understand what is required to sustain it. And you were correct, the entire soul of a god will be enough to ensure Kovalith survives forever. If one of us must be sacrificed for this, let it be me."

"Father," said Elyn. "I'm dying. Please don't do this for my sake, there's no point. Let me be the one."

He turned his eyes, reassuring yet sympathetic, to Elyn. "Daughter, you are only dying in this world. This isn't the end for you. I regret that I don't have the skill to heal your broken form but let me save you in a different way. I will assume your burden, and you will join your mother in the Etherian. She waits for you."

Bythe gestured to the sky. Elyn looked up and saw the figure of Maelene once again, her face beautiful and loving and framed with long, flowing hair. Next to her stood the small figure of Naya – made whole and healed again through the Etherian – her youthful face beaming with excitement.

"Elyn, Elyn!" Naya waved enthusiastically just like she would back in Tiet. Elyn laughed through tears.

"And Vale," said Bythe. "Let me give you the life you finally deserve — the life I should have given you long ago."

"But, father, you'll no longer exist," said Vale.

Bythe smiled. "Yes, but you both will."

Vale stepped forward and took Bythe's hand.

"I've always loved you. Even through all those years in my childhood, I still loved you. You knew this, didn't you?" she asked.

"I knew, Vale. And although I loved you in return, I only showed it through self-indulgent thoughts. That wasn't enough. I should have acted. Fortunately, fate has given me one final chance to remedy this. I will not waste it."

Vale placed a hand to her mouth and shook her head, trying to comprehend what she was hearing. "This can't happen. No. It's not fair," she pleaded, stepping closer to him as though it would keep him from leaving.

Bythe's eye's shone with affection and he placed his hand on her shoulder. "I would stay with you, but this is the only way for me to atone — and to save you. It is just, considering all I have done to this world and what I have done to you."

Vale shook her head, then hugged him. Bythe closed his eyes and returned the embrace.

"The judgment is set. You may not interfere with it," barked Khanem from above.

Bythe sighed and gently extracted himself from Vale's hold.

"I can interfere, and I will gladly pay the price for doing so," Bythe answered with a ring of defiance in his voice.

"Brother, what are you doing? Stop this nonsense and return to us," said Pia.

"Please, brothers and sisters, give me no orders now. You claimed I would see wisdom once I returned to you and you were correct. I see now that I was never your equal and my attempts to redress my inadequacies have done too much harm to these people. I have almost destroyed those I loved. I have been an ambitious fool. Grant me this small act of atonement and let me have peace," Bythe answered.

The ground shook violently and two warehouses next to the marketplace fell inward as if made of sticks. The *ovoid* surged forth and the ruins of Fairhaven were enveloped in a wave of sickening light.

"Then farewell, brother," said Pia as if she could not understand her own words.

"It is time. Come, Elyn," said Bythe, extending his hand to her.

Elyn turned to Vale and the two sisters embraced for the final time.

"I love you, Elyn."

"And I love you, Vale. Please, make sure you live a good life for us both."

Elyn kissed Vale on the cheek, then broke away to walk over to stand next to their father.

As both Vale and Aleasea watched on, a nimbus of colors enveloped the figures of Bythe and Elyn. Elyn vanished first, her physical form faded slowly then seemed to evaporate upward to the gods waiting above. It seemed as though Vale could briefly hear the mingled joy of Elyn and Naya on the wind. Bythe stood alone for a moment.

"Goodbye, Bythe" said Maelene from above. Bythe looked up at her and nodded a silent farewell, before a wave of red light swept over him and he vanished forever. And the gods watched as Bythe finally achieved his superiority in a manner totally incomprehensible to them.

The light of the *ovoid* flickered for an instant, then went dark. The violent tremors threatening the world instantly ceased, and the gods of Kovalith faded into the sky, never to be seen by mortal eyes again.

The air of Fairhaven was completely still, and Vale and Aleasea stood shrouded in the blanket of the unnatural quiet that followed. The Ageless took Vale's hand and held it in silence. Both women stood in the ruins of their old world, mourning the price of the new world dawning and wishing there had been another way.

·   ·   ·

The Ironhelm seemed surprisingly calm when Vale emerged from the makeshift infirmary that had been set up in one of the ballrooms on the outer edge of the city. She was dressed in the black and gold livery of a Commander's dress uniform, it had been a long time since she'd worn it, but she found herself fastening the clasps and straps as easily as she had when she was a girl. She intuitively reached for Elyn, but she felt nothing — there was nothing to reach out with. That part of her life – that part of her – was gone now, and she realized it would take a while to get used to.

There was something strange about the shadows on the street before her. She shielded her eyes against the early morning sun, looked toward the center of town and saw Domitus was listing to one side, a crack splintering the center of the structure almost all the way to the top. Vale was so astonished at the sight, she didn't notice Ethan as he walked up beside her.

"It happened when Bythe sacrificed himself," said Ethan. "Nobody's been hurt as far we I know, but we're evacuating the whole city. We don't know how long it's going to stand."

Vale nodded. The Ironhelm would fall with Bythe, and his monuments would also fall with him. It seemed fitting. She turned and looked at Ethan's face. It was haggard, as if he hadn't slept in living memory, yet his eyes still shone with tearful joy when he looked at her.

"I'm so sorry, but I thought I'd lost you," was all he said.

Vale stepped into his arms and held him as tightly as she had ever held anyone. She decided in that moment that she would never let go of him. That she needed to accept the love while there was still time to share it. That the distractions and overcomplications of life were no longer an excuse for avoiding her own happiness. He gripped her back just as fiercely, and they stood locked in that embrace for the longest moment of their lives. She took in a deep breath, then gently stepped back from the man she finally loved.

"Alright, well, before we get too carried away, I have some business to take care of first, don't I?" she asked.

A playful smile brightened his face at the promise, and he assumed the role of the loyal officer once more.

"Right this way, Commander," he said, and gently placing his hand on her back, he escorted her along the street toward the main entrance to the city.

The streets were filled with ordered lines of people slowly filing out of the city. Helmsguard wearing the purple sashes of Arbek lined the streets, ensuring order. The occasional broken wall or smashed doorway were the only signs of the previous day's battle.

"Where's the Outland Alliance?" asked Vale.

"We asked them to withdraw outside the city. I thought it might be harder to maintain order with a half dozen different armies roaming about like an occupying force."

Vale looked around at the ordered scene before her.

"I can't believe you restored control. I thought civil war was about to erupt."

Ethan shook his head. "We all saw what happened. We witnessed it through Ferehain's portal. I think he intended it to serve as a punishment as he ended the world in front of us. As it turns out, it had the opposite effect."

"You all saw the gods leave us," Vale said.

Ethan nodded. "The people have had enough of gods, and there wasn't any serious will to support Ferehain in the rank and file soldiers — not outside the Unity Assembly anyway. Once Ferehain murdered them, half of the Helmsguard refused orders to keep fighting their countrymen, and the other half openly joined us. That's not to say it's over, mind you. We may have put down this coup without much bloodshed, but we need a new government and a new leader quickly, or we'll just have delayed a civil war."

"Indeed, we do," said Vale. She decided it was time to start building the new world.

After several minutes they arrived at a squat, marble building with functionless columns adorning the facade. It was a small municipal building, designated to the administration of the Sheriffs. It was now the site of a meeting that would decide the political landscape of a new empire. They were saluted by the Helmsguard at the door and allowed to enter. To Vale's mild surprise, there was no table nor a formal agenda. Instead there was a simple gathering of people in the center of the large circular room. Vale immediately recognized Nadine and Jason, but she hadn't expected Exedor and Lady Sarele among the others. All conversation stopped as she entered, and every face turned in her direction. Ethan stepped forward.

"I present Lord Vale, Daughter of Bythe, and heir to the Iron Union," Ethan announced.

The snap of a dozen mailed fists striking their breastplates filled the room, and every face in the delegation nodded their respect to her.

Vale approached Jason and Nadine. Their red-rimmed eyes betrayed a night of sleepless grief over the death of their friend. There was nothing to be said. No words could fill the emptiness they all felt. So it surprised Vale when Nadine steeled herself and closed the gap between them. She looked into Vale's eyes, seeing her old friend but also understanding the stranger beneath the familiar face.

"She's part of you, isn't she?" Nadine asked.

Vale nodded. "I'll carry her with me always."

Jason also stepped close, as if seeing Vale could give him the chance to see Elyn one last time. He smiled, and his laugh was edged with sorrow. "You know, I used to tease her about needing me to protect her. But in the end, she was far braver than any of us, wasn't she?"

"She always was," said Nadine. "We just didn't know it, but we should have."

They each nodded in silence for a moment. Sarele and Ethan quietly joined the group.

"Lady Sarele," Vale said. "I thank you. This wouldn't have been possible if not for you. Thanks for coming to our aid. It can't have been easy."

Sarele shrugged. "Thank my son. Somewhere between his promises of political power if I overthrew Ferehain, combined with his threats of what he'd do if I didn't help, he managed to get his way."

"You made the right decision. I'm in your debt," Vale said.

"Well, you need to remember that when you're dividing the spoils of your new empire," Sarele answered, and Vale didn't need empathy to know she was very serious.

"That won't be a problem," Vale said.

"And so, I now have to look into the face of my best friend when I negotiate with the Iron Union," said Nadine. "That's going to give you an advantage."

"You won't have to worry about that. I won't be leading my people," answered Vale, and the surprise on Nadine's face was mirrored on the others. She held up her hand to forestall the flood of questions before continuing. "I'm no longer a god, but I was for a time, and I'm still the daughter of Bythe. It's not right for another god, or near-god, to sit on the throne. This isn't what our people deserve. The age of gods is over. This is a time for change. I can't carry on in my father's name, even if I had the heart for it, which I don't."

"Then who's going to lead the Iron Union?" asked Nadine. "There'll be chaos without a leader and that'll threaten the stability of everyone."

"That task will fall to Ethan, not me. He's certainly earned it," Vale said.

Ethan's head swung around and he looked at Vale in astonishment.

"Apologies, Baron," Vale said with a half-smile. "It's punishment for performing so admirably as my second-in command all those years and also for saving my life."

Nadine looked at Ethan warily. "The House of Mac-Soldai? Are you confident the Iron Union will accept their leadership so peacefully?"

"The Iron Union will no longer exist, and the federation of its states will no doubt want to govern themselves," said Exedor, as he quietly inserted himself into the conversation. "It's what the Prodigals have long fought for. But Arbek and the House of Mac-Soldai have currently seized power, and they'll emerge as the strongest voice in the discussions that will now follow. I offer my services to negotiate this transition with the

Prodigals, and we can discuss the details of my position in the new government at a later time."

Vale shook her head with disbelief. She knew there would always be men like Exedor in the world, and there was likely always going to be a need for them.

"Indeed, there's going to be a lot of negotiation and diplomacy needed," said Sarele as she slowly digested the proposal. "But with your public support, Vale, combined with the right compensation provided to the right people, I think we can facilitate a smooth transition to my son."

Nadine turned her stare to Ethan, and it was cool. Her confidence faltered for a moment.

"I can't ever forgive you for what you did to my father, and I won't ever forget what happened after that . . . but I also know what you did for me — how you probably saved my life — and that despite all your mistakes, I know you're still a decent man. I just don't know if that makes things better or worse." She sighed and ran her fingers through her hair, as if clearing her mind of grief. "But if we're to be the new leaders of this world, I think we can find a way to respect each other. I know I can do that much for Elyn."

"Thank you, Nadine," Ethan said softly.

Jason didn't say a word, but the two solders locked eyes for a moment before Jason nodded briefly. It was all that needed to pass between them. Nadine and Jason then turned to Vale. They looked at her strangely, still seeing the friend they had known, then walked away. Sarele and Exedor likewise retreated to start haggling over the finer details of the transition. Vale turned to Ethan and - much to his surprise - stepped close to his body, guiding his arms around her waist. She rested against his chest and breathed all of her tensions out.

"Did you really mean what you said, about me taking command?" Ethan asked.

"Why wouldn't I? Do you think I should be stuck with all the responsibility? You're damned right I meant it. It's all your problem now. Let me know what the job's like."

"Well, I wasn't expecting so much commitment so early in the relationship. And I was only going to buy you dinner tonight."

Vale laughed. "I don't want to carry the weight of the world anymore. I just want to truly enjoy my own life now — a life with a different meaning. I owe Elyn that. Is it really too much to ask?"

Ethan gently kissed the top of her head and cradled her. "Of course not. I think you've earned whatever you want."

Vale smiled, then looked up suddenly, glancing around the gathering for someone who should have been there, but wasn't.

"Where's Aleasea?" she asked.

"Nobody seems to know," said Ethan, following her gaze. "Once she knew you were safe in the infirmary, she left the city. Understandably, no one was willing to try and detain her. But don't worry, I'm sure you'll see her again."

Vale looked out the door and felt the pain of another small loss, but she smiled, nonetheless.

"No, I won't," she said.

EPILOGUE
THE FINAL TESTIMONY OF ALEASEA OF THE AGELESS

The land of Kovalith did indeed change that day, and a new world began from the remnants of the old. Such change did not take hold immediately, nor did it grow with a planned and steady purpose, but I have learned to hold faith in a noble outcome when such change is led by good people with selfless intent. To my relief, my faith was largely rewarded.

In the five years that have passed since the Fall of Bythe, the Iron Union's transition into the Iron Federation has been relatively peaceful. The stars of the gods never returned, and the night skies were dark from that day forth. While people were fearful at first, they adapted quickly. The Ironhelm cities – the last creations of Bythe – were evacuated and rebuilt, as the towering and decaying citadels were removed from each city. The damage done to the lands has been largely restored, and many still praise Bythe's sacrifice for this miracle. I am forced to concede that this is likely the final act of the gods on this world, and I take relief that his act was one of healing.

Baron Ethan of Mac-Soldai was unsurprisingly elected to serve as the first Chairman of the Iron Federation, a post he continues to hold to this day. I am pleased to note that he has served with admirable control and restraint, as is needed from a good leader forging a new direction. Within the first year, the Fortress of Krag briefly entertained its own insurrection and dream to rebuild a new Iron Union, but the campaign was far from enthusiastic and was quickly defeated by the united forces of Mac-Soldai, Ciro, and Alovat. The cunning Exedor proved his value more often than expected in these early years, and while it was clear that Ethan could never fully trust him, it was a better strategy for Ethan to keep him close rather than set him free.

Eventually, the Iron Federation found its feet and grew into a stable alliance of independent states, an act mercifully aided by the patience and wisdom of First Minister Nadine of the Outland Republic. While many forces agitated for war against the old enemy, Nadine held firm against them, honoring her word to work with Ethan for the betterment of both their people. Like Ethan, Nadine faced her own small insurrections; however, she enjoyed the support of Warmaster-General Zain of Roy, not to mention her husband, Field Marshall Jason of Fairhaven, who controlled the bulk of the Alliance's armed forces between them. As such, Nadine's insurrections were more political than militant, and she proved herself more than capable of handling those.

Perhaps the smartest change was not wrought by political strategy, but from genuine compassion. The hitherto desolate lands encompassing Outpost, Wheatsheaf, and Klyph were granted autonomy under a joint agreement between the Iron Federation and the Outland Republic and assigned to Lord Vale at her request. It was Vale who granted the new nation the title of Leon, and it was Vale who set her mind to rebuilding the towns as a gateway between former enemies. Within two years, Outpost had been almost completely rebuilt, with its waterfront position serving as an excellent trading post between east and west. With increased trade came increased capital, and Vale proved herself to be an effective economic tactician, growing both Outpost and Wheatsheaf into thriving centers of commerce. The marshlands are now being reclaimed and even the crevasses of Klyph are to be refilled by a brilliant young engineer from Fairhaven. Leon is no longer a war-ravaged wasteland. It is now the center of the world, and it is fitting that Vale is the foundation of this.

While I do not wish to make myself the focus of this account, I feel it is necessary to document my role in the closure of this era of Kovalith. I am deeply shamed by the actions that were forced upon me and the destruction that was unleashed in my name. However, I also understand I was nothing more than a tool for Ferehain to use and that such actions must never again be permitted. For three years I travelled the breadth of Kovalith, to seek out all such Artefacts of the gods, to ensure they would not be manipulated by one like Ferehain. I cleansed Kardak of its horrors and traversed the Render until I finally returned to The Tower. It was a cold and dark place once more, separated from the kai of the gods, nothing more than a construct of stones. Here, I unleashed the height of my power for the last time, and the last edifice of the gods descended into oblivion. We are alone. Our gods have now truly left us.

Eventually, I returned to Fairhaven, which I have decided will be my home. I do not know how long I will live. Am I still ageless or will I grow old and eventually die? This adventure of discovery now lies before me, and I will not disclose the destination here. Not unlike Vale, I dedicated my time to acts of rebuilding and found my calling in Fairhaven and Sanctuary. To my delight, I discovered that other Ageless had survived the Desecration, Kaler among them. While I will never again allow myself to be worshipped – or even observed – by the people of Fairhaven, I decided to use my power to regenerate what was once poisoned. Sanctuary now thrives as a lifeblood to the wilderness, and my Ageless now move throughout the lands, not as feared sorcerers, but as teachers. Kaler now tells the story of the young woman he once misjudged and mistreated so terribly. He ensures her name will never be forgotten. A garden has been built on the grounds where the Temple once stood, and a tree now stands at its center, planted in memory of Elyn. There are nights when I go to that tree alone, to rest my hand upon it, and in those quiet hours I feel she is near to me.

I admit that, on occasion, I have succumbed to curiosity and used my Oraculate deep within Sanctuary to peer into the lives of those who now live in this new world. I see Jason and Nadine, smiling as they watch their infant daughter chase their large, lilac-colored cat – almost as large as the young girl herself. They laugh as the cat flees the affections of the enthusiastic young girl, who stomps awkwardly across their living room with arms outstretched, and I know her name is Elyn. I see Vale, dressed in the dark clothes of a noblewoman, overseeing the reconstruction of Outpost and Wheatsheaf, proud of a new life. I see the people from both east and west honoring her, not as a god, but as a leader who has sacrificed everything for them and would do so again. And I know they truly love her. I also see the love she shares with Ethan, but on that, I do not pry.

There are days when I miss the young woman who was like a daughter to me, who later became my closest friend, but I do not weep for her. I know she watches me still. There are days when I even miss Ferehain and lament the dark paths that separated us in the end. But I will not lead a life of regret, and I push these thoughts behind me.

When the day ends and I have a moment to reflect, I feel pride. Pride in Vale and the work that continues in her name. Pride at the brighter morning that waits for the people of this world. But most of all, I feel pride when I remember the name of a timid young girl from Outpost who I had the pleasure of meeting so long ago.

ACKNOWLEDGEMENTS

We've come to the end of a very long journey, and I sincerely thank each and every person who has taken it with me — including you. I clearly remember first dreaming up Valeyn's story twenty years ago, lying on a couch one afternoon, smiling at the outrageous idea of writing a fantasy trilogy. It hasn't been easy, and it took much longer than I expected. But after many deviations and endless revisions, I'm very proud to have finally told the story I set out to write. I hope you enjoyed it.

I'd like to thank Pamela Taylor, an editing machine if one ever existed. Thank you once again for improving my collection of words. A shout out to Reagan and the team at Black Rose Writing. Thanks to my brother, Andrew, for being on this journey from the very beginning. These characters have come to life between us over the years, and it's sad to say goodbye to them. But you've made this possible.

And to my beautiful wife, Anya: only through your unwavering encouragement have I been able to complete this work. This trilogy exists because of you. Thank you so much for writing this with me.
Finally, to those of you reading these last words: a story only exists as long as there is someone to read it, and that means you have created this with me over the course of several hundred pages. I genuinely thank you for that. You've made me very proud.

About the Author

Christopher Monteagle is a lifelong fantasy reader and writer of fiction in various forms. Growing up in outback Australia with no running water, electricity, or—needless to say—television, Christopher was introduced to books by Tolkien and Herbert to pass the time. He soon began writing his own stories and became immersed in the worlds of fantasy and fiction. *The Final God* is Christopher's third novel.

The Godless Trilogy

Note from Christopher Monteagle

Word-of-mouth is crucial for any author to succeed. If you enjoyed *The Final God*, please leave a review online—anywhere you are able. Even if it's just a sentence or two. It would make all the difference and would be very much appreciated.

Thanks!
Christopher Monteagle

We hope you enjoyed reading this title from:

www.blackrosewriting.com

Subscribe to our mailing list – *The Rosevine* – and receive **FREE** books, daily deals, and stay current with news about upcoming releases and our hottest authors.
Scan the QR code below to sign up.

Already a subscriber? Please accept a sincere thank you for being a fan of Black Rose Writing authors.

View other Black Rose Writing titles at www.blackrosewriting.com/books and use promo code **PRINT** to receive a **20% discount** when purchasing.